The Goddess Called

The girl in the room began to scream. High, piercing, frightened screams, cut through with pain, shame, and hopelessness. As Gaultry stood in the dark passageway outside the brightly lit room, a red cloud descended across her vision. Something moved in her—something more than her own volition. The palm of her hand—the hand that held the sword—went cold. A touch like a dagger of ice lanced through her arm up into her brain. She found she had crowded against Tullier, that she was fighting him to open the door, and then, suddenly, she was in the room.

The girl on the bed cried out, struggling against her attacker to hold back his knife.

"Thunderbringer! Thunderbringer! Oh Llara! Don't leave me!"

Something in Gaultry responded—something she did not control. The sword was in her hand, the man's broad, gray-tinted back before her, the girl still screaming . . .

"A rousing, and very readable, fantasy adventure that largely stands alone, while leaving plenty of room for more, much anticipated, adventures."

—*Locus*

"The highly satisfactory sequel to Reimann's *Wind from a Foreign Sky*. Readers will quickly and pleasurably find plenty of action, complex, but plausible motivation and characterization, and well-done world building in the second Tielmaran Chronicle."

—*Booklist*

Tor Books by Katya Reimann

A TREMOR
IN THE
BITTER EARTH

▼

Katya Reimann

A Tom Doherty Associates Book
New York

This is a work of fiction. All the characters and events portrayed in this book are products of the author's imagination or are used fictitiously.

A TREMOR IN THE BITTER EARTH

Edited by James Frenkel

Map by Ellisa Mitchell

A Tor Book
Published by Tom Doherty Associates, Inc.
175 Fifth Avenue
New York, NY 10010

Tor Books on the World Wide Web:
http://www.tor.com

Tor® is a registered trademark of Tom Doherty Associates, Inc.

ISBN: 0-812-54934-1

First edition: June 1998
First mass market edition: March 1999

Printed in the United States of America

0 9 8 7 6 5 4 3 2 1

In memory of William Pomerance and L. Parker Lesley
Two wise men

Acknowledgments

My first thanks must go to the members of my writers' group: Paul Ferrari, Ed Seksay, Jill Smith, and Cecilia Tan. They challenged me, supported me, and didn't stint in their criticism. I owe much to their help.

Second books pose new challenges: thanks also go to Jim Frenkel, my editor, for helping me face them; and to my agent, Shawna McCarthy, for taking the time to explain.

Other friends were a tremendous support. Leah Bateman, with great humor and patience, put up with the most.

Lastly, I owe thanks to Tom Doherty. His support helped make this book happen.

—K.A.R.

MONTEVIA ROAD

BISSANTY EMPIRE

LAKES COUNTRY

North

AVERIOS

Great River Bas

River Dolorosa

Bassorah

Feeder

Dunsanius Ford

THE NEEDLES

Fructibus Arbis

Murver Sopra

Locatus River

Balik Sirti

GREAT MARSH CRESCENT

High Plateau

Lemu Valley

Clarin's Seat

Aciers

Ilana's Kettle

Haute Tielmark

BISSANTY FINGERLAND

HIGH ROAD

Lourdes' Manor

Pontceil

TIELMARK

BOOK ONE

▼

Prologue

Tullier's first arrow killed the fair-haired knight. His second, loosed as he broke clear of the brush, took the neatly liveried groom high in the shoulder but did not finish him. That took a third arrow. By then Corbulo, Tullier's journey-master, already had three kills to the boy's two, and he'd paralyzed the servers' lady with a special black-tipped dart.

"Quickly now!" Corbulo urged.

The two assassins, novice and journey-master together, rushed down the slight incline to close in on their prey.

Tullier, running full out, quivered with ill-controlled excitement. The ambush had gone so easily—every detail, every reaction, anticipated by his master. Smooth as an exercise, steady as a practiced form, yet here were five corpses on the ground, the tang of blood in the air, and the strange bedraggled-looking Tielmaran lady, Destra Vanderive, with her tangle of brown hair and her sun-darkened skin, lying paralyzed against the bole of the great chestnut.

The assassins reached the broad shadow of the chestnut. The big tree where the Tielmarans had made their picnic had given no shelter, and the ambush had come without warning. That showed in the blank expressions on the dead knights' faces, their empty sword hands.

Destra Vanderive heaved her willow-thin body against the tree, struggling without success to gain her feet. Her dark eyes were wild with fright. Her younger son, stiff with shock, buried his head in her skirts and suckled her limp hand, as if hiding his face meant that nothing could harm him.

His brother, a bare handspan shorter than Tullier, met them at the edge of the tree's shade, brave but helpless.

"The Great Twins beg you, have mercy!" he beseeched them, and threw wide his hands in supplication.

Corbulo paralyzed him with a second black-tipped dart. The boy dropped facedown into the fallen chestnut flowers with an anguished cry.

Tullier, half-sick with the joy of victory, hardly heard him. He stopped at the corpse of the fair-haired knight: an older man, with silver at his collar and sleeves. Stooping, he plunged his Sha Muir knife into the body, below where the arrow had taken the man in the chest. Blood slicked the blade's thunder-bolt figure—the Goddess Llara's sign. This, after so many years of preparation, was his first kill as a Sha Muira. Wetting his fingers with blood from the blade, Tullier marked his right shoulder with four short lines. *Great Llara*— He closed his eyes, tried to imagine the face of the gray goddess turned towards him, splendor and joy rising at her servant's first blooding. *This kill is for you; for the Emperor; for Bissanty*— He had trained more than a decade for this moment. Pictured it in its perfection, its glory—

"You almost missed your second man."

Breaking his prayer short, Tullier's eyes flicked to his second corpse—the groom—then across to his journey-master. The broad-chested man, swaggering in full Sha Muir garb, moved quickly among his own kills, imprinting his blade with the three deaths. Unlike Tullier, Corbulo did not pause to mark his shoulders. The tall journey-master merely wiped his knife on the skirt of his robe and sheathed it. Shoulder-marking was for novices, that gesture told Tullier.

"Finished there?" he asked. "Or are you taking the other one too?"

Tullier lifted his chin. "I'm finished." Set to him as a question, he couldn't—he wouldn't—mark his other shoulder with the blood of the second man he had killed. Not now. Not with Corbulo giving him such a sly look, dark eyes smiling down his nose to see if his new novice would mark his every kill, however contemptible, to the Goddess's name.

Corbulo was right, however hard it cut him to admit it. Tullier had rushed, and in rushing he'd fumbled his second kill; Great Llara would know. Unlike the knight, the groom had carried no weapon. It would mean nothing to dedicate that death to her.

Tullier sheathed his blade, his first thrill draining.

Lady Vanderive's guard had not been the challenge for which the young novice had primed himself, and even so, he'd managed to bungle one of his kills. The boy glanced, frustrated, at the rapidly blanching face of the knight he'd shot down. One kill for Llara. A second missed through clumsiness, right there for his master to see. For no reason, no reason at all, outside of his own haste.

He had been cautioned that killing freemen would be harder than dispatching slaves. Warned that first-timers had to guard against haste, fear, and a kind of panicked admiration for those who struggled to preserve their lives. Already he'd failed to heed the first of those warnings.

He glanced around the little clearing, trying to convince himself that the rest of the mistakes would be easier to avoid. Fear and admiration? Though hurry had marred this first taste of freemen's death, Tullier could not see how it differed in its essentials from culling slaves in a practice yard. Corbulo's careful planning had reduced it to that. Spread among the fallen clusters of carnelian-and-white chestnut buds were the pathetic remains of a picnic lunch: linen napkins, fresh white bread and early spring fruits, children's toys. Though the knights had been armed, the picnickers had been ready only for a day of pleasure. Corbulo, leaving nothing to chance, had waited until they had unpacked their luncheon and laid aside their weapons before striking. The lady's knights had died as they'd sported with the children, unarmed even with a stick.

Corbulo, Tullier thought, might have let one of the knights live long enough to fight. The Sha Muira would of course have prevailed, but the young apprentice might at least have learned something, facing such an enemy. Now all that remained was a babe in a folding canvas cradle, paralyzed children, and a bird-thin woman, also paralyzed, who was powerless to stop them. Where did glory for Llara lie in these killings? He could not see it. As he stood by the fresh corpse of the knight, the musky scent of crushed chestnut flowers mixed with the tang of blood. An inexplicable bitter gall choked his throat.

"Disappointed, youngster?" Corbulo pushed by, making for the slumped woman. "Don't be. There is more than death to Llara's honor here. For those who can abide it."

"I'm not sad for them," Tullier said angrily.

"Then why that clumsy second shot?"

Corbulo did wait for an answer. Moving on, he bent over the woman, turned back a fold of skirt, and exposed her younger son. The child's eyes were clenched shut, his small body tightly curled. Without a moment of hesitation, Corbulo raised his hand, sighted a dart from his wrist-launcher, and shot the child in the base of his spine. The boy, instantly paralyzed, whimpered and lost his grip on his mother's hand.

"Bastard! Oh, Goddess—" The words were a strangled noise in the mother's throat, but something in their tone caught Tullier's attention. Anger was there, as well as fright. The boy's interest sharpened. This was something unexpected. The woman's thin body had little extra flesh, and the paralysis poison had strength enough to fell a well-grown man. She should not have had the breath to resist.

"Help me," Corbulo said brusquely. He wrested the limp child's body free of her skirts.

Tullier, uncertain, reached for his knife.

"Not that," his master stopped him. "We must strip them."

The boys were dressed in boiled wool jackets, embroidered tunics, and soft trousers: nothing that would have marked them as gently born in Bissanty, where the nobles wore only silk and fine-stuff. Tullier heaved the older boy up by his shoulders, avoiding eye contact. Remembering the boy's brief, doomed stand, Tullier found himself comparing his body to the boy's as he worked. The novice was short for his age, and lightly built, while the boy was sturdy and long-limbed. The jacket Tullier pulled off the boy's back would almost have fit his own shoulders. He tossed it aside, something in him made angry, and split the tunic with his knife, deliberately ruining it. When he was done, the boy lay face-down on the fallen chestnut flowers, his smooth skin puck-ered with cold, a strand of silver links on his neck his last adornment. That had to come off with the rest. Not sure what to do, Tullier dropped the silver into the babe's cradle.

"The baby too?" he asked.

Corbulo, finishing with the younger boy, looked round, saw Tullier standing at the cradle, and made an angry gesture. "Llara's eyes, stop hurrying," he snapped. "What's rushing you now?"

"I wasn't—" Tullier protested.

"You want to argue?" The words rang with disbelief.

Tullier shook his head, recognizing the warning, however unjust. For a moment, he saw his master as the woman or her sons would see him: the lean menace of his figure, the blood-colored robes, the flapping braids, and, worst, the cruel set eyes, glittering in the death's-head mask of black-and-white paint. The paint-masked journey-master had every advantage over Tullier, with his youth and naked skin, with nothing but his own will to conceal his expression. Staring into his mas-ter's poison-rimmed eyes, Tullier discovered he had already overstepped a boundary.

"I want only to serve," the young novice said, forcing him-self to speak humbly. "Llara's light in you—please tell me what to do."

"You're pestering me," Corbulo said, again unfairly. "Just keep out of the way and watch me. I'll tell you when I need you."

The clearing settled around them. Tullier, pretending to

look at everything that wasn't his master's face, watched the
older man covertly, struggling to read his mood. The unfairness wasn't like Corbulo, and that was dangerous. The
ambush had been a success. Tullier's mistake with the groom
had not jeopardized that success. Why then was his master so
angry, so full of nerves?

Corbulo, no longer paying attention to his novice, stood
over the older boy's body and pulled a box from a pocket
deep in his robes: a wooden box, with stylized carvings of
reeds around its sides. Touching a hidden spring, he popped
the box into separated halves.

The swiftness of the man's motions had the smoothness of
practice. Yet something in Corbulo's manner told Tullier he
was not comfortable with the box or its contents. He was too
delicate, too careful in his movements. Inside the cased halves
were two coiled straps, supple red-tanned leather with black
edges. Uncoiling these straps with elaborate care, Corbulo
used the first to bind the younger boy's ankles.

The leather, touching the boy's skin, seemed to burn it. An
acrid tang sprang out, strong enough to overpower the musky
scent of chestnut blossom. Tullier could sense magic. A
strong prayer had set the spell on the leather. He bent forward,
trying to understand what he was seeing.

"Keep yourself busy." Corbulo glanced at his novice, his
voice sharp. Tullier had a confused sense that his master did
not want him watching, that despite his instruction that Tullier should watch, he was doing a thing he wished to finish
without witnesses. "Give thanks to Llara that everything so
far has gone smoothly. Goddess help us with this next—"

With a sudden powerful heave he jerked the strapped boy
up by his ankles and lashed him, head down, to one of the
chestnut's low branches. The acrid scent grew stronger. It
smelled of burning, of ritual power.

Tullier, with all his training, could guess neither the ritual's
purpose nor the source of its power. The ugly burnt odor did
not smell like Llara's magic. . . .

"Go on," Corbulo said roughly, seemingly reading his
apprentice's doubts. "Bless Llara for letting you observe

this." With the first boy secure, the journey-master nervously ran the second strap through his fingers and bent to bind the bigger boy. Now Corbulo was the one who was rushing, almost clumsy.

"Thanks be to the Thunderbringer," said Tullier, eager to demonstrate his obedience, but bewildered. The upended bodies, the way the ankles were strapped, reminded him more of stock hanging in a butcher's slaughteryard than of human bodies readied for death. He saw no signs of the Thunderbringer or of the rites of death as he had been taught them. Only the prayer that Corbulo called him to recite was familiar. He began: "Great Llara, our thanks for this kill, proof here of Llara's favor—"

Corbulo's next action cut Tullier's prayer short. A shocking, sharp interruption, as he drew a knife across the first of the boys' throats. There was nothing in the kill: just a slash with his knife, repeated for the second boy. A slash and a quick end.

"—proof here of Llara's favor," Tullier repeated, "and of Her Blessing on us." The boy stared at his teacher, appalled. The journey-master should not have made his kill with his apprentice's recitation unfinished. Not after he had specifically asked Tullier to recite the blessing—

"These young ones should have been locked behind warded gates." Corbulo wiped his knife on one of the discarded jackets and pushed it cleanly into the sheath on his thigh. He would not meet Tullier's eye. "It's a sign of Llara's support for us that they weren't. Don't be displeased, boy, that this part has gone so smoothly. It's not Lady Vanderive's fault Tielmarans are fools who left the treasury door of her blood unguarded. This has gone smoothly, thank Llara, smoothly. Bless the Great Thunderer for that."

Smoothly? Tullier shot a skeptical look at the fast-draining corpses, and then at his master. Corbulo was repeating himself too insistently. Something had gone awry. This was not the way of death that Tullier had been taught. There was something unpleasant here. Something concealed, something beyond what a master should keep from his subordinate.

"I thought Lady Vanderive was our target." The question was out of his mouth before he could quell it.

"She is."

"I thought she was our *only* target. You told me Bissanty was bringing Tielmark to heel, that we were here to teach Tielmark it is not free, not safe from Bissanty aggression."

"So?"

"This—" Tullier gestured at the strung-up corpses. He hesitated, but the words had to be spoken. "There is no hope in me that I could finish this work if you were to die." Novice stared at journey-master. For a moment, neither moved.

This was Tullier's inaugural mission. He had been well drilled in its terms. No Sha Muira could return to the home island with any part of his mission uncompleted. Because of this, the Sha Muir code decreed that a novice's first mission should be limited to a task he might hope to accomplish unaided, in the unlikely event that his master failed him.

Corbulo's eyes slipped away from his novice's. The older man sank to his knees, as if he meant to pray. "You want to know too much too soon," was all he said, avoiding Tullier's question. "Beg Llara for your answers, not me."

Tullier, dumbfounded at his master's refusal to give him a direct answer, had no choice but to drop to his knees and join him. He turned his eyes to the sky, seeking to empty himself for Llara. But he could not concentrate. His mind raced, question piling up on unanswered question. In such a state, he could not hope to feel Her touch.

Corbulo had completed twelve journeys as a Sha Muir warrior. An auspicious number. One mission for each of the gods. Back at the Sha Muira stronghold, Tullier had rejoiced to be paired with a master so distinguished as Corbulo. Now, with his master's strange withdrawal, Tullier was left to guess—wildly—what his master's strange responses might mean for his own future. Had the Arkhons decided to test Great Llara's love by assigning Corbulo a peculiarly perilous thirteenth mission? Was there truly great honor to be earned in this mission, or only damnation, in calling on a magic power outside the Gray Goddess's? If so, why had they seen fit to risk a novice with him?

This was Corbulo's first venture to Tielmark, the Bissanty Empire's southern neighbor. It was unusual, the older man had told him, for the Emperor to order a full Sha Muir envoy to the Free Principality of Tielmark. More than unusual. Unheard of. Despite its backward ways, Tielmark had once been a Bissanty possession, dignified as the fourth quarter of the Empire. In recognition of this, only shadow-envoys— spying ventures with no killing—went to Tielmark.

Corbulo had been frank with Tullier when they'd met for the first time, heeding the journey-herald's call. "I don't like this mission," he had told him. "You won't either, by the time our work is through. My thirteenth mission has been highly honored—our orders come from Emperor Sciuttarus himself. Unfortunately, Llara's will is such that this distinction may bring us more trouble than good. This mission won't simply be to cut throats."

Tullier, overwhelmed to learn that Llara's Heart-on-Earth had personally ordered their venture, had barely attended Corbulo's warning. Now, confronted with his master's nervous manner as he readied the Tielmaran lady's sons for ritual death, it took on new meaning. Corbulo, even before he had been told the full details of his envoy, had, the novice suspected, guessed that neither returning to Sha Muira Island to take up a fourteenth venture nor dying in glory for Llara would come easily. If the unfamiliar magic in the ritual belonged to some other God, not Llara, Corbulo's anxiety suggested that the dark journey-master was not certain that Llara approved its use here.

The baby sat up in the cradle and began to wail. Corbulo, deep in prayer, his braids fallen over his face, ignored it. Their situation, deep in a thick, moss-darkened forest, near a running stream, was over two miles distant from the rambling stone house where the woman who lay at their feet served as lady. No one would hear it. But the cry rasped on Tullier's nerves. Why should Corbulo be so cautious about the rest, where Tullier might have learned so much, and so casual about this? The boy unsheathed his knife.

The child tottered and stood against the canvas side of its cradle to greet him. It—she—was pretty, sturdily built like her older brother, with deep brown eyes and ash-blond curls: more toddler than baby. Between sobs, she reached out a chubby hand, too young to know better. Tullier offered her the edge of his blade.

"Not yet," Corbulo snapped coldly. "That's bait for another trap. Leave it."

Behind them, the child's mother made a protesting sound.

"Bait?" Tullier sulked, turning from the child to his journey-master. "What are you keeping from me, Master?"

"There's some at the Hold who claim you as the pride of your class," Corbulo said coldly, obsidian dark glittering in his eyes. Even on his knees, he inspired fear. "Yet here you are, running your mouth in front of the living. Look at her. Do you think she does not hear you?"

Tullier turned away, suppressing an unexpected stab of alarm. He stared at Lady Vanderive, hating her, wondering how it was that he kept on compounding his mistakes, when so much of the situation lay under their control.

The woman had fallen back on the grass. Before the dart's poison had set in, she'd thrashed her skirts over her knees, exposing slim ankles and long coltish legs. Staring at those pretty legs, Tullier felt his face go hot. She won't be living long, he told himself, teasing her by moving the knife still closer to the baby. Yet, once again, Corbulo was right to rebuke him. In the expressive brown eyes she had passed to her children, rancor mingled with her fear. She had calmed enough to stop fruitless struggle, to concentrate her all on what she could do—which was to watch them.

One of the first lessons at Sha Muira Stronghold, a thing impressed on the youngest classes, was a demonstration of the raising of the dead. To the bloodthirsty circle of students, sometimes the demonstrations had been humorous, occasionally they had been almost sad, but the greater lesson had been that even the most profoundly mutilated corpses would find the means to communicate their assassin's name to their questioners, when they knew it.

There was only one punishment a journey-master could mete to a novice on his first mission. Tullier had to stop compounding his mistakes.

"You said bait," Tullier said briskly, trying to retrieve himself. "That doesn't tell me what you next require. Am I in your way? I'll stand with the horses if I am in your way."

Corbulo shook his head, laughing malevolently. "You can't escape so easily," he said. "You must play your part, as well as I." His tongue touched his lips, a nervous, too vivid shock of red in the painted mask of his face. "Stop hurrying, and follow me. Llara will watch over us."

Tullier froze. A dizzy wave of dread swept from his brain to his gut. He did not know if it was the nervous tongue, or the words, but he sensed with a deep and sudden certainty that his master was terrified; like a slave waiting for the cut of death, Corbulo was terrified.

Terror for a Sha Muira came only from one source: turning from Great Llara's path, losing Her favor. If his master was afraid—his apprentice must accept that he would have to share that fate.

What was in the fallen woman, in her sons, that might make a Sha Muira cross Llara's will?

Compared to the Bissanty nobles with whom Tullier was familiar, the lady was unimpressive: her wool dress somber, the hammered silver of her necklace a touch barbaric. Her hands were callused like a farming wife's, her broad face was pretty, but not exceptional, and the thin body did not inspire Tullier's young passion. She seemed hardly a sight to compel a Sha Muira to terror.

Yet Corbulo was so frightened he was almost visibly shaking.

Tullier instinctively drew closer, craning to see, to understand, without unduly drawing his master's notice. Gods' glyphs ornamented the boys' bonds. A pattern of stylized deer in flight alternated with an unfamiliar symbol: a broken spiral, bound round by a white circle. It was not the Gray

Goddess-Queen's magic. One of the other *twelve*, then. Perhaps Huntress Elianté, Llara's oldest daughter. Elianté and her twin, Emiera, were the highest of the gods worshiped in Tielmark. He flicked an impatient look at the Tielmaran lady, desperate suddenly for her to be dead so he might have a hope of prying answers from his tight-lipped master.

Corbulo, prayer finally completed, rose from his knees. The last item from the carved box, a bone-bladed knife, was in his hand. He flourished it twice in the air, tracing a circle. The pommel, like the red straps, bore the broken spiral sign, encircled by a white rim of enamel.

"Give me your hand." His journey-master, looking up, did not seem surprised by Tullier's closeness. The acrid scent of the leathers was stronger now, past burning to bitter ashes. "The casting needs a taste of blood—your blood. And then we'll have some of the baby's."

Tullier, trying to prove himself true to his training, did not hesitate. He held his hand out, careful not to flinch as his master seized it.

Corbulo drove the blade deep into the boy's palm.

An unpleasant shock of power flashed through the knife into Tullier's sinewy arm and on down through his spine. It was power as strong as any the boy had felt standing before the main shrine on Sha Muira Island, bowing to Llara in Her darkest aspect. It numbed something deep in his body, low in his hips. He quivered involuntarily, shaken. Blood welled from his palm, looking strange—purple and dark—against the pale ivory of the blade. There was something eager in the way the bone edge sucked up the blood, something nauseating and strong. The magic was not under Corbulo's control.

"It wants more," Tullier said faintly.

"It's getting more." The journey-master jerked back the blade and stooped for the baby. The mother twitched, but the baby was too young to anticipate the threat. Her infant gaze fixed on the journey-master's face, intrigued by the hard contrast of the black-and-white paint. She stopped crying. Corbulo touched her thigh with the knife so slyly she hardly knew that the blade had gone in and out.

As the baby's blood spread on the bone edge and touched Tullier's, the whole of the bone blade went tar-black.

"Virgin to virgin," Corbulo intoned. He rotated to face the hanging bodies. "Blood calling blood." Bowing his head, his long braids falling forward, he braced himself: knife hand raised, the fingers of his free hand spread. It was as if, at that key moment, the journey-master felt off-balance.

"Witness my act, Great Twelve above!"

The knife drove into the older boy's chest, under the breast-bone, deep enough to pierce the heart. A draft of wind swept the sultry, unseasonably warm air, and there was a clash, as if of thunder, though the sky was brazen blue, cloudless. Corbulo moved swiftly to the second boy. Again, the blade swept down. Again, the great clash rang out. The leaves of the chest-nut and of the other trees shivered and sighed. The chatter of the stream faded.

Where the two corpses of the boys had hung, two young deer swung, raggedly butchered, tied by their hind legs to the tree. They swayed gently in the last tags of wind.

The bone blade, once more white and clean, was clasped in Corbulo's hands, its tip pointed to the sky. Tullier noted dark patches of sweat on his master's robes. Black paint from Corbulo's face had trickled onto his neck, staining the collar of his robe.

Wiping his neck, Corbulo gestured for Tullier to approach. The journey-master stood proudly to his full height, shook his braids back over his shoulders, and turned to the woman. For a moment, Tullier's heart lifted: the fear had left his master. He was once again Sha Muira, death-bringer, with no doubt in him.

"You were born for this death," Corbulo said, addressing her. "Pray to your gods and welcome it." He curled his painted fingers around the curve of her white arm, marking her flesh with poison. That instant, she was dead. She was too ignorant to know it. A Bissanty woman would have been screaming, anticipating the curdling pain of the poison that would soon bring her the horror of dying by Llara's black curse. Tullier would have sneered at her ignorance—but at that moment, the Tielmaran woman's composure was greater even than his master's. Corbulo, something relieved in him, was gloating. "Think on the sweetness, pretty one," he was saying. "You'll be Tullier's first woman. I'm giving your death to him. You'll make him a true Sha Muir man. He'll try to be gentle, and he'll likely be fast—but you'll have to help him, or you may find him fumbling."

The blood dropped from Tullier's cheeks. Names! The journey-master had named him! Not only had his master mixed his blood with the babe's to work the magic, but now he had named him to the lady's face! He almost cried out, the shock of betrayal was so great.

"I've done nothing." The woman fought to answer smoothly, but with her thick, poison-swollen lips and half-paralyzed lungs, her words came out a foolish stutter. Her angry-hurt eyes shifted from Corbulo's painted death's-head mask to the transformed corpses of her sons. "They did nothing either."

"You were born, they were born." Corbulo propped her, half-sitting, against the tree. Her thin body was as limp as a puppet. "That's enough. Blame your mother's mother for the legacy of bad blood that she imparted to you. And yourself, for birthing a new generation. Tullier and I are here to break a prophecy—if we can't, we'll at least make a cull that will weaken its strength."

Lady Vanderive's eyes widened, filling with enlightenment and wrath. "My children," she choked harshly. "Killed for my blood." Somewhere deep within her body, she made a mighty effort to collect herself. Her tongue protruded from her lips. One hand shifted, the fingers fumbled, sketching a spiral sign—similar to that which Corbulo had used to cast the spell, but not the same.

For all her callused hands, she was not a strong-looking woman. With the dart's poisoned tip deep in her body, with the dark stain of poison on her arm where Corbulo had touched her, she shouldn't have been able to move or speak.

"I won't die for you." With great effort, she forced out the words. "You can't have that. Goddess in me, you won't break prophecy through me."

There was magic in her. Magic strong enough to resist Sha Muir poison. Corbulo had given Tullier no hint that there was magic in their intended victim's blood. Alarmed, the boy shot his master a doubting look.

The Sha Muira were Great Llara's tools, the dagger in Her left hand to balance the sword—the Imperial Army—that She held in Her right. But prophecy was something that bound even the gods' actions. It could not be right for the Bissanty Emperor, even as Llara's Heart-on-Earth, to interfere with prophecy.

He watched, blood pounding at his temples, as his master dragged the Tielmaran woman to her feet and tied her by her wrists to another of the chestnut tree's thick branches—near enough to the transformed corpses of her sons that she could almost have touched them. Corbulo lashed the woman's arms high over her head, posing her so her breast jutted forward.

Back at rocky Sha Muira Island, Tullier would have sworn on his soul that his loyalty to the cult was beyond questioning. His training was the path that would lead him to Llara. Life and death were as one, in service to the Goddess-Queen. In Her name, every fear could be met and conquered. A glorious river of silver fire awaited those who served Her. To die in Llara's name and feel that everlasting fire was something to be welcomed, an eternal banishment of fear and pain. What need of threats or bonds, compared to the fear of earning Her displeasure and losing that silver fire?

At the last Sha Muir ceremony, prior to the start of his mission, Tullier's spirit had rebelled against the seeming distrust that motivated the final binding. The priests, masked with gold for the ritual poisoning, had counted the black pearls onto the silver salver, impassive, seemingly unaware of his kneeling figure. The final test: to voluntarily consume the Goddess-blessed poison that would last the course of his mission.

He had flattered himself that he needed no poison vow to assure his loyalty, that he would voluntarily choose death over failure if his mission miscarried. But even with his eagerness to fight and die in the Sha Muira name shining bright in his eyes, the Arkhon priest had proffered the plate of poisonous black pearls, implacable. It was only the presence of Corbulo at his side, invoking the name of great Llara as he took each pearl from the silver salver, crushed it between his teeth and swallowed, that had steadied Tullier to submit. If Corbulo could count, with steady fingers, the antidote beads that were to be strung on his life necklace—one to void each pearl, one to keep the poison at bay each day as they fulfilled their mission—so must Tullier.

Now, watching Corbulo ready the woman for death, Tullier understood that the poison bond existed to free the Sha Muira to perform their duty. The hanging sword of death and pain gave them liberty to fulfill their duties without regret or hesitation. And where they failed—the poison would take them to Llara, and another Sha Muira would follow and succeed, taking to himself the Gray Goddess's glory. The poison gave them steadiness, surety.

"They'll come to avenge me," the woman said. Her voice, little more than a whisper, had cleared.

"We're counting on it," Corbulo told her, rubbing the knife along the curve where her ribs gave onto her stomach. "Your avengers have been hand-picked. And if they don't come"— he shrugged—"your daughter's life should serve as a more adequate lure." He nodded to the cradle. The baby, sensing the attention, giggled, moved, and caught his eye.

"Watch!" Tullier cried. As the journey-master's attention slipped, the woman's expression contracted with a tremendous focus, tremendous rage. "Watch her!"

She lunged onto the proffered knife.

The blade was too close, too full of hungry magic. Although her hands were bound high over her head and she had little leeway, it was enough. The blade nicked her front. When Corbulo tried to jerk away, the knife hissed and twisted, eager.

It was over.

"Bitch." Corbulo slashed the corpse with the knife, dragging the blade so it carved jagged gouges in her skin. "Blood-cursed bitch." Standing back, he hid the knife in his sleeve and turned angrily to his young novice, but not before Tullier saw, with a dropping heart, that the edge of the blade was broken, the knife ruined. "That's the wages of too much talk," Corbulo spat. Fear ran high in his voice. "Load the boys onto the spare horse. I'll carry the babe."

Leaving the young woman's corpse hanging from the tree, they went to get the horses. Moving the transformed deer-boys was hard work. The packhorse, smelling the tainted metal scent of blood and magic, fought against the loading.

There were questions the young novice wanted to ask—so many questions.

From Corbulo's mood, he guessed it could be worth his life to ask them.

More than anything, Tullier wished he knew what prophecy the pair of assassins had been sent to Tielmark to subvert.

chapter 1 ▼

When Gaultry Blas, the young Huntress
Witch of Arleon Forest, arrived at the three sacral hills
where Princes of Tielmark celebrated the feast days of the
Goddess Twins, her position at court could best be described
as ambiguous. Certainly, she was a hero, her accomplishments manifold. She had defeated Tielmark's traitorous
Chancellor in single combat, had broken the Bissanty bond-
magic he had laid upon the Prince, and had stood upon the
coronation stone of Tielmark to choose the Prince's new
bride. For a woman raised in an isolated rural cottage deep in
the southern border forest, these were exhilarating feats. But
they also frightened and confused her. They had changed the
course of Gaultry's life irrevocably, not least because they
revealed her heritage—which was to serve and protect her
Prince's destiny. Long-dormant magic coursed, strong and
potent, in her blood, magic that could safeguard Tielmark, the
Prince, and even the Great Twins' rule over Tielmark, should
she so choose to use it.

Yet with the Chancellor dead and the Bissanty threat laid,
Gaultry found herself adrift in a confusing web of court poli-

tics in which her fabulous powers had little relevance. Benet, Tielmark's Prince, had rewarded her stunning acts of magic with a courtier's favors. He had gifted Gaultry and her twin sister, Mervion, with ample accommodations, horses, a falcon, and generous stipends. Gaultry and her twin had been chosen to perform in a ceremonial capacity on feast days such as this, when Goddess Twin Emiera's benediction was supplicated to bless the spring planting. But such rewards and sinecures, which made no active use of either sister's talents, had only served to compound resentment towards them, stirring envy and satisfaction among those who had been less active in thwarting the Bissanty incursions.

Ironically, Gaultry had helped the Prince renew the godpledge that would protect Tielmark from powerful Bissanty, its northern imperial neighbor, for a full cycle of rule: fifty years. Fifty years, Gaultry thought wryly as she reached the flat top of Feeding-Hill, would be a long time to laze at court waiting for her services to once again truly be necessary.

She turned slowly on her heels to survey the sacral land that spread around her. The sun shone warmly on her face and the light breeze brought a tang of fresh sea and plant scents. Despite all her worries, she found her mood lightening. For three hundred years, Princes of Tielmark had celebrated the Goddess Emiera's planting day at this site. Today, at least in part because of her actions, the Prince could celebrate it once more. The green hills stood on a small rise of land that separated the rugged coastal cliffs from the thin band of forest that extended inland towards the Dousallier hills, east of Princeport, Tielmark's capital city. It was an ancient site, with a history that reached deep into the years of Bissanty occupation. Clarin, the founder of Free Tielmark, had consecrated the ground in the Great Twins' names on the site of an even earlier Bissanty outpost. Gaultry, drinking in the beauty of the day and the fabulous view of the green hills and sea, could not help but feel proud, thinking on the part she had played in denying the Bissanties' efforts to reclaim this land for their powerful thunder-goddess, Mother Llara.

Supporters and detractors of the new Princess, loyalists to

the Prince, and Bissanty-sympathizers who had survived the purge, stood clustered together on the hill in the strong morning sun, waiting for the noon ceremonial. That was when everyone would renew their vows of service: to the Prince, to Tielmark, and to Tielmark's god-wrought freedom. Gaultry was not surprised that some of them appeared openly uneasy.

The Prince was there with his new Princess to dedicate himself, body and bride, to the spring planting. The supplication to the Great Lady Emiera was Benet's first formal act as a Free Prince of Tielmark, a Prince who had escaped Bissanty bonds and claimed the Great Twins' Blessing on his marriage and his rule. But despite the joyous nature of the occasion, the Prince had summoned his court to the sacral hills with a grim warning: without renewed pledges from every landholder, he would pray for the Goddess to wither the crops in their fields. This was no empty threat. Benet's god-pledges meant that he was joined in mystic marriage to the land. He had the power to damage the harvest if he withheld his blessing from the sacred ceremonies. Though some men grumbled that there was space between prayer and the gods, few were willing to chance it. The hills were near overrun with courtiers and their servants.

Gaultry found the pomp and the elaborately colorful preparations overwhelming. In the village near the forest cottage where she had grown to womanhood, Lady Emiera's Feast meant a scanty meal comprised more of the roots and dried legumes left over from winter than of the thin new produce of spring. At the Prince's feast, by contrast, gaily-laid tables groaned with the weight of early harvest gifts, drawn from all quarters of Tielmark. If bounty and expense counted as indicators of a people's loyalty, the Prince proved himself well loved today.

The many closed and nervous faces among the Prince's courtiers spoke otherwise. Some, grown accustomed to the loose leash of a sorcery-bound, weakened Prince, had little reason to celebrate Benet's recovered strength. Others felt that Benet's fallibility, in falling prey to Bissanty wiles, had yet to be redeemed. On a cloudy day, the dark faces would hardly have been noticed. Today, the sweet scent of spring and sea combined with the clear blue of the sky to make the discord among the Prince's people uncomfortably conspicuous. Many of the discontented were not even Bissanty collaborators.

For Gaultry, the most disturbingly unhappy face was that of Tielmark's newly restored High Priestess. Dervla of Princeport's shrill voice and her ill-suppressed anger could be heard even from where Gaultry stood at the hill's seaward edge, drawing her eye to the thin woman as she thrust her way aggressively through the throng on Feeding-Hill, in open argument with the Master of the Tables about the assignment of places from the Prince's table downwards. Though dressed in splendid robes as befitted the day, and crowned with a wreath of ash branches—Emiera's signifier—the High Priestess's face, beneath the budding twist of branch, was pinched and sour. As the top-ranking priestess of Tielmark's Twin Goddesses, confident in her Prince's readmission to Their favor, some part of Dervla must have found the day a glad one. But as a politician who felt that her modest role in the Prince's reinstatement had served only to diminish her influence, Dervla seethed with the frustration of unfulfilled ambition.

Sensing the young southern woman's scrutiny, the unsmiling priestess turned. Her eyes narrowed. Gaultry, caught staring, answered the woman's hostile glare with a foolish guilty smile. Dervla, seeing that smile, abruptly dismissed the tablemaster and pushed a man out of her way, moving towards Gaultry, anger evident in the tense lines of her thin body. The High Priestess was not above lashing out at those whom she imagined had detracted from her personal share of glory. From the chill in the High Priestess's pale almond eyes as she approached, Gaultry could see that whatever had focused the woman's ill-humor, right now she had decided to hold Gaultry responsible.

"A fine feast day to you," Gaultry greeted the priestess, bowing her head. She wanted to be conciliatory, though she had never liked Dervla. Before the Prince's reinstatement, the priestess had seized every opportunity to challenge Gaultry's part in the struggle to defeat the traitor Chancellor Heiratikus and his Bissanty-backed insurgency. Now she was foremost among those whose conduct made Gaultry feel out of place at court.

"And to you," the priestess said shortly. "Such a crowd. Lasalle is struggling to find everyone places at the tables. Those the Prince did not call should have stayed at home. This is a Princely rite, not a sideshow gawkery!"

"People want to see the new Princess."

"They should have stayed home. I'm sure their own people are missing them. Indeed . . ." The pale eyes fixed on Gaultry. "I'm sure Paddleways Village must miss their homegrown huntress-lady twins."

"People in Paddleways are preoccupied with their planting now," Gaultry said, taking two steps up the hill to meet Dervla on level ground. The lanky young woman was a good head taller than Dervla, and she knew Dervla disliked the physical advantage it gave her. "Along with the rest of Tielmark. Oats, wheat, brown barley, and rye. Hunting is probably the last thing on their minds, so they don't need me. I doubt they miss Mervion either. They know her duties lie here with the Prince. Paddleways has its own priestess to play the lady's part on Emiera's Day."

Dervla cocked her ash-crowned head toward the young huntress, the almond eyes unreadable. "It's a small village," she insisted. "They must miss you. Both of you." Dervla's supercilious expression went well with her thin ascetic's body. Her taut, active movements, and her carriage somehow suggested that righteous denial of the flesh should be taken as an example by all around her. But despite her self-conscious denial of excess—or perhaps because of it—the priestess had a poor understanding of the hard simplicity of working life in a small border village.

Or how little a part Gaultry and her sister, living deep in the border forest with their eccentric forest-bound grandmother Tamsanne, had ever been of it.

"Neither of us will be returning to Paddleways any time

soon," Gaultry told the priestess stiffly. "Not while the Prince wants us here at court."

"Or the new Princess," Dervla said, unusually candid in her bitterness. She disliked the Prince's new bride, who, like Gaultry, was not court-bred. "But what is it that you are hoping to accomplish by staying?"

"The Great Twins know better than I." Or you, Gaultry felt tempted to add. "In the meantime, Mervion and I are here to serve Benet in anything he asks of us." The priestess was a fool not to see that her point had been won long past, at least insofar as Gaultry was concerned. Her few short weeks at court had taught her—all too quickly—that there was no regular service she could hope to offer her Prince for which there was not someone else who was better trained, better habituated, more ready. "We're being a help today," she added, defensive in spite of her pride. "My morning began before dawn. I was out with the branch-cutting party."

"Physical labor," Dervla scoffed. "Don't pretend you believe that's your calling."

"Work finds me as it may." Gaultry rubbed her palms together, conscious suddenly of the skin she had chafed dragging branches, and beginning to lose her patience. "I wish it were my place to smooth the Prince's path with magic and prayer," she added. "Unfortunately for me, my calling is not so easily defined."

Dervla's thin cheeks reddened. "Don't mock my vocation," she hissed, an expression on her face that made those around them draw hastily away. "There is nothing easy in channeling the power of the gods."

Gaultry, aware of the worried attention they had drawn from those who had been casually listening, looked round in dismay, surprised that Dervla was so ready to make a public show that she took the young woman's every word as an uncloaked insult. "I respect your power, High Priestess," she said. "The Great Twins' light is strong in you."

"You!" Her words served to make Dervla angrier than ever. "You respect power, and only power! And I have power enough to put you in your place!" She reached out and seized

Gaultry's wrist, forcing the young woman to feel the green heat of holy magic that coursed like renewing fire through her whip-thin body. "By the Huntress and Lady both," the priestess said, shaking with effort as she drew up her strength, "don't think you can mock me. If you have acted where others could only hope to serve, don't flatter yourself that it was of your own planning."

Whatever Dervla's weakness for posturing, she had earned her place as High Priestess through merit. Gaultry, her senses overborne by the woman's power, felt her resentment and with it her resistance abating before the river of Goddesslight. But she would not bow without a struggle. Dervla's attacks, her tests, were no longer the surprise they had once been. Even as her head dipped in submission, half-mastered, a painful warmth spread through her chest as her own magic lashed to life, rousing against the bullying. The flare of magic was golden, intense, and barely under Gaultry's control. "Huntress help me!" Gaultry fought to speak, "I never offered you any such challenge!" She struggled to rein back her counterassault. "Leave me be!"

Power flashed between them. Gold magic seared green, driving it back. Dervla dropped Gaultry's wrist, rebuffed. She spread her fingers to dissipate the pain, and shot Gaultry a venomous look. Gaultry looked away, her own ears ringing as though they'd been boxed. She panted, still struggling to quiet the instinctive surge of power, wishing angrily that Dervla would learn to leave her alone.

"If you truly loved great Elianté and Emiera," Dervla said, disingenuously mild, "you would understand your duty to submit."

Gaultry, her face flaming, had no answer. If the thin priestess refused to admit she did not quite command the power to force either Gaultry or her sister to submit to a subordinate role in Emiera and Elianté's priesthood, there was little Gaultry could do about that. Priests often disapproved of those who called magic from the gods without first surrendering their lives to religion. Gaultry had encountered such prejudice before, and she knew there was little she could do to change it. But Dervla's stubbornness stemmed from more than this, and again there was little Gaultry could do. Although Gaultry and her sister called magic from the Great Goddess Twins—weak magic, that Dervla could easily have suppressed—a second, stronger source of power fortified that magic, a source that enabled even an inexperienced huntress-witch like Gaultry to face down the High Priestess of Tielmark.

Gaultry and Mervion were throwbacks. They had been born with Glamour-souls, an atavistic primitive magic. Glamour was a raw and dangerous force, which both sisters were struggling to control and to understand. When the gods first created humankind, they had drawn human flesh from their own bodies, and formed it in their own image. Because of this, their new creation at first proved more powerful than even the gods had predicted. The gods each wielded distinctive creating fire: green for the Twin Goddesses Elianté and Emiera, silver for their mother Llara Thunderbringer, red for Father Andion the Sun, and on through all the Great Twelve. Born of god-flesh, the gods' new playthings inherited a pale echo of these divine powers: a new, golden fire called Glamour. Glamour-power manifested itself in the human body as a second soul, a soul of molten creative fire that bestowed mingled torture and beauty on its possessors. It had alternately destroyed and exalted those who had possessed it.

The gods acted swiftly to purge mankind of Glamour, drawing all they could of that golden power back into themselves. Now, less frequently than once a century, a throwback was born with a Glamour-soul. It was unheard of for twins to be born to Glamour . . . until the birth of Gaultry and Mervion Blas.

As children, unaware of their latent power, the Blas twins had prayed to the Great Twins for their magic. During the events that led up to the Prince's marriage and his Godpledge, the threat to their lives had awakened their hidden strength. But they were still fledglings, trying to learn to use their power safely. If used incautiously, Glamour-magic was almost certain to consume them with its wild creative force.

Gaultry gave Dervla an unfriendly look, realizing that the High Priestess had chosen to goad her, aware of the risks the young woman faced when she drew on the power of her new magic under duress.

The priestess, refusing even to acknowledge that she'd challenged the younger woman, gave herself a little shake and tucked her stung hand into one of her voluminous sleeves. "Benet wants you here at court," she said, jerking her shoulders in a resigned shrug. "As if either you or your sister is suited to serve him in that capacity. I can't worry about that. He'll learn better soon enough."

Gaultry, still sick from the lurch of raw Glamour-magic, did not trust herself to answer.

"Look—" The older woman pointed, spinning away. "The thrones are almost ready."

Below, in the gentle bowl of land between the triad of hills, a wide circle had been cleared in the glossy grass. A little beyond the circle's perimeter, workmen were weaving ivy and flowering branches into twinned chairs where the Prince and Princess would sit to accept the obeisance of their courtiers. The seats and chair-backs were complete, only the armrests left unfinished. The priestess's manner as she gestured to the thrones was carefully cool. They had come to the reason for Dervla's hard feelings—at least for this feast day.

"Your acolytes cut those branches," Gaultry said, tentative.

"Indeed," Dervla said lightly. Something in her eyes hardened. "As they have done for decades past, and will do for years to come, when you and your pretty sister have left our Prince's court."

Gaultry waited, silent.

"They want you to stand at their shoulders as they accept the season's branches, don't they?"

"They" meant Prince Benet and his wife.

"Me and Mervion together," Gaultry corrected her.

"You and your twin," Dervla said resentfully.

"Had Your Veneracy chosen some other young women to be supporters to the Prince today?" Gaultry asked. "Be assured, Mervion and I did not put our names forward for the role. If Tielmark regards twinship as a sign of the goddesses' favor, it is nothing we asked for. The Prince simply apprised us that he wanted twins in tribute to the Great Twins. His exact words were 'True twins for the Great Twins,' if you must know."

Here was the crux of Dervla's problem. The gods were cruel. Those who wished to serve were not always those who were chosen. And to those who wished for freedom—it was not always granted. "Mervion and I will not refuse our Prince's orders," Gaultry said.

Dervla's eyes were like flint. "I am Tielmark's High Priestess. When Benet calls the Great Twins, he should look to me first for advice."

"I'm sure he does look to you first," a new voice broke the conversation, a dry crackle of a voice with a sharp ironic edge. "But Benet is his own man—and his wife and others are there to clamor for his attention after you have had your say."

Gaultry turned to face the new speaker. For a moment, the dazzle of sun off the sea blinded her. Gabrielle Lourdes, the Duchess of Melaudiere, seemed to emerge in a disconcerting glitter from that blaze of heat and blinding light. Her robes were ancient-looking white and blue silk, but a shining surface on the cloth mimicked the light of the sea behind her, so the effect was grand rather than shopworn. "You look in an awful temper, young Gaultry," the Duchess said lightly. The deliberately mild expression on her aged face disarmed the words of their potential sting. "What's Dervla been saying?"

"Your Grace," Gaultry welcomed her, relieved. "Best joy of Emiera's Day to you. We were speaking of the ceremony."

The Duchess was a woman who had fulfilled her ambitions, only—as she had once told Gaultry—to come to regret that ambition had ever ruled her. In current court debates, she and Dervla, putatively allies, were in fact at constant loggerheads in the struggle to reestablish the balance of the Prince's power. By Tielmark's law and customs, Gabrielle of Melaudiere should have been at a disadvantage in this struggle. She called her magic from Allegrios Rex, the Master of the Sea, rather than from Tielmark's patron Goddess Twins,

and that allegiance alone could have deprived her of a full
voice on the ducal council. But in a full fifty-year cycle of
Tielmaran politics, that loyalty had seldom, if ever, proved a
hindrance to the old Duchess. She had served the Prince's
father, uncle, and grandmother staunchly, many years before
Dervla had risen to her position of prominence. Those experiences had taken the Duchess from a desire to share the
Prince's ruling power through to a belief that for Tielmark to
prosper the Prince must be strong and even willful, exercising
his divine connection to the land without well-meaning but
ultimately destructive mediation. She approved of Benet's
instinct in keeping Gaultry and her twin at court, though
Gaultry sometimes felt that part of Melaudiere's approval
stemmed from her amusement in seeing Dervla's plans so
constantly set at odds. Just at the moment, however, the
young huntress felt only gratitude at her intervention.

"You were speaking of the ceremony?" the Duchess asked,
her sharp blue eyes shining with mischief. "I hear Gaultry and
Mervion will support the Prince's throne this year. Who better?"

"Who better?" Dervla said. "If my own acolytes won't do,
no one."

The old Duchess grinned, wolfish. "Can you wonder that
the Prince prefers real twins at his back? Consider what befell
the last pretenders on the night the Prince was married."

The last pretenders, called by the traitor Chancellor to stand
in for Great Elianté and Emiera at the Prince's marriage-
ceremony, had been torn limb from limb at the commence-
ment of the cataclysmic events that had restored Prince Benet
to power.

"Those false priestesses were none of mine," Dervla said.
The skin tightened around her mouth. "They had sold themselves to Bissanty."

"So they had. And the Great Twins extracted the highest
penalty for their false witness." The Duchess shook her head
sadly, though her eyes remained intently on the priestess.
Gaultry, who had moved to stand beside her, marveled at the
old woman's appearance of mildness, even as Dervla's com-

mand of her own temper slipped. "Benet knows Gaultry and Mervion are loyal," the Duchess continued. "It's a Prince's job to know that—even when his highest advisors cannot agree."

"They're untrained—"

"Is that your worry, High Priestess?" The Duchess laughed. "That our rustic border witches will shame our Prince on Great Emiera's highest day?" The taunt against her upbringing made Gaultry redden, but she held her tongue and let the Duchess finish. "You know as well as I, all that is called for today is two pretty girls to stand at the Prince's shoulders. The holy day's power lies in the sacrifice the Prince makes on Emiera's Hill—not in what his nobles bring him."

"Don't pretend to teach me the Great Twins' ways," Dervla spat back. "I know, better than you, Sea-Preacher, where Emiera's eyes turn. But I won't sit by and let Benet ruin his chances to make Tielmark truly invulnerable to Bissanty incursions. My own choice had its merits. I had planned that Palamar Laconte should stand service at the Prince's back."

"Palamar?" the Duchess said softly. Something in her darkened, a storm moving across a deceptively calm sea. "The same Palamar whose grandmother was Marie Laconte, who took the Brood-blood vow with myself and five other fools? So—" She moved herself, subtle yet unrelenting, to pin Dervla against the sea cliff's edge. "You don't like seeing Tamsanne's granddaughters playing Tielmark's standard-bearers, but you'd decided in your own mind to bring Brood-blood back into the Prince's Court."

Dervla cast a single glance at the sparkling sea. Then she mastered herself, took a step forward, and closed the space between herself and the old woman. "Tielmark is ruled by prophecy," she said. "Any Prince who ignores that will shatter his own rule. But prophecy can be bent, re-formed. This recent wedding bought us fifty years, a new cycle before the Great Twins once again descend to us to demand their fee. We can't let ourselves slip, let untrained innocents blunder and ruin our plans. Not like the last time."

"Like the last time?" the Duchess said. Her pose of calm

dropped away, and Gaultry saw that she was deeply troubled. "You weren't alive the last time these matters were debated. Your own mother should have counselled you better about the last time. The Common Brood was formed the last time—the most powerful sorcerers in the land, all dedicated to Tielmark's service by a Princess's pledge-bond, sworn through that bond to endure the chains of a prophecy that bound them to that service. We—even you, High Priestess—are pawns of that prophecy, not its master. Prophecies are for Princes to form. Princes, and Kings, and the gods themselves. And perhaps the rare god-touched lunatic. Lay you claim to that last?"

The wail of a deerskin horn postponed Dervla's answer. The sound of the horn rose, a gasping cry, melancholic and triumphant both, across the green of the hills and out to sea, silencing the throng on the seaward hill and the three women who stood, a little apart, at its edge.

A column of white smoke wafted skyward from the center of the grove of ash trees on Emiera's Hill—the westward of the inland hills, where the Prince and his wife, hidden from the crowds, were making sacrifice. The solid, tightly formed column rose, higher and higher, holding its form, like a great mounting spire that drew the heavens nearer the earth. Up it went, and kept on rising. To Gaultry, it seemed it would reach up and touch the blue bowl of the sky, the train of the gods' territory.

"The temper of the day itself was a good augury," the priestess said flatly, her eyes on the smoke. Unfriendly resignation colored her voice. "Even so, I've never seen such a height. It cannot be disputed."

"What is it?" Gaultry caught at the duchess's sleeve. She had expected the smoke, but not this great rising spire. "What does it mean?"

The old woman stared across at the silver trunks of the high ash grove, rapt. "Somewhere up that hill," she said, "the Prince and Princess are on their knees, embracing, and praying as one soul to Great Emiera to bless their land with healthy crops. It looks to me like Emiera heard them." The Duchess threw back her head and laughed, shaking the weight of age and care from her shoulders. Her fierce blue eyes were bright with pleasure. "Benet and Lily have fed a fire Emiera wants all the Great Twelve to witness. She's agreed to honor their prayers—now the Great Summer Lady makes notice that none of the gods should prove that promise a lie. Tielmark's farmers will rejoice come autumn."

"Only if Elianté's Harvest goes well," Dervla interjected dampeningly. "A good crop helps no one if it can't be harvested. And come autumn, it will be the new Princess, not Benet, who sets the holy timber to light."

"Another of your doubted ones, the untrained?" the Duchess said humorously. Lily, who had been born into a poor fisher's family, had served the Prince as his laundry-girl before she had married him. "Why worry? She has all summer to learn the service."

"Enough talk," Dervla said grimly, pushing her robes up her arms to reveal thin white wrists. "I must go to my Prince. The fire will be burning itself out by now. He will need me to consecrate the ashes." She pushed past old Melaudiere and onwards up the hill.

"She never mentions the Princess," Gaultry said, staring at Dervla's dwindling figure, "except to criticize."

The Duchess shot the young southerner an amused look. "Dervla likes a bloodline she can recognize," she said. "On both sides, back through the generations. Which is bound to frustrate her in Tielmark, where the gods want common blood enriching our gentlefolk's cradles. Poor Dervla! Though she's loyal to Tielmark, and Tielmark's gods, her heart's desire is to be the center of a well-defined court circle, where everyone stays neatly in place."

Gaultry stared up at the spire of white smoke. "That's the last thing Tielmark needs," she said. Tielmark, a land of freeholding farmers, was too poor and too preoccupied with the cycles that governed farming to support an extravagant court. It needed a Princess like Lily, who was worn and lean from the poverty she had suffered as a child, but spirited and proud beneath her unimpressive looks. Such a Princess reminded her courtiers daily that true wealth lay in the land and the people, not in court games and personal amusements. "Tielmark's court needs its Bissanty influence purged," Gaultry said. "The land will benefit from Lily ruling at Benet's side."

"As I would expect you to say," the Duchess said. "Considering that you were the one who thrust her into Benet's arms on Prince's Night."

"I can't claim that honor," Gaultry protested. "I had no idea what I was doing. I thought I was picking her at random from the assembly. I never guessed that she and Benet were already lovers, that Benet wanted her for his bride. Only the Great Twins knew the truth. They moved through me that night."

"And you wonder that Dervla envies you?"

"How can she?" Gaultry said with simple honesty. "The power of the Great Twins that is in her—it's like a river of green light. Mervion and I—we love the Great Twins, but we don't have anything like that."

"Your strength is from another source," the Duchess answered dryly. "You don't need to beg a god for power. Dervla is not alone in envying that."

The High Priestess had reached the top of Feeding-Hill. As she walked over its crest, out of their sight, she cast a last look backwards and shook her head.

Melaudiere, squinting in the bright light, stared after her and sighed. "Dervla is a bitter woman. She sees change, and she cannot hold it back. The High Priestess serves Tielmark to keep the status quo. You and your sister together signify a new force—perhaps a new era. Dervla fears you."

"But we're all blood of the same brood," Gaultry protested. "Even if we don't like each other, the pledge we share binds us to a common purpose—supporting the Prince. Dervla's mother made that pledge. So did Tamsanne, my grandmother. And so did you—"

"We have Brood-blood in common," the Duchess agreed curtly, "but there is no agreement as to what the Brood-prophecy signifies. Protecting the Prince—what does that mean? We all agree that Tielmark must be purged of the Bissanty plague that makes its resurgence at every cycle. How to achieve that, no one knows. But certainly the Bissanty will not wait fifty years before they come at us again. We have to anticipate that threat.

"Dervla would rather call for aid from young Palamar, who's like a lapdog whining among her skirts, than from a pair of country-grown independents like you and your sister, who might argue with her and even form your own plans. Look—"

Gaultry looked, and saw that the Duchess had drawn her dizzyingly close to the cliff's edge. Below, the turbulence of the waves glittered and chopped. The surf had carved jagged gaps in the shoreline cliff, the white stone crumbling a little more with each new tide. Land-bred Gaultry had never felt the power of such a sea, and she turned alarmed eyes to the Duchess, unnerved.

"Although Tielmaran Princes have worshiped here for centuries," the Duchess said, "one day the sea will claim these sacred hills. The Great Twins love this land, but a day will come when this small piece, at least, will be forever lost to the force of the water."

"Dervla fears she is this cliff," the old woman continued, staring downwards, "and that you and your sister are the new power dashing against her, a power that will crumble her strength. You have done nothing"—the blue eyes bore into Gaultry's, a hint of accusation in their depths—"to convince her otherwise."

chapter 2

It was warm in the sheltered bowl among the three hills. Gaultry had stood behind Princess Lily's shoulder for more than an hour now, her sister at her left, behind Benet. She was hot and bored. The branch-receiving ceremony was repetitive and dull, and she had had enough of it.

The Duchess had been accurate in her description of the day's service. While the Prince's earlier sacrifice had tugged at deep forces in the land, this ceremony—despite the fact that clusters of young leaves from Elianté's oaks had been entwined in Gaultry's hair, and Emiera's ash fronds in Mervion's—this ceremony had no more scent of the sacred than any other court receiving line. Gaultry and Mervion were required to do nothing more than stand quietly, without open apathy, while the Prince and his lady smiled and gave brief thanks to those who shuffled before them. Any pretty girl, Gaultry thought restlessly, as the sweat gathered uncomfortably at her temples and her spine, could have performed this function.

The air was heavy with flower and plant scents, released by the day's heat. After the fresh breezes that had touched her at the top of the hill, the air felt unbearably still. The line in front of the Prince seemed to be moving more and more slowly. A stout knight with iron-colored hair, accompanied by his lady, kneeled gracelessly before his Prince, his movements deliberate but clumsy as he offered his pledge and branch. Long moments after, a slim gentlewoman, equally leisurely, replaced him. Gaultry's attention wandered from the long queue of supplicants to the white-garbed acolytes who took over the branches once the Prince had accepted them.

Dervla's complaints notwithstanding, her acolytes were active participants in the ceremony. In six couples, three pairs of men, three of women, they were busy helping the Prince with the courtiers' offerings—the green branches that Gaultry and the wooding-crew had cut so early that same morning, before the first dew had faded. Dervla's acolytes were responsible for the construction of the woodpile that would later be set alight as a celebratory bonfire. At first, in their sweeping white robes and smoothly coifed hair, the young acolytes seemed elegant and serene. This impression dwindled as the bonfire pile grew. The twelve, men and women both, became increasingly flushed and sweaty, as if unaccustomed even to the light work of carrying single branches. So much for the High Priestess's disdain of manual labor.

Gaultry could not help but grin; then, remembering that one of these acolytes might have taken her place at the Prince's shoulder, she gave them a closer look. Which of the women was Palamar Laconte, Dervla's Brood-blood woman? The Duchess had described Palamar as a lapdog. With this in mind, Gaultry's attention fixed on a timid-looking woman, a few years older than herself, with ash-blond hair, chubby arms, and a face that was pink with unaccustomed exertion. The woman trotted back and forth beneath the unrelenting heat of the sun with cumbersome armfuls of green branches, increasingly awkward, her expression fixed and solemn, a little mournful.

A lapdog. Staring at the young woman's clumsiness, Gaultry felt she could begin to understand why the High Priestess so resented Benet's decision to have the Blas twins stand at his shoulders as his ceremonial supporters. Dervla wanted to impress the Prince and the people of Tielmark with her power, yet her chosen acolytes, on this day of high ceremony, did not appear impressive.

The pledge ceremony was indeed little more than a fancily dressed receiving line, but the importance of the vow, made on a day when Emiera looked down, could not be underestimated. Among those who crowded this queue—surely there were some who had little intention of keeping the day's vow. Benet, who had proved himself over-trusting in the past, must finally have tired of glib promises. Now, although he greeted his subjects with a welcoming smile, his general demeanor was stern. By requiring his courtiers to remake their pledge to him on this day, he meant to advance them a warning: those who broke faith with Tielmark's Prince risked breaking faith with the gods, and there would be a price.

By choosing Gaultry and Mervion to support his shoulders, he reminded his court: where Benet had need of a lapdog, he had two strong Glamour-witches to serve him. An impressive display of power indeed, that he could call on such strength so casually. Gaultry, staring at the elaborately curled mass of wheat-colored hair at the back of her Prince's head, felt this realization like a blow. Her heartfelt desire to do her Prince service could condemn her to a life of dull court service—the very idea brought a chill to her spine, even as she felt her sweat spreading.

"You can't jump the queue." An irate voice returned her attention to the line of perspiring nobles. Dervla's senior acolyte, a glum-faced man of about thirty, had stopped, his arms heavy with branches, to reprimand one of the waiting supplicants. "You're out of rank."

"If I am," a deceptively mild voice answered, "I doubt it is your place to tell me so."

Three brothers, young-looking knights at the front of the line, cast quick looks at the speaker. Recognizing him, they mumbled the Prince a hasty pledge, thrust their branches into the senior acolyte's already overloaded arms, and departed in a hurried confusion that left the speaker abruptly alone at the head of the queue.

"My Prince," the man bowed formally to Benet. "I have traveled hard to pledge myself to you today." It was Martin, the Duchess of Melaudiere's grandson and Gaultry's closest friend at court. He had been away from Princeport on the Duchess's business, and had not been expected to return until well after Emiera's Day was past and gone. Out at the cliff, when she and the Duchess had been alone, his grandmother hadn't mentioned that Martin had returned. Gaultry cast her eyes about, trying to spot the old woman's blue and white dress. Had Melaudiere withheld that information intentionally, or had she not known?

The tall warrior was still dressed for the road, in travel-stained gray and green livery—Melaudiere's colors—of the plainest cut. With his cropped black hair, short as any common soldier's, the acolyte had mistaken him for an untidily accoutered house-guard. But no house-guard could have conveyed the arrogant chill that Martin emanated—or would have stood before his Prince, cutting a senior acolyte with such a terrible smile.

Dervla's man eyed the soldier's long, muscular body and deep chest. Amid the shuffling crowd, Martin stood very much apart. He moved with the rangy strength of a warrior who had seen many seasons' service. There was a hard wolfish stamp to his features: broad, battle-battered cheekbones, deep-set measuring eyes. Not a man to take lightly.

Belatedly, recognition dawned. "Martin Stalker." The acolyte paused to gather his nerve. "If you are here on your grandma's service, you must go to the back with the retainers."

Martin laughed. "Emiera take you. It's custom, not right, that makes the hierarchy here. Even so—" The soldier bowed past the acolyte's shoulder to where Benet and Lily sat watching. "The Prince put me here today, in recognition of recent service. Ask him if I must go back in line."

The acolyte wheeled around, openly nonplussed. "My Liege?"

Benet raised his right hand, palm outward, and nodded at
the acolyte. His mouth quirked, suppressing a smile. Just
short of his quarter-century, the Prince had the look of a man
young for his command, with a plain, smooth-featured face
and straight dark brows. At his jaw and temples, the strong
bones of his forebears were beginning to show through, but
still, he could appear deceptively gentle. "I am your Prince
today because of this man's sword," he said calmly, his
words, in their calmness, a greater rebuke than harshness.
"This man would stand foremost among my knights—if he
would only agree to accept the commission."

Gaultry could not help but enjoy the acolyte's confusion.
The commission the Prince wanted Martin to accept would
have been a reward for Martin's heroism in stopping a blade
before it opened Benet's throat. Martin's refusal of that honor
meant that the Prince's gratitude, rather than any formal court
order, determined how the Prince would receive him. It certainly made for difficulties in the ordering of a receiving line.

The tall soldier bowed to his Prince, closing his lips in
something like a grin, though Gaultry could see that he found
the attention the acolyte had drawn to him somewhat embar-
rassing. He thrust his branch into the hands of the nearest
acolyte, a nervous girl with a fallen mop of chestnut-colored
hair. "I am through with titles, Your Highness. But never, I
hope, with your service." He genuflected deeply. Then, raising his head, he let himself look past the Prince's shoulder to
meet Gaultry's gaze.

Gray eyes locked on green. For that brief moment, he drank
in the sight of her: the crown of oak, the cropped green
smock, her naked feet and arms. She stared back, trying not
to smile and break her pose of detachment.

"I and mine will always serve you," Martin told the Prince,
his eyes still fixed on Gaultry. He bowed again and was gone.

"Foolish man," Benet murmured, quietly so that only his
wife at his side and the women at his shoulders could hear. "I
would help him if he would let me."

Gaultry flushed, and shot a sharp look at the back of
Benet's head. She did not want the Prince to meddle with

Martin's affairs, particularly insofar as they related to herself. She and Martin had already suffered from too much interference.

Before the Prince's marriage, there had been an incontestable bond between herself and Martin, but it had been a bond that neither of them had volunteered for. It had started with the magical geas that had been laid on Martin, compelling him to serve as her protector. That bond, even before they had come to know each other well, had created a quicksilver passion between them. Her pains and fears, magnified, had been his; she, striving to loosen a bond she resented, had been forced to a heightened awareness of his feelings. The intensity of those shared emotions, amplified by the dangers they confronted in their struggle to protect their Prince, had at times infringed upon their duty to Tielmark and the Prince. It had been a relief to them both when, once the Prince was restored to power, the geas had faded and left them free. Or at least she had hoped that it would be a relief. With the geas gone, there was no aching press of magic forcing them to unravel the tangled skein of their emotions. Surely they both were grateful for that!

Gaultry cast a troubled look at Martin's back, watching him withdraw to the tent encampment that had been erected beyond the ground of the hills. One part of her had to acknowledge that she missed the geas. Too many tangles of emotion had risen between them for her to feel pleasure in the new distance they now shared.

The least-tangled skein was the fact of Martin's long-estranged wife, the woman to whom he had ceded his property and title when he had forsworn his family name.

The most-tangled skein was the occult tie of Rhasan magic that still bound them.

The Rhasan was wild magic, older than the Great Twelve, and said to rule even godly fates, when the gods resorted to using it. Decks of Rhasan cards dated back to the dominion of the wandering tribes, the peoples who had passed through Tielmark before it had become a sovereign land with god-pledged borders. Although empire had come and overlain the old wanderers' trails, and later Tielmark had come, a free nation, jealous of its boundaries and forgetful of the powers that had ruled before Empire, through political tides of change, the Rhasan decks of the ancients had never waned in strength. The cards were ever a temptation and a danger. They revealed the deepest desires and fears of the human soul and, by so doing, transformed its future.

Gaultry and Martin had shared their Rhasan cards. In some way that meant they had shared their futures. Another draw from a Rhasan deck might set that link asunder—but Gaultry did not want to submit to another reading. Not if the only reason for so doing was to break her tie to Martin. Her gaze followed the big soldier until he disappeared among the tents. Pleasure and irritation flickered through her, as they so often did when she considered the tangle of their connections. It was easy for a man with a sword to know how to serve his Prince. For herself and her sister, nothing would be so simple.

She looked up to the heights of the two landward hills: Emiera's, to the east, with its crown of silver ash trees; on the west, Elianté's, with its massive oaks. She had visited Elianté's grove two days earlier and had walked among the thick trunks, admiring how the leaves had already grown lush enough to create a closed canopy. Standing beneath that canopy, memories of her past life on Tielmark's remote south border had pierced her. How fine it had been to run wild in the border woods, to hunt, to cast arrows to the wind, to enter proudly at her grandmother's door, her game-bag heavy on her shoulder with a week's meat. Her grandmother had kept her innocent of the knowledge that her free life as a deep forest hunter was illusory—hers and Mervion's both. Before they were born, before even their long-dead mother was born, Tamsanne had pledged her own blood, and theirs, to the Prince's service. That blood, it seemed to Gaultry, utterly determined their futures.

As she stared at the trees that hid the tops of the Twin Goddesses' hills, a flood of refreshed resentment against Tielmark's High Priestess rushed through her. Dervla's spiteful words against the Blas twins, her insinuations and petty insults, were less than meaningless. Dervla knew that a pledge made fifty years past bound the young women to their Prince; she could not pretend that she did not know it.

She was bound with the same blood-bond.

Seven sorceresses had made that pledge and now it bound them with the strength of prophecy:

The path of the Prince of Tielmark will run red with the blood of the Common Brood.

Beneath the sheen of her sweat, Gaultry shivered. Although that simple declaration should have formed a two-edged prophecy offering Brood-members both glory and doom, to date, only one of the edges had presented itself to the Brood-blood. Three of the original seven of the Common Brood were dead before their time, and eight of their children. Four of the latter had been battle-deaths; two of these—the Duchess of Melaudiere's sons—as they cleared the ground before their Prince in battle.

In Gaultry's generation, the Brood's grandchildren, three lives already had reddened the Prince's path. The most recent, a girl driven to madness by the traitor Heiratikus, Tielmark's half-Bissanty ex-Chancellor, had thrown herself from the castle battlements to a slow death on the paving stones of the terrace below. That Prince's Path, as the terrace below the battlements was called, was still dark with the stains of fresh Brood-blood.

Gaultry looked up to the crest of Feeding-Hill. The Duchess of Melaudiere stood alone at the hill's side, silhouetted against the broad reach of the sea, not far from where they had first spoken. Her blue and white sleeves fluttered in the wind, giving her the look of a stark old bird.

It was the Duchess of Melaudiere who had taken Gaultry to see Lady D'Arbey's death-blood. Gaultry stared up at the old woman, remembering.

The Duchess had come to see Gaultry in her chambers two days after Martin had left for Haute Tielmark on his grandmother's business. The young woman had been suffering at

Martin's absence—not least because she had argued with him over a matter of no importance before he'd set out on the road. Answering the Duchess's knock, Gaultry eagerly hurried the old woman into her salon, hoping to hear word of her grandson.

At first the Duchess settled comfortably into the best divan in the salon, fanning herself with the edge of one sleeve and speaking to the young woman of Martin's younger days, before he had gone to war. Then, apparently artlessly, the old woman suggested that they take a turn together through the palace grounds, to escape the heat.

Melaudiere brought her to a broad walkway beneath a high battlement. "This walk is known as the Prince's Path," she said. "And here is the stain of Lady D'Arbey's death-blood. And that," she added, pointing, "is the spot from which she jumped." The Duchess's description of how the young woman had lain, undiscovered for long hours as her lifeblood ebbed away, was no less brutal. "Lady D'Arbey was Dervla's niece," the Duchess concluded. "Imagine Dervla's feeling of guilt when she realized that tie was not sufficient to protect her."

"Why have you brought me here?"

The girl's blood had flowed and dried in stages. Although the stains had been well scrubbed, the dark pattern where the in-curled body had huddled was painfully obvious.

"This is the worst yet that has happened to our blood." The sharp blue eyes met Gaultry's, their expression revealing the woman's sense of her own power—and her own helplessness. "Chancellor Heiratikus understood the importance of the Brood-blood prophecy. He thought he could twist it to bring himself to power in Tielmark—but as he was Brood-blood himself he only drew the circle tighter, and brought on his own death.

"The Brood wasn't formed to make us all perish miserably in the Prince's service," the Duchess said grimly. "Our founder, Princess Lousielle—if only you could have known her—was no friend to suffering. Though she is fifty years dead and gone, she haunts the edge of my sleep. Her bright eyes, the fire of the goddesses in her, still lighten my shadows. Knowing today what I did not know then, knowing that I would live to see my sons die, I would still make my pledge to her.

"Pain was no stranger to Lousielle, and she was determined that it should not triumph. You are too young to understand. Fifty years ago, there was none of this pretty dancing for power and influence. Bissanty had all but subverted our free rule. Tielmark was free in name only, and desperate for the god-pledge that would keep us independent from Bissanty. I have shown you the scars where my own father cut me, sending his blood-pledges to Bissanty. Lousielle suffered worse. She watched Bissanty doctors torture her weakling father throughout her childhood, living in dread of the day they would finish with him and turn their attentions to her. When her father was finally gone, Bissanty regents ruled her, and she knew that the day would come when her own usefulness would end, and they would kill her in her turn.

"But despite her dread, she believed in the Great Twins' love, and she comforted herself that if she could only fulfill the sacred pledges to close the fifth cycle of Tielmark's rule, Tielmark's strength as a free nation could be rebuilt. Every day of her life, she fought to preserve her sovereignty, but everything was done in secret, where no one could comfort or praise her. When it came time to marry, she suffered her regents' choice—a Bissanty-bred popinjay—because no one in Tielmark stood up to protect her.

"That marriage almost brought her to despair. In the eyes of the Great Twelve, Tielmark is a sovereign nation, protected by the Great Twins against secular incursions. Our Prince's body is married to the earth in payment for this generosity. That is a Tielmark's goddess-pledge: our Prince must make a spiritual marriage to the earth, sacrificing himself for his people. If Lousielle married a Bissanty man, that pledge would be broken, and Tielmark would revert to Bissanty rule. Lousielle knew that with the death of free Tielmark, the suffering she daily endured would spread throughout her land, to every farmhouse.

"She had to find some way to prevent it. But how? Bissanty spies were everywhere. As the days slipped by, bringing her wedding closer, she saw, with joyless clarity, the fate that lay ahead—for her and for Tielmark. She had no freedom. Little power. It was inevitable. She could not escape the marriage, and her Bissanty consort would get a child on her of mixed blood—a child half Bissanty, half Tielmaran, a child fated to return Tielmark to the slavery of Bissanty rule.

"She foiled that." The wrinkles around the sharp blue eyes filled with tears, softening Melaudiere's expression. She clasped Gaultry's hand against her wrist. The younger woman felt the old scar where the Duchess's father had marked her, so many decades past. "I have a secret for you," the old woman said. "A secret known only to Lousielle's blood-sworn witches. Today I want to share it."

"I don't want it," Gaultry started to say. "I don't want to think of Tielmark helpless and weak."

The Duchess ignored her, though she dropped her voice to an intense whisper. "Lousielle was close-guarded by Bissanty foes. But the night before the wedding, she found freedom for a few short hours. Escaping from the palace, she descended into Princeport.

"There is a madhouse in Princeport. Just outside the city gates, near the walled pathway that leads down from the Prince's gardens. And that was where brave Lousielle went. Afterwards, a madman ranted to all comers that he had taken the Princess to bed, that the Great Twins themselves had stood at the foot of his bed, there in the midst of the common ward, and smiled as he seeded a child in her womb."

"Did she—?"

"Who believes the ranting of a madman?" Melaudiere said simply, avoiding a direct answer. "The Bissanty courtiers certainly did not. They crowed loud, declaring all was won, that the day was coming when Tielmark would once more bow beneath the Imperial yoke. Every appearance suggested that they were right. Nine months after the Princess's marriage, she gave birth to a healthy daughter. Lousielle nurtured that child to adulthood, punctiliously observing every outward expression of submission.

"But the strain of desperation and madness that had seeded a child in Lousielle's womb united with Lousielle's princely blood, and the gods spoke to her, calling her to make prophecy. She waited, resisting the call, letting it grow and strengthen. When her daughter finally trembled at the brink of womanhood, she knew it was time to act. In secret, she summoned seven sorceresses to her. She called us the Common Brood, guardians of the common blood of Tielmark, the blood that must run in the veins of every Prince. We were chosen for our strength, for our magical powers, and for the trials we had suffered at Bissanty hands. Lousielle knew, long before any of us, how desperate we were to pledge ourselves, how keen we were to invest our lives in anything that offered hope and purpose.

"She warned us to hesitate before we made our promise. 'Before your work is finished, you will regret your pledge,' she said. 'You will be martyrs as well as saviors, so think before you swear.' Those words only made us wilder to serve her.

"I am sure Lousielle guessed we wouldn't understand the full extent of our promise. Most of us were young, and beneath our veils of suffering, overconfident. Speaking for myself, she was surely right. Unlike the Princess, we had yet to suffer the birthing of our own children. Unlike Lousielle, with her young princess-child Corinne, we knew nothing of the pains of watching the strength and beauty grow in a child born to blood-pledges and a forespoken fate. Your grandmother Tamsanne, perhaps alone of all the Common Brood, suspected the full extent of what Lousielle intended—but you will have to have that story of her, at a time of your own choosing."

The two women stood on the stone path, staring downwards at the dark stains. When she next spoke, the old woman's voice was harsh with pain. "Of course the pledge outlasted our generation. I lost two sons and a grandson to the

Prince's path. It seems that none of the house of Melaudiere can soldier by their Prince's side without opening their life's blood to him. Martin—you cannot know what I felt when he moved under the sword blow meant for Benet on Prince's Night. I was sure the moment had come for his blood to flow in the Prince's service.

"That is the lesson of this blood." The Duchess delicately scuffed at the stained pavement with her slipper.

"We must find a way to fulfill the Brood-pledge, or more of us will die, while Tielmark is made no stronger against Bissanty encroachment. And this business of Heiratikus's—there is a self-defeating strain of ambition in the blood of the Common Brood. I fear sometimes that we will all be dead before we turn to help our Prince." She made a movement with her hands. Gaultry, sensing magic, drew back. That made the Duchess smile. "I am not Dervla, seeking to test you like that. My tests run on other lines—do you remember Tielmark's flag song?"

"It's about Briern-bold," Gaultry said. "Every child's hero-prince. The children still sing it on market days, when the girls play their circle games."

"It's not just a children's song," Melaudiere said. "Any song that lasts two hundred years has more meaning to it than that." She pursed her wrinkled lips—

> *I watched a blue flag flying high*
> *The Prince was in his glory;*
> *I watched a flag of purple die*
> *The Emperor in his fury.*

The Duchess's voice was high and reedy, but not unpleasant.

> *The crimson King came to the field*
> *To help blue make its stand;*
> *The gods they bowed on every side,*
> *And held the bordered land.*

"It's history, as well as a game-song," the Duchess prompted Gaultry. "Who was the crimson King?"

"A Lanai tribesmen. Instead of fighting us, he came to help." The Lanai mountainmen were better known for fighting Tielmark than for aiding it.

The Duchess shook her head. "He was more than that. The Lanai have many tribes, but only one that rates a King. That King was Algeorn, of Far Mountain. When Briern was making his last stand, Algeorn unexpectedly ran his troops east from Lanai to ally against the Bissanties. Their combined armies drove the Bissanties back.

"The gods had sent Algeorn and his troops across three high massifs to thwart the breaking of the Great Twins' border-pledge. After the battle, the Lanai King married Briern's sister and brought her back to the mountains. She bore him many heirs. Her blood is strong in the King of Far Mountain to this day."

"I never liked that part of the story," Gaultry said. "No one ever asks if Briesinne wanted Algeorn."

The Duchess gave Gaultry a hard look. Gaultry wanted to squirm and turn away, but instead she stared back, stubborn, trying to show the older woman she could understand duty and fate but still not think it right that a marriage should be determined by those forces. The Duchess, reading the young woman's look, shrugged. "I sang Briern's song to remind you how the gods act for a Prince who honors his pledges—and for a King who honors his. Algeorn did not want an heir, until he met pretty Briesinne. If the gods made him cross all those mountains, it was as much to find him a marriage-partner as it was to help our Prince. While Algeorn's line reigns, no Bissanty soldier will ever stand within the borders of Far Mountain. And while his line does honor to the gods, his blood will never lapse.

"A Prince makes a spiritual marriage to the land," the Duchess continued. "His rule is manifested in the color blue, emblematic of this spirit-sacrifice. Purple is the color of Empire, for the sacrifice the Emperor makes of his soul.

Blood, for the raw body, is a King's pledge. And in the eyes of the Great Twelve, red is the King's color.

"For fifty years, the red path in Lousielle's prophecy has signified the Brood-blood's death in the Prince's service. But Lousielle hoped that there would be more in the prophecy than the brutal slaughter of her most talented magicians. Lousielle knew she would not live to see her daughter break the Bissanty stranglehold. She dared to hope that a coven of sorceresses, bound in blood-pledges and shared memory of suffering, together might find a unity that could transform Tielmark's ruler from a Prince into a King, to finally free us of the threat of the Bissanty Empire's encroachments.

"Gaultry—" The Duchess took hold of the girl's strong young hand in her brittle, aged-claw fingers. "You are angry that your grandmother hid your blood heritage. Your own Prince's court confuses you, and you cannot see clearly how to act. But perhaps Tamsanne knew best. She taught you— you and your sister both—to know the feel of freedom. To you, Bissanty was a distant bugbear, not an ever-present threat with a hidden stranglehold closing in on your throat.

"You and your sister alone, of all the Common Brood's blood, were able to close the sixth cycle of Tielmark's rule and remake the Prince of Tielmark's strength. Not Dervla, or myself, or any of the others who would have liked to have acted. Now that your magic has waxed and you have grown in power, it may be the pair of you who will determine Tielmark's fate—and your own, in deciding whether it is the crimson of kingship or the red of your own blood which you will choose to spread on the Prince's pathway."

Tugging Gaultry's hand, the Duchess pulled her so they stood together on the stained stone of the terrace, rooted on that blood, on that stone. "You never knew young Lady D'Arbey. Two forces came together to kill her.

"The first was the ambition of the Brood-blood, in the traitor Heiratikus's fervid dream of power." She looked again at Gaultry, and the young huntress was amazed to see an expression almost like guilt in her face. "Some might say this was a just return. The Common Brood had betrayed his mother,

Melaney Sevenage. She was one of our own, yet we were all eager enough to let her hazard her life so that our own skins would not be put at risk. When the Bissanty agents she had befriended discovered that her heart was truly Tielmark's, we had a chance to save her. Instead of acting, we argued about what should be done. Our hesitation—if not our cowardice—allowed Bissanty agents to seize and destroy her, in the confusion following the closing of Tielmark's fifth cycle of rule.

"But Gaultry—we of the Common Brood have faces. We are here for you to see and judge, as your own intelligence and wisdom will allow you. The second force that killed Lady D'Arbey is a force more implacable than ambition. It has no face. It is the Bissanty Empire itself. Their land went bitter when Llara ceded Tielmark to the Great Twins. The Emperor, Llara's own heir, never acknowledged the Thunderer's concession—nor did any of his sons after him. In her turn, Llara seems to have punished Bissanty's ruler by breeding dissention among his heirs. Now Bissanty hungers for our lands, imagining that their return will heal the rift between goddess-mother and Imperial-son."

"That's like the flags," Gaultry said, frightened by the old woman's tone and uncertain what it was in the woman's words that had made her frightened. "Or the colors of rule. Those things are symbols. They aren't real."

"They're real enough to those who want them to be real," the Duchess answered. "Just as real as it is for us to be standing here, on the Prince's Path, with the red blood of prophecy staining the stone beneath our feet.

"Take my warning or ignore it as you like." The Duchess abruptly released the younger woman, more stern than sympathetic. "At least you will not die like the others, who never had the luxury of this warning."

"The crimson of kingship or the red of your own blood." Amid the stuffy heat of the receiving line and the aromatic balsam of the fresh cut branches, the Duchess's words whirled and seemed to echo in Gaultry's head. She shook herself and tried to smile, to concentrate, to ignore Dervla's creeping acolytes and the cringing line of courtiers. Melaudiere wanted too much from her, she thought angrily. The old woman demanded that Gaultry understand everything at once, that she see her way clear to helping the Prince in a way that didn't involve standing stupidly at his back or politely following his orders. Yet the Duchess reproached her at once when she tried to stand up for herself, as she'd done earlier, with Dervla. . . . Why had the Duchess singled Gaultry out? Was it because she saw some critical weakness in the younger woman, some fault in the young huntress's character that needed to be shored up?

Why indeed did the Duchess reserve her lectures for Gaultry, when Mervion too needed to find a way to serve the Prince at court? Gaultry glanced sideways at her sister. Mervion stood, calm and still, behind Prince Benet's chair. A twinge of jealousy touched her. Mervion's appearance alone was answer enough to that question.

Although she had been on her feet as long as her sister, Mervion exhibited none of Gaultry's impatience. She projected exactly those qualities the Prince must have hoped the Blas twins would project: confidence and serenity. Her calm, intelligent eyes surveyed the Prince's presenters with polite attention, and there was a slight smile on her lips for anyone who cared to return that gaze. Despite the heat, she looked light and fresh. Her golden hair, shot through with red undertones, shone like a crown, the thick braids entwined with the young green ash boughs. Although she had worked as diligently as Gaultry through the morning, she appeared rested and fresh, ready to meet any challenge. She looked as if she were in complete command of all her faculties. Gaultry, by comparison, felt wilted, sweaty and red-faced. Her hair, which she wore shorter than Mervion's and was therefore harder to pin up, had fallen down around her ears and shed at least one cluster of oak leaves.

But the differences went deeper than dress. If Mervion looked confident and perfect, to Gaultry that outer beauty was merely a reflection of the stronger composure that lay within.

Staring at Mervion, Gaultry felt she implicitly understood why Melaudiere and Dervla should choose to focus on her rather than her beautiful sister.

When they lived with their grandmother in her lonely border cottage, Mervion, as older sister, had been the leader, the sister who chose consciously to challenge herself, to seek new knowledge, new spells, new answers. Gaultry—she could admit it now to herself, after the past weeks of adventuring— had been the timid one, preferring the familiar life of the forest, the fixed seasons of the wild game's movement, the predictable round of the weather's turns. Tamsanne had once said that each had found her own path, coping with their mother's early death, their father's apparent abandonment. Mervion had turned outward, Gaultry inward. Where Gaultry had shied from human contact, running deep into the forest to try her strength against deer, foxes, and wolves—animals from which she soon learned to take power and knowledge— Mervion had made the human mind her study, disciplining herself to probe its strengths and weaknesses. Long before either sister had left Arleon Forest, Mervion had already readied herself for a wider society. She had often pestered Tamsanne with her questions, doing all she could to learn of life beyond the forest.

The past weeks had been brutal to Mervion. Her eager departure from the safety of her grandmother's cottage had exposed her to unexpected peril at the traitor Chancellor's hands. If she had not possessed the advantage of her hidden Glamour-soul, her blood would have mingled with young Lady D'Arbey's on the flagstones of the Prince's path. Indeed, if Gaultry had not broken the habits of behavior that had stood for years to guide the sisters, leaving her beloved forest to offer her sister her aid and support, even Mervion's Glamour would not have been enough to save her.

That awful time was past now, and Gaultry had no intention of turning back to it, searching for retrospective answers. Mervion, like the Prince, had survived defeat and learned from it. Like the Prince, she was stronger, more certain in the course she must take for Tielmark's and her own protection.

When Dervla and old Melaudiere spoke to Mervion, they spoke politely, their respect almost as great as if they were addressing Tamsanne herself, and not one of her granddaughters. Instead of allowing herself to be drawn into their arguments, Mervion had kept her distance, answering their attempts to bully or confuse her with a ready tongue and steady head.

Mervion's understanding of what the Prince wanted, and what Tielmark and its court needed, so far exceeded Gaultry's own that the younger twin found it impossible not to defer to her elder's judgment. Indeed, it was Mervion who had insisted that they appear for the Prince today, when Gaultry had balked at displaying herself. Now, Gaultry could see that however dreary the service, it had a function. The Prince needed his court to understand the power that was his to draw on. Watching Mervion, Gaultry was torn between pride and envy at her sister's unmatchable aplomb.

Mervion's eye suddenly met Gaultry's, as if she sensed the ramblings of her twin's mind. The older twin smiled, and Gaultry, caught battling her tangle of thoughts and new ideas, blushed and smiled wanly back. She knew that Mervion must be bored too, but there was nothing in her sister's relaxed stance to betray her feelings. The young huntress was hot, bored, and sweating—and knew that she had managed to conceal none of these things. She wished it was in her to look so serene and certain.

At the same time, looking into her sister's calm face, Gaultry felt regret at Mervion's ability to hide her emotions.

Though the young twin loved her sister dearly, she could not help but wonder if Mervion had forgiven her yet for being the twin who hadn't needed rescuing on Prince's Night.

▼

The Prince rose from his seat and reached for his wife's hand. The last branch had been piled atop the great bonfire stack, and the cheeks of those who had participated in the ceremony were bright pink from prolonged exposure to the unseasonably warm sun. The seemingly interminable receiving ceremony had at long last reached its natural end. "Not long to the feast now," Benet said, his voice amused as he noted Gaultry's weary expression and the way she had begun to shift her weight from foot to foot. "The show of support cannot but please me, nevertheless, I too had begun to believe it would go on forever. You must be ready for some time off your feet."

"I am, my Prince." Gaultry bobbed her head in a short obeisance, embarrassed by her sovereign's solicitude. Mervion, at her side, bowed with her, somewhat less jerkily.

"Rest then, both of you, and enjoy the day's beauty. Emiera has smiled. Let's hope that will continue." He turned to Lily, his fingers tightening possessively on her arm as he drew her, with unprincely informality, close to his side. "Where's

Dervla when you need her? Have you spotted her in the crowd yet, sweeting?"

That was as much of a dismissal as the Blas twins needed.

"It went well, don't you think?" Mervion's words were not quite a question, so Gaultry nodded without answering. "It was better than I expected," Mervion added softly. To Gaultry's surprise, her twin sounded both relieved and slightly tentative.

She shot her sister a searching look, but Mervion's face revealed no hint of inner discomposure. The sun had reddened the bridge of her nose and brought an unhealthy flush of pink to her cheeks, but her appearance was considerably less sweaty and uncomfortable-looking than that of anyone else in the crowd. "What do you mean?" Gaultry said, inelegantly blotting the thin material of her own smock against the running perspiration on her arms. "Everyone was admiring you. I was the one who looked like a sweltering fool up there. Isn't the heat affecting you at all?" she fretted. They headed out over the gentle saddle of ground that let onto the tent-ground that flanked the hills. Ahead, the brightly-colored sides of the ladies' changing tent hove into view, promising a welcome relief from the sun. Gaultry picked up her pace.

"Looks aren't everything," Mervion muttered, as she lagged a little behind. "I'm just as uncomfortable as you are—"

"Elianté take me," Gaultry interrupted, spotting the man who stood in the shadow of the tent's front awning. "What's Martin doing here? If he thinks I'm going to stand out in this sun a second longer just to chat—" From his stance by the tent, the tall soldier waved. Gaultry waved back before she thought better of it, then broke into a smile, admitting to herself that she was pleased. Returning her smile, he strode out to meet them. "What were you saying?" she asked, turning to Mervion.

Her sister frowned and raised her delicate brows. "It wasn't important. It can wait." Her eyes flickered to Martin. "If you two want to talk, you had best make it quick. The feast will begin soon, and we're supposed to be in our seats well before the Prince arrives."

Trust Mervion to know the protocol, Gaultry thought. And trust Mervion, she could not help but think, to let herself be ruled by it.

Mervion, as if sensing her sister's unkind thought, gave Martin a cool and not entirely friendly nod, and walked on towards the ladies' tent.

"You're back early," Gaultry greeted him. "Benet was pleased."

"Only Benet?"

She smiled, her eyes daring him to repeat the question, and looked him over. Since she'd seen him make his pledge, he had tidied himself and shaved, but he had not had a chance to change out of his dusty traveling clothes. Away from the Prince, he looked tired. There was a tightness to the skin around his eyes, and he walked with the stiffness of one who had been too long in the saddle. Gaultry wondered how hard he had ridden to return in time for the ceremony. Very hard, she guessed. "Will you be staying after the feast, or will Melaudiere be sending you off again?"

"I don't live only to serve her," Martin said irritably.

"Sometimes it seems like you do," Gaultry answered. Then she reached for his hand, regretting that she had spoken sharply. It wasn't Martin's fault if his grandmother had pressured her in his absence.

Beneath her fingers, his hand felt brazier-hot. So hot, in fact, she almost dropped it. She looked up into his eyes, alarmed, and saw a poorly-concealed urgency in their gray depths. "What's happened to you?"

"Gaultry," he said. "We don't have much time, but I wanted to catch you before the feasting. There may not be time after. The news from the western border is hard to read. Wraiths and rumors, and none of them bringing good tidings. My best guess is that this summer's campaign will be a long one."

Gaultry shivered. Since he had first wielded a sword as a

soldier, Martin had fought twelve campaigns against the Lanai mountain people, one for each of the Great deities. This season would be his thirteenth—a lucky number, she tried to assure herself. Glamour's number. "Will you have to go back?"

"Very probably." Martin took her other hand, letting her feel how the burst of unnatural heat was flushed throughout his body. "But that's not what I want to talk about." He glanced around, as if to satisfy himself that no one was near enough to eavesdrop. Aside from a few stragglers, they were momentarily alone. "Can you feel the torment in me?"

"How could I miss it?" It was not the hotness of fever, nor even of magic. It was as though Martin was pumped high with anger, or strong emotion, so high that he could not come down. Yet his voice, despite his impatience, gave little hint of the physical strain his body suffered.

"Do you remember the geas?" he asked abruptly. "Do you remember how the geas formed?"

Her eyes chastened him. For one terrible moment, she thought she might break into tears. "Why speak of that today?" she said bitterly. "Is the sun shining so bright, you cannot bear to see anything happy?" The geas had been her father's death-wish. He had killed himself on Martin's sword, to free himself from the torturing maze of spells in which the Prince's traitor Chancellor had bound him.

"I wouldn't bring it up willingly," Martin said. He released her hands, and shot her an impatient look. "I'm trying to explain to you something that is happening, something important. I'm not sure when I'll get another chance to do so."

"Go on then," she told him.

"Ten years ago, my brother died. It was too much for me to bear. Yet somehow, in some way, his death brought closure to the four years of terrible pain I had suffered, dating from the time of my father's death. With Morse gone too, I had lost or forsworn everything that had ever held value to me. My wife was lost, my land rights, the very name to which I had been born. Morse had left me Dinevar, my father's sword. That noble blade in my hands, come to me in that way, was the last thing I wanted. But somehow, despite my despair at this last sorrow, Dinevar gave me the strength to continue. With Dinevar in my hand, I found the strength to close my heart and return to battle, and with that return I became a new person. A battle-man. A field-stalker." He was speaking quickly and angrily now. Some part of him clearly wanted to pace, to escape her, but he forced himself to stand before her and finish his explanation. "I did not care if I died. Perhaps because of that, I lived. Months passed, then years. It did not matter. I lived only for the battle-field, the long summers of fighting in the high mountains.

"This winter, when my grandmother told me the Prince was under threat from his Chancellor, those words had little meaning to me, save that I could see my way clear to my next duty. And then—and then the New Year came. There was that crazy hunt, with the Prince riding out like a man possessed, Heiratikus clinging to his tail like a spider, and all the rest of us chasing the largest he-boar that I had ever laid my eyes on. You've heard the stories. The kill was a living nightmare, with dying dogs, wounded men, and a boar who would not die. And then, in the middle of all that confusion, a gray-bearded madman on a broken-down horse threw himself on Dinevar's blade and killed himself.

"You know the trauma I felt in that moment. You have seen the images the old man forced on me—of you and your sister, your raw anger at what you thought was the old man's abandonment of you. The magic ripped open my heart, my emotions. Such feelings were so unfamiliar to me. I felt suffocated, but the geas would allow me no respite. It tortured me, relentless, until that moment when I found you, lying wounded in a ditch, with Heiratikus's outriders standing over you.

"I was transfixed. Your father had last seen you when you were a child. I was unaware that I had been sent to guard twins. I knew only that I had been bound to the protection of a mewling child, and I had raged against that, thinking that such service was beneath me.

"When I looked down at those men, and saw they meant to

dishonor you, and that you were a woman grown, for a moment, I could not comprehend what I was seeing, the picture was so far from anything I had imagined. In you, I saw everything that I would ever want to protect."

Gaultry, staring at his wild face, felt a chill run through her. She remembered well their first meeting. The men who had attacked her had been far less frightening than Martin. She had thought that he had come to kill her.

"I got rid of the men," Martin said. "I came down into that little hollow, and I touched you." He raised his hand and brushed it lightly against her cheek. "After that, I wanted the geas. It let me feel your every need, your every murmur, and it left me with the fierce desire to answer those needs." He smiled, rueful. "You have fewer selfish needs than many I have known, Gaultry. You made me need to serve my Prince again. To feel passion for that service."

"Why are you telling me this?" Gaultry said angrily. "Why now, here, so publicly. Couldn't it wait for another time?"

He shook his head. "It can't wait. We've been apart two weeks—it's already been too long. And the geas has been dead almost a week longer."

"What are you saying?"

"With the geas gone," Martin said bluntly, "There is a chill in all my senses. I cannot feel as I did. My greatest pain is not that I have lost—it is that I can remember." He met Gaultry's eyes, and she was shocked to see the depth of the sorrow in the fierce gray eyes. "What I felt—surely it cannot all have been owed to magic. Surely my years as a warrior do not mean that I have stifled my capacity to love, to feel passion." He stared at her, helpless. "I am angry, my body is hot with emotion, but my mind is not heated with it. On the field of battle, this detachment serves me well. But it does not help me now, when I look upon you, and feel the touch of desire, and know that touch does not transmit itself to the deepest reaches of my heart and mind." He paused, then swung his arms out in a defeated gesture. "So much has been left unresolved here at court, and I want to stand by you. But perhaps we should not see each other again until I have resolved this."

Gaultry stared at him, her mind spinning. "It was not only the geas that held us together," she finally said. "Our ties run deeper than one completed casting." Not caring if he rejected her, she reached out and pressed her palm against his chest, above his heart. He shivered at her touch. He had not exaggerated his dilemma. For all the angry heat that ran through his body, the throb of his heart was only marginally accelerated. "I think," she swallowed, and tried to steady her voice. "I think I do not want you to struggle with this yourself."

"Then you don't understand what I'm telling you." He put his hand over hers, unthinkingly crushing her fingers in his powerful grip. "I am not the same man who you kissed in the darkness on the borders of the Bissanty Fingerland. The geas is not in me. I cannot feel what I felt then—"

Gaultry stiffened. "You've already said that," she said testily. "Why rub my nose in it?"

Her acerbic words did more to shake him from despondency than any sympathy she might have offered him. Martin grinned feebly.

"At least I can still make you smile," she groused. She pulled her hand free. She did not want to believe that the man she had grown almost to love did not exist, except through magic.

"This is more than just the geas being gone," he said seriously. "How can I escape the control that my life as a soldier demanded from me? My heart, my head, and my body feel like they're in separate closed boxes."

"Your Rhasan card said you were a wolf, not an automaton," Gaultry reminded him. "Maybe you are looking in the wrong place for your answers. But for now—" she nervously looked over her shoulder, realizing suddenly, as a group of prettily-dressed feast-goers brushed past them, that time had flown. "But for now, we both need to ready ourselves for Emiera's feast. We'll have to worry about this later."

"I'm glad I found you," Martin said. He did not say whether he meant now, or earlier. He kissed her fingers and released her. "I cannot tell you how unpleasant it is to be half-alive once again, to feel myself shutting my emotions away. I can barely find pleasure, even in serving my Prince."

Gaultry hurried towards the tent, hoping Mervion would have had the kindness to lay out her formal clothes for her. Her thoughts were not, however, on dresses and fripperies. Her thoughts were on Martin.

If she didn't know better, she would have thought he was once more acting under the influence of a powerful spell.

"**D**o you see old Melaudiere and Dervla up there on the hill, watching us during the branch ceremony?" Gaultry asked. She was in the ladies' tent, changing out of the green smock she had worn for the ceremony. Her fingers shook as she undid the laces at her bodice. "Dervla lectured me beforehand. She wanted her own girl at the Prince's shoulder." Just now, she would have talked about anything to distract her sister from her nervous state—anything, of course, that wasn't Martin.

"You can't trust either of them," Mervion said. She was out of her smock, standing naked against the tent wall, fussing with her hair in front of the little mirror someone had placed there. She splashed some water into a bowl to cool her arms and face before reaching for her dress. Gaultry, it seemed, was not as late as she had feared. Perhaps that was why Mervion hadn't noticed how upset she was. "If anything, the fact that Dervla's so open about her ambitions should make you think better of her."

"Melaudiere wants the Prince to rule—"

"Gabrielle of Melaudiere is a clever old fox. She knows you're in love with her grandson—Martin who was bound to you, Martin who shielded you while you fought for the Prince. Telling you that the health of her grandchildren is her greatest care and ambition is a calculated gambit."

Gaultry's cheeks burned. She wanted to tell her sister that her feelings for Martin were reciprocated. But she was no longer certain that was true. "That's easy enough to say. Whether it's fair or not is another matter. The Duchess aside, there are certainly bonds between me and her grandson." She had to struggle to keep a tremor of fear out of her voice. "Whether they can be used to manipulate either of us is another story. Matters are complicated. I would not say it is love that Martin and I share."

Mervion dried her hands and turned away from the mirror. "Then why deny love so vehemently?"

Gaultry scowled. She simply was not ready to share the details of her conversation with Martin. "I thought we were talking about whether the Duchess could manipulate me or Dervla." She threw her smock on a nearby chair and reached for her leggings and tunic. A gift from Melaudiere, they were gray and green, the colors of the old woman's house. For Gaultry, accepting the Duchess's generosity had seemed simpler than wasting precious days with a tailor fitting her out in new court clothing. Now, considering the dress as a partisan statement, she was less certain that had been a clever choice. "Why is everything at court about allegiances?" she complained, sitting to pull on her leggings.

Mervion shrugged, sensing in Gaultry's words acknowledgment of her advice. "Button me," she said. She turned her back and let the subject drop. The Blas twins were the only women in the changing tent who did not have servants, and they were now among the last getting dressed.

Gaultry threw her tunic over her head, yanked it down, and turned to help her sister with her dress, glad of the excuse to stand where Mervion could not read her face. She did not want to talk to her sister about Martin. His struggles were his own, and he had not given her leave to share them. Besides, she resented Mervion's insinuation that she was vulnerable to a shrewd-minded grandmother's manipulations. Finishing with her sister's last button, she sighed. Probably she resented Mervion's insinuations because she feared they were true.

"Where do you suppose Dervla has seated us?" Gaultry shrugged into her jacket. She wanted to change the subject. She would be at her sister's side for the remainder of the day. It would not be fair to Mervion if she allowed her feelings for Martin to ruin Mervion's day too.

"We're at one of the lower tables," Mervion said, reaching out and smoothing a ribbon that had tangled in Gaultry's hair. "But I spoke with Lasalle, and he put us on the seaward side of the hill. We'll have a nice breeze there, as well as a good view of the High Table."

Her sister's careful forethought came as no surprise to Gaultry.

They reached their places just as the deerskin horns blared to announce the Prince and his inner court's procession. There was no time to greet their tablemates—only time to slip into their places on their assigned bench. With six-a-side to each table, coming late meant they were stuck with the awkward middle pair of bench seats.

The procession was very fine. Dervla, in the long green robes that marked her as High Priestess, led the way, her gorgeous velvet train carried by Tielmark's young rulers, Benet and Lily. The priestess looked regal and correct, her expression formal. The Prince and Princess, supporting the rich cloth of the train that symbolized their lands, seemed lighthearted and happy. They looked out across the assembly with smiling faces. Benet whispered something in Lily's ear. She laughed and ducked her head. They were quite a contrast to Dervla's severity.

Behind them, in order of precedence, came the seven dukes of Tielmark, each with a pair of retainers. They seemed to be competing for a place of pride as the most magnificently dressed, in silks and velvet and gold braiding. This year, Gabrielle of Melaudiere led the council of seven: Benet's recognition for her service to him in the past month. Like Dervla, her expression was formal and severe, her robes of state long and flowing. She had chosen Martin and his younger sister Mariette as her retainers, and was walking slowly, a little stiffly, her eyes fixed on her Prince's back. It seemed to Gaultry that the heat was affecting her.

"Melaudiere might come to regret keeping her heirs so

close by her," Mervion murmured, soft enough that only Gaultry heard. "It emphasizes her age, don't you think?"

At first Gaultry, who had only admiration for the Duchess's grandchildren, could not see what Mervion meant. She saw only a rugged pair of soldiers: Mariette, a lean woman with high, athletic shoulders and long arms; and Martin, now shaved and dressed with the polish required for his seat at the Prince's High Table. They were a pair to ennoble any courtier's back. Then she looked again at the Duchess, and understood what Mervion meant. Their strength emphasized the old woman's slipping hold on life, the stiffness of her walk, the brittle delicacy of her aged bones. Gaultry wanted to tell her sister that the Duchess was too proud to live for anything but the future, but she wasn't confident she could guess the old woman's motives. She stared at Martin, trying to see a shadow of his former upset, but he had, to all appearances, completely recovered.

"Sit." Mervion tugged her shoulder. "The Prince has taken his place. Along with everyone but you."

Gaultry stepped hastily across the bench and slid into her place, mindful that she had made her feelings conspicuous at a moment when she most wanted to hide them.

"Dervla's acolytes are at the table just below the Prince's," Mervion commented.

Gaultry shrugged. "Dervla made the seating, didn't she?"

"She did. But she didn't think of everything. If she wanted them to look impressive, she should have put them at the table on the Prince's other side. They're out of the breeze and sweating like pigs where she has them." Even from their low table the first prickings of a sweat stain were visible along the spine of the ash-blond woman Gaultry had decided was Pala-mar Laconte.

"You're the only one who isn't," Gaultry said testily. It was easy enough for Mervion to make fun of Palamar. The girl's face was splotchy, her physical discomfort from the heat all too evident. By contrast, Mervion, in her sparkling white dress and peach-glow skin, looked indecently cool and fresh.

Even the flowers in her hair had maintained their crispness. That had to be a spell, Gaultry thought resentfully. Little magics like that came so easily to Mervion that Gaultry often thought she must not realize that she was using them. "It's hot. Why shouldn't people sweat?"

Nine courtiers shared their table. Dervla had done her work well. Gaultry was not familiar with a single face. If Dervla meant her to feel isolated, she had succeeded. She let Mervion do the introductions. Her sister, she discovered resentfully, already knew half the names.

One seat, opposite the twins, was still empty.

"We should be twelve for the Great Twelve," Gaultry said, noticing the empty place. She wondered if Dervla had the gall to have deliberately arranged such an asymmetry. "Who's going to make up our number?"

"That would be me." The late arrival, hoving into her field of vision, sketched a quick bow. Gaultry frowned. This man she knew too well.

"Coyal Torquay." She could not keep the distaste from her voice. "What are you doing here?" Gaultry had first met the young knight on the opposing side of a battlefield, a scant week before the Prince's marriage. Then he had been the traitor Chancellor's personal knight and champion, under orders to destroy her escort and take her prisoner. That had been before Gaultry discovered her Brood-blood and her Glamour-magic. Back then, Coyal had been almost strong enough to take her.

"There's no one from Torquay's house here," the man said. His voice was carefully expressionless. "My name is Memorant. Coyal Memorant. Torquay is forsworn. Or hadn't you heard?"

Gaultry looked down at the table. She had heard. But she had put it from her mind, thinking that she and Coyal would not cross paths again. With the downfall of the Prince's half-Bissanty Chancellor, Heiratikus, Benet had purged the rest of the Bissanty faction at court. The gentry who had been open in their support of Heiratikus had been stripped of titles and lands. Others, against whom no disloyalty to Tielmark's crown could be

proven, had simply been relegated to the outer ranks. The Prince
had denied them the chance to renew their pledge today, though
he had not been without some mercy for their diminished position at court. He had invited these outcasts to demonstrate their
loyalty to Tielmark by participating in the summer campaign
against the Lanai—Martin's news that Tielmark should ready
itself for a long campaign aside, rumors were already flying that
the Bissanty meant to push the mountain tribes hard against Tielmark's borders this year. "I cannot give you your honor back,"
he had told them. "But you can take it back yourselves on the
field of battle." Some, rising to the Prince's challenge, had
already ridden far west to Haute Tielmark's border. Others had
stayed at court, determined to outride the scandal by denying any
admission of guilt.

Coyal Torquay had chosen the latter course. Despite his
prominent court position under Heiratikus, the brilliant young
knight had numbered among those against whom no disloyalty to Tielmark could be proven. There had been whispers
that his father's influence had saved him. Coyal himself had
squashed those whispers by publicly quarreling with his sire
and renouncing his rights to the family name. That he had the
brass to attend Emiera's feast did not surprise Gaultry—
though she noticed that he had not quite had the effrontery to
attempt to renew his pledge to the Prince before Benet wanted
it. That he had the nerve to get himself seated at the Blas
twins' table—

"Memorant?" she said harshly, still flustered by his unexpected appearance. "If your memory is so good, you have
great gall to seat yourself here with me and my sister." His
new name was a curious choice. Those who forswore their
family-ties often took on work names. That was what Martin
had done when he had left his wife and become a field-
stalker—one of the desperate men who wandered in no-man'-
s-land between army lines, drawing the enemy troops into
battle. It was not so easy to determine what might have
prompted Coyal to name himself "the remembering one." Did
he mean to rebuke himself, or the Prince who had relegated
him to such an ambiguous position?

"Gall?" Coyal made a short bow. "Why gall? Where better to start repairing my fortunes, than at the feet of the woman who brought me down?"

The young knight had a manner that Gaultry had difficulty outfacing. Despite his fearsome reputation, Coyal was young and boyishly handsome, with flowing golden hair and a sensuous red-lipped mouth. He simply did not look like a devious traitor. His manners were exaggeratedly casual, as though a warrior's focus was nothing to him, but that seemed more a matter of a young man's vanity than a reflection of any more serious flaw. As always, he was elegantly dressed, his hair, worn long in chevalier's locks, glossy and fine, the lace at his wrists and throat crisp.

Distracted by the man's handsome looks, Gaultry found it hard to dredge up the memory of the battle lust that had been in Coyal's face during their last fight, and harder still, in front of a crowded table of gaily-dressed courtiers, to maintain her animus against him.

"Sit then," she said awkwardly. "I won't try to stop you."

"You are kindness itself, lady." Coyal bowed. Gaultry struggled to control a rising blush. She wished Martin were at her side. Coyal would not play such a game with her if Martin were present. Despite her ambiguous feelings toward court politics, she had no desire to help the young man climb back into favor. He had offered her so much harm—and yet here he was, pressing his advantage, as though the trouble between them had been nothing more than a passing difference of opinion—less even than a quarrel.

"I thought you would not refuse me. For that, I have brought two fair sisters a commemorative present." A neatly dressed page, on Coyal's cue, slipped up to the table and held out a fresh armful of branches. Willow branches, tied with ribbons that matched the clear color of the young knight's blue eyes. "Some say willow is for sorrow," he said, taking them from the boy. "Others for memory and remembrance. But I say it is for forgiveness. What say you?" His mouth curved, as if in a confident smile, but there was a hunger in his eyes that belied his attempt at lightness.

"Why should we—" Gaultry started.

Mervion, interrupting her, reached out and took one of the offered branches. "In Arleon Forest, we say willow is for the kindness of spring." She tucked the branch into her hair.

Which left Gaultry isolated, if she was to deny him.

For politeness, she followed Mervion's lead. "It's for a spell that makes the foxes dance," she said. "Nothing higher than that." Mervion touched her leg under the table, a warning to watch her words. Gaultry pretended to ignore her.

Coyal pushed into his narrow seat on the bench opposite Mervion and Gaultry, making himself comfortable between two stout bench-partners, who protested feebly but ceded him the space when the steel plates at his shoulders pinched them. Like everyone else at the feast, the young knight had come up on Feeding-Hill without his weapons. But ceremonial armor was part of his warrior's gear, and he had chosen to keep it with him, even though it was a feasting day. The fealty badge on his shoulder was a blank disk of silver, defiantly polished to mirrorlike brilliance. He had served Chancellor Heiratikus well and honorably, but now that the Chancellor was dead and disgraced, he was a knight without a master. His insistence on appearing with high bracers, greaves, and a short armored coat revealed his fierce, disappointed pride. *Memorant.* Gaultry hoped his memories were lessons well learned. If Coyal had ever paused to question the Chancellor's authority or motives, the young knight might easily have escaped this fate.

"You're asking me to be your lady?" Mervion's laugh returned Gaultry abruptly to the conversation.

"Why not?" Coyal was asking. "You and your sister both. In the eyes of the Great Twins, who better? I'm astonished to find that I'm the first to seek the honor."

Gaultry glared at him, furious that the manners of court wouldn't countenance reaching across and giving him a good shake. "You're not the first," she said, "and I doubt you'll be the last. Why seek to curry favor where you know you're not welcome?"

"You'd have to prove yourself worthy first," Mervion

interrupted, overriding her sister's objections. She twined the ribbon that tied her willow branch round her fingers. The gesture suggested that she was seriously considering accepting him. Gaultry touched her sister's hand under the table, trying to forestall her. She was furious with Mervion for playing Coyal's game.

"Anything," Coyal said. "Name the task. The more impossible the better—"

A sudden sick shudder through Gaultry's chest prevented her from cutting the young knight with angry words. It was a jolt of magic, painfully strong, not directed at her, but powerful enough to impact her. "Huntress help me!" she gasped, the pain giving her voice a hard edge. "What is this?"

Mervion gave her an impatient look, then frowned, realizing that something more serious than pique at Coyal had prompted her sister's outcry. "What's wrong?"

The young huntress tried to scramble up from her bench. Some thing, some magical casting, threatened the Prince, even as he sat at his High Table, surrounded by loyal courtiers. The stab of magic that had alerted her seemed to pin her in her seat, holding her back. She was helpless, spellcrippled, her skin slick with sweat, the color blanched from her face. Rage at this unexpected powerlessness leapt in her. Coyal, his back to the Prince's table, saw the expression in her eyes and mistook her intent. He stood, his hand going for a hilt that wasn't there at his hip.

Mervion tugged at her hand, not understanding, trying to hold her in her seat.

"You're making a scene," she said. "Tell me what's happening—"

"The Prince," Gaultry rasped. "The Princess." Her legs were leaden, her sight blurred. The last remnant of her focus was on the small procession just arrived at the Prince's table. Three pairs of serving men, each shouldering a roasted deer on a long stake. The young venison was gaily decorated with strings of flower and spice, a special preparation for the Prince's table. An unnatural light glinted off the glazed skins of two of the three deer. "The deer are spell-poisoned,"

Gaultry said, trying, and failing, to point. "They'll poison the Prince. Don't let him so much as touch them."

Mervion jumped to her feet. Unlike Gaultry, the queer spell-sickness had not affected her. "Don't fight." She pulled up her skirts and clambered easily clear of the bench. "I'll go."

"Quickly!" Gaultry pleaded.

"What's happening?" Coyal was already up from his place at the other side of the table.

"It's the Prince," Mervion said. To Gaultry it sounded as though she was speaking from the bottom of a well. "He mustn't touch his venison."

"The carving knife is in his hand—" Coyal said, turning over his shoulder to look.

"We must stop him!"

Then Coyal and Mervion were gone, leaving the table in an uproar. Gaultry, ignoring Mervion's order, stumbled out of her seat after them.

The sight of the Chancellor's ex-Champion and Mervion dashing towards the Prince's High Table created pandemonium. The young knight moved like a man dangerously possessed—he had no need to shove, the crowd simply melted open before him. Behind him, courtiers jumped up from their seats, increasing the confusion. Mervion, trapped by the crush, threw her hands out and called a spell. Gaultry saw her sister draw in the casting—saw it in the preternatural glow of energy that swept through her sister's body, gold and green entwined: Glamour and the Great Twins' magic together. Already, she noted with reflexive envy, Mervion had taught herself to mix the two as one. A bolt of shining gold-green fire arched over the crowd. Reaching the Prince's table, it crested and broke, sheathing the serving men and the venison which they had laid on the Prince's table with a pale glow. Princess Lily threw herself across Benet's lap, shielding her husband with her body. Benet jerked back the hand that held the carving knife, barely avoiding slashing her.

"What treason is this?" he shouted, furious, one arm reaching to shield his Princess. "To break Emiera's Feast—"

Sunlight flashed on metal. The Prince, still holding his wife, angrily stood up, glaring to his left and right. Gaultry, trying to push her way forward through the crowd, had the impression that Mervion's magic, seeking only to protect the Prince, had flushed out daggers and short-bladed weapons from all the ducal retainers—men and women who had been expressly commanded to attend the Prince's table unarmed.

Benet's rage increased the chaos among the lower tables. In the confusion, someone rammed Gaultry in the shoulders, knocking her to her knees. She slipped down between two bodies, clutching vainly at backs and belts to catch herself. A man wearing boots stepped on her wrist, crushing down with his heel. She gasped in pain. Suddenly it was not the Prince's safety that concerned her but her own, as she fought against being squashed by the panicked crowd.

Three times she rose to one knee, and three times she was knocked back. *Call a spell,* she told herself. *Call a spell to make them quiet.* The corner of mental calm she managed to conjure gave her a point of focus; she threw her mental strength towards it, gulping back tears.

Before she could act, someone else's magic surged around her. Old-tongue shouting cut across the mob, enforcing a palpable calm in its wake. The man who'd unthinkingly trapped Gaultry beneath him drew back; the press of bodies shrank aside. Even the bridle of unfriendly magic that held Gaultry in its clutch withdrew, allowing her to regain a degree of equilibrium. "Let me up!" she called weakly, clutching at the ankle of a woman who had been pushed almost onto her body.

The woman, glancing down, recognized her. "Rennie!" She pulled anxiously at the man with the boots. "It's the Prince's Glamour-witch! You're killing her!"

In the small space that cleared, Gaultry scrambled woozily to her feet.

Over the crowd's heads, she saw that Mervion and the Chancellor's ex-champion had reached the Prince's table. Coyal had yanked one of the young bucks away—it was on the ground, its trappings of spring spice trampled underfoot. But the Prince's guards, catching him from behind, had prevented him from pulling the second deer out of the Prince's reach. At the young knight's side, Mervion was up on her toes, scanning the crowd, trying to spot Gaultry. "My sister said you were in danger." She was trying to appeal to the Prince, trying to calm him. "It was not our intent to needlessly cause disruption—"

"Shame!" The High Priestess called, loud enough to drown Mervion out. "Magic summoned in anger, and knives at the Prince's table!" Scarcely a member of the seven ducal retinues had come to their master's table without hidden weaponry. "Emiera sees you! You have shamed yourselves!"

As Dervla ranted, the Prince was staring, a furious expression on his face, at the blade that rested in the hand of a young ducal server, a bare four paces from his shoulder. Gaultry, closing on the table, was just in time to hear the Prince's words to this young unfortunate.

"Is that blade to protect me or your master?" Benet asked dryly.

The young retainer, one of the Duke of Basse Demaine's supporters, paled, and thrust the weapon into the sheath he had concealed in his shirtfront. "My Prince," he stammered, "I am ashamed . . ." It was easy to underestimate Benet, until his temper rose and he revealed the anger and hidden strength that ran through him like sharp wire. Looking into the Prince's face, Basse Demaine's man ran out of words.

Benet's orders to the dukes had been specific. Emiera's Feast was the first holy day at which his new wife officiated as Princess of Tielmark. He had wanted the occasion to be free of confrontation, had commanded that his inner court should bring no weapons within the bounds of the sacral hills. The dukes had obeyed the words but not the spirit of his injunction. Though their own hands were empty, every one of their retainers had come to the table armed.

Having vented his ire at the young retainer, the Prince turned to Dervla, his face dark with his displeasure.

"That's enough words from you," he cut short Dervla's harangue. "Drop your spells. This mob that calls itself my court must learn to calm itself." His hand clasped Lily's, and his young wife pressed it to her cheek, in plain view, against the accepted custom. "Redress is no matter for my High Priestess on the highest day of the Goddess Twins' peace.

"As for the rest of you . . ." Benet glared at the courtiers who had stood around him. "Are you children or men, that you take such upset at a single woman's call?"

Despite the agony that churned in her, it warmed Gaultry to watch him take charge of his court with such boldness. Benet had been two weeks without a Chancellor. The traitor Heiratikus had discouraged the Prince from addressing his own court, and Benet was still awkward when it came to public speaking. Many had claimed that he needed to appoint a new Chancellor quickly, for need of a mouthpiece. But what the Prince lacked in formal address, he made up in his mettle. His dukes, responding quickly to their master's display of anger, snapped orders to their servers, shamed and eager to get the weapons out of sight.

"Now"—the Prince turned his angry face to Mervion and Coyal—"what means this sad interruption, on such a propitious day?"

"My sister—" For once Mervion was flustered. She started again. "There is a spell upon your table, Highness. This man and I sought to protect you."

"A spell?" the High Priestess interrupted. She scanned first the table, then, as though a spell might naturally center there, the Prince himself. "On this table? I see no darkness here. What makes you think that the Prince is threatened?"

Gaultry broke free from the crowd and reached her sister's side. "The deer are poisoned!" she said loudly. "Cry mercy to Elianté the Huntress if you can't see that!" She glanced down at the young deer Coyal had jerked from the table and shuddered. From afar, she had only been aware of a strange light, glinting off the honey-glazed skin. Close to, something in that cooked flesh brought a crawling sensation to her spine. The back legs of the deer that had been tumbled out of the Prince's reach were bound with a strap, now blackened from the cooking fire. The faint trace of a glyph could be seen through the scorch-marks: a broken spiral. It reminded Gaultry of

Elianté's mark, in her incarnation as Spring Hunter, killer of cubs in their dens. Yet even as she made that connection, she sensed that identification could not be correct. This magic had a darkness that did not belong to the Great Huntress.

"Can't you feel it?" Gaultry shivered, staring from Mervion to Dervla, then farther down the table to where Gabrielle of Melaudiere was sitting, her thin white hair fallen forward on her face. "Am I the only one who can feel it?"

"If there is a spell," Dervla sniffed, "the caster must have named it to you, young Gaultry, to ensure you could feel it. Myself, I don't see or feel a thing."

"Who says it has to be named magic?" Mervion said sharply. "If Gaultry can feel it, it could be because she's spent her life in the forest, running with deer, and hunting them. Who better than my sister to know if a kill has been poisoned? That she can see it, and you cannot, need have nothing to do with a spell-caster naming power to her. When did you last touch a deer's mind, High Priestess?"

"One needn't run naked in the forest to know the taste of the Great Huntress's prey!" Dervla rejoined nastily. "I am familiar with the savor of fawn and yearling!"

"Then why can't you feel this!" Gaultry interrupted. She did not understand what was happening, only that something was dreadfully wrong. "It's so strong, the very smell of the flesh is making me sick!"

"We can have it removed—" Benet interjected, raising one hand.

"No! Don't touch it!" Barely thinking what she was doing, she grabbed for the second deer's hock, meaning to drag it out of his reach. The hot grease that lay on its flesh, the heat of the cooking fire, seared her hand.

"Leave it," Benet said angrily, reading the pain on her face. "I will call a servant—"

"Don't touch it!" Gaultry panicked and jerked again at the heavy venison, ignoring the pain. Her fingers slipped on the grease, on the glazed honey, and then hooked at last on the leather strap that bound the deer's ankles. It broke, and fell free.

A thunderclap of magic shook the air. There was a great swooshing intake of wind. The Princess began to scream. Benet's face blanched with shock, though he had enough wits about him to cover his wife's eyes. Gaultry, a distant, burning sensation in her hand, looked down.

A shock of revulsion rocked her. Her hand had hold of the ankle of a very young child. A boy. A boy of seven or eight years. He was naked and brown, the cooking twine on his body tied so tight it cut deep into his young flesh.

For a moment panic held her so tightly she thought it was a spell, a spell that wouldn't allow her to let go of the boy's ankle. Then she realized it was only panic; she could take her hand off the child's leg. She could.

She did.

Then she turned away from the child's corpse and was violently sick.

chapter 4 ▼

Gaultry, gracelessly hunched over as she heaved her breakfast onto the grass, missed what happened next. A slim figure, a boy who moved with a predator's quickness, darted up to her back. But for Coyal's reflexes, a dagger would have taken her between the shoulders. Faster even than the assassin, the young knight caught Gaultry's attacker by the wrist and spun him away from her back.

The would-be assassin, one of the boys who had carried the desecrated corpse to the Prince's table, twisted his wrist free and struck at Coyal's face with the dagger. "Llara take you, meddler! Die in her place!"

Coyal barely turned his head in time to take the cut along his cheek rather than through his eye socket.

"Protect the Prince!" someone shouted.

Melaudiere's grandchildren were the first to react. They jumped up from their places and vaulted across the table, scattering dishes and forks. Mariette, younger than Martin and slightly swifter, made it across the table before him. She interposed herself between the fighting and the royal couple, clearing a space with the sweep of her long dagger. Martin, just behind her, went straight past, striking directly at the assassin. The boy disengaged from Coyal a split second before the big soldier's blow came down. Catching the force of Martin's blade on his knife, he executed a complicated flashing roll with his weapon, spinning himself clear. The court spontaneously widened the circle of open grass around him, overturning benches and tables in their haste.

"You're all afraid of me!" the boy shouted. He sounded strangely joyous. He laughed as he feinted towards his attackers, testing their strength, his strange ice-green eyes drugged bright. In his hand his blade dipped and rose like a living thing. Coyal, despite the superficial nature of his wound, did not seem to concern the boy now that he had new challengers.

That was not vainglory—Coyal was out of the fight. The young knight, his face livid, backed clumsily away and knocked into Gaultry. His hand was pressed to the cut on his face. Blood seeped through his fingers, staining them an unhealthy off-pink color. "I'm poisoned," Coyal called. His voice sounded flat. He slumped to the ground, the strength leaving him. "Don't let his blade touch you—"

Gaultry, turning and calling for Mervion, found that her sister had already pulled the man's hand away from his face, was already chafing his wrists, trying to keep his circulation going. "Oh, Great Emiera, it's desperately strong." Mervion, busy with her hands, had no awareness of her sister. "Will even a spell be enough to save him?"

The stranger, after a dismissive glance to assure himself that his first mark had fallen, turned to Martin. "You're next," he crowed, lashing out.

Martin, cold as ice, did not wait for him to complete his swing. He met him with a vicious counterslash, all the weight and force of his body in his blow. In a shocking explosion of gore, the boy's shirt and arm split open from wrist to elbow. A nauseated look slipped across the boy's face. Then, astonishingly, he recovered himself. He transferred his knife into his unwounded hand, and ducked back—only to find his retreat cut off by Mariette.

She struck at his neck. He twisted, escaped the blow, delaying a death that now seemed inevitable.

The boy glanced from one to the other, rising indecision on his face. His glacier-pale eyes flickered to Gaultry, where she stood on the sidelines, clumsily mopping her face. He would have moved towards her, but Martin, sensing his intent, blocked him. The boy scanned the crowd, as though seeking relief, but there was no one there to answer the sudden, unspoken plea. Every face was turned against him.

Someone in the crowd tossed Martin a length of thick cloth, a horse's saddle blanket. Never taking his eyes from the young assassin, the tall soldier wound it over his fist, making a shield.

As the boy watched Martin, Mariette struck, once again going for the boy's throat. Again, his extraordinary reflexes caught and turned the blade. With a grunt of effort, he hit back, opening the front of her tunic. He might have had her then, but Martin pressed in from the rear, forcing the boy to break his assault. The boy stumbled, disoriented. The pain from his wounded arm was beginning to slow him. The crowd murmured, hungry for his death. They sensed the kill would not be long coming.

"You cannot have my blood!" the boy shouted suddenly, seeing death closing in. "I am Sha Muira! You will not kill me!" He threw down his weapon.

His words had an immediate effect. To Gaultry's astonishment, Martin and Mariette, instead of seizing him, exchanged a quick look, nodded, and hastily backed away. Around them, the crowd was almost falling over itself in its hurry to widen the combat circle. "What's going on?" she asked as Mariette, also rushing, bumped against her.

"Just back away," Mariette said, pushing at her. "That boy could practically kill you just by looking at you."

"What do you mean?" Gaultry said. "He's not even attacking now."

The boy fumbled in the breast of his shirt, tearing buttons as he opened his collar. He yanked out a necklace of milky-looking beads and snapped its thread, pulling it free of his shirt.

"I commit myself to death!" he proclaimed. He threw up his hands, offering the necklace to the sky. "As I have committed my body twice before to Great Llara who watches above, my protector!" The stones began to let off smoke, angry black smoke that wreathed between his fingers. The boy's hand was on fire. He paid it no heed.

The smoke spread ever swifter, winding down the boy's arm like a writhing nest of snakes. Gaultry looked into the boy's face. The boy was doing his best to hide his pain, but she could tell that he was hurting badly.

"What is it?" she cried out. "What's happening?" No one seemed to hear. All were fixed on the boy's death-dance. He was trying to cover his involuntary lurching with graceful movements, a bizarre choreography that bespoke preparation for this particular death, this particular agony. Mariette was nearest her. The young swordsman had bruised her knee, and she was leaning over, pressing her fingers against her leg to dull the pain. Gaultry grabbed at her. Mariette at least she could make answer. "Tell me why you stopped fighting. Why are you letting him kill himself? Don't we want to know who sent him?"

"If the boy is Sha Muira, Bissanty sent him," Mariette answered grimly. "And as for letting him kill himself—he's already dead. The Sha Muira are always poisoned—he just let the poison have sway in his body." Keeping her eyes on the boy's writhing figure, she rubbed her knee, grimacing at the pain. "That prayer necklace was his antidote. Without it, nothing can save him."

"Why doesn't anyone stop him? You or Martin could spare him this."

Mariette gave her an impatient look, wiping her dark, sweat-heavy hair out of her face. "He's Sha Muira, thrice committed to death. His death belongs to Mother Llara—not to us."

The beads were bare cinders now, cinders that crumbled from the necklace string with a sparking sound like fat popping in a fire. The boy's face arched in agony, but still he made no sound. Around him, the crowd grew strangely quiet, almost respectful, waiting for the end.

Gaultry stared into the young face and felt a surge of revulsion. The boy had neither prepared nor cast the spell that had lain on the slaughtered boy who had been served to the Prince's table—that much, she would have been ready to swear on. He had an assassin's training—but beneath this, he was a dispensable tool in a greater power's hands. If the boy died now, it would be for his loyalty to those thankless hands.

She felt as if she was the only one watching him now, as if she was the only one who could see his pain. Sensing her attention, the glacier-green eyes turned to her, just as a lash of pain hit him.

A dazzled jolt of recognition stabbed her. Ritual ruled the boy—but beneath that ritual, something in him called to her. Not the trained assassin, readied for death, but the primitive animal force that ran through him, deeper than training. It desperately wanted to survive. Responding to that desperation, Gaultry reached out, probing the boy with all her magic. The boy's suffering was a palpable thing, drawing her forward, demanding her sympathy. Then, quite unexpectedly, her magic found an animal focus, and a vision burst across her.

A starved puppy, with black fur, was crying in the boy's soul. Odd, glacier-green eyes, the color of glass, the color of deep winter ice, told her it was the young assassin himself. She could see every rib in his young body, the thinness of his dark hair; the unsatisfied cold of him. There was a leash on his throat, but the leash had been severed. Now it tangled round his puppy-legs, hampering his efforts to free himself.

She shook herself free of the vision, badly frightened, not sure what had crystallized her magic so that she could see him in this way. His trust had been twisted, used against him. Now, despite the stoic will with which he attempted to welcome his own demise, he was dying, and dying badly. Whoever had abandoned him must have known that his death would be painfully prolonged.

The ugliness of that drove her to action.

"Mervion!" Gaultry called. "I need you!" Somehow Mervion was there, reaching out to her through the crush of the crowd. Gaultry grabbed her sister's wrist and pulled her into the trampled ring of grass.

"What are you doing?" Mervion resisted, trying to free her wrist.

"What are *we* doing," Gaultry answered. "We're saving this boy's life. You have to stop the poison. I know you can do it—use the magic in me to do it. Use even the power of my Glamour."

"I had barely enough power to help Coyal—" Mervion started.

"Use everything from me," Gaultry cut her short. "I don't care." Around them the crowd had dissolved into a mob. The mob's focus was all on the boy who had threatened to defile their Prince. "You can heal him. Take a piece from my Glamour-soul. Save him."

"What if I can do what you want?" Mervion asked. "It won't be popular." They were standing over the boy now. He had sunk to his haunches, weakened, though he continued to make graceful gestures with his hands. The necklace string had frayed almost to nothing. His head lolled, the pale green eyes were staring and blank. He barely knew they were there. "Gaultry, the poison is not what you think—it has Great Llara's blessing on it. He doesn't want to be saved. He thinks he's going to his Goddess. It may take half your Glamour-soul to bring him back—or more."

"I don't care," said Gaultry. "Just try. The rest we'll sort out later." She stooped and dragged the boy's in-curled body clumsily against her own. *Great Huntress,* she prayed. *Great Huntress Elianté. Benevolent Lady Emiera. Assure me now that what I do is right.*

A gold arc of light flashed across her vision, blotting away the crowd. She saw, as if in a mirror, a dazzling golden face, the skin airily thin, the eyes, like burning stars, slanted and unfriendly. It smiled, teasing, mocking her. It was her own Glamour-soul, her second soul. The soul that powered her magic.

As if at a great distance, she heard Mervion singing, working the casting. Gaultry threw herself mentally open, pulling her sister in past all her barriers. There was a new shyness rising in her, an awareness of her mental nakedness, even before her beloved twin, and she hesitated, trying to beat back the unfamiliar sensation. She forced herself to conjure the image of the starved black dog. That helped her quash the pangs of fear.

Mervion was deep within her now. Gaultry sensed her sister's presence, her surprise, a tentative pause like an indrawn breath, as she encountered the image of the ragged, ill-grown dog, protectively clasped in the golden Glamour wraith's arms. *Is this wise?* Mervion's query echoed uncomfortably through the young huntress's skull, setting her teeth on edge. *Are you so sure you want to champion him?*

Gaultry could not find the strength to answer. She tried to focus the image, but her strength seemed to fail. Mervion had to trust her. That was all. Letting this boy die was not fit retribution.

She wished she had Mervion's gift to form whole words, whole sentences of communication, not just this blunt throb of empathy, these crude images that showed where her loyalties fell.

I see what you want. Mervion's presence seemed to stroke the young dog's back, to ruffle its thin pelt against the grain of its fur. *The poison is strong; only the fire of a Glamour-soul can quell it. But you are asking more than you realize, sister—not only was the poison blessed by Llara Thunderbringer, the God-Mother, but the boy took it willingly.*

I don't care. Just do it! Gaultry's fear was strong enough that words crystalized and formed at last, powerful enough to command. *We mustn't let him die.*

Gaultry was not sure who performed the next magic: Mervion or herself, forcing Mervion to start the spell. The ethereal woman of gold, Gaultry's Glamour-soul, ripped brutally down its center. The right side of the soul thinned to nothing as Mervion drew it away, leaving Gaultry with an aching gap in her chest. Then Mervion was gone, the dog image was gone, half Gaultry's second soul was gone, and the moment of agony closed, like a roiling whirlpool coming to an abrupt surcease, leaving only calm unruffled water.

Gaultry opened her eyes. The young assassin boy's face was inches from her own. His eyes, clear of pain, were wide open, focused. They were filled with an expression very like horror.

"Your name is Tullier," Gaultry told him, loosing her hold on his body. His name had come to her in the moment she'd opened her eyes—she could have known more, but she blocked the knowledge away. "That little I know." She took his hand in hers, the hand that had held the ruined anodyne necklace. Her thumb brushed away a last dark ash. "Your body is still running with poison, but it can't kill you. Not now. You're borrowing half my second soul. You can't die unless I will it."

He stared up, disbelieving. "Nothing can stop Sha Muir poison."

Mervion put her hand in Gaultry's and pulled her sister to her feet. "He's only parroting what he's been taught," Mervion said wearily. "The fact of his life and health will have to convince him."

"Thank you, Mervion." Gaultry was suddenly aware of the tiredness in her sister's face and voice, a tiredness that seemed strangely like defeat. "I knew you could do it."

"Did you?" There was something unhappy in Mervion's smile, something Gaultry did not understand, but she roused at Gaultry's words and gave her sister a look that was full of tenderness. "I'm glad. I want us to share our magic—"

"Always," Gaultry agreed.

For a moment, it seemed to Gaultry that she, Mervion, and the boy were a quiet center in the eye of a turbulent storm. At their backs, Martin and his sister restrained the crowd, aided by the Duke of Basse Demaine's retainer and one other man. Then Mervion broke the moment, standing away from Gaultry and wiping her hands on her skirt.

"They've taken Coyal out to the tents," she said. "I want to go to him. Maybe I can help him, now that I see how the poison works."

"I should go," Gaultry said. "He saved my life."

Mervion shook her head. "Stay here. See what they decide to do with this one. I think he's going to need all the help you can give him."

Smoothing her hair and dress, Mervion stepped briskly away through the crowd. Gaultry stared after her, wondering at her sister's changeable mood. It almost seemed as though Mervion was disappointed in her. That was a disturbing thought, and she was grateful when the chaos that remained on the hill distracted her.

The bonfire would be lit at the day's closing, but Emiera's Feast was over.

Still impaled on the cooking stake, the corpse of the young deer-boy sprawled grossly on the Prince's table. The two deer that had been brought in with him lay on the ground where they had been thrown by angry hands.

The Prince stood in front of his table, staring at the corpse. It had been a narrow escape. The royal pair were supposed to be pure of human death on this day of the Goddess's Feasting, or the Ash Hill sacrifice to Emiera would be rendered invalid. He had sent the Princess to the women's tent, telling her to wash herself. But when Dervla suggested he should absent himself with his wife, he exploded.

"Not until the body has been cleansed. I'll turn my back on a clean corpse, but not on this foulness! I won't hide from this—no god would want that."

"Then move aside and give me room to cleanse it."

The Prince shot her an angry look, but he saw her logic, and gave way.

Choosing three acolytes to help her, Dervla stripped the Prince's table of its cloth and garlands and laid the body out on its back. One of the acolytes was sent for a bowl of water from the spring on Elianté's Hill, and a second was dispatched to Emiera's Hill for fresh ash branches. Then Dervla, having shrugged herself out of her robes and the long velvet train, revealing the simple priestess's vestments that she wore beneath, took a cloth, invoked a prayer to the Great Twins, and commenced the ritual cleansing.

As she worked, the crowd on the hilltop calmed. The seven members of the ducal council dispersed their retinues to help clear the hill while they remained with their Prince, embarrassment mingled with curiosity in varying degrees on their faces. Each of the dukes, from Victor of Haute Tielmark, a great yellow-haired giant of a man who ruled Tielmark's westernmost province, to Gabrielle of Melaudiere, had been shamed, thinking too much of themselves when their attention should have been on the sacrificial bond their Prince was making to ensure the bounty of their harvests. In more than one face Gaultry could see a hint of relief that disaster had intervened to draw attention away from the armed servers they had brought to the Prince's table.

Dervla gently stroked the body with damp cloths, intoning holy words, snipping free the tightly drawn cooking twine and removing the garlands of rosemary. The scent of cooked meat was unpleasantly heavy in everyone's nostrils. Finally, the job was complete, and all that remained was to remove the horrible stake that had been brutally pushed through the body, head to hips.

The priestess, gripping the stake, braced her hands. A nervous movement fluttered through the watchers. The struggle to remove the stake, which was well-cooked into the body, would be an ugly thing. Dervla, glancing up, and ever sensitive to a crowd's mood, shifted her hands.

The spell formed with a shock of green power: a small, focused fire that crept along the wood, reducing it to ashes. The high priestess, permitting herself a satisfied smile, widened the casting so it flared out to burn the tainted herbs and flowers that had ornamented the boy's body. There would be no remnants, no blighted sprig that might be stolen and twined into a fetish to give the Prince bad dreams. As she finished and the magic dropped away, the crowd sighed with relief.

"What about this one?" Gaultry asked, pushing up to the front of the crowd, the assassin boy still at her side. One of the two remaining deer was still tied with a leather bond across its hocks. In the reverent hush that had fallen around the table her voice sounded overloud.

The Prince gave Gaultry a hard look and let his gaze slip to the young stranger. "Guards! Remove the murderer to a secure holding." His men, perhaps guilt-ridden because of their earlier inaction, moved quickly. Two men in gauntlets and long mail sleeves jerked the boy from the young huntress's side.

"Your Highness," Gaultry began, shocked to see their roughness. "He is a prisoner—"

"You've overstepped yourself, Lady Blas," the Prince said coldly. "This boy is no longer your problem."

Gaultry's nerves were already ragged, and the rebuke was unexpected. Watching one of the guards chop the back of Tullier's neck with his hand, something in her snapped. "Without me, there'd be a mouthful of boy-flesh in your mouth," she said wildly. "And you still haven't listened to me! What about this second one?" She gestured to the smaller of the remaining deer.

"Second one?" The Prince's face was white with inheld fury. "High Priestess?"

"It's a deer, Your Highness," Dervla said. "Goddess in me, it's a deer."

"Gaultry—?"

"Put a bite of it in your mouth then," Gaultry dared him, furious. "That should make the gods love you."

Benet took a step towards the deer, as if to answer her challenge. He made an angry gesture. "On any other day, I would not hesitate. But today, for Great Emiera's sake, I cannot meet that challenge," he said. "So you had best prove, Lady Blas, that what you claim is real, lest my deference on this matter be proved poor judgment—if not weakness."

With the shock of the first discovery and the fight, no one had bothered with the other deer. They had been drawn back a little from the table, but otherwise, nothing had been done with them.

She stared at the slim animal legs and the half-burnt-through bond that bound them, and tried to swallow. With the first one, she hadn't known. There had been fear and wonder at the spell, and a strong musky stink with animal-spirits twined strangely all round it, and she had somehow known that a thick cover of spell would crack open like a gross chrysalis, revealing a frightful transformation. But she hadn't known exactly what awaited her inside the cocoon of magic. This time, she feared that she did.

"Please," Gaultry said, reluctant to appeal to Dervla's good graces but unwilling to go ahead with things as they stood. "Please, can we cleanse it first?"

Dervla gave her a wintery look. She still did not believe the deer was anything other than a deer.

"I mean no offense," Gaultry said, struggling to keep a respectful tone. "Neither to yourself nor Your Highness." She made the Prince a slight bob.

Dervla, with an impatient gesture, ordered a servant to clear the table refuse from around the second deer. The core of the Prince's court held its breath. Then the priestess, moving quickly, immolated the cooking-stake.

"There's nothing more to be done," she said. "This piece of venison—"

"Take off the leg bond," Gaultry said. "That's where the spell is."

She forced herself to watch. Dervla, after looking carefully at the fire-hardened bond and trying to read the god-glyph, cracked it apart with a knife.

The corpse seethed and changed its form. A ripple passed through the air; a ripple of the ghostly deer-spirit that had been trapped in the tortured flesh. Gaultry reeled back, newly horrified. It was little wonder she had been able to recognize the spell. Her greatest joy as a spell-caster had come from such spirit-takings—one animal's swiftness, another's strength. Whoever had disguised the boys' bodies in deer form had also trapped animal-spirits in those bodies, a ploy intended to confuse anyone like Dervla or old Melaudiere, who might otherwise have detected the human corpse.

She shuddered. The frenzied deer-spirit that had passed her

had once belonged to a living animal, now insane from its long tenancy in dead flesh. It did not surprise her that she had felt its pain, even down the hill. Who could have done such a thing?

The child who lay, lifeless, beneath Dervla's hands, was older than the first deer-boy. In all other respects they were similar enough to be brothers.

"Put him on the table next to the other," Dervla said. She wiped her hands vigorously on a clean cloth, agitated. "And send someone for more water."

The priests pushed between Gaultry and the corpse, unfriendly. Some of the table leavings that still festooned the second body were there because they had been too haphazard as they'd tried to make the table clean for the first boy's corpse.

Gaultry stepped out of their way, almost bumping into Martin, who had come up behind her.

"They took your assassin boy to the priestess's shriving room," he told her quietly, as he reached out to steady her. It took all her self-control not to clutch at him, she was so grateful for his presence. "It's the only secure building between here and Princeport. They've sent two priestesses to bind him."

"Tullier can't escape," Gaultry whispered back. "Mervion fixed it so he can't escape."

"So much the better. Your sister, with some help from Dervla's acolytes, has managed to stop the poison in Coyal. She could have used your help there, I think. He's still off his feet—and she's not as strong as you seem to think she is, after all she's been through these past weeks."

The rebuke stung, all the more because Gaultry did not believe it was justified. Martin did not understand how strong her sister was, how resilient! But Coyal—thinking on the young knight, Gaultry felt tears threaten. "The Memorant saved my life," she said. "Just a heartbeat before, I was cursing him for his court airs. I kept remembering our last fight—"

"If Coyal ever learned to think as quickly as he acts, he'd make a better man," Martin said. "But today—thank the Great

Twins for his quickness." He took her hand and pressed it briefly to his cheek. "I thought my heart would stop when I saw that dagger striking for you."

"I didn't even see it—" Gaultry, her hand warm in his, wanted to return the gesture, but Dervla's voice interrupted her.

"About time!"

The timid ash-blond woman had finally come with the water. On the way she had run and slopped the water against her front. She looked wet and miserable. Taking one glance at the woman's shy rabbit face, the high priestess lost her temper.

"Did you manage to bring me anything?" she blazed. "If so, bring it here!" All the spleen she had not been able to vent on Gaultry came spewing out. "Do you think the Prince wants to sit here all day, waiting for us to complete the ministrations? Bring it here, Palamar."

Palamar Laconte, granddaughter of the Common Brood, ducked her head beneath Dervla's admonishment and scuttled to the table, losing still more water in her hurry. "I didn't mean to spill it," she protested. Then she saw the boys, dropped the basin, and began to scream.

"Reiffey!" she cried, "Darden! Oh, Great Twins, make it not so!"

Dervla went white. With a gesture and a troubled look, she sent two of her acolytes to quiet the woman. "My Prince." The High Priestess swung around to Benet. "I'd advise you to join your wife and leave us to honorably bury these dead."

"Who are they?" the Prince asked, turning his face to Palamar. "Who is she?"

"She's seed of the Common Brood," Dervla answered curtly. "And so were they. From Palamar's reaction, these boys must be the sons of Palamar's sister, Destra Vanderive."

Another red stain had been cast across the Prince's path.

chapter 5

▼

What happened to them?" The initial shock
faded from Palamar's eyes. Her soft face curdled with
hate. The young acolyte turned on the High Priestess and
grabbed at the front of Dervla's vestments. "You promised
me," she said, physically jerking the older woman off-
balance. There was something terrible in seeing this shy-
faced woman possessed by such wrath. "After you let my first
sister die, you promised it would not happen to my family
again. You promised me and I trusted you. Even after Lady
D'Arbey fell to her death, I trusted you."

"Palamar," Dervla protested. "I protected you after the
Chancellor killed your sister. I would have protected Lady
D'Arbey from him too, if she had let me. This—no one
expected this. No one could have prevented it." Her eyes
dipped sideways to the Prince, as if to calculate his reaction
to this new upset. Her composure in the face of Palamar's
hate was almost incredible.

"Great Twins!" Palamar screamed. "Don't pretend this is
not your fault! You promised me that my sister Elsbet would
be the last Laconte to pay blood for Tielmark's throne! You

promised me!" One of Dervla's priests caught at her robe, trying to restrain her, but Palamar's distress gave her the strength
to shake herself free. "Where are Destra and her daughter?
Where is my brother Regis? Can you look me in the eye and
tell me they are safe?"

Dervla, watching the expression harden on the Prince's
face, suddenly had had enough of Palamar's outburst. "With
the power I have wasted on you, Palamar Laconte, I will
thank you to shut up!"

"I have a right—"

Dervla whipped forward and caught the younger woman by
the throat, her long white fingers digging into Palamar's soft
flesh. Palamar shrieked, incoherent with pain as well as rage.
Green eldritch fire lashed from the High Priestess's hands, a
choking noose to silence Palamar's protests. The raw display
of power sent a new wave of panic through the watching
crowd.

"Order!" the Prince shouted, his face white as ash. "Order!"

The priestess, immersed in her casting, ignored him. Benet,
not one to be easily put off, seized her shoulder, shouting in
anger when the sting of magic bit him. Dervla, coming
enough into herself to recognize the touch of her Prince's
hand, jerked free and pushed Palamar down with her wiry
strength. The acolyte, in frenzied panic, rolled her eyes
towards her Prince. Her mouth bobbed open, beseeching and
pathetic.

"Let her go!" Benet ordered. Dervla, focusing and tightening her spell, did not listen. Something in her manner suggested a spider, tethering a fly. The spell spat into life and
sprang clear of its caster.

Palamar's eyes glazed. Her body slumped. Dervla, weakened briefly by the casting, barely had the strength to prevent
the woman's head from striking the edge of the table.

The acolyte was unconscious. An enraged look suffused
her features even in her sleep. Dervla and the Prince each had
a hand on the young woman's shoulders. They panted angrily,
their faces a bare hand's breadth apart.

"You disobeyed me," the Prince said icily.

"She was hysterical." Dervla refused to back down. "When she calms herself, she can say whatever she likes. But I won't have my own servant speak to me in such tones. Not in front of a full assembled court."

"That is no excuse for your action," Benet said. "This woman was hysterical, but by her words it seems you gave her reason. Did you offer her family a protection that you could not supply?"

"I protected the Lacontes the best I could, but there is no all-encompassing guard against the fate that threatens them," Dervla flared. "They're Brood-blood. So am I. Unlike the much vaunted Lacontes, I have never whined against that pledge. Your great-grandmother swore us to a hard fate, my Prince. Not all of our blood have the strength to fulfill our promise of service. If I have failed in my attempt to help the weak, it is no fault in me. Omnipresence, to shield the weaker Brood-blood, is beyond me."

"If you exaggerated your influence or power, you did this young woman no good service." The Prince fixed the High Priestess with a hostile stare. "Worse than that, you betrayed a sacred trust. The Great Twins have been kind to you, Dervla of Princeport. They have lavished magic and power upon you. You must learn to satisfy yourself with that—any false promise you made this woman was beneath you."

Dervla crossed her thin arms on her thinner chest. "My Prince is wise," she said, her pose speaking that she thought oppositely. "As his subjects cannot act for him, I trust he has his own plan to safeguard those sworn to serve him with their life-blood."

Benet took one angry step toward her, then controlled himself. "I bow to you, High Priestess. You serve me well, in so graciously reminding me where my duty lies. Of course, I owe the Common Brood my protection. Heiratikus killed two of the Brood-blood before my marriage, now we have two deaths more. Bissanty will not stop there, I'm sure. I know the prophecy—so, by now, does half my court. Rest assured, High Priestess, if the Emperor thinks he can thin your blood with impunity, I will make him regret it.

"In the meantime, we must introduce measures to protect you. I have let you all run free, to risk your skins in any venture, too long." His eyes scanned the hilltop, numbering those present of the Brood-blood. "Poor Palamar; Melaudiere and her kin; yourself; the Blas twins; these two bodies. Is that half the number of the Brood-blood thread that hangs between me and Tielmark's destiny?"

Dervla, seemingly unwilling, shook her head. "The Brood's children are widely dispersed. Even I am uncertain how many are still alive."

"They must be called to Princeport, and we must make a reckoning." Benet looked sorrowfully at the corpse of the older boy and let out a long sigh. "Would that I had the wisdom to know what my foremother Lousielle intended in pledging the Brood to this sad fortune. But this we know: the Brood-blood's fate is tied to Tielmark's. For too long, that fact has gone unexamined.

"Perhaps I should put the Brood under house arrest for its own protection—and mine—until this matter is settled. Great Twins, that would make for a happy court!" Benet let out a harsh laugh, then cut himself short, recalling his many listeners.

"If these last deaths are not on your head, Dervla of Princeport, I'll take them on mine. I should have expected the Emperor to retaliate against our recent triumphs. And perhaps"—he looked at Palamar's awkwardly slumped body and then, accusingly, at Dervla—"perhaps I can offer a more scrupulous protection to those of the blood who are yet alive."

Dervla frowned, but did not challenge him.

"For now, let's make a peaceful burial for those who are already gone." The Prince stretched his hand towards the young corpses, as if in blessing. For a moment it seemed he would touch the cooling flesh, deliberately desecrating the purity of his earlier sacrifice. A restless flutter passed through the watchers. Benet's harsh manner frightened them. This was not the gentle Prince they knew, so obviously in love with his land and his wife, so determined to acknowledge and expiate his past weaknesses. Would he destroy his pledge to

Emiera to emphasize his sense of responsibility for these children's deaths? Surely that was not fair—

Relenting, Benet withdrew his outstretched hand. His left hand traced a spiral on the palm of his right, the sign of the Great Twins.

"Finish with the bodies, High Priestess. Attend to your duties. The Great Bonfire must be started. I—" He stared round the table, looking tired beyond his four-and-twenty years. "My decision concerning the Brood-blood must wait. I must attend to my wife."

"**H**ouse arrest?" Gaultry said. "Would they really put us under house arrest?" In the Prince's brief absence, the ducal council had convened at the tent encampment for an emergency deliberation. Martin and Mariette, as their grandmother's retainers, had gained admittance to the first part of the discussion, but the latter part had been limited to the council of seven alone. By Martin's terse report, the temper of the parley was trending toward gathering the Brood-blood together to put it under guard.

"No one wants to be responsible for more bodies dumped on the Prince's doorstep."

"Would that mean we would be locked into a room with Dervla?" Gaultry did not think she could stand that.

Martin shook his head and grinned. "Nothing so extreme. But even Grandmère is convinced that the Bissanties have decided to take action to eliminate the Brood-blood before it has a chance to make Lousielle's prophecy anything other than its own bloody doom. Too bad the best idea anyone's offered to counter that so far seems to be herding us together where one sorcerer's firestorm could do in every one of us." He shrugged. "That's simple pandering to the Prince's own first impulse. I'm sure they'll think better of it as they debate—not least because Grandmère won't consent to such foolishness.

"They are also trying for a head count. Grandmère reckons there is near a score of Brood-blood living, counting those of us who came to attend the Prince today. Thus far, all the council has decided is that runners must be sent to warn the Brood-blood kindred that Bissanty may have sent Sha Muir killers to stalk them."

"They sent all the retainers away when they began to argue whether those of us here today would need a special escort to take us back to Princeport," Mariette put in. "Also, they're trying to decide on the appropriate punishment for your young assassin."

"They're going to kill him," her brother said bluntly. "Someone needs to be made to pay for today's horrors. All they need to argue there is how they are going to put him down."

"But he barely did anything!" Gaultry said, shocked. It had not occurred to her that saving the boy from one death would only mean preserving him for another. "He's only a child. Besides, we stopped him from poisoning Benet."

"No," Martin said firmly. "You are saying that only because you don't understand the Sha Muira code. If your boy was trusted on a mission, there's none of the innocence of a child left in him. Once a warrior swears his allegiance to Sha Muir law, he is alive only for Llara's service. He cannot exist outside the cult." Soldier-cold, he looked levelly into Gaultry's eyes to ensure that she followed what he was saying. "The boy would have killed you. I'm sure the only reason he didn't kill Benet today is because the Emperor ordered our Prince a slow death—he was to be poisoned by a voluntary, if unwitting, act of sacrilege against the gods' creation.

"Those are the reasons the boy's death shouldn't trouble you, but there are other matters that the dukes have to take into consideration. Today's crowd, ripe with renewed pledges to Benet—and to Tielmark—cannot do other than demand swift and mortal vengeance for this insult. Anything else leaves the suggestion that they are in sympathy with Bissanty."

"I want to talk to him," Gaultry said. "Maybe he'll tell me who sent him."

"The Bissanty Empire sent him." Martin was losing his patience. "You aren't listening to me."

"I am," Gaultry said, "but it's hard to understand. Your words don't fit with my picture of the boy. When he was dying, I saw more than that in him."

"You're seeing what you want to see, because you have never seen the Sha Muira act. Your boy—he's young. This is probably his first mission—don't think that makes him less vicious than a full Sha Muira. He has to prove himself, so it makes him worse. You feel bad only because you have yet to see him in the full swing of action. The Sha Muira have no conception of remorse or pity.

"The Emperor sometimes sends Sha Muira among the Lanai. The Lanai call Sha Muir envoys *the black devils*. With good reason. Full-fledged Sha Muira paint themselves with contact poison—they'll do anything to increase their efficiency as killers. Beyond poison and faith, they have no desires. That's all," Martin finished. "They are a weapon, not a people."

"We'll see," Gaultry said. "I want to talk to the boy all the same. Maybe you're right—but my instinct told me to save him—the same instinct that made me see through the spell on the Prince's table. There was something animal in him—something real, alive, and suffering. I can't turn my back on that."

For a moment, it seemed that she and Martin were alone. She could feel the heat of Martin's body, the heat of his eyes, as he stared into her, holding back his first angry response. Her heart jumped. Perhaps her words were reaching him.

"Gaultry," he finally said. His anger had dropped, and his voice was rich with a self-mocking humor that she found at once familiar and confusing. "You have a ruinous capacity for changing things by refusing to understand them. No wonder poor Grandmère has been struggling to make you understand her vision. Allegrios Rex! You're making even me feel pity for that boy—and I have witnessed Sha Muira atrocities."

"I want to see him, Martin." She did not understand him in this mood, but while he was so, she knew he would refuse her nothing. How could he believe that the connection between them had been broken?

"So we'll go see him," Martin said, nodding at his sister that he wanted her to join them. "At least I can count on you not to reproach me if you come to regret this choice."

The shriving house was a low-eaved building that faced the sea. The Goddess Twins smiled: one of the men set to guard the would-be assassin owed Martin a favor. For a shilling and a handshake, he agreed to let them enter.

The building was opened only twice in the year. Although it had been decked with fresh garlands of flowers and ivy, a damp odor of mildew and mold pervaded its single window-less chamber. The boy sat on the edge of a canvas cot, opposite the door, huddled near the pale heat of the single candle that had been left him. He had been stripped of the blue-and-white livery he'd worn to carry the bespelled corpses to the Prince's table and left with only a short length of cloth to pull around his hips and a clumsy bandage for his wounded arm. The boy had that arm clasped between his knees, trying to keep it warm. As the door opened, he looked up at Gaultry with poorly concealed alarm.

His nakedness and the clumsy bandage made him look younger than ever, younger and more vulnerable, his skinny shoulders bowed with cold and pain. Then he recovered himself. He flexed his good arm, displaying the tight muscle that lay beneath his pale skin. Gaultry could not tell whether vigorous conditioning or simple lack of food had winnowed the flesh from his body.

"What a bag of bones!" Mariette said bluntly. "Imagine bribing guards to get a look at this! And such a small squib of a Sha Muira to send to our Prince's court! What could his masters mean by it?"

"They knew we'd kill him," Martin said. "Why waste a good man on a mission that has no hope of success?" Gaultry could see that he and his sister were trying to play to the boy's weak points, as they had done in the earlier fight, tempting him to strike out—this time verbally—so the other could set a barb in. "The Sha Muira like to get the utmost advantage from their flock, even as they cull it. Isn't that right, young one? What did you do to make them decide you weren't a keeper?"

The boy's pale eyes were empty, expressionless.

"He's in shock," Gaultry said, trying not to show sympathy but finding it hard not to stop them from baiting the boy. "He's still seeing his own death."

"Don't soften," Martin said. "It's not shock that's running through him. He's only wondering why he didn't take more of us with him before dying, the poisonous little rat."

"Remember this." The tall soldier loomed over the young assassin, hand on his sword's hilt. "He didn't offer mercy to Lady Vanderive's children. The Sha Muira stifled any mercy he might have been born with in a decade or more of training. At least he won't beg and expect it in return, will he?"

"Don't talk like that," Gaultry said. "We don't know if he had anything to do with that." All the same, she could not help but look at the boy and ask, "Did you? Did you kill them, see them die?"

"He won't answer that."

"Don't interrupt—he might!"

"Why am I alive?" The boy's voice was so soft Gaultry could hardly distinguish the words. "I am Sha Muira. We are the last god-blessed arm of Bissanty," the boy whispered. "Llara Thunderbringer watches us. Her poison—and her blessing—should have taken me by now. Why am I alive?"

"He has a tongue! Can we coax him to say more?" Mariette's laugh sent color flooding to Tullier's face. The boy closed his lips and refused to speak further.

"The boy is right," Martin said. "Llara Thunderbringer, Queen among the gods, does bless them. The Sha Muira are notoriously successful, even as they are steeped in treachery and deceit. And the Goddess-Queen watches out for her own—for Sha Muira, the door to her hall is said always to be open."

Martin shot Gaultry a look of reluctant admiration. "You

don't realize what you and your sister accomplished by stopping this boy's death. It's an impossible thing. Sha Muira don't know trust. Every one of the envoys they send out from their home island leaves the stronghold with a body that is riddled with poison, and only a limited number of prayer-beads to hold back the poison—one bead for each day they are due to spend away from the island. They can't go home unless they successfully complete their mission. Which is why this little rat can't believe that he's sitting here alive and well, with no shadow of death hanging over him."

"Sure he can believe it," his sister said. "Look at the way he's watching Gaultry. He thinks she's his new angel of doom. He's just gearing himself up for the first shock of pain he's sure she'll bring him. Pain is the only master he can imagine."

Gaultry gave Mariette an anxious look. "Is that really what I've committed myself to? Torturing this boy? I hope not." She sat wearily on the edge of the cot, keeping a distance between them. "What can I say? The magic that showed me there was a spell on the Prince's deer showed me that there was something in this boy worth saving. I'd do it again if I had the choice."

Tullier had turned his white face to follow the young huntress's movements. Now a small smile passed his lips. A smug smile, as though he thought her words revealed great weakness in her.

Gaultry folded her arms. Goddess Elianté, she thought. What had possessed her to save this cold young murderer's life? Why had she imagined they might share a hidden sympathy? Compared to this boy, she had led a sheltered, idyllic life, nurtured by her grandmother's love, constantly paired with a supportive and loving sister. As a huntress, she had learned early what it was to kill, but with that learning had also come respect. The bent of her magic, which had sent her dancing with foxes and running with deer, had forced an early empathy between herself and her prey. This was an empathy that the young Sha Muira killer would never have known—and his prey was human, rather than animal.

"The magic that binds you wasn't done for mercy," she told him. She forced herself to look him in the face. Her image of him as the starved young hound had retreated. The reality of the young boy, with his precociously wiry legs and arms, his heavily callused killer's hands, was all too evident. With the confusion of discovery past, the instinct that had moved her to bind the best part of her magic to this murderer made less and less sense. If she tired of the obligation and retrieved her soul and magic, he'd die a painful death, a death that would be on her head now that she'd chosen, with Mervion's help, to interfere. Further, if the ducal council decided to call for his death, she would be forced to withdraw in any case, or allow the destruction of half her Glamour-magic. She stared at the boy's hard features, wishing that she'd had the chance to consider these aspects of things before acting.

"Probably you're right to smile," Gaultry told the boy. "I was naive to stay your death. I should have listened to my sister's doubts. But I wonder why your masters were so determined to send you to such an early doom. Did you imagine that there would be a safe retreat for you from Feeding-Hill?"

"If that other hadn't interfered," Tullier said coolly, refusing to answer her question, "you would be dead now."

"He means Coyal," Martin said. "At least Sha Muira see virtue in being truthful." He grinned, not above relishing the look of dismay on Gaultry's face. But when he bent over the boy, there was no humor in him. "If you had touched a hair on this woman's head, you would not have died for Llara—you would have died for her. Remember that. She and I are bonded. As sure as my weapon was in breaking your guard, her death would have become yours."

Gray wolf's eyes fastened on pale green. Something passed between the two as men: a message, or a cool reading of the other's depths. Though the boy showed no fear, he was the first to look away, his good hand moving reflexively to cover his bad arm. Martin, a look of cold satisfaction on his face, stood back.

"He still imagines that Llara's death is coming for him—probably in the form of whoever partnered him on this venture, rather than from our ducal lords. Whatever hold you put on him, Gaultry, the little rat doesn't comprehend it. He still thinks he can complete his mission. He thinks he can retrieve his honor before his old masters." Martin vented a bitter laugh. "What it is to be a child and have so little understanding."

The boy's eyes blazed. "I can," he said. "Goddess Llara in me, I will return to her faith."

Gaultry lunged then, and seized his shoulders, her hands hot on the cold of his skin. "Don't fool yourself," she said. She looked deeply into him, letting him see a hint of the power she held, even with half her Glamour-soul gone. "Don't try to fool yourself. You underestimate the noose that's snared you. You were on a leash before—now you're enmeshed in a many-stranded web." She turned to Martin. "Give me your knife."

"It's got the boy's blood on it still." Mariette reached and put her hand protectively over the blade's pommel where it jutted from her brother's belt. "Which means, effectively, that it's poisoned."

Gaultry held out her hand, insistent.

Mariette exchanged a nervous look with her brother. When he shrugged, she eased the blade from its sheath and gingerly handed it over. "Be careful," she said. "It needs proper cleaning before it'll be safe."

"All the better." Gaultry took the blade from her and held it out to Tullier. "Here is a knife," she said. "Use it as you will."

The transformation was instantaneous, and all the more shocking for that. The blade was out of Gaultry's hands; the boy was off the bed; his back was against the wall as he hefted the weapon from one hand to the other, familiarizing himself with its balance. His mouth twisted, as if in prayer, and suddenly Martin's curved blade was a talon, an extension of the assassin, utterly deadly. He whipped around and faced the huntress, a look of triumph passing through him—

—A look that sagged into puzzlement. He tried to strike. Something turned him away. He tried again, and again failed. He turned the blade in his hands in a dance of death. But he could not turn the motion toward Gaultry—or toward Martin, or even Mariette. Trying to strike, he turned himself in a frantic circle, round and round, like a dog chasing its own tail.

Martin, who had jumped up the moment Tullier had seized the knife, drew back and rolled Gaultry a curious look. "What's he doing? Are you blocking him?"

Gaultry stared, fascinated, as Tullier's frustrated, determined motions became ever smoother and faster, but still no more effectual. She shook her head sadly. "Does he look like an outside force is stopping and starting him? No. It's more complicated than that. He's stopping himself in his own head. He just doesn't recognize that he's doing it yet."

She met Martin's eyes. "You were wrong to say he has no mercy or conscience.

"He has mine. And my conscience would never allow him to kill me. Or you. Or even himself."

chapter 6

▼

Watching Tullier exhaust himself in his dance with Martin's blade sobered the Tielmarans. The boy refused to understand that he could not attack them. Refused, and tried and tried again. His young face stretched in anguish and self-hate. "Llara take me," he panted, desperate. "Let me turn the blade! Let me finish this!"

"This is not right." Mariette broke the Tielmarans' silence first. "We should not see this. Allegrios mine! We countenance torture, watching this. We can't let this go on."

"The blade is poisoned," her brother reminded her. "We can't touch him while he's swinging it like that—there's too much room for an accident. Wait until he gets tired."

Mariette shook her head. "This is too cruel. It's torture. Even a Sha Muira—"

"If it's torture," Martin answered, "he's doing it to himself. The harder he learns that lesson the better. We have to let him find his new limits. Trying to coddle him won't help."

Tullier's conditioning was deep, his boyish will fearsome. As he began to understand the fruitlessness of direct assault, his movements became wilder, more frenzied, as if he hoped he could, by introducing random gestures, subvert the magic that prevented his attack. He seemed unable to grasp that this battle was against something that was internally wound round his senses. As defeat was forced on him, his pale eyes lit with a desperate gleam. Gaultry, recognizing despair, felt a twinge of pity. The dagger would have been in the boy's own guts now, but her Glamour-soul would not permit suicide.

Finally the boy flopped onto the cold flagstones next to the cot, his skin sleek with unnatural dark sweat. Gray tears tracked his cheeks. He seemed unaware that he was crying; or as if he didn't understand tears, did not know how they revealed his dawning sense of helplessness. His confusion made him again seem younger, more vulnerable, but when Gaultry moved to touch him, Martin grabbed her shoulder and hauled her back.

"Are you mad?" he said coldly. "His body is purging itself of poison." When she tried to pull away, his fingers bit into her shoulder, bruisingly hard. "Don't you understand anything I told you about the Sha Muira? They are a race apart— by choice. The poison that's inside him—he consumed it deliberately, knowing it would kill him if his mission failed. Whatever you and Mervion did, Gaultry, you robbed its power to kill him. But that doesn't mean it won't kill you if it so much as touches your skin. You can't risk getting close to him."

The muggy air of the shriving room and the intensity of Tullier's emotions were overwhelming. Faced with the boy's outburst, a sick feeling welled in Gaultry's stomach. His passion for death—to deal death or to inflict it on himself—was beyond her experience. In some far-removed part of her brain she could sense, like a shadow of pain, the piece of her Glamour-soul that Mervion had bound to him. That piece should have been cut away cleanly by Mervion's spell. Gaultry herself had deliberately blocked it away, the moment it had sent Tullier's name bouncing back to her. Just now, however, the intensity of Tullier's will echoed it to her: she could feel the heat of its power as it stretched to consume the poison.

"You're right," she said to Martin, sagging against his hand. "I think the poison in his blood would kill me. Elianté in me, what can we do?"

"Bear up," Martin said roughly. Though his voice was unsympathetic, his manner was gentle as he let go of her shoulder and wiped her hair from her face. "What are you thinking, making such a display for our guest? Look at him." He gestured toward Tullier, who sat pressed against the cold stone floor, panting with distress. "He's a murdering animal, but, Gods on us, he's having trouble enough accepting what is going on without you losing your composure. Whatever you and Mervion did, he's your responsibility now. You don't have the luxury of panicking."

Something flickered in Tullier as Martin spoke, and he pulled himself up. "Tell me." His voice was a cracked whisper. "Tell me what you did. Why am I alive?"

Gaultry looked at Martin, who shook his head, "Don't look to me—I didn't help you with that spell."

"I'm not sure myself what Mervion did," Gaultry said, a trifle guiltily, "only that I gave her little choice as to whether or not she should do it."

She crossed the room to the winded boy's side and sat down near him.

The poison on his skin was like oiled ash. Beneath the sweat and smear of blood from the long cut on his lower arm, he smelled of sour incense, heady and strange. His wounded arm trailed at an awkward angle from his body, its clumsy bandage wet with fresh blood. In his unwounded hand, he loosely clasped Martin's knife to his chest. She picked up a clean bandage, and covered her hand with it. Then, tentative, she reached out to him. "Martin will want his blade back."

He handed it over, his dulled eyes never touching her face.

"There's a beauty in your training," Gaultry said. She gingerly wrapped the knife in the bandage and passed it to Martin. "But while you live under my protection, you'll have to find a new purpose for it.

"We are taught that the human soul is indivisible, that it cannot be separated from the human body—unless death takes it." Gaultry touched her heart, where her grandmother had often told her that the soul was seated. Tullier would not meet her eyes, but he watched her hands intently. That made her feel the puppyish presence in him. Heartened, she continued. "In all my living years, I believed that this was how life was ordered, that there was no other way.

"But human-souls—like animal-spirits—can be separated from their bodies. And there is a power in them—a shadow of the Great Twelve's magic—that has a strength almost like a god-prayer."

Tullier's eyes flickered across hers, then retreated. "You can't believe that," he said.

"I wouldn't," she said, "save that I have seen it in action." Something cold seemed to brush her as she remembered the moment when she had fully understood that the human-soul could be cleaved from its body. Even now, the horror was fresh. Perhaps, she thought numbly, it should not have struck her as such a revelation. From an early age, she had possessed the power to draw animals' spirits from their bodies, leaving both unharmed, while she augmented her strength with various qualities drawn from those spirits. However much she respected that power, she had always taken her right to enact it for granted. The discovery that the human soul could be manipulated in a similar way should not have shaken her. All it took to steal a soul was more power, or the knowledge of a carefully laid spell that could invoke that power.

Gaultry shivered again. Even with her second Glamoursoul, she knew she did not possess the power to wrest a soul from its body. That was a power that should be left to the gods. It gladdened her to think that Heiratikus, who had shown her that the human soul was vulnerable, was dead, his terrible spells dead with him. Gladdened her, even as she had learned to make use of what he had taught her.

"The power of a soul can counteract even the blessing of a god. Indeed, to save you from Llara's poison," explained Gaultry, "I lent you a piece of my second soul. It's the part of my soul that creates magic. Mervion set that piece inside of you, to counteract the poison that permeates your body." She paused. Tullier showed no reaction to this astonishing news, though she could sense, even from her place on the floor, that Martin and Mariette were shocked to learn what she and her twin had done.

"Did you come to Tielmark knowing about Mervion and me?" she asked. "Did you know we had Glamour-souls?"

The boy's glacier-green eyes focused, something in his expression tightening. He did not answer. She wished she could touch him then, wished she could reach out to her bound soul-half and connect with the stream of his private thoughts. Fear of the poison on his skin joined with conscience to hold her back. She already had one powerful leash on him—more control would not be right. "That piece of my Glamour-soul is twisted round your soul now, counteracting the poison that would otherwise consume you. It will stay there until the poison in your body has burned away.

"But a Glamour-soul is not just any magical casting. Though it has the power to burn Sha Muir poison, it is not just an insensate spell, acting in you without awareness. It has something of my heart in it, and something of my conscience. Already you've discovered how little impulse I have for self-destruction."

For the first time, Tullier's face showed fear. "I'm to be your puppet, then," he whispered. "You control my life. Already, you've torn me from Llara's path."

Gaultry frowned. "I hope not. Your faith is your own problem."

"If you won't let me kill—"

"If that's your soul's desire, I'm sure you'll eventually find something that your soul and mine can agree needs destroying." She drew back, contempt mingling with a sudden dread. His soul would learn something from hers, but what would hers learn in return?

Turning away, Gaultry found that she was alone with Mariette. "Where's Martin?" she asked, half relieved to find he had not been there to see her moment of fear. Already so little of the situation was under her control.

"The boy needs some clothes," Mariette said. "And a

proper dressing for his arm. Also—he's gone to find out if they've made a decision about what to do with this young scoundrel, down in the tent encampment."

Gaultry tried to hide her alarm. "Do you think they'll want to act quickly?"

Mariette did not look hopeful. "Yes," she said. "I think they will. But if you want to keep him—maybe you can pull the knife trick again and have him dance for them. That should give them some assurance that he's toothless."

"You think I've overreached myself, don't you? I don't know why I thought saving Tullier would help—"

"You believed what you did needed doing," Mariette said. "It's something no one could have expected, least of all those who sent the boy here to taint Benet. While I myself wouldn't have argued for saving him—" She flashed a smile, her irrepressibly sunny nature breaking through, and shrugged her high shoulders. "It won't have been anything the Bissanties expected, and you're right to think that there's value in that. Grandmère at least will take that into account when she votes."

As they spoke, Tullier staggered off the floor onto the cot. He was white with shock and moving clumsily. The bandage slipped from his arm, revealing the clammy bloodstained lips of the wound that ran from his wrist to his elbow. Simultaneously, his hip cloth began to slide. He clutched at both with his good hand and sat abruptly, looking miserable, unable both to coddle his wounded arm and keep his loins covered. Mariette, spying his distress before Gaultry, smirked, torn between taking his dilemma seriously and mocking him. "I'd offer to give you a hand," she quipped. "But I have no taste for poison—and I've seen worse than that which you have to show me there between your legs." Her tone was not unkind. The early sympathy Tullier had roused in her during his thwarted knife-attack had remained. Gaultry, who had never had brothers, wished she too could be so lighthearted about the boy's show of modesty. Instead, she was simply embarrassed. "Stay with him for a moment," Mariette said breezily, unaware of Gaultry's discomfort. "I'll run and get something for that arm." She ducked out the door, calling for one of the guards to help her.

Left alone, the boy and Gaultry exchanged a fidgety stare. "You could use a wash," Gaultry said awkwardly. Without Martin or Mariette present, she found she did not know what to say. The possible imminent arrival of a messenger from the Dukes or the Prince, demanding his death, hung between them. Gaultry guessed the boy would neither accept nor desire comforting. Happily, Mariette was not gone long.

She returned with a bucket of murky water she had fetched from the shriving house's rain barrel, a sponge, and some strapping. The activity had further lightened her mood.

"Here." She slopped the bucket at his feet. "Martin will bring you something to wear, but in the meantime, why not clean up that arm?"

Tullier, his expression hooded, followed her suggestion. He washed and bandaged his wound with a fieldsman's efficiency, as though his Sha Muir training had taught him that along with killing. Gaultry, who had feared that Martin had shattered the boy's arm with his single savage sword blow, saw with relief that the boy could move his wrist and fingers—stiffly, but not with the sharp pain that would have suggested a break. The worst of the bleeding had stopped.

After finishing with the wound, the boy began to use the sponge to wipe at the ashy slick of poison on his skin.

"We'll have to leave word to make sure everything he touches gets either burned or cleansed," Mariette observed. "Carelessness with that would be a foolish way to lose lives."

The boy, squeezing the sponge into the bucket, pretended not to hear. "I wonder how this will end." The lean swordswoman crossed to the door and looked across to the curve of the hill, beyond which lay the tent encampment. "Once Prince Benet understands what you and Mervion did to save this boy, he's not going to be happy."

"If he gives me a chance to explain, Benet will be on our side," Gaultry said hopefully, coming to stand next to her. "I won't ask him to condone what this boy did—only to find out more before he orders action."

"I don't think the Prince will approve of your having even a small part of your Glamour-soul tied up in this boy's flesh," Mariette said hesitantly. "He's going to think it means you've given your power to Bissanty. That was my first reaction."

"If I were Benet, I'd find more to worry about in the fact that his entire cabinet of dukes brought armed retainers to the table against his express wishes than in anything Mervion or I did today to protect him. Not a man or woman among their retainers came to the Prince's table unarmed. Not even your grandmother's. At least I respect his office—"

"Benet asked too much. The country's unstable. People will arm themselves. But your argument feeds my point. What can Benet do about Grandmère and the others? He can't sanction all seven dukes beyond what they themselves agree to submit to."

"Very nice," Gaultry said. "With the most important of his titled nobles flouting his authority, why is anyone surprised that people question Benet's claim to the Great Twins' respect?"

Mariette raised her chin. "That may be so," she said. "Though if I, Martin, and the others had actually followed Benet's direction you and Benet both would certainly be dead now. I'm just trying to prepare you for the worst—which is what's probably going to happen. Benet won't want the only Glamour-magic in Tielmark tied up, even partly, in the body of an enemy nation's assassin."

"The boy will die if we take my Glamour-soul back," Gaultry said worriedly, speaking softly in the hope that he would not hear. "We'll have to appeal to the Princess. Lily won't force us to kill him." Even as she spoke, the young huntress wasn't sure. Lily trusted her, and perhaps even owed her a personal favor, but there was a limit to what Gaultry could ask of that trust.

Across the room, the boy slumped against the wall, his head bowed with fatigue. With his arm properly bandaged, he looked more pathetic than ever. She could not have stood by watching him die without trying to save him, or at least to ease his death pain, but now she had to consider how much further she was willing to take this matter in order to aid him. Would she defy Benet for him? She didn't want the boy to die—at least not until it had been proved that he had done something that warranted that fate.

She shifted uneasily, thinking of the horrible cooked corpses of Palamar's nephews. What part of the responsibility did Tullier share for that deed? Those boys had been too young to fight. Had Tullier helped kill them? From what Martin had told her, it seemed only too likely he had played some part in that execution—though nothing had been proved against him, as yet.

There were other reasons that today's action concerned her. Beyond even scruples, barely acknowledged, was the frenzied eagerness that had thrust itself on Gaultry, compelling her to save him. She would not confess it to the others, but a part of her—the bored part of her that had tired of dancing attendance on a court-bound Prince—had thrilled to Tullier's pain and need. She had welcomed her descent to the vision world, where her Glamour-soul appeared to her as a golden woman, Tullier as a skinny green-eyed dog. It had been no great surprise when Martin had told her that the boy's body was envenomed by Llara's blessing. From the first moment she had faced the black poison that possessed him, she had sensed that the spell needed to counter it would have to be very strong. At that moment, it had seemed natural and easy to call to Mervion, knowing that between them they might have the power to subdue it.

Would that pride in power prove her undoing? If Tullier was killed before she took back her Glamour-soul, she would suffer the death of that part of herself, and her clumsy attempt to save him would exact a great toll. A warning her grandmother had first given her when she was a child learning to spirit-take from animals came to her. *The potential for a successful casting was no good reason to summon a spell.*

She shivered. She had been a mischievous child, and there had been many occasions for her to face the truth in that.

"But I was not trying to take a bird's flight here," she murmured. "It was right of me to try to spare him pain, if not to save his life."

"What's that?" Mariette had come up quietly to her side, catching her last words.

Gaultry gave her a defiant look. "Neither Mervion nor I entirely understand what we've done today, using our Glamour to save a Sha Muira. We've had control of our Glamour-magic for scarcely a fortnight, and we'd never even heard of Sha Muira—or at least I hadn't. Perhaps we shouldn't have done it. I have an empty place in my chest where there should be power, and I may find myself defying my own Prince— whom I love to serve—for a boy who probably hates me for trying to save his life. You and Martin will probably tell me that I should have thought of this before merrily handing half my new power away to such a young miscreant.

"That won't stop me from being glad I did it."

Martin burst into the priest's shriving room and strode to the cot. His long sword clanked at his waist, his shoulder scabbard was loosely buckled, as if he had been running with it. He had put aside his Festival clothes for a sturdy jacket in his grandmother's green and gray.

"You're dressed for traveling," Mariette said, startled. "What's wrong?"

Ignoring her, Martin went straight to Tullier. "Your partner's in Seafrieg, isn't he?" When the boy did not immediately answer, the big man flung a bundle of clothes on the cot and reached for the boy's arm.

"You can't touch him—" Gaultry interposed herself, and Martin grabbed her instead.

"Palamar woke up," he snapped, pushing her away. She could not believe the coldness in his eyes.

"I don't care if she did," she said, trying not to let him see how he frightened her. "You still can't touch him."

He stepped back, raking his fingers through his hair. "Fine." He fumbled with the buckles of his shoulder scabbard and pulled his blade up from his waist. "I'm still going to have it out of him." Scabbard properly buckled, he unfurled the folds of his traveling cloak. "Let me tell you what Palamar said." He took Gaultry's hand. "She's stopped screeching at Dervla, but she's no less hysterical. There's a third Vanderive child. A girl. They checked the last deer that was to go to the Prince's table—yes, they agreed it would take you to know for sure, but the third deer was male, and it didn't have bonds, so that's probably safe. But Palamar had a letter from Destra Vanderive, the children's mother, not two days ago. Destra was in Seafrieg, visiting Helena. Helena Montgarret. Now do you see why he has to tell me where his partner is?"

Gaultry pushed Martin's hand away as if it had stung her. Martin's estranged wife, Helena, made her home in Seafrieg—the County on the Eastern Seaboard where Martin would have held title, if he had not ceded his name and possessions to his wife and her young son more than a decade past. What did it mean, that Helena's name was coming up now—just when Martin had been telling her how difficult it was for him to sustain the feelings that had been born under the geas?

"Helena should be safe," Mariette said, trying to cool her brother's temper. She shot Gaultry an anxious look, then turned back to her brother. "They're only after Brood-blood."

Martin rounded on her. "Not everyone knows Helena's son isn't mine, Mariette. And the Sha Muira are killing children."

"I'm not a child," Gaultry said softly. "Tullier tried to kill me too."

"Gaultry." He faced her, his eyes shadowed with guilt. "They may already be dead. Because of me. Because of the blood that runs in me. I have to help them."

"You're not thinking clearly." Without realizing what she was doing, she had once again seized his hand. With that contact, she could feel the raging determination rising in his body, as if he had already girded himself for battle. Yet his eyes were still cool and steady. A pang of jealousy, deeper than anything she had known she was capable of, twisted in her breast. She struggled to subdue it. "If you have to run to Helena, I'll come with you. I can help."

Martin shook his head, already withdrawn from her. "You can't help me protect Helena. That would not be right."

He turned back and leaned over Tullier. "Were you in Seafrieg?" he asked. "Was Helena Montgarret's son your next mark?"

"I don't know," Tullier said. His eyes flicked to the bundle of clothes. "I don't know anything about Tielmark, save that it is populated by louts and fools. I'd like to dress now, if I may."

Martin, with an obvious act of will, curbed his temper. "Tell me what you can and you can have the clothes. On Llara's word, tell me."

They stared stubbornly into each other's faces. After what seemed like an interminable time, something in Martin's expression forced Tullier to answer.

"The Vanderive baby isn't dead." Tullier stared into Martin's dark eyes, a confused expression on his young face, as if he did not quite believe that he was giving Martin his answer; as if he was seeing something that he respected but could not quite recognize. "She's alive, if you can say that being a piece of bait is living. I don't know about any plans for your son."

"But your partner is at Seafrieg?"

Tullier nodded. "Maybe not yet—"

"Dress yourself," Martin said roughly. As Tullier reached for the bundle of clothes, the big soldier caught at the boy's shoulder and swung him back so their eyes met once again. "Your old life is over. Let's see what you make of the new one."

The boy looked from Martin's hand where it touched his bare flesh to the soldier's hard face, and then back to his hand. A shiver passed through him.

"I'm poison to you," he said, his voice reluctant, touched with self-loathing.

"Maybe," Martin answered. "And maybe I can pass through a cleansing flame and lose the poison. I must risk something in return for what it cost you to answer me."

"You idiot—" When Mariette would have interceded, Martin waved her back.

"He's got to learn that there are more choices than life or death. Why shouldn't he have two decades' head start on me there?

"Gaultry—" Martin turned to her, his expression darkening. "Grandmère is still arguing, but the other six are clamoring to hang him. I know you won't allow that—we can't allow that. Follow me to Seafrieg. Once I've finished my business with Helena, I'll meet you on the road. We can argue with the Prince together."

"I won't follow you anywhere," Gaultry said. "I'll come with you now." Did he really believe she would allow him to run off to Helena alone if she could help it?

"Where I go, you cannot follow." Martin unsheathed his sword. "Watch Gaultry for me," he told Tullier. "That's a better cause than the one you've left."

Ignoring Gaultry, he turned to his sister. "I left Helena and the boy unprotected," he said. Something in his voice told Gaultry that he was asking Mariette a question. "That's unforgivable. I have to try to reach them. That's not a choice."

"Do what you want." Mariette's answer was inexplicably bitter. Her face had paled and was set beneath her riot of dark curls. "Helena already has the best of Seafrieg. Why shouldn't she take the rest?"

"I never intended to deny you Seafrieg—"

"Nor Dinevar either?" Mariette, suddenly angry, raised her hand as if to strike him. "More choices than life and death? Don't look to me for permission. Just do it. You cannot leave Helena."

He raised the blade with a single smooth movement. Dinevar was the noble blade he had inherited from his brother, the last part of his legacy. Mariette would have inherited it—and the County of Seafrieg—if Martin had not acknowledged Helena's son as his heir before throwing away his right to the title. Gaultry could see she had no place in this debate. Swallowing her pride and worry, she stepped aside to let them have it out.

Brother and sister together stared at the shining blade. Then Mariette turned her face away, as if she could not bear to look at it.

Dinevar had been forged in magic fire. Martin, hardly noticing that Mariette had turned away, seemed fully absorbed by it. He flourished it over his head. "For Tielmark!" he cried, summoning its magic. Along the blade's flat, six runes winked to life, lighting the darkness of the priest's shriving room like wicked pricking eyes. Martin ran his fingers over the sixth rune, the rune closest to the blade's hilt. The rune spat with gathered power and sheeted his hand with pale blue light. "Allegrios mine, give me your power!" he called.

Gaultry's throat closed. She watched that pale light run up his body until he was entirely sheeted by light, as if by ethereal armor. Mariette's face, turned back to watch in spite of herself, was terrible to see. Dinevar shone brighter than ever, its edge outlined by white flame.

"Take it!" she shouted suddenly. "In our father's name, take it!"

Martin, within the sheath of light, nodded to acknowledge her. Dinevar hissed. The light pulsed, blinding-bright. Then, with a flash of light, the blade shuddered. Whether by Martin's hand or another force, it swept down, striking the earthen floor. With a howl, the magic in the blade released itself. The blade collapsed in on itself in a cascade of scintillating blue shards. As she threw her hands up to protect her eyes, Gaultry thought she saw a widening circle of white at the core of the blue cascade.

When the blindness retreated, Martin was gone. Only the shards of Dinevar, lying shattered on the ground, remained.

Mariette burst into tears. "It wasn't enough for him to give Seafrieg away! He had to destroy Dinevar as well. All for his precious honor!"

It took long moments for her to once again gain command of herself. Then, as if to make up for her outcry, she was angry with Gaultry. "You should have stopped him!"

Gaultry gave Mariette her coldest frown. She had little

desire to be drawn into the middle of this particular family battle. "What was I supposed to do, beg? You know he wouldn't have listened." She would never compete with Martin's wife for his loyalty. Never. "Martin can make his own choices."

"That wasn't a choice!" Mariette choked. "That was suicide! Breaking Dinevar to go after a Sha Muir envoy alone! She's not worth it!"

"You don't mean that," Gaultry said, trying to find the words that would calm her. "Whether or not she's worth it, Martin had to go. He wouldn't be your brother if he could stomach sitting safe in Princeport, not knowing what was happening in Seafrieg . . ." Gaultry's voice faded. "I'm going to have to see Mervion before I go after him." She turned to Tullier, her resolve taking form even as she spoke. "Finish dressing, Tullier. We're about to embark on a journey."

"You're not a fool to go after him." The Duchess of Melaudiere caught up with them as Mariette's man was saddling their horses. "But you are a fool if you think you're doing it for him."

Gaultry was in no mood for riddles. The old woman seemed exhausted. Gaultry did not understand how she had ferreted it out that they were leaving—or why. But she did know that she was in no mood for a lecture. "He's your blood," she said curtly. "But he's my friend. I have to go."

"You have to go," the Duchess nodded. "But not for those reasons. Gaultry—child—this is about Tielmark, not about Martin. I love him too, but there are matters of greater consequence than one man's life." Her words were an accusation.

Gaultry was not going to argue. "Maybe. But my fate is tied to Martin's. Tamsanne read our Rhasan cards together. So my concern must be for him first, if I want to survive." She guessed she sounded pompous, but she did not care. As she fumbled with the saddle, she thought back to the night of the Rhasan reading, clinging to any assurance that Martin and she retained some link, that they would one day be together again.

Gaultry had expected to draw the Huntress card. The Huntress was the card Tamsanne had pulled for her, years before, on the eve of her woman's first blood. She liked that card: the self-sufficient woman standing proudly in the forest that was the source of her strength. When Tamsanne had pulled the Orchid card for her, with its shimmering purple leaves and hint of burgeoning power, the unfamiliar image had come as such a shock that she had at first resisted its implications. The Orchid was the deck's thirteenth card, a number both lucky and unlucky. Glamour's number. She shrugged. In her own mind, she still thought of herself as the Huntress, not the Orchid.

But even now, it was the memory of Martin's card that haunted her. Martin's card had been the Black Wolf.

The Wolf could be a good card for a soldier: a creature of passionate energy and fears; intelligence warring with might. But in Martin's card, it had appeared in its darker incarnation: the Wolf as the self-devourer, gnawing its own tail. Just as Martin gnawed at himself now, torturing himself for events he could not control.

"Going to Seafrieg may destroy Martin," Gaultry told his grandmother, leaving her Rhasan memories behind to glare in the old woman's face. "You won't stop me from trying to prevent that."

The Duchess gave her a hard look. Gaultry, fumbling ineffectually with the stirrups of Mariette's spare saddle, sensed that the old woman wanted to shake her—or test her, as Dervla had done earlier by matching her sorcery against the young huntress's. But the Duchess had a different style. She would not confront the younger woman in that way.

"This is not about Martin alone," the Duchess said. Her voice sounded desperately tired. "It's about Brood-blood. The time has come for us to act—before the Bissanties trace every one of us to our graves. Your search for Martin won't end in Seafrieg. The Bissanty are getting clever. They have learned they can't force us, after 300 years of trying. They could have murdered the Prince today, but they sought only to taint him—to taint him with the very flesh that is sworn to his protection. They are seeking now to disgrace us in the eyes of the gods—or to subvert our prophecies and our god-pledges. This day's plotting is about Bissanty finally taking heed of the prophecy Lousielle brought to life on her deathbed.

"Before the Prince was married, the Bissanties had a Brood-blood puppet—Heiratikus, the traitor. Now, with Heiratikus dead, someone—perhaps even the Emperor himself—has decided to thin the Brood-blood. My guess is, they'll try to bring home a new sample or two of the blood to keep for themselves.

Gaultry, frustrated in her attempt to fix the saddle, gestured for Mariette's man to take over. "What are you telling me?"

"Helena is nothing but a lure," the Duchess said. "A lure, like the missing Vanderive sister and her baby."

"They want to kill Martin—"

"If they wanted to kill," the Duchess said, her voice deliberately cold, "they could have done that today. Your boy there, Tullier, would have been told to do it himself. But that performance we saw in front of Benet—he had no death target. He was just there to spread terror. You were in his way, he would have killed you—but if he had specific orders to finish you, our defenses would not have been enough. He would have come in the dark and done it quietly—a far better way to get such a job done. They must be planning to capture another Brood-blood. They need another puppet."

"Martin is no puppet!"

"Indeed. But if you plan to go after him, I'd suggest that you ready yourself for a trip to Bissanty. The journey will be shorter than you imagine. We have agents in Bassorah City— the capital—they can help you."

"Bassorah?" Gaultry said. "Seafrieg is as far as I plan to travel."

"You and your twin are the only ones who can travel to Bissanty with a hope of returning alive," the Duchess said seriously. "The Bissanties have no mercy. But you or Mervion—you have Glamour. Even if they take you prisoner, they'll want to keep you alive.

"We must go on the offensive. We can't sit back this time

and let Bissanty build new strength against us. If Martin is taken to Bissanty, you must follow him there.

"When you find him you will have two choices: rescue him or kill him. For Tielmark's sake, you must not leave him alive in Bissanty hands."

Gaultry stared at the old woman, stunned by the enormity of what she was asking. "It won't come to that," she said. "We'll catch up to him in Seafrieg and that will be the end of it."

The Duchess shook her head. "My grandson is a fool, and I was a greater fool not to see that Helena was still a weakness to him. You'll go to Bissanty. Perhaps I should thank the gods for that—you'll learn why we have to fight them, so long as we have breath." She coughed, as if to emphasize her words. "They won't be a distant specter, a force to be spoken of as past history. You'll learn what it really means to hate them, as all the old Brood did. Maybe that will give you the impetus to change things. I can at least die hoping so."

"Seafrieg," Gaultry said determinedly. "I will meet Martin there."

"You'll have to move fast to do it," the Duchess said. "And don't forget, Benet's men will be on your tail. Even if I twist him round to approving your journey—the Prince will not be pleased that you have taken his would-be assassin along with you."

"I have to take Tullier," Gaultry said. "I'm not leaving him here to have the mob string him up."

"So be it," the Duchess said. "But remember, when it comes to land, only a King or an Emperor can bargain with the gods. Not a Prince. Keep that in mind."

The old woman kissed her granddaughter, gave Gaultry a last nod, then turned and left them.

chapter 7

If they don't catch us tonight, we'll reach Seafrieg the day after next." Mariette set her candle on the shelf by the wide bed with its puffy goose-feather mattress and bent to pull off her muddy riding boots. "And as they haven't caught up with us already, I doubt they'll find us tonight."

Gaultry, standing by the window with her hand on its iron latch, stared out into the inn's dark court. Theirs was the last lighted window. Even the angry innkeeper whom they'd woken to gain entrance was returned to bed, his light extinguished. The cobbled court was empty, the night sultry and absolutely still, a continuation of the day's unseasonable warmth. "I didn't get a chance to speak to Mervion properly," she said guiltily. "Tending the Memorant exhausted her, and we were in such a hurry." The room around her felt suddenly stuffy, claustrophobic. She fumbled with the latch and pushed the window open.

"Grandmère will keep her eye out for her," Mariette said shortly, kicking off her first boot as she unlaced her second. "Someone has to explain to Benet that we aren't bucking to commit treason, dashing off as we did before he could give us our curfew. I can't say I envy her the task. Particularly when it comes to justifying our taking *him* with us." Her hands busy, she gestured to Tullier with her chin. "But Mervion set the spell—her explanation may come close to satisfying him."

Tullier lay hunched in the middle of the broad bed, tucked under the thin sheet with his knees folded tight to his chest and a slightly self-conscious expression on his face. He'd undressed down to a borrowed undershirt. Something in the set of his boyish shoulders suggested he was suffering an attack of shyness.

"We couldn't have left him," Gaultry said. Across the yard, the stable door was locked and securely bolted. "The likelihood that Benet would have demanded Mervion undo the spell and let him die is enough justification for bringing him."

"I'm not afraid to die," Tullier spoke up.

"So you keep telling us." Gaultry, annoyed, pushed the window open a little farther and refused to look at him while she spoke. "We'll try to make finding that fear your first lesson."

Long hours of riding had tempered Gaultry's initial ardor for the journey. Gaultry was a poor and inexperienced rider. Her mount's animal-sensitivity to her magic compounded the problem. The beast had taken an early dislike to her. She had spent the late afternoon and long hours of the evening trailing Mariette's horse, struggling to persuade her own animal to mind her. Young Tullier, to her annoyance, had proven a more than able horseman. Throughout the ride, he had kept his horse precisely at the flank of Mariette's horse, never deigning to turn his head to watch Gaultry and her struggle, but always quite aware, it seemed, of the difficulty she was having keeping up. The hours that Gaultry had spent staring at the smooth movement of the pair of rumps, always a little farther in front of her than she wanted, had given her ample opportunity to regret the expedition on which she had so hastily embarked, and her own weaknesses as a member of Martin's support party. She couldn't ride, and she would have to resort to castings to defend herself from a brawny street-bully, let alone fend off a trained assassin of the Sha Muira. She was a decent shot with a hunting bow, but had only the rudiments of a warrior's training. With half her Glamour-magic tied up in Tullier's body, the force of her spell-casting would be relatively feeble. To her disquietude, the farther she rode from Princeport, the less certain she was that she should have left it. If the Duchess had agreed to help her protect Tullier, surely she could have stayed and argued to turn the tide of court opinion? Her parting with Mervion also had been dissatisfying. She had not argued with Gaultry about her decision to follow Martin to Seafrieg. But she had seemed tired, distant, and angry about the unfolding drama with Tullier. Probably, like Martin and Mariette, she thought it served her sister right to have backed herself into a panicked corner.

She thought again of Martin, and how he had come to her with his troubles. No, she had no choice but to follow him to Seafrieg. "You shouldn't leave the pane open," Tullier said as Gaultry left the window and came round to her side of the bed, pulling her jacket off over her head without unbuttoning it.

"I'm sweltering," Gaultry said. "It should be all right. We're high up, and there's nothing to stand on under the sill."

Tullier didn't answer, but his expression said clearly he thought her a fool. Gaultry and Mariette exchanged a glance. Gaultry saw in Mariette's eyes that she agreed with the boy, though she said nothing out loud, to save Gaultry's face. The huntress got up, resenting that she had to take advice from a child—a child who was the next best thing to the enemy—and closed and locked the window.

"There," she shrugged. "You're the one who is sleeping in the middle. I'd think you'd want it open." The room had only the one bed, large and roomy enough for three, and Mariette, though she claimed to understand the nature of the magical hold Gaultry had on Tullier, had insisted that they put him in the middle lest he try to make a run for it during the night. Like the closing of the window, it was a matter of good security—even if it meant Tullier under two sheets so he wouldn't sweat on them, and everyone cramped and uncomfortable.

Tullier himself seemed to be less than overjoyed by the arrangement.

"Have you never shared a bed?" Mariette asked. She laughed at his prim expression as she clambered in on her side.

"Never with one who should be dead at my hands." He glanced at Gaultry.

Even with the thinness of her bed-shirt stuck to her spine with sweat, coldness seized her. "From all we can gather, you yourself were supposed to die at the Prince's table this forenoon," Gaultry reminded him. "So at least one of your compatriots has already had something like the experience."

Tullier turned his face away and fixed his eyes on the ceiling.

Gaultry didn't press him.

A small noise woke her. A noise like a mouse, scratching among the sheets. The long square of moonlight that lanced in through the window told her it was late. Even the crickets had quieted. Under the thin sheet, her body felt hot, restless. She lay quietly, resenting the closed window, the stale-horse body odors that permeated the room. The mouse sound came again, across the bed, on Mariette's side of the pillow. Without turning her head, she rolled her eyes to look over at Tullier.

He was fully awake. His eyes, though hooded by darkness, were wide open. He stared intently into the shadow by the room's rickety wardrobe, the deep shadow that concealed the room's only door, transfixed. Gaultry, following his gaze, saw only darkness. Her eyes flickered past the boy again, trying to guess his thoughts and what had woken them both. The extra sheet they'd lain over him to shield themselves was wrapped tight against his body, cocoonlike, only his arms and head poking out over the whiteness of the cloth, pale skin hardly darker than the dinginess of the white.

The small mouse sound came again.

Then a sound that might have been the barest whimper of distress.

Gaultry flung herself to the floor, dragging the top sheet with her. A short arrow—a dart—caught in the sheet and came with her. She felt it stick in her shirt, but it had, barely, missed her skin.

"Master!" Tullier's voice came out as a shriek, whether of fear or excited pleasure Gaultry could not determine.

A guttural word in a language Gaultry couldn't understand snapped back and silenced him.

Gaultry, more by reflex than by design, called to the half-dampened river of power that ran within her. Even with half her Glamour-soul missing, the power pooled in her hand like a roil of water. She threw it, merged into a bolt of green-gold light, directly at the shadow.

It struck the wall, the door, the floor, and set everything aglow with unnatural glittering color. Everything save for the tall figure at its center. He—it was a he—repelled the light like water meeting oil. His black silhouette was a figure in a waking nightmare, hands outstretched and fingers curved like talons, a crest of wild braids standing outwards from his scalp.

Gaultry scrambled for her knife belt.

The dark figure stepped forward. The glow from the wall and door glistened off black hair and oily jet-black skin. He was tall and thin, and moved with a fluid gait. His robes, beneath the eerie green and gold of Gaultry's light, were rusty brown, with streaks of white at the lower skirts. At first, in a shock of horror, she saw the man's face as the naked bone of skull, then she saw eyes flashing in the dark sockets and realized the effect was created by paint and poor light.

"Tullier Sha Muira," the apparition said, this time speaking so Gaultry understood him. "Ready yourself for Llara's Last Banquet."

Gaultry glanced at the bed. Tullier sat, very upright, his thin body clearly outlined beneath the sheets, pale green eyes huge in his narrow face. Mariette was curled at his side, her glossy black curls in disarray across her pillow. A dart with a long, fine shaft had pierced her low in the abdomen, pinning the sheet to her body. The mouse sound Gaultry had heard had been the movement of Mariette's fingers as she scratched weakly at the dart's shaft. A dark stain spread on the sheet, down from where the dart had taken her.

"Tullier is mine now," Gaultry snapped, trying to divert the dark monster's attention. "You can't have him." Panic stabbed at her. The knife was not in her belt. Mariette's weapons were on the far side of the bed, out of reach.

The man Tullier called Master ignored her. Two long strides brought him to the foot of the bed. The face paint hid his expression, but there was something odd in his manner: a whisper of hesitancy—not fear, something else. Awe? "You shouldn't have allowed them to prevent Llara's last blessing from taking you," he told the boy. From his words and demeanor it was clear he marveled to see the boy alive. Marveled, but did not offer mercy for the miracle.

There was something in his hand. A cluster of withered flowers on a shrunken brown-pink stem. The tall Sha Muira threw it on the bed. It bounced and came to rest between the two hills made by the boy's legs under the sheets.

"My death token, for the Arkhons." Tullier's voice was anguished. "What are you doing?"

"They'll never see it. You never lived to take it."

"You owe it," Tullier said. "You owe it on your word. I made my kill. My place at Llara's table—" Shock robbed the boy of his voice.

"Sha Muira was lost to you when your body poison failed," the man hissed. He flicked a dagger from a hidden sleeve-sheath, smooth as a cat extending its claws. "Even now it should be rotting your guts. The pain alone should have killed you."

"I've done nothing disloyal," Tullier said, his young voice shaking, his fingers rigid on the sheet. "I did not ask to be saved. Llara above us, I want to come back to you, I want the Thunderbringer's bounty—"

His Master leapt, a cat pouncing.

Gaultry cut the light of the magic spell and threw herself at his back.

At first, the loss of light disoriented everyone. Gaultry struck Tullier's attacker and fell with him into the enveloping softness of the goose-feather mattress. She found herself grasping loose handfuls of robe-cloth. The material was rough and stiff. It smelled of dry blood and long-dried sweat. Somewhere in the dark to her right, Mariette moaned in pain. The man beneath her twisted in his robes like a cat inside its skin and slashed upwards with his blade. She wrenched the cloth on his back, trying to hood and blind him with his own clothes, and heard rather than felt her own shirt rip as he tagged her with the knife. The flat, not the edge, touched her skin, and she realized then that he was only toying with her. Panting and desperate, she tried to thrust clear, but the enveloping looseness of the mattress made retreat awkward. She bumped clumsily against the headboard with her face, knocking her teeth against the wood hard enough to daze her and to bloody her lip. As she shook herself, briefly muddled, she half heard her attacker laugh.

He could see her in the dark. Her heart gave a sickened shudder. He was laughing at her confusion and pain.

"Mariette!" she shouted, fright curdling through her, fright combined with desperation. "Stop him, Mariette!"

The dark outline of the Master assassin lunged.

Someone moved on the bed. The assassin grunted, but kept coming. His blade slid past her cheek, a whisper of a wet kiss. She imagined she felt the damp of its poison on her skin, burrowing like acid.

Then, so quickly that she almost missed it, a slash of moonlight from the window caught the silver of the blade as it spun from the assassin's hand and flew across the room.

Something kicked on the bed. A reflexive, repetitive motion that stilled gradually and quieted. "Oh God!" someone cried. Gaultry could not tell if the voice was male or female.

Collecting herself, Gaultry stumbled and half fell free of the bedclothes. She blundered over to Mariette's side, hunting

for the candle. "I'm coming," she said. "I'm getting a light."
An acrid urine odor reached her, underlain with the tainted
metal smell of blood. "Elianté in me, wait for me. I'm hurrying!" She found and fumbled with the tinder, muffed it, and
tried again. At last the candle's flame flared up, strong and
true. Gaultry, trembling, straightened and turned to the bed.

Mariette lay on her back, her face pallid, her eyes turned to
Gaultry, pleading. The sheet over her belly was dark with a
ragged star of blood. Tullier, at her side, sat rigidly, propped
against the headboard. His frozen expression betrayed neither
fear nor relief. His Master's painted death's head lay cradled
in his lap, tightly embraced by Tullier's thin arms. At first she
mistook the embrace for sadness, for affection. Then she saw
the dart and understood that it was Tullier, not Mariette, who
had cut short the man's attack. One of Tullier's hands still
gripped the dart—that dart that he'd snatched from Mariette's
belly in the darkness. He had rammed it deep into the big
artery that ran up through his former Master's neck, connecting his brain to his heart. Blood soaked the boy's lap and
the sheets surrounding him—his Master's blood. The Sha
Muira's legs twitched, convulsive, but his body had otherwise
quieted.

"Tullier!"

"I should kill you too," the boy rasped. "If I could, I'd kill
you too, and then I'd be free." His face, set with shock, was
filled with horror at the turn events had taken. If the boy had
envisioned escape, and with it his return to Sha Muir service,
that prospect was gone.

"That's enough," Gaultry said, shaken by his intensity.
"You've come through this in fine shape. Elianté's mercy—
look at Mariette! We must stop the bleeding."

"If you want to help her, you'll have to move her first,"
Tullier said, his voice toneless. "There's enough poison in my
Master's blood to kill her a thousand times over."

"She's not poisoned already?" Gaultry threw the sheet off
Mariette's body, her hand moving to cover the horrible belly
wound. Across the bed, Tullier stared, face unreadable, his
pale eyes set. "The dart wasn't poisoned?"

"That? A paralysis drug? She'll recover from that. It's nothing." The dead voice, the stillness of him, unnerved her.

"Why should I know that?" She pushed the blood-soaked bedclothes to Tullier's side of the bed, her relief giving way to the luxury of anger. "How in the Great Twelve's names could I know that!" Spatters were everywhere; Mariette had surely already been poisoned. She would have to try to call a spell, a spell about which she knew nothing, a spell Mervion could have called without thinking—

Near to tears, she dragged Mariette out of the fouled bed and laid her on the floor. "You're going to be fine," Gaultry told her, trying to reassure herself. "We'll stop the bleeding and you'll be fine."

The swordswoman stared up, her eyes bright with tears of pain. A strain moved through her body as she struggled to rise, but the drug in her body defeated her. Gaultry patted her arm, awkward.

"It looks worse than it is." She dragged a pair of trousers off the back of a nearby chair and used them to cushion Mariette's head. "Now—" She clasped Mariette's hands over the wound. "Hold your hands there if you can. Tullier says you're going to be all right." When Mariette responded by exerting a slight, if palpable pressure, she sobbed with relief.

"And you?" she asked Tullier. She stood up and wiped her face. The boy lay in a bloody nest of sheets, his dead Master's head still lodged in his lap. "Can you get up now?"

The boy stared down at the face of the man he'd killed. Almost reverently, he brushed the lank hair away from the dead man's face, his fingers smearing the mask of black-and-white paint. "I've found something that your Glamour-soul would let me kill," he said. He sounded surprised. "And I wanted it—"

"Get up now, Tullier. It's over." Gaultry, in her distraction, was not listening.

Tullier crawled stiffly out of the bed. The cluster of crumpled flowers was in his hand, the waxy buds broken almost beyond recognition, hand and battered flowers both slick with his Master's dark blood. In the light of the candle, Gaultry could now see that they were chestnut blossoms. She frowned, wondering what the flowers signified, guessing it would do no good to ask. "I've done nothing disloyal," Tullier had told the dark man. "I want to come back with you, I want Llara Thunderbringer's bounty." Everything in the boy had yearned to join again with his Master, even at the price of his own death.

If she hadn't cast the room into darkness, into the blind thrusting realm of willful intuition and reaction, she doubted Tullier could have brought himself to act against the man, even after he'd given back the sprig of chestnut.

"Stay away from the bed," she told the boy again, her manner deliberately terse. She did not feel up to bandying words with him. "For all you know, prolonged exposure to his poison can kill you now."

This time Tullier obeyed her.

The innkeeper was predictably furious when Gaultry roused him from his bed to send for a healer who could both tend Mariette's wound and exorcise the poisons that had soaked from the dead assassin's body into the mattress of what had been one of his nicer feather beds. Furious and suspicious both.

"I should have never opened my doors to you!" he shouted, struggling to throw a coat over his great tent of a nightshirt as he emerged from his chambers into the hall. He had a pleasant face, with even features and a mouth that would normally have curved in a congenial grin, but the two interruptions to his night's slumber, the second so disastrous, had broken his temper. "Demanding a healer at this hour!"

"We wouldn't be needing a healer if you'd kept your doors locked tight," Gaultry shouted back. Something in her was relieved to be dealing with the rightful anger of a wronged innkeeper. "We'll pay for the ruined bed, if that's what's bothering you." She made the traveler's sign with her hand, emphasizing that her intention was not to take undue advantage of his services.

Glaring, he roused one of his lads from a cubby by the stairs. He muttered something to the lad that Gaultry didn't quite catch, something that sent the boy running out to the stables.

"Don't insult me." He made the traveler's sign back and passed a hand over his face, aggrieved. "Can it be my fault that you brought death to this house?"

"It's no one in Tielmark's fault," Gaultry said. "This man was sent here from Bissanty."

"Bissanty!" The man paled. "In my house? Great Twins protect us!"

Coming with Gaultry to the chamber where the body lay, the big innkeeper burst ahead of her into the room. "Emiera in me! The blood! Can only one man be dead?"

Even with the window open, the corpse had already made the room foul. While the Sha Muira master had lived and breathed, his faith for Great Llara had held the poison in his body at bay. Now it ran free in his corpse, brutally scorching his flesh. The smell of rapidly advancing putrefaction, combined with the heat, made the room almost unbearable.

"We have to move Lady Montgarret to a fresh chamber." Gaultry knelt by Mariette's side to feel for her pulse. She was relieved when the young woman shifted her head to greet her, struggling to shape her lips into a reassuring smile. Though there was a tremor like a fever in the woman's body, her blue eyes were alert, and the blood had begun to crust on her stomach. "We've sent for a healer," Gaultry told her.

"What about him?" the innkeeper asked.

"Tullier?" The boy was standing near the door, slick with poisoned blood from his lap downwards. "He can't touch anything until a priestess comes."

"Madness! He can't stay like that until she gets here. The blood on him—" The innkeeper swung his head from Mariette to Tullier and back again. He came to a quick decision. "Leave that one there. I'll call some men to take her to a more wholesome resting place. The boy"—he nodded at Tullier—"the boy should go out to the road and clean himself at the

well there. Emiera blessed it, this winter past. It should do to
clean him. He can't stay like that."

"He can wait for the priestess," Gaultry said. "I won't risk
poisoning your well."

"Have some mercy." The innkeeper gave her a disgusted
look. "The poor lad's in shock."

It had not occurred to her until that moment that the
innkeeper had no idea that Tullier was Sha Muir trained.

Afterwards Tullier and Gaultry lay side by side on a narrow
loose-mattressed bed, staring at Mariette's sleeping body. The
innkeeper had found her a cot, so they were still all in one
room. The thin gray light of dawn slanted in, but it was still
too early to be up.

Tullier had not lied. The black rime on the dart had been a
paralysis drug, not poison. After Mariette slept away the last
of the effects, Gaultry had hope that she might even be well
enough to ride. At least so the local priestess, a shy woman
with gentle eyes and hands, had told them.

After she had attended Mariette, the priestess cleansed the
dead assassin's body. With the aid of several of the inn-staff,
she had removed it, along with the poisoned bedding, to her
own cart for later burial. The priestess had also, thankfully,
asked few questions, and had been satisfied with their explanation that they were on the Prince's, and Melaudiere's, business.

The dead man's belongings now lay between the huntress
and the former apprentice assassin. It was an odd collection:
four daggers of assorted sizes; a dirty length of garrote-wire;
a handful of evil-smelling powders in a silk pouch; the wrist
sheath with the cunning spring device from which the assassin had propelled his weapon; a purse that was heavy with
gold imperials and silver Tielmaran shillings; a necklace with
eleven openwork silver beads. Most interesting to Gaultry
was a narrow wooden box, its veneer dark with age, carved
with a stylized reed pattern.

The sheath with the spring fascinated Tullier. Gaultry let him play with it while she examined the box.

There was also a withered bouquet of six chestnut blossoms folded into a black piece of silk, but, unlike the sprig the man had thrown onto the bed, it appeared to hold no interest for the boy.

"If Mariette is well enough, we'll ride again when she wakes," Gaultry said. Turning the box over and over in her hands, she could hear something bumping around inside, but still she had not discovered the trick for opening it.

Tullier loaded the shortest of the daggers into the spring device. "They said I was too young to be trusted with one of these." He wound the contraption's straps around the slim wrist of his unwounded arm and primed the spring. "What will they do with his body?"

"Bury it at the crossroads." She picked up the wooden box and gave it another cautious shake. The contents had begun to rattle, as though they had slipped free of a protective fold of cloth. It was not the sound of metal.

Tullier, still playing with the spring sheath, was watching her covertly. She could feel that, in the way his body tensed, in the way the clicking of the spring became repetitive.

The province of Gaultry's magic was the beasts of the deep woods rather than its plants, but it had been a long night, and frustration could twist her powers to new ends. She was irritated by Tullier, by herself, by the carelessness that had left them vulnerable to the Sha Muira attack—even by Mariette, for not waking in time to escape wounding. Smoothing her hands along the wood, she channeled that ill-feeling, feeling for the last hint of sap in the wood, the last vestige of life. The stylized pattern of reeds helped. Increasingly intense, she rubbed her hands on the box's carved surface, picturing banks of wild reeds as they grew along a river, as they shifted in the play of water, in the wind. *Remember,* she told the box. *Remember the spring, the uncurling leaves of a fresh season's life, alive even now outside these windows. Remember what it was to live.*

The box emitted a creaking sound, and shifted. Tullier looked over, his narrow face startled, but still disdainful.

That look, the rasp it gave the huntress's nerves, gave a focus to Gaultry's anger. *Remember!* she told the box, suddenly fierce.

It shattered into kindling, in shape not unlike the reeds she had pictured. A scrap of leather dropped onto the bedcover, together with a broken, bone-bladed knife. Even cracked, its edge was murderously sharp. It came to rest on the bed with its edge sliced cleanly into the cover.

"What's a Sha Muir assassin doing with this?" Gaultry stared, astonished. "Aren't you all dedicated to Llara Thunderbringer?" At first, she thought the pommel was sculpted in the shape of Huntress Elianté's birthing sign—the broken spiral that a lord's gamekeeper might carve on the hood he put over a coop of pheasant chicks to protect them while they gained in health and strength—right up to the moment when they were released to be hunted. Then, taking it into her hand, she frowned. It was not Elianté's magic. The god-glyph was not quite right—

The blade felt emptied, preternaturally cold. More than that, there was an angry void in the yellow-white bone, an emptiness so profound it made the hairs rise at the back of her neck.

"Do you know what this is?"

The boy stared, his expression deliberately blank and cold. She mentally cursed herself for having blurted the question.

"I'll tell you what it is," she went on, pretending she had not intended her words to be a question. "It's a burned-out husk. It was used as a focus for a spell. A spell of astounding power. See the sign on the pommel? I'm not sure exactly what it is, but it's like one of the Huntress Goddess's signs—the Huntress in her incarnation as the mother who sacrifices her young to the hunt. That's what the broken spiral means. But there is a silver circle banding it, and a black one as well. That could be the White God Tarrin's sign. I've never seen them together like this." Tarrin, one of the twinned war gods, was not much worshiped in Tielmark.

Tullier, concentrating on the mechanism of the spring sheath, did not seem to hear her words. He made a sharp, snapping motion with his wrist, clicking the release catch. The loaded dagger darted out, faster than he could catch it. It speared the bedcover between his knees.

"It takes practice," he said, ignoring her as he retrieved the dagger and fitted it back into the sheath. "Corbulo was so smooth. He could catch it in his hand or fire it at a target. Whichever came first to his purpose. For him, it was second nature. Beyond practice into mastery." He snapped his wrist a second time, and missed the catch again.

Gaultry watched him for a moment, saying nothing. After a while she let her attention drift across to Mariette, out the window, forcing herself to be casual as she let him practice. The bedcover was dented with many false starts, and he began to catch the blade two times out of three. The first light of a watery, overcast sun was peeping in at the window. Mariette, still asleep, sighed and moved restlessly on her cot.

Corbulo. His Master's name had been Corbulo.

She risked a covert look at the boy's closed, secretive face.

He was pledged to the Great Mother Llara, and he was young and had been kept so ignorant that he imagined calling magic from another god was a betrayal. She didn't blame him for that. Her grandmother, Tamsanne, had seen to it that her own upbringing had been so provincial that she too had once imagined that owing favor to one goddess—or pair of goddesses—had meant that the others were not there for her, would never extend their favors. Since she'd left the security of her grandmother's home in Arleon Forest, she'd learned differently.

Tullier would learn differently too, if he lived long enough. But for now, if it meant he would give up information that would otherwise have remained hidden, she was not going to be the one to teach him.

Corbulo. A man's name. It was their first shared secret.

chapter 8

Bellaire was a pretty town, tucked between two craggy headlands with a sheltered harbor and a fine view of the sea. Today, with the sun high overhead and the air shimmering with unseasonable heat, the vivid green of the headlands made a striking contrast with the shining blue-gray shield of the sea. The town, though small, was an important harbor. Tielmark's rocky eastern coast had few secure ports, and Bellaire's, by every measure, was the best of them. It had the deepest harbor and the sweetest water. Though the town itself had never been large, in Bissanty times it had supported a massive fortified encampment, the earthworks of which could still be seen on the southern headland.

The old Bissanty presence could also be seen in Bellaire's aqueduct, visible from the High Road for miles before the town itself. Unlike the abandoned earthworks, the aqueduct, an ancient, much-repaired series of arches, still functioned. It wound inland for miles, following the course of the road. Gaultry and her companions rode the last miles into town in the cool shadow cast by the great arches, listening to the gurgling water running above them through the deeply weathered channel in the brick. Here and there, the worn seals of the Bissanty sorcerers who had mixed the aqueduct's mortar could be seen, embossed into the tile fancywork that decorated the joints of the arches.

"Bellaire gets ships from as far as Cosicché Island," Mariette said as they reached the top of the last hill before the road sloped down between grassy pastures into the town, "though mostly it's Chlamanscher traders on their way to or from Bissanty. Tielmark has water for them, and perhaps summer bales of our shepherds' wool. Usually they just want our water. Bellaire would be a bigger town if it had something better to trade."

Gaultry, looking down across the dark slate roofs of the town to the masts of the graceful ships in the harbor, quivered with a strain of unexpected excitement. Out in Arleon Forest, the stories she'd heard of Cosicché Island had seemed exotic and unreal. The journey to Cosicché, the last island before the great pillar of the gods rose from the southern sea, had seemed farther than anyone would ever travel. The troubadours, describing Cosicché, made it seem mythical; for the forest dwellers, the world did not exist beyond the bounds of Arleon Forest.

Yet here she was, staring down at ships that had traveled the world over, ships that might be bound for any of the lands that she had once considered so distant. Though her legs ached from two long days of riding, a fresh eagerness to travel farther still took her. Today they had passed through unfamiliar grassy country, land that was flocked with herds of unsheared sheep and skinny black cattle. Tomorrow—she could get on one of those ships and head for anywhere. It was a thrilling thought. In the distance, studding the harbor, were ships that might have touched far Cosicché's shores, might have sailed to the gods' own pillar, their crews staring up through the mists to see the flashing walls of the Great Twelve's palace.

Her delight in the charming townscape and harbor with its strange streamlined ships and their high carved decks was cut short by the look of pain on Mariette's face. The swords-woman had reined her horse to Gaultry's side, as if to ask a question, when the pain cut her short.

"What's wrong?" Gaultry asked.

Yesterday's long hours of riding and the tense night they had endured at the second inn had not been good for Mariette. They had tried to set watches, but the attack by Tullier's master the night previous had unnerved everyone, and no one got much rest. That morning, Mariette had been unusually demure as she'd dressed, categorically refusing to show her wound as they'd pulled on their clothes in the pale light of early morning. Looking at her now, Gaultry wished that she had insisted that Mariette let her examine it.

"It won't be long now," Mariette said, ignoring Gaultry's question. "Will you smile at Martin first or scold him for jaunting off to rescue Helena without you?"

"How far is it to Seafrieg?" Gaultry said. For Gaultry, as for Mariette, certain questions had no good answer.

"Two hours, riding. We should reach the house by mid-afternoon."

"Do you think Martin will be there?" Gaultry asked. "What would happen if he's finished already in Seafrieg and come down into town?" Gaultry looked over at Tullier, where he sat self-assuredly, the usual cool expression on his face, on the tall pony they'd secured at the last way station. They had plied him for more information as to what Martin would have encountered when he'd arrived at Seafrieg's stronghold, but he had maintained a stony silence in answer.

Mariette sucked at her front teeth, shaking her head. "I wish I knew. Too bad we can't beat it out of our young lad here—there's a handy willow. We could have him cut his own switch." Where Gaultry struggled not to press Tullier with questions that he wouldn't answer, the swordswoman, disregarding her pain, had taken to teasing Tullier with suggestions that they curb him like a naughty schoolboy. At first Tullier had stiffened when Mariette had offered to beat his story out of him. More recently, he'd become accustomed to her manner, and learned he could ignore her prattle with impunity. Something like a humor had begun to rise behind the coldness of his eyes when she teased him.

And this time, he surprised Gaultry by actually acknowledging that Mariette had spoken. "We went past switches in our training years back," he said, deadpan, his eyes fixed on the town and its ships. "Willow will do you no good."

"No good? Might it at least bring some color to your pretty white cheeks?" Mariette twisted on her saddle to face him. Her horse shied—a small shy, but enough to give her a hard jerk. Her grin vanished. She pressed a hand to her stomach, over her wound.

"Mariette—" Gaultry started.

"I'm fine." The swordswoman shook her head and reined in her horse. "I'm fine. If I wasn't fine, I'd be the first to tell you." She swore softly at the horse, all the while clutching her stomach. It took her longer than Gaultry liked to see for her to compose herself, but finally she looked up and pointed, only a little white-faced, across town to a tall, whitewashed lodging-house that stood by the road where it meandered out of town to the south headland. "There may be news of Seafrieg at the Tête-de-Garret," she said. "We can stop in there before pressing on. It's Helena's property now, but if Martin left Seafrieg to come back this way, they'll have news of him there."

They detoured around the town center, keeping to the High Road that girdled the high end of the town away from the harbor. The town was larger than Gaultry had guessed from her first glimpse. Even so far back from the water, the houses were tightly packed together, painted with a strange, blue-tinged whitewash, their roofs shingled with nubbly dark stone. The townspeople, with closed and unfriendly faces, stopped their work to watch Mariette and Gaultry passing by on their tall horses. In a town that should have been used to strangers, it was unsettling. Gaultry rode as close as she could to Mariette, conscious that even her horse knew she was clumsy and poorly in control.

They turned a corner between two whitewashed shops and came out into a square that was paved with the same nubbly stone that shingled the roofs. A cluster of townspeople by the well in the square's center turned to face the strangers. This time the faces were openly disapproving.

"What are we doing wrong?" Gaultry whispered.

"Get off your horse," Mariette said, suddenly realizing what the trouble was. "Get off. That's a black armband there. Something terrible has happened. The whole town is mourning." She scrambled off her horse as she spoke, pulling up the hood of her cloak to cover her jumble of dark curls. Gaultry, hastily sliding down, mimicked the gesture. At first Tullier was slow to follow, then he too caught the dangerous turn of the crowd's mood and quickly moved to make himself inconspicuous.

"Who's dead?" Mariette handed her horse's reins to Gaultry and accosted the incipient mob's leader, a big man in a square butcher's apron. "And why aren't you at the funeral?" Something changed in her as her feet touched the pavement. Her nose went up, arrogant, and the blue eyes flashed. Her grandmother Melaudiere's commanding mien shone in her, and for a moment, Gaultry seemed to see the Duchess herself, as she must have been, near the height of her power.

The man's expression shifted. "Lady Mariette! Great Twelve give thanks! Did the Countess call you—" Mariette, who was in line to rule as Count of Seafrieg after Martin's wife's son, waved his embarrassment aside.

"Who's died?" she repeated, this time both more polite and more confident.

"Father Piers." Around him, the crowd murmured, hands everywhere sketching the Twins' double spiral. "Our High Priest. Of poison. The Black Men called him out to Seafrieg and cut him down with a poisoned sword. We didn't know. Then they came back to Bellaire, brazen-faced like men with nothing to hide, and set sail back for Bissanty. Yester-morn. They went out with the fishing fleet, on the morning tide. The harbormaster didn't know to stop them. When riders finally brought the news of what had happened, there were no ships in port to chase them."

"It wasn't only our good father," a woman behind the butcher cut in. "Eight other men died with him."

"Five castle knights," the butcher said, answering the question in Mariette's face. "And three innocent servers."

"And they killed Lady Vanderive afore that, and all her guard with her," someone else added. "That was before—"

Gaultry jerked around to look at Tullier, but the boy's face was already carefully blank.

"And Piers is being buried today?" Mariette asked. "That's quick."

"The good father and the others too. There was no choice," the big butcher said, distraught. The crowd nodded its agreement. "The poison rotted them from within, and the weather has been unforgiving. Too warm to keep even a sound corpse aboveground."

"Has anyone seen my brother?" Mariette asked.

No one had seen anything of Martin. "But the Countess leads the funerary procession. They're interring Father Piers now, out on Garret Head." The butcher gave the party's horses an unfriendly look. "The horses are too noisy. However, Lady Mariette, if you walk quickly, you'll reach them before the interment finishes. Perhaps she can tell you."

Mariette thanked the man. "We'll walk," she said to Gaultry, quietly so the butcher and his mob wouldn't hear. "To respect the dead. But this is bad—"

"Who is Father Piers?"

"Piers Laconte." Mariette shrugged her high shoulders. "You may not know the name. But you'll have heard of his mother—Marie was one of the Common Brood, along with your grandmother and mine."

"More Brood-blood dead," Gaultry said grimly. "Now how many of us are left?"

Mariette shook her head. "Maybe Grandmère knows. But the Laconte blood at least must be running thin. With old Piers and Destra gone, that leaves Palamar—who should be safe in Princeport for now—her older brother, Regis, and, just maybe, Destra's infant daughter. I don't know of any others."

Tullier made a sudden motion, inadvertently drawing their attention.

"Did you know?" Mariette asked bluntly. "Did you know they were going to kill the priest?"

"I didn't," Tullier said. "I had nothing to do with it." He sawed at the pony's reins, trying to get it to follow their horses. The beast resisted, giving him an excuse not to meet their eyes.

"He didn't know," Gaultry said, looking at the stubborn set of the boy's head. "If he did, he wouldn't lie. He'd keep his mouth shut. Isn't that right, Tullier?" Her frustration made those last words a taunt. Tullier didn't rise to it.

It was a half mile to the headland. No great distance, but under the hard sun of midday, Mariette could no longer hide the distress her wound was bringing her. Gaultry cast her a worried look.

"This has gone far enough," she said. "You should be up on your horse. Tullier and my being afoot is enough respect."

"I am a Montgarret." Mariette gave Gaultry a level look, though the skin around her eyes was taut with pain. It was the look the lean swordswoman had had on her face when Martin had broken Dinevar. "I won't let Helena see me shirking my duty. Not if it's Piers of Bellaire who is dead. I'd cede my own name first."

"You wouldn't be the first Montgarret to rush to forswear your name on a point of honor," Gaultry snapped. "And look where surrendering his name got Martin."

Mariette clenched her hand on her stomach. "What Martin did was right for its time and place."

The graveyard overlooked the sea. It was a bare, windswept place, the markers erected in ragged rows under worn earthwork walls. They heard the singing first: the leading voice a perfect liquid silver, rising sorrowful and resonant on the breeze up from the water, secondary voices joining in on the end lines. The sound was so pure and sweet, Gaultry felt her throat tighten and something in her chest respond, expansive. Then they came out from behind a stunted line of trees and spotted the new grave, a paler mound of earth, shot through with flinty rubble. The burial cortege was large, officiated by two elderly men in white smocks. Between them stood a slender, black-clad figure.

"That's Helena," Mariette muttered. Gaultry started, an ache almost strong enough to be pain twisting in her. Helena was the singer with the haunting voice.

A black veil covered Helena Montgarret's head and shoulders, not quite hiding the silver-blond of her hair.

"She's beautiful," Gaultry said softly.

"Maybe," Mariette answered. Her generous lips were closed in a flat, disapproving line.

A tall, thinly built boy, perhaps a year or two younger than Tullier, stood by Helena Montgarret's side, swinging a censer on a brass chain. One of her black-gloved hands rested lightly on his shoulder, possessive.

The boy's hair was a mop of rumpled silver-blond, already long enough for braided knight's locks. But he was not quite ready for manhood. He swung the censer with childish intensity, making an even pattern with the thin arcs of smoke. Gaultry could not help but stare. Though Martin had told her this was not his son, she could not help but search his young features for a trace of Martin's looks, his gestures.

His mother's voice had the entire crowd in tears.

"Wait here," Gaultry told Tullier as they entered at the low cemetery gate, within sight of the mourners. "Hold the horses and wait here. It would be asking for trouble to bring you to the graveside."

Tullier didn't protest as she pushed the reins into his hands.

Lady Helena watched, unblinking, as Gaultry and Mariette crossed the burying ground and joined the queue of townsfolk who were waiting to pay the dead priest their last respects. Passing over Gaultry, whom she did not know, her dark eyes fixed on Mariette. Her voice slipped on a single note, then she regained control.

Close to, it was evident that Martin's wife was exhausted. Despite the clarity and strength of her voice, her shoulders drooped. The hand that rested on her son's shoulder was there to steady herself, rather than to possess him. Gaultry felt a twinge of guilt at having interpreted the gesture otherwise. Beneath her thick, silver-blond hair, Helena's brows were unusually dark and expressively curved, lending her a gentle look, but there were lines of hard-won maturity around her eyes and mouth. Gaultry had been told that she had been celebrated as the most beautiful woman in Tielmark the year Martin had married her. With her head set proudly back on her neck, and her throat opened in full song, it was easy to see why she would have been named so. Gaultry didn't doubt that Martin's marriage to this woman was over—more than a decade was past since their separation—but thinking of Martin, young and still openhearted, marrying such beauty, made her choke.

Consumed by these thoughts, she reached the side of the grave before she had prepared herself to face it. She stared down into the yawning pit. The coffin was simple, built of ash planks fresh enough that they were still moist with sap. Already the chalky earth half obscured the entwined spiral symbols of the Huntress and Lady that had been carved onto the lid.

The bent woman in front of Gaultry sobbed and shuffled forward. "Father," she whispered in a voice like crumpled paper. "You blessed my children's children." With her gnarled, work-hardened hands, she threw a double handful of earth onto the coffin's lid. "The Great Twins give you peace." Mumbling a prayer, she passed on, pressing a silver shilling into the hand of one of the white-smocked priests.

Gaultry stepped forward.

The stench from the grave hit her like a physical thing. Even the pungent, oversweet censer-smoke could not mask it. Only a spell could cover this rotting death smell. Tullier's journey-master, Corbulo, had left the same odor, less intense, on the innkeeper's sheets. Gaultry gagged and stooped to seize a handful of earth, eager to do her duty and be away. Then she saw that Lady Helena was watching her—Lady Helena who sang, standing so near the grave that the death smell must have been thick in her throat, but offering no hint that the stench caused her any distress, and that brought Gaultry to a stop. Jealously, she wanted to prove herself in front of this woman. To her face, she could not hurry.

Gaultry approached the edge of the grave, so close the earth gave slightly under her feet, and held out the handful of crumbled flint and chalky gravel. Closing her eyes, she invoked the Great Huntress. *Let Martin not be dead,* she prayed. *Let me stay on his trail until I find him, as he stayed on my trail and found me. He fought his hardest to protect me. Let me not turn from this path until we are once more as one, as portended by the Rhasan.*

Heart in her throat at her madness—it went against sense and custom to mention the Rhasan in a prayer—she threw the handful of earth into the grave blindly. It rattled on the coffin.

"What did you pray?" Mariette grabbed her elbow. "Gaultry, what did you pray?"

Gaultry opened her eyes and looked down. Her handful of earth had spread across the coffin, white crystals against the darker gray of the earth. On the coffin's lid, the entwined goddesses' symbol blazed with white fire.

"I wish I had prayed for your health," she said. Mariette's sudden movement had clearly pained her. "I wanted—" The words would not come. "Martin—"

Across the grave, though the song had not swayed, Martin's wife's eyes were following her. Gaultry, meeting those eyes, realized that Helena somehow knew her prayer had been a challenge. She felt her bravado shrivel. Her display of jealousy at a pious man's graveside suddenly seemed inexcusably petty.

"Talk to Lady Helena for us both and find out what's happened," Gaultry told Mariette. "I can't take this. I'm going to find Tullier."

She walked away quickly, blinking back tears.

Back by the gate, she found the horses, but no Tullier. He had tied the horses to a post and wandered to the seaward side of the cemetery. Here Bissanty names mingled with Tielmaran on the markers. When at last she found him he was standing over one of these markers, his finger tracing the worn engraving of the Goddess Llara's thunderbolt sign that marked its top.

"Was that your lover's wife?" he asked, knowing it was her without turning.

"Martin's not my lover," Gaultry snapped, and then berated herself for admitting even that much. "What are you doing?"

Tullier took his hand away from the stone; his eyes were fixed on the sea and the distant horizon, beyond which lay Bissanty. "I've never seen a place where people interred their dead and put stones up in their memory. Look at that one—" He pointed without looking to the stone where he had lingered. "*Llara, hold my son. I loved him well.* That one was there years before Tielmark's rebellion."

Gaultry, stumbling on the uneven ground, went to read the inscription. The stone was so worn she could barely distinguish the dates. "Longer than that," she said. "By a cycle or two. Another fifty years and it will be gone. What do the Sha Muira do with their dead? Dump them in a ditch?"

Tullier shrugged.

"You're not going to make me believe they do that," Gaultry said. "A ditch?"

"Sha Muira Hold is on an island," Tullier said coldly. "With the sea all around us, do we need to waste hours scrabbling up the earth?"

"I don't know," Gaultry said. "But I guess the Bissanty man who put up this boy's stone thought the effort was worth it."

A gust of wind caught Tullier's black hair, hiding his face. He wasn't going to let himself be seen looking at the marker a second time.

"Gaultry Blas! Lady Gaultry Blas!"

Gaultry looked up. Helena Montgarret's son ran towards her, waving his arms. Behind him, the funerary cortege had dispersed. Only a handful of mourners remained by the grave.

"Come quickly! Lady Mariette's fainted!"

Gaultry sprinted past him. She had desperately wanted to avoid Martin's wife, to avoid Martin's putative son. Now there was no choice. By the time she reached Mariette, she was already laid out on the grass. One of the priests had pulled her shirt free from her leggings, revealing the shallow curve of her white stomach and the ragged puncture mark of Corbulo's dart. The puncture was small, but the mass of bloodied compresses which someone had pulled from inside Mariette's shirt and scattered on the grass evidenced that it had not stopped bleeding in the day and a half that had passed since she'd received it.

"Idiot!" Gaultry snapped, kneeling on the grass by the attending priest's side. "Idiot! Why didn't you let me help you?"

"She's a Montgarret." Lady Helena's speaking voice was sharper than her voice in song. "They weren't born to ask for help. Or to accept it."

"We'll stop the bleeding." The priest fussed with a prayer-book and fresh compress. "She is very weak. When did she receive this wound?"

"Two nights past." Gaultry pulled Mariette's head gently into her lap and stared down into the glazed blue eyes. "You should have told me."

Mariette shut her eyes, and managed to shake her head.

"The Montgarrets are famous for their stubborn streak," Martin's wife commented, her voice annoyingly calm. "And for their foolhardy nature. I take it you're the Brood-blood huntress of Arleon Forest? Where is your twister-woodie twin?"

Gaultry looked up. "I'm Gaultry Blas," she said gruffly. "What happened? Did the Sha Muira attack you as well as the Vanderives? Martin—" She stumbled saying his name. "Martin thought you were in danger."

Lady Helena shook her head. "They didn't want me," she said, "or my young Martin either." She nodded at the boy who had run for Gaultry. "Tielmark's Brood-blood has no secrets from the Bissanty."

The young huntress forced herself to look at the boy. He was plainly his mother's child. He had his mother's delicacy of feature: the graceful dark brows, the expression that shifted disconcertingly between gentle and supercilious. Court-bred, Gaultry could not help but think. It was strange to see the pair of them out in the harsh sun, presiding at the death ceremony of a modest priest who held a parish on the hard rocky coast. Gaultry glanced down at Mariette, smoothing the woman's tumbled hair from her face. Even on the ground in pain, Martin's sister had a steel in her that suggested she would hold up well against pirates, against storms, against whatever challenges might meet the Countess of a wild and rocky coastal holding. It was strange to think of Martin's family-holding passing away to this delicate-looking woman and her line.

"Did Martin find you?" Gaultry asked. "What happened?"

"What happened? What didn't happen? Now, or in the past days? First there was the news of poor Destra's death. They found her hanging from a tree, torn open by a sharp blade. Then, on Emiera's Planting Day, four Sha Muira broke into my house. They killed—" Lady Helena faltered, "They killed some of my finest men and walled themselves into the old keep. They had the Vanderive baby with them. They sent a lock of her hair to poor Father Piers, drawing him to us from Great Emiera's altar.

"Piers—I've known Piers since I was a child, since before he took the Great Twins' cloth. He was a gentle man. He had no chance against them, but little Marina was his niece, so he must have felt he had no choice. They cut him down with black arrows even before he reached the door. His body lay in the sun on the front stoop for half the day—no one dared to shrive his corpse with Sha Muira still in the house.

"Martin arrived in the evening, as the light was fading. He came into the hall in a crack of magic. The Sha Muira weren't ready and he knew the house as they did not. He killed one, wounded another."

She gave Gaultry a look that showed a bitter twist. "Eventually they got clever. They forced him to surrender by threatening my life."

"And?"

"When he surrendered, they riddled his body with black darts."

"He's dead?" The pain of it cut Gaultry like a knife. Not dead. Her mind would not accept it. Surely she would have sensed it if Martin was dead—

Martin's wife shook her head. "Not dead. They took him prisoner. They sailed on yester-morn's tide. Didn't you hear that in Bellaire when they directed you here?"

Gaultry whirled and stared out to the sea, the great brooding plain that she had looked on so lightly as she'd entered Bellaire, imagining the joy of travel. A silver gull, wheeling high overhead, let out a mocking call. Everything around her receded: Mariette's sprawled figure, Lady Helena's cool face, the concern of the priest as he ministered to Mariette's wound.

The Duchess had warned her. She had not listened.

Let Martin not be dead, she had prayed, bending over the dead priest's burial pit. *Let me stay on his trail until I find him, as he stayed on my trail to find me.*

To honor that prayer, she would have to follow her beloved out onto the surging breast of the sea.

It paid to be careful what one prayed for, Gaultry thought. One never knew when the gods were going to listen, when they were going to answer one's prayers.

"When's the next ship that leaves for Bissanty?" she asked.

There had been no one with sufficient authority to argue with Gaultry's decision, and the coin from the pockets of Tullier's dead Master meant nothing stood in her way.

Mariette offered a token resistance. "I can't stop you from going," she said, speaking from her sickbed at the Tête-de-Garret. "It's not worth calling you a fool, because that won't stop you. If I could come with you, lend my sword to your protection—" She pressed her hand again to her side, her voice trailing away. "Your poisonous rat is going to have to protect you. I hope he's up to it."

Tullier actually inclined his head and acknowledged the epithet—if not the duty.

"I'll manage," Gaultry said. "With the Twins' luck, I'll more than manage."

"If you make it to Bassorah, you may have help. My grand-mère's agents. Arnolfo's family is there."

"That's lucky."

"Who's Arnolfo?" Tullier asked.

"One of the old Duchess's men," Gaultry said. Arnolfo had been part of her escort on the long ride she had taken to Haute Tielmark to waken her Glamour-magic. She smoothed Mariette's sheet. "That's the best news you could have given me."

"I know Bassorah," said Tullier. "Gaultry won't need help there."

Mariette rolled her eyes. "I can just imagine the help *you'll* give her. What will it be? A knife in the ribs or the back?" She started to laugh and choked with pain instead. It took her a moment to recover herself for more words.

"If Tullier knows Bassorah he can help you find Arnolfo's house. It's in the city's old quarter. Somewhere near the new triumph bridge."

Frighteningly, that was the only resistance Gaultry encountered. She had become accustomed to having companions who argued with her, who told her that she was foolish, that she didn't take the time to think. But instead, all she had to do was ask the innkeeper for a captain's name and suddenly it seemed that Bellaire was full of hotheads, all eager to avenge their priest's murder—particularly if their actions meant putting someone else's neck on the block rather than their own. The innkeeper was noncommittal when she asked which captains were reliable. She had to interview them herself and try to cut through their boasts and stories without any aid. It was a daunting task indeed, for someone like Gaultry, with her limited experience of sailors and their customs. Even more frighteningly, it took almost no time to get the logistics sorted, and soon she could muster no more excuses for delay.

They sailed with the tide at dawn, the morning after Mari-ette's collapse.

CODA

Mervion leaned over Coyal Memorant's bed. His eyes were swollen with deep bruises—already yellowing—and his body was feverish, but the wracking pains that had shaken him for three days had at last abated. The gash that ran from his brow to his ear had finally scabbed. She smiled faintly and dabbed at the cut with a fresh cloth, remembering his pride and swagger when he had first presented himself to her and Gaultry at the feasting. Coyal possessed the breed of innocent, unquestioning vanity that was almost guaranteed to raise her sister's hackles.

Herself—she found it charming. Despite his punishing experiences at court, the young knight was still not wholly suspicious of the world. He was not a stupid man. He simply had no wish in him to acknowledge the ungenerous nature of those who resented his talents rather than appreciating his demonstrably fine abilities. That he had continued to fight for his place owed a good deal to his refusal to back down in the face of a faction of the Prince's courtiers who, envious of his early success in achieving high rank, were only too pleased to have witnessed his downfall.

"You're more trouble than you're worth," she told him, not caring whether or not he could hear. "And more like my sister than you know."

When he recovered and the swelling subsided, the new scar wouldn't detract from his looks. She had seen to that.

No one had liked it when Mervion had moved the young knight to the fine suite of rooms that she shared with her sister in wing of the summer palace. She herself would have preferred not to have made so overt a gesture of support for the recent outcast. But in the two days he'd languished in the

Prince's hospice, no one had come forward to oversee his nursing. His quarrel with his father, his renunciation of the family name, were still too fresh. Combined with the prominent position he had held in the traitor Heiratikus's court, his troubles were too much on the new court's mind for anyone to risk the association.

"That's the Blas twins for you!" Mervion said, rueful, straightening her back to relieve the tension in her shoulders. "Taking up with every court traitor and assassin. We're an unstable force, don't you know! Benet shouldn't give us any trust!"

"I wish for once Dervla would say that to our faces."

Dervla. In the past days, Mervion had come to better understand why Gaultry so disliked Dervla. If the High Priestess did not see how an act would benefit her, she would not do it. It was true, the High Priestess had helped Mervion slow the course of poison, but she had refused to offer Coyal nursing—or even the services of one of her acolytes to help nurse him. After two days, when Coyal's health was declared stable, Dervla had ordered the young knight's removal to the inn in Princeport where he had lodged since being stripped of his rank.

If Mervion had not been in the room when the order had gone through, she would not have involved herself any further with the young man's predicament. She would have let him go and thought her duty done.

But she had been there. She had seen Coyal's swollen and feverish body hoisted by uncaring hands into the flimsy litter, the look of alarm in his young page's eyes as he realized that his ailing master was now fully his responsibility.

"He has coin," Dervla had said, merciless. She hadn't even wanted to spare him a blanket for the trip through the streets. "The worst is over. He doesn't need to be here in the palace."

"His act saved Benet's goddess-pledge!" Mervion had protested.

"And I, on the Prince's command, saved his life. The rest he must recover himself."

Following the litter out into the court, Mervion had redirected its bearers to her own rooms. Then she had ordered a pallet be laid in the little workroom next to the salon. "And there you will stay," she had told him. "Until you open your eyes and tell me where you want to be taken."

That act of generosity had sealed court opinion against her.

She looked down at the young knight's swollen face and grimaced. "It's a good thing you need constant nursing," she said. "With Gaultry gone, there is little to fill my time, yet by the Prince's order, I cannot leave."

Events had moved swiftly following the upset on Emiera's Feast Day. The Prince had issued a command that ordered the living residuum of the Common Brood to convene at court. "If the fate of Tielmark is bound to the Brood-blood heirs," he had said, "I will not sit by and wait while they are cut down around me."

Behind closed doors, a fierce discussion with the Duchess of Melaudiere had followed concerning the precipitate departures of Martin, Mariette, and Gaultry. Rumor had it Benet had threatened Gabrielle Lourdes with demotion from the ducal council if she did not instantly send for Gowan, the heir to her ducal title—and Martin and Mariette's first cousin. Everyone had been a-buzz, wondering why the Duchess had been so insistent in her arguments.

There, at least, Mervion knew more than the rest of court.

"She doesn't want Benet thinking poorly of any of them. The old biddy wants Gaultry for her grandson Martin," she told Coyal, pressing a fresh compress to his seeping eyelids. He was closer to consciousness now, she sensed, and talk pushed her loneliness away. "There would be a bloodline for the court-genealogists to follow!" She could not help but grin, imagining her sister's horror that the old woman could regard her as a broodmare, but this she did not say aloud. "Needless to say, the Prince owes her. He was willing to be convinced that her grandson hadn't been foolhardy, and that Gaultry— and Mariette—had to follow him. Emiera only knows how she won him to the idea that the Bissanty assassin should go with them.

"But they're having no easy time rounding up the Brood-blood. The High Priestess is preening herself—you'd think her mother had been Princess herself rather than one powerful witch among seven. Dervla accounted for her mother's heirs in no time. She keeps reminding the Prince that this is the opposite of old Melaudiere—and it *is* notable that the Duchess, despite her promises, has yet to bring her youngest grandson to Princeport.

"They've sent to Arleon Forest for Tamsanne. With two days gone, the messenger will have yet to reach her." Mervion pulled the compress away and threw it into a bucket. Later she would take the contents to the chapel and burn them. She had learned the hard way that even a pair of days did not lessen the potency of the Sha Muir poison. Luckily for Coyal, he was strong and hardy. With the poison slowed, he would be able to purge it before it killed him. But even now, the residue was potent enough to blister the skin on her hands if she touched it directly. "Knowing Tamsanne, she won't come running. She doesn't travel anywhere without planning first." She pictured her grandmother, in her tidy border cottage, receiving the Prince's messenger, and couldn't help but frown. To Mervion, it had always seemed that the cottage, and the life her grandmother lived, were half in another world. A harder world, a world more full of magic than this, always faced across the border of the Changing Lands—the magic lands across the river where magic ran on the wind and through the trees, wild and treacherous, sweeping up human souls and animal spirits alike. It was hard for her to imagine Tamsanne leaving that place.

"Palamar Laconte's brother is proving troublesome too. County Tierce is only two days' ride, but he already sent a pigeon saying he'd be delayed. You know him, don't you?" The Laconte holdings were separated only by a river from those of Coyal's father. "What would make him delay, with one sister collapsed in hysterics and a second murdered, her children with her?

"Julie of Basse Demaine should arrive tomorrow. Apparently she sent word that *her* heirs are staying at home. Some past scandal means the Prince isn't grumbling.

"And that, so far as the Prince can do anything about it, is all that he can call of old Princess Lousielle's Common Brood. Three of the old witches dead and gone, three come to court—once Julie Basse Demaine and Tamsanne get here. The seventh witch—Richielle, the goatherder—she's disappeared. Dervla keeps telling the Prince she's dead. No one's seen her at court for fifty years, since the close of the last cycle, when the Common Brood put old Princess Corinne on the throne. Not"—Mervion arranged a fresh cloth on Coyal's face and stood back—"not that there is anything to make of that. Few at court knew where Tamsanne was holed up during those fifty years either."

She sat down by Coyal's side and pressed her hands to her temples. Keeping her spirits up was a constant struggle. Princeport was a prison. With Gaultry gone, her isolation was almost complete. How much longer would she be able to keep up her pretense of strength and calm, when every day brought new slights, new isolations? When the messenger had been sent for Tamsanne, Mervion had requested that the messenger pass by her half-brother's house and leave word there of the new happenings. Dervla—she was sure it was Dervla—had seen to it that the court functionary who approved such requests had denied her. "Gilles and Anisia Blas are not high in the Prince's favor," the secretary had informed her. "Any messages sent to them must be at your own expense." She had not had the strength to argue the unfairness of that, even knowing that her failure to rise to the defense of her brother and his young wife, Anisia—with whom Mervion had been imprisoned for several weeks before the night of the Prince's marriage—could only mean more rumors, more gossip.

"If only I could recoup my strength!" she said aloud. "I'm tired, and everyone here is relentless." Partly, she knew her troubles were her own fault. After the painful ordeal of the Prince's wedding, Mervion had been determined to conceal her fears and weaknesses from her younger sister. Her success in so doing had been all too complete.

"Wake up!" she chided Coyal. "Wake up and at least keep me better company!"

The young knight stirred but did not wake.

Leaving his side, Mervion began to pace.

She did not blame Gaultry for making her escape from the stifling round of court-politics. But she did wish that her younger sister had not left so precipitously. There was much that Mervion would have preferred to share with her, had she known they were to be separated. Things Tamsanne had told her. Things she suspected about Dervla, the Duchess, the Prince. Things about the spell she had cast to protect the boy assassin—she wished Gaultry had given her the time at least to tell about that.

Now it was too late.

Book Two

▼

chapter 9

▼

"They'll give you passage all the way to Bas- sorah City."

Gaultry looked past the Tielmaran Captain to the Bissanty slave-ship. It was an ill-proportioned, boxy craft that wallowed low in the water off what she had recently learned was the port side of the Tielmaran fishing vessel. For a full day they had gained on this ship. The Captain had strode the deck, cursing and yelling, making her crew duck and run—anything to trim the ship to a smarter course. Gaultry, despite her fear of the sea, had felt her mood lighten. A hunt felt much the same on land or sea. Now that they had caught up with the ship, however, her mood had changed again. This time not for the better.

This was not Martin's ship. It was merely a ship that would follow where he had gone, which the Tielmaran fishing-ship would not.

"They say they'll give us passage?" The Bissanty ship was broad, built of stained dark wood, its dun-colored sails striped with the black double line of the Emperor. "So easily?"

The Tielmaran Captain, a hard-faced woman aged somewhere between thirty and fifty, shrugged. The winds had been against them to catch any north-bound vessel, and she well knew, even if Gaultry did not, that she had proved her mastery of her craft in overtaking even this lumbering tub.

"Three gold imperials turned the balance," she answered. "That, and the look of your boy, standing there at the rail."

Tullier's eyes were on the Bissanty ship, but Gaultry knew he was listening.

"Is he so notable?"

The Captain spat over the rail. In Bellaire, two days' sail behind them now, she had wavered between eagerness to give Gaultry passage and suspicion, looking on Tullier and noting the Bissanty stamp of his features. "They recognize their own brand of arrogance," she said. "No one in Bissanty has that unless they've lorded it over slaves and lived the soft life."

Tullier's ears might have reddened, or it might only have been a glint of light off the bright sea.

"We'll cross to them," Gaultry said.

"Good. We have the coracle ready."

"The Huntress will thank you for bringing us this far."

"Tell her to join the Sea Lord in his bed." The Captain gave her a broad smile and shook Gaultry's hand to fare her well. "And give us a good harvest of fishes."

No sailor would have called the sea rough as Gaultry and Tullier descended to the tiny sheepskin coracle that danced in the fishing-ship's shadow, two sailors waiting at its oars. But to Gaultry, every wave threatened to swamp the light craft as it bobbed and swayed in the crash of foam. Reaching the last rung of the ladder, she stretched out her foot to catch the boat's side. One of the sailors offered her a hand. He grinned at her nervous face, amused, as he swung her into the safety of the boat.

"Let the Huntress fill the Sea Lord's bed," she muttered, disliking her awkwardness as she stumbled to the seat the sailors had made for her up in the bows. "And let this huntress gain the far shore."

Tullier, sliding in next to her, did not seem at all disturbed by the boat's motion. Riding, sailing, fighting—he never showed hesitation. Gaultry, sitting by him, struggled not to show how the swell of the surf unnerved her. She had never been so clearly in the Sea God's hands. Then, staring at the top of Tullier's head, she recollected how shaken he'd been by the Bissanty headstones at Bellaire's headland cemetery.

She could resign herself to his physical self-assurance if she kept that memory before her.

The sailors began to row. Working steadily, they soon moved the coracle out of the waves that drove against the parent ship into the relative calm of open water. Gaultry, settling a little to the rise and fall of the boat, twisted to see where they headed. The sun, high above them, glistened on the water, making everything shimmer with light. Ahead, the Bissanty ship rolled in the surf, clumsy. The stout two-masted vessel bore much complicated rigging. The smocked faces of the sails were trimmed by many lines. Lashed high on the main mast, where the rigging met with the mast-cap, was a copper replica of Llara's thunderbolt.

Two red sunburned faces framed by oiled black hair stared down from the officers' quarterdeck; a handful of sailors with darker bronze skin waited at the top of the rope ladder that had been dropped over the ship's gunnels. A rank of oars—twenty in all—jutted, low to the water, from the side of the ship that faced the coracle. The oar ports that were not in use were tightly shuttered.

When the coracle came within a hundred yards of the slaver's side, a gust of wind slapped Gaultry with her first whiff of a slave-ship's stench: blood and sweat, tar and urine, all mixed together and made old with salt. The ship rode low, with shuttered ports, because it was full of unwilling human cargo.

"This ship was at Bellaire?" she asked. "Tielmark's law allows such a ship to rest in Bellaire?"

"Two days in the outer harbor," one of the sailors confirmed. "With a stink like that, the harbormaster would hardly let her in closer."

"With a cargo like that, why would he let it stop in Bellaire at all?"

"The ship paid to use the harbor. It is not his business to judge the freight."

For all the broad expanse of water that spread around her, a wave of claustrophobia swept across her. Gaultry understood bondage. Anyone who worked with magic knew—and, if they had any sense, they feared—the snares presented by the higher powers. The gods would grant fabulous powers to their disciples in return for the surrender of free will. And some kinds of magic bondage could be imposed involuntarily. A geas compelled its victim to its service. Prophecy stalked its players, relentless, until its fulfillment. But these bonds, however terrible, shared a reciprocating reward: the love of a god. In the stink and misery of human slavery, there was no promise of a god's love, or, worse, of a god's notice. One could serve in utter misery and die unnoticed—

You have looked in the face of your own deity, she reminded herself, trying to steady her faltering nerve. *Elianté and Emiera together gave you their blessing. What man does to man should not make you falter.* She clung to that thought like a prayer, like a spell that would bind her so she wouldn't betray her physical revulsion to the Bissanty crew.

Tullier looked up, his glacial eyes intense. Something in his young assassin's body sensed her dread and could not help but respond—like a dog smelling fear on a man once-bitten.

If you can't stomach Bissanty ways, you should turn back now, his expression seemed to taunt her.

For a moment, that truth sorely tempted her. She could still retreat. She need only give the word to these sailors, and they would take her back safely to the Tielmark ship. Only her own will would send her to risk herself in Bissanty lands.

The Duchess had said she did not understand the Bissanty threat, that she had no sense of its proximity. Was this what she meant by those words?

The young huntress closed her eyes and tried to steady herself by picturing Martin's face. For a moment, he seemed near her, encouraging her with his gray wolf's eyes, the curve of his mouth. She would board this ship as a passenger, she reminded herself. Martin, ahead of her on another such ship, was a prisoner.

A sailor called from above, jerking her out of her reverie. A Bissanty voice. Gaultry's eyes slitted open. They had already arrived at the slaver. A rising wave slapped the fragile coracle along the ship's barnacled side. One of the sailors reached out, swearing, and pushed the sheepskin-and-wicker craft out of danger.

"Travel broadens the mind," Gaultry said, meeting Tullier's puzzled look. The boy could smell that her fear was gone, and that made him confused.

She gave the sailors who had rowed them across a handful of coppers, then turned to climb up the sea-sprayed rope of the ladder.

What was it in Tullier that made the slaver Captain bow and scrape? With one look in Tullier's face, the Bissanty Captain quickly ordered a change in the arrangements he'd made for their quarters.

"Does he think you're still Sha Muira?" Gaultry asked as they waited for the ship's boy to clear the pair of shuttered bunks next to the galley. "Is that why he's afraid?"

Tullier shook his head. "He thinks I rank him," he said. "That's reason enough for him to change our bunks. If you like, you can insist that they put us down in the hold. We'd be next to the cargo."

"I don't expect people to submit to me without thinking," Gaultry said. The thought of beds next to the slave hold repulsed her, but Tullier's easy acceptance of the Captain's reflexive recognition of his apparently innate ascendancy was also repugnant. "When they do, I want to understand the reason."

"Bissanty form is the reason." Tullier scowled. "Can't you leave it at that?"

"Not really. Even if you do rank him, why should he have to upset his ship for you?"

"He's afraid if he doesn't I might prove my position by forcing him."

She gave him a long look. "I wouldn't do that to you," she said softly. Tullier glowered, and turned away. They both knew she had the power to force him to submit. He didn't need her to constantly tug on the leash to remind him that it was there.

Their bunks were in the bow, next to the galley and the chicken coop, two body-length slots built into the ship's side. The wooden shutters that served as doors could be folded back, letting a pleasant breeze in to air them. The top bunk, though inconvenient, had a slightly better view of the deck, as well as a narrow vent. "I'll take the top one," she said, hefting her bag up. She didn't mind the bird coop smell. Clambering in, she stowed her bag and, swinging her legs over the bunk's edge, took a close look at the ship, getting her bearings.

At the boat's rear, on the raised quarterdeck, the Captain was in conference with his officers and the Master of Sails. The Captain and Master were leather-faced seamen; the quartet of sunburnt officers standing by them seemed callow, lacking even the carriage of trained warriors. They were, however, handsomely dressed. Gaultry guessed they kept the ship's wizened laundress busy.

"It looks like from here on in I'll be carrying your bag," Gaultry said. They were traveling with two bags as well as the long bundle of cloth that held Gaultry's bow. "And you're going to speak up and tell me how to make myself inconspicuous. From what I've heard, Bassorah City is big enough that we both can disappear into it. But not if I'm standing out like a Maypole dressed for Emiera's dancing."

"You won't like your choices," Tullier said nastily.

She didn't. In the Empire, women had less freedom than Gaultry was accustomed to. Except for those born to the highest of the nobility, women were considered little more than readily exchangeable family property. Traveling with Tullier, it became clear, would make her presence less questioned; in Bissanty, single women did not travel unaccompanied.

"You can't be my slave," the boy said coolly, "unless you intend to brand your back with the Emperor's mark. If you had a sword—and knew how to use it—we could pass you off as an eccentricity: a barbarian bodyguard. Of course, the most natural thing would be to disguise you as my whore."

"Really." Gaultry gave him a cold look, trying not to let him see her surprise that he thought he was old enough to travel with a paid sex-companion. "Young Bissanty gentry must be precocious. No, I fancy I'll play your nurse. Or better still, your duenna. That is, if you really think you're old enough to be taking a lover."

That shut up Tullier for a while.

Brand your back with the Emperor's mark. When the "cargo," as the Bissanties called it, was brought on deck, Gaultry realized that Tullier had meant his words literally. The "cargo" was seventy war captives from a battle being fought far to the south, its fallen warriors sold on both sides to the Bissanty slavers: forty men from one desert tribe, and thirty soldiers of mixed gender from the other. More than half bore battle-wounds, in varying stages of recovery. Despite this, every captive had been branded on the right shoulder blade by a square with a cross running in from its corners, the sign of Empire. Beneath the slaves' rags gaped poorly healed burns, still raw and tender.

Weakened as they were, many of the new-made slaves were still fighting their change of status. To discourage this, they had been chained together in strings of three. The chains made it difficult to move and impossible to run, though several trios had adapted remarkably well to their bonds' limits: these walked, almost gracefully, in eerie synchronicity.

It took Gaultry longer to see that a number of the three-somes had been fitted with metal rings, pierced through the fore-flesh of their tongues. These seemed to be the more aggressive groupings. One trio of men suffered the further indignity of having a braided line threaded into their tongue-rings. That trio's massive center man looked as if he would challenge any comer. He had an angry face and an unhealed cut at the side of his mouth. When he spat on the ship's deck, his tongue-ring didn't show, it had been pierced so far back in his mouth.

"A slow learner," Tullier commented. "He must have fought it, more than once, and ripped out his ring. I doubt he has more than a tag of tongue left." He flashed Gaultry an interested look. "Does it upset you? He's from Chauduk. They're harder on their women than anything Bissanty offers."

"If he's still fighting," Gaultry said, "it's because he has hope. Why should that upset me?" It upset her. She was a hunter, and she understood that the fire of life was strong enough that even the most untamable of wild creatures could linger in a cage for years and years, prisoner of its own misery as much as the bars. In Gaultry's experience, creatures which could will themselves to death merely for the loss of freedom were few and far between.

She prayed that if she were discovered and taken prisoner in Bissanty, she would find herself one such.

"Chauduk and Ardain are fighting again." The ship's cook had come out of the galley on the pretense that the chickens needed feeding. He had a garrulous nature—he would talk to the hens, or his pots, or anything. Instead of resenting that he'd had to cede his bunk to them, he seemed pleased to have their company. "And selling slaves on both sides. But even chained, the sides stay apart—Master," he added hastily, catching Tullier's eyes and making a sketch of a bow to apologize for having opened his mouth before he'd been invited to speak. The chickens, Gaultry was amused to see, got only a handful of grain before the little man began to tie up the feed sack.

"Who's getting the best of it?" Tullier inquired.

"This season? Chauduk. Another month and it will be too hot in their lands for fighting. But there's always next winter."

"What makes them fight?" Gaultry cut in. The man shot her

a surprised look. She remembered that she was supposed to be letting Tullier talk for her.

"A valley that has water. That, and the Chauduki belief that any tribe that allows its women to ride into battle transgresses against all the Great Twelve's will. Look—" He pointed. "There—that's a real curiosity. That woman used to be a Sharif—an Ardanae war-leader. They're almost never taken alive."

The woman was at the center of a trio, shackled between a stout, patient-looking man and a girl with a bandaged ankle. She was tall and lean, with the well-muscled legs of a rider. Matted black hair hung in cords to her hips. Unlike the man with the ripped tongue, her carriage was collected rather than angry. Despite the ill-matched heights of these chain-partners, the trio was one of the smooth-moving ones. They had been actively pacing up and down the deck, the girl with the bad ankle leaning heavily on the center woman for support.

"They say Sharifs can speak in the heads of those they trust," the cook added. "It makes them fearsome leaders. Maybe that's why those three walk so well together—she could be calling marching time for them in their heads."

The slave woman, sensing she was under observation, turned her head and locked eyes with Gaultry. The Sharif's eyes were an unexpected golden color, tawny and intense, like sand and sun combined. Her expression was shuttered, but beneath the proud line of her jaw Gaultry could see a terrible boil on her throat, and her skin was patchy with dirt and ill-healed cuts and sores.

"She's not well," Gaultry said.

"She was almost dead when the Chauduks caught her." The cook, beginning to acclimate to Gaultry's manners, cast Tullier a careful look before he answered. "To take her they had to kill the rest of her war party, down to the standard-bearer. By Ardanae custom, their Sharifs are more highly regarded than their war flags."

So the woman truly had been a leader. She had watched her own warriors die at her feet, vainly sacrificing themselves to protect her freedom. Gaultry doubted that such a woman would find it easy to stomach the life of a slave.

"Will you be needing the ship's larder for your Master's laundry?" the cook asked her. "The officers' laundress uses the sailing-master's cabin, but I expect you won't be spending much time up at that end of the ship."

Gaultry, stuttering inwardly, just managed to make herself acquiesce. "A splendid idea," she told him.

Laundry proved to be the least of the duties that the Bissanty crew expected her to take on for Tullier. Wash his clothes, serve his food—the cook, whose name was Arion, was openly surprised that she didn't insist on tasting his food for him. It was, she supposed, an excellent rehearsal for the trials that lay ahead.

It was not, however, a satisfactory way to tread through the entirety of their passage.

"I'm bored and you must be too," she told Tullier the morning of their third day aboard the slaver. "We both need exercise. We can practice sparring—I'll partner you. I want to learn something about knife-play."

"You'll have to ask the Captain first," Tullier said crabbily. He had not adjusted well to sleeping in his little bunk. "Any fighting aboard ship might upset his cargo."

"What, by giving them something to watch? They've been stuck in their chains for more than a month. Besides being miserable, they must be more bored than the rest of us. If anything, the entertainment will quiet them."

"Maybe," Tullier said. "But that aside, they won't see why we're bothering. I outmatch you. Why should I set my skills against yours?"

Gaultry jumped down from her bunk and laughed. It was amusing to discover that Tullier could prefer sulking to acting. That quirk jibed oddly with his self-image as the implacable Sha Muira warrior. "I don't imagine they'll have any trouble believing that you'd take pleasure from humiliating me."

Something in Tullier's face moved, a tenseness of muscle along his jaw, a tightening of his mouth. "You're trying to insult me," he guessed.

Gaultry grinned. "I'm trying to think like a Bissanty. What's the difference?"

The boy went white. For an awkward moment, Gaultry was sure he was furious with her, in the next, she decided he was simply upset. Her words, spoken in innocence, had unbalanced him as badly as the worn tombstones out on Garret's Head. Something in her words had touched a nerve.

His expression hardened. "I'll teach you something," he said. "I'm sure if I ask, the Captain will give us permission."

The Captain did agree, with a few provisos. They could not fight, of course, while the slaves were on deck, and they had to limit themselves to the small area in front of the galley— the cooking-deck, as Arion was wont to call it.

Gaultry was outmatched from the first moment. Tullier was too intent on punishing her for it to be proper training. At first, he wasted his effort, trying to hit her woundingly hard— Gaultry could see that in his face—but he soon discovered that those thrusts inevitably missed, daunted by the leash of her Glamour-soul. Then, to Gaultry's dismay, he made the discovery that so long as he was not trying to actively wound her, he could hit her as hard as he liked.

It was a painful rout—her rout, with Tullier dogging her round the deck, leaving her no room to lash back as he jammed the flat of the wooden practice knife into her gut, the soft flesh of her upper arms, even the side of her throat. Taking the offensive was out of the question. The best Gaultry could do was steel herself to take the hits. The half dozen gulls that accompanied the ship, living off galley scraps, perched on the bow-rail, shrieking and crowing, watching them with bright periwinkle-colored eyes. Their leader, a bullying male with a crippled foot and a crest of black feathers like a sort of scar on the side of his head, gave a gurgling hiss of approval every time Gaultry took a hit.

"Beg for quarter," said Tullier, still angry. He had cornered her against the hen coop. She shook her head. He drew back, choosing his opening, savoring her helplessness.

Sweat trickled on his brow. He wiped his face with his hand to clear it, and his hand came away slick with oiled ash.

It had been more than a week since the Feast of Emiera, yet Tullier's sweat was still dusky, poisoned with Sha Muira black. The sight of the poison made him swear. "We'll break now," he said. "I need to clean myself."

Gaultry, grateful for the respite, leaned back against the chicken coop. Her body, like Tullier's, was sheeted with sweat. Thankfully, Mariette had insisted Helena supply them with some extra clothes for their journey to Bissanty. Her shift was ruined—their blades were edged with tar, and Tullier had marked her again and again. If she forced herself to keep the knife-play up, it would be in rags after the week of sailing it would take to reach Bassorah City.

Tullier was already back, ready to start again.

"How many times have I died?" she asked.

"Is it worth counting?" Tullier sneered. He sauntered cockily to the tar bucket, dipped his blade, and wiped it on the bucket's rim.

Gaultry's rein on her temper was slipping. She did not want to sit out a long fortnight's sail washing his clothes and dancing attendance on him, but if he would not settle to the sparring, and train against her without vendetta, she was not going to have a choice. The punishment—his gleeful relief that he could finally stick a knife into her gut, so long as the edge was not turned to wound her—was too much.

At least, she noted with relief, they would not be able to practice much longer today. The noon sun was high overhead, the sky a bright shield of unrelieved blue. The grates over the slave hold lay open, airing the fetid lower deck, and the slaves were due for their noon outing. The closest grate was set so the cargo had a view of the kitchen deck, and Tullier and Gaultry as they fought back and forth. When they had first begun to fight, there had been a lone trio sitting there, waiting listlessly for their afternoon exercise on the upper deck.

Now it was crowded with more heads than Gaultry could easily count. The Captain had told them that their knife-play must not excite the cargo—perhaps, she thought, they would have a scuffle and prevent her and Tullier from going on. But those watching, perhaps guessing that the diversion would come to an end if they were at all rowdy, were unusually silent. Both Chauduki and Ardanae had crammed the small watching space, their interest temporarily overriding their mutual aversion.

The big ripped-tongue Chauduki man and the Sharif had taken the best viewpoints. Those two, Gaultry had come to recognize, were the two factions' leaders. The Sharif, meeting Gaultry's eyes, gave her an almost imperceptible nod. The ripped-tongue man . . .

He smiled unpleasantly. If he had any tongue left, Gaultry guessed, he would have licked his lips salaciously. Opening one hand, he spread his fingers, then made a fist—a god sign with which she was unfamiliar. But the man's intent was clear. He wanted to see her on her knees. Even though he had been enslaved himself, he wanted to see her brought down. The Chauduks believed that it was unholy for men to meet women on the field of battle—and a worse transgression for men to fail against them. Tullier's ability to dominate her pleased him.

"Giving up?" Tullier said.

"What do you imagine I'm trying to learn here?" Gaultry asked him. Her eyes were still on the big man down on the slave deck. What did he know of the true balance of power between herself and the boy? What must he think, seeing her in retreat before him? The man, sensing her animosity, her seemingly helpless anger, ran his hand over to his crotch, then pointed at her directly.

Tullier was too inflated with the easy hits he'd been scoring to appreciate the change when she wheeled suddenly back to him, bright color in her cheeks.

"What do I think you are trying to learn?" he taunted. "Nothing, beyond the lesson that you'll never beat me."

"*Never?*" Gaultry stuck her wooden blade into her sash, freeing her hands, and flashed him a look that warned him of her anger.

Tullier, who had been trained to know what anger did to an already outclassed opponent, laughed. Above him the gulls on the bow-rail cackled, laughing with him. They were clever

birds, clever and naturally aggressive. They had chosen a side
to back, and they took open animal pleasure in watching their
side prove victor.

The blood pounded at her temples. "You shouldn't laugh at
perceived helplessness," she told Tullier.

"You can't stop me," Tullier said. "I have found the limit
to your leash."

The black-headed gull, shrieking mockingly, swooped
across the deck.

She spun it out of the air with a shaft of magic, and had it
pinned to the decking where she could reach it before it
guessed what was happening. It pecked at her, vicious. She
grabbed for its throat. It was too fast—as she caught it, it
slashed her palm with its bill. But then she had it, the body
beneath the natty black-and-white feathers startlingly strong
as it twisted to free itself, smacking at her with its wings. She
met the pale blue of its eye and thrust a casting at it. It
squawked again, this time in fear.

Her taking-spell, fueled by her fury, ungently ripped its
spirit free. She threw open a channel and drew it roughly
inwards, ignoring its croaking cries of dismay. Panting, she
opened her eyes. In her hands, the bird's warm, feathered
body was a dead weight. She set the little body down by the
rail and stared across at Tullier. A quick, birdlike motion. The
five gulls that remained on the bow-rail, gawking down,
sensed what had happened. They took to the air, crying, in a
flutter of wings and flashing tail-feathers.

Gaultry attacked.

She was no better at knife-fighting, but she was faster now,
and Tullier had become overconfident. He adjusted his style,
countering her sudden, animal-fast movements, but he did not
understand the change in her. The gull, quickly grasping that
the knife was its new beak, and sensing that it could avenge
the indignity acted on it by fighting, squalled forward.
Gaultry let it ride over her senses, not caring what Tullier saw
of her, of the magic in her, of the bully-gull's spirit shining in
her eyes. She was using her longer reach to her advantage
now, pressing him. Tullier lunged, she countered—

Tullier's knife spun out of his hand, and she was in past his guard, bright and murderous. Throwing down her own blade, she stepped back. If the play had been with real knives, his guts would have been pouring onto the deck. Gaultry, shaking, brushed herself down.

The gull still wanted to fight, but she was finished with fighting. She reopened the channel and showed it the way out. The bird-spirit flew hastily back to its body, took possession, and launched itself into the sky, squawking insult upon insult down at her as soon as it was safely aloft.

There was a new line of tar across Gaultry's chest. She brushed her fingers against it, relieved that there was no new bruise. Tullier's last thrust had missed its mark. "That's enough for the day," she said. "The Captain will want to bring the slaves up soon."

She looked back into the slave hold. The ripped-tongue man was gone. But the Sharif was there. Golden desert eyes met wild forest green.

Neither woman's mouth changed, but Gaultry knew that they were sharing a smile.

The cut the gull had made in her palm took four stitches. But it wasn't her knife hand. Gaultry let Arion sew it up for her—despite his occasionally unpleasant Bissanty expectations she was coming to like him.

The next noontime, when Gaultry told Tullier it was time to practice, the session was no more than that, and no less.

Tullier won every bout.

chapter **10**

▼

Bassorah City was one of the wonders of the world. Founded on three small hills that rose from the center of a great salt marsh, it had grown to dominate the land surrounding the confluence of the Great River Bas and the Lesser Polonna. Generations of Bissanty Emperors had laid foundations of granite deep in the mud down to bedrock, conquering the marsh as they had the land around it. Colossal monuments celebrated a thousand years of imperial glory: monuments faced in white, black, and exotic gold-streaked marble brought down from high mountain quarries as imperial tribute. As the Great River Bas wound its leisurely way toward the city, up from the sea, the Empire's capital city was visible from miles away, its red tile roofs, white towers, and monumental spires rising high above the dusty dun and green of the marsh and the scattered hummocks that dotted the great marsh plain.

For a full day now, from the ship's decks, Gaultry had watched Bassorah rise over the sparseness of the salt marsh, looming ever closer as the river turned one great oxbow bend after another.

Her first impression of Bissanty had been that sparseness: straggling villages spread back from the river's edge; stretches of rough marsh land, alternately dry and mucky; dusty, gravel-bedded roads beaten by sun and wind, unsheltered and open to the wind, discouraging travel.

The thought of the great city lying in wait at the marsh's center worried her more than she wanted to admit. Bassorah sucked the lands around it dry of imperial tribute and trade. From what she had observed so far, that flow citywards of material wealth seemed to take something else along with it. In comparison to Bissanty, Tielmark was, she knew, a poor country. But that poverty bred a spirit of community throughout Tielmark's farmlands that was most striking, in Bissanty, for its evident absence. It was not that Tielmarans were selfless. Gaultry had known numerous greedy farmers in her life. But their poverty had habituated them to taking care of resources that were held as a common stock. These were customs which the Bissanty peasants, ravaged by taxes and powerful traders, seemed to have forgotten.

When they had first left the open sea and begun to wend their way inland, she had asked Tullier why there were no trees. He had laughed, and told her no peasant would leave a tree standing that wasn't guarded behind a noble's walls.

"But you can pollard trees," Gaultry had protested. "Pollard trees, and everyone can have wood, year after year."

Tullier didn't know what the word meant. She had to explain the process of cutting canes, leaving the bole of the tree to thicken and send up new shoots, and she still wasn't certain he had taken her point. That was when she discovered that he didn't know the most basic information about how to grow food, how to hunt for game so fields and forest weren't depleted, how to hoard up a supply of fuel for a long winter— or for a season of cooking fires—the things that Gaultry, bred to the thin but hardy life on Tielmark's southern border, understood almost without conscious thought. And now she was headed for a city that would be full of people bred to life with slaves, to life with an army that was led by a hereditary class of soldiers—men quite distinct from the gentry and courtiers who filled the halls of the Imperial court, supplicating the Emperor for his favor.

But Tullier had told her that in Bissanty all byways led to Bassorah, that the business of Empire ran through the great capital like grain through a sieve. If they wanted to discover where Martin had been taken or tidings of the new plots being laid against Tielmark, the place to start lay somewhere within the cramped quarters of Bassorah City, with its seven bronze gates and its guarded river locks.

The city's inner harbor, once the envy of far-flung nations, had silted full. The Empire's maritime business had drifted down the tidal stream to Bassorah Port. Now only slave-ships wound their way along the ever-narrowing channel to the city proper, where they unloaded their cargo at Slaves Wharf. Llara had a temple there, a slavers' temple where a small sect of her priests thrived, their chief duty being the laying of the goddess-bond on incoming slaves. The priests of the slave-bond temple—wealthy, affluent men who enjoyed the pleasures of city life—refused to move their shriving house south, out of the city. It was a measure of their sect's power—and its intransigence—that the long channel to the inner port had been kept dredged for more than a century for their convenience.

Which meant that Gaultry and Tullier were fortunate to have shipped on a slaver. Unlike other trading craft, it would come to berth inside the city walls. They planned to jump ship when the ship entered Bassorah's inner harbor. They needed to come to land inside the city gates, Tullier had told Gaultry, where they could most easily melt into the bustling population of the city and disappear.

The Captain might have guessed their intention to leave the ship early, before they'd met the customs men—Gaultry was quite sure that Arion, the cook, knew—but so far restlessness among the cargo kept his attention from them. The seventy war-prisoners had taken the first brands and metal bonds of slavery fresh from the trauma of defeat and capture, but the long sea voyage had given many a chance to recover from their battle-shock. As the ship neared the city the prospect of submission to the Bissanty goddess and forsaking hope of a return to their native soil seemed increasingly to prey on their minds. Five—two Chauduki men and the members of one Ardanae chain—ripped out their tongue rings in the course of disruptions that Gaultry and Tullier heard discussed, in gruesome detail, via Arion's complaints that they required special feeding.

"Is the god-bond so strong?" Gaultry asked Tullier when the news came that the Chauduki trouble-leader had lost another hunk of tongue getting hauled back through an oar hole which he and his chain-partners had secretly enlarged.

They had just finished a practice session and come to Arion for a drink and some dinner. The sun slanted low across the marsh. A light wind brushed the marsh grass with gentle gusts, making their seeded tops ruffle like waves. Another day and they'd reach the city. Down on the slave deck forty slaves were rowing, two to each oar, ten to each side; Chauduks on the port side, Ardanae on starboard. Though she couldn't see the Sharif from where she stood, Gaultry knew exactly where the woman sat. She and her chain-partners rowed the stroke oar on the starboard side of the boat.

Her question caught Tullier off guard. He nodded, but followed the nod with a frown, making it clear he didn't want to give a longer answer.

"How strong is it?" she pressed, taking the dipperful of water Arion held out to her. The practice sessions had been good for them both, once he had stopped trying to hurt her. Without the relief of exercise, their anxieties might have grown intolerable. It was over a fortnight since Emiera's Feast, and Tullier, incredibly, was still seeping poisoned gray sweat. Having half her Glamour-soul in him had begun to feel increasingly stressful to her. There had been times when she had been overwhelmed by loneliness, times when she had longed to reach out with her own power and tear away the caul of magic that Mervion had used to seal Gaultry's soul-piece in place over the tormented center of Tullier's poison. But the practice sessions Gaultry and Tullier had shared helped with that—the two halves of the Glamour-soul, riding their own souls, had brought an inevitable sense of intimacy between them—and to Gaultry, a sense of renewed resolution to bide her time, to wait for the return of her power. She had tried—and sometimes it had been hard—to respect his privacy, to check the flow of energy that ran between them, broken soul calling its missing half. But the practice sessions had inevitably brought them closer.

"They're slaves," he finally answered. "You shouldn't think that their lives are more than that."

At times like this it wasn't so hard to remember what life he'd been born to.

"So they are," she said, sorry she had opened the subject in front of Arion—though the cook, recognizing the signs that their tempers were flaring, had already retreated discreetly to the galley on the pretext of refilling the bucket. "And so were you to the Sha Muira. And so you still are—to me—if you want to insist on thinking about your bondage to me in those terms. What I want to know is what the god-bond *does*. Tell me about that."

"Llara's bond will lock them to Bissanty soil," Tullier said. "After the god-bond, they won't be able to move without the blessing of the man who owns the soil they're tied to."

Gaultry turned to stare at the white towers of Bassorah, still so far away beyond the long sloping curves of the marsh. Martin was somewhere in that city. The thought of him made her chest tighten.

"Will they do that to Martin?" she asked.

"Not if they have plans to return him to Tielmaran soil. We can't brand our soldiers, you know. Slaving your friend would limit the scope of how they could use him."

"And only Bissanty landholders can own slaves?"

"True." Tullier looked away. "Not every slave settles to his or her first Master."

"And then?"

"If they don't settle, their Master can always bless them a new bonding where they can find a better peace. To the rock of Sha Muira Island, for preference."

"What happens to them there?"

"Gaultry," said Tullier faintly, "how do you imagine it is that we learn to kill?"

It was hot in the Bassorah marshes. After a week of clean sea air, it seemed a sickly, suffocating heat. Gaultry's lungs felt heavy as she looked across the marsh, picturing the men and women who labored in the ship below.

She had not come to Bissanty to risk her mission by challenging a practice that had been ongoing for a thousand years. She had come for Martin. For the Brood-blood. For Tielmark.

"I doubt either the Sharif or that big Chauduki will ever learn to settle," she said aloud.

Tullier hesitated, then nodded.

Gaultry knew so little about ships that she had not at first wondered that the slaver's officers had no obvious employment. She'd assumed that they were aboard to keep the slaves in order, but the four high-born Bissanties spent most of their time in their cabin, preoccupied with card-playing and drinking. Without asking, she gradually came to understand that they functioned more like guests than actual members of the crew. Though they wore swords—expensively wrought, silver-traced blades with elaborate basket handles—and they took a spectator's interest in her knife sessions with Tullier, they themselves had not stooped to practicing aboard ship. From what Gaultry could see, maintaining the quick polished speed of a fencer's step did not concern them. She thought of Mariette and the fierce practices the young noblewoman put herself to with her arms-master. She wished Tullier had seen Mariette and her practice sessions. It would have left him with more respect for Tielmarans' skills at arms.

On the morning before the ship was due to arrive in Bassorah, the ship was heaved to at an unmarked stone pier. The quartet of officers appeared on deck, readied to disembark. At first Gaultry did not understand what she was seeing. There had been trouble in the ship overnight: two of the crew had been injured trying to calm a scuffle in the slave hold. If ever the ship had need of armed men, this passage along the last stretch of river before the city marked that time and place. But the intention to disembark was plain: pulled back from the pier, two fine coaches awaited—overtly luxurious coaches with painted panels, gilt, and brocade curtains.

The hardworking Captain and his crew—Arion, the cook, included—lined up by the taff-rail in honor of their departure. As the officers came past them, they went down on their knees, their leathery sailors' faces shuttered and cold.

The officers minced by, chattering to each other, failing to acknowledge the obeisance in their obvious eagerness to be off the ship.

"Another six months!" Gaultry heard one of them say. "Llara in me, can the title be worth it?" His affected manner— and piercing voice—made her think he spoke for the benefit of the knot of men who waited beneath them on the pier, rather than for his fellow officers.

"My brother did it," another answered, equally loud. "And now he's posted in the Crown Prince's train. Outlast the boredom and the travail, my dear. You'll make it to the Pallidon's court yourself."

"All for Empire's service," said a third. "Nothing is too great for that."

Something in that last quip made them laugh, a humor that the crew, judging by their sullen faces, did not share.

The quartet walked noisily to their coaches, laughing, relaxed, their days on the ship already behind them. The Captain did not allow his crew to move until the last of the officers had boarded and both coaches had churned away through the dust of the road that led into the marsh.

"A better lot at least than the last rogues we were lumbered with," Arion muttered, climbing stiffly to his feet. His place at the end of the line meant he was safely out of the Captain's earshot.

"Hoy! Captain a-ship!" The business with the officers completed, a man now came to the front of the pier and waved. He was darker-skinned than the pale, pinkly sunburned officers. His clothes were elegant and fine, though the tight trousers he wore made his thin legs look storklike and frail. A pair of heavy, well-muscled men attended him, along with a more elegant servant and a short-legged boy who clutched a heavy ledger and brought up the rear. "Captain Odipo! Are you ready to give an accounting?"

"Angolis Trier." The Captain gave his crew a sharp look, gesturing for them to return to their duties. "Welcome aboard."

He left the Master of Sails to direct their launch and retired to the great cabin with the thin-legged man and his entourage.

"Weren't the Bissanty officers along to control the cargo?" Gaultry asked when Arion came back to his galley.

The little cook grimaced. "They wouldn't have lifted a finger if Kurkut himself had come up on deck to slit their throats." Kurkut was the ripped-tongue Chauduki warrior. "Perhaps not that bad. They're the Sea Prince's men, and they have to prove themselves by making voyages. Some are better than others. This last lot were just lazy."

"The Sea Prince?" Gaultry asked.

"You don't know anything, do you?" Arion started to fill a bucket with onions from a nearly depleted sack. "It's a wonder *he* has thought fit to bring you here." He nodded towards the bunks to where Tullier sat, stropping a knife against his boot.

"We have only one Prince in Tielmark," Gaultry said, smiling. "That's not so hard to keep track of."

"Harder than you'd think," Arion said. "Peel those." He pushed the bucket into her hands. "We call your Prince usurper, you know. Here in Bissanty, we have our own Tielmaran Prince. Not that he gets to do much in the way of ruling, mind you."

"Why do you bother keeping the title at all? We're not the richest land. Why even deign to bother with us?"

"We have no choice," Arion said. He made the thunderbolt sign with his hand. "Llara made the Empire to have five Princes. One for each of the wind's four quarters, and one for the land's center. Tielmark is still our southern quarter, whether or not the Emperor controls it." He gave Gaultry an intent look. "Our Emperor, Llara's Heart-on-Earth, still must prove he owns Great Llara's blessing on his rule by seeding five sons. One of them still gets titled Prince of Tielmark."

"We've been free of you for three hundred years!" Gaultry said, trying to take him seriously. "Our Prince is descended straight from the last Bissanty Prince's line. How can you call him usurper? Besides, our Prince is bonded to our soil by a gods' pact. What sense does it make to deny him?"

"The first Tielmaran usurper forsook the blood of Llara— his own Imperial blood—to own Tielmark. Break your god-pact and the blood of Llara—the fifth Imperial Prince—will be there to reclaim the land."

"Well," Gaultry said, grimly chopping onions, "less than a month back, our Prince reaffirmed the god-pact, so Bissanty plans are going to have to wait. It will be fifty years before Tielmark has another opportunity to break its pledges to the gods. Your so-called Tielmaran Prince will have to be patient."

Arion dumped a measure of salt into the onions and gave them a stir. "Don't be so hot," he said, amused. "Do you think any of us aboard this ship cares whether our lackland Prince regains his princeship? You asked about our Princes—I told you. None of it has anything to do with our daily lives— unless the Emperor gets a bee in his bonnet and sends us along to be killed on your border."

"That's hard for me to understand." Gaultry, finished with her task, put down the bucket. "In Tielmark, we care about our Prince. If only because he makes sacrifice and brings our harvest to bear fruit."

Arion, bending to retrieve the bucket, rolled his eyes. "Our slaves make the harvest sacrifices for us here. What has the Emperor to do with such low things?"

Gaultry went hot with involuntary rage. That Arion should speak so carelessly of sacred roles and duties! Then, realizing that he had intended no insult, she forced herself to laugh. "No more, I would guess, than your gentry has to do with the practical running of a ship."

Arion opened his mouth to answer her, and then closed it. "I would not compare the two so," he said softly. "But the comparison might be made." By a coltish provincial from Tielmark, his eyes told her.

"So your officers were men of Bissanty's Sea Prince." It would be safer to return to their original subject, Gaultry decided. "Is the Sea Prince Bissanty's Eastern Princeling?"

Arion pointed to the striped standard that ran at the top of the ship's main-mast, above the gold-and-black flag of Empire. "Just so. He rules the sea-trade and the great and lesser archipelagos. That's his burgee."

"So the Sea Prince is the Emperor's son?"

"In a sense."

"What does that mean?"

"The Sea Prince is Siri Caviedo. The Emperor's uncle." For a second time, the cook sketched the thunderbolt with his hand. "Praise Llara, our Emperor is short two sons. His uncle and his brother will continue to hold title as Prince until he seeds more heirs."

Gaultry nodded. "I suppose I knew that," she said. "Being short sons means your Emperor's children can't inherit the throne, right?"

"It means nothing of the sort," Arion said. "It only means that they have to wait. Sciuttarus is young. He will get more sons, Llara willing." He dumped the onions into the largest of his stew pots and began to sift in flour to thicken the broth.

"How old is he?"

"Forty-two." Arion smiled. "We are of an age, the Blessed One and I. And my wife gave me a daughter last winter. Get me that flour sack—there, by the left cupboard."

She did as he directed, cutting the top off the bag with the knife she'd used for the onions. "Who is the man with the Captain?"

"That's Angolis Trier, Prathe Lendra's steward."

"And who is Prathe Lendra?"

Arion almost dropped the flour and sifter into the pot. "He's Master of this ship. And most every other ship that's come out of Bassorah this spring." His face paled beneath his ruddy tan—more reaction than he had given in any of their talk about Emperors and Bissanty gentry. "You must know his name—"

"Why should she?" Tullier was at the galley door, staring in with a furious expression. He seldom took part in Gaultry's and Arion's exchanges. His interruption now came with a vengeance.

"No reason." Arion, hearing the temper in the boy's voice, gave Tullier a nervous bob. "Leave me to my cooking!" he said to Gaultry, his voice growing shrill. "I don't have time for this chatter!"

"What was that about?" Gaultry followed as Tullier stalked back to their bunks.

"You don't know anything." Tullier was genuinely upset. "You're going to get us both killed."

"Do we have business with this Prathe Lendra?" Gaultry asked. "That's not a Bissanty name. Is he a foreigner?"

"A foreigner in all but power," Tullier said. "Llara in me! Who is Lendra? He's the man who petitioned the Emperor to end the Sha Muir charter. He claimed our envoys were bad for trade."

"I'd imagine this Prathe Lendra must be right about that," Gaultry said dryly. She could not imagine why Arion had answered her questions about the Emperor and his kin with such calm, only to panic on hearing Prathe Lendra's name. "I'd think even a distant King would hesitate before doing business with a power who thinks it's a god-granted right to send assassins down on those who oppose them."

"Bissanty is not a Kingdom," Tullier said. "It is an *Empire,* ruled by the get of the Supreme Mother. Prathe Lendra did himself great dishonor by attempting to dissolve Llara's own temple."

Gaultry had become familiar with the fixed expression that sometimes came to Tullier's eyes when he spoke of Sha Muira and the Great Thunderbringer. It came when he most missed the bond of poison, the comradeship of faith. She preferred not to push him when those feelings ruled him. But there were also times when it would have been wrong for her to back down. "Those things may be true. But regardless of whether or not Prathe Lendra has any honor, he clearly has power, and all Bissanty, even those who believe in Bissanty's goddess-given rights and powers, are afraid of him. Which is why it is his name, and not the Emperor's, that makes a man like Arion tremble."

The ice in Tullier flared to heat. "It's not like that!"

Gaultry, deciding there was no sense in continuing the conversation, bent to check the single bundle she'd made of their belongings. She'd wrapped everything in a piece of sailcloth she'd bartered from one of the crew. Weatherproof, but not waterproof.

But Tullier had not finished. "You're depending on me to help you through the city," he hissed. "You have to listen to me. You may already have exposed us."

This was the most upset that she had seen him. "Are you saying Arion will betray us because I asked him who Prathe Lendra is? What does he care?"

"He doesn't give a damn that we're planning to avoid the customs guards," Tullier said. "No one does. There are a million heads in Bassorah City. What's two more, or less? But if we know so little of his Master's business that we might interfere with it—it could be worth his neck to not pass that on. Lendra is a vindictive man. If we were to cross him, and Lendra later discovered our cook had failed to report us, Arion could see the bite of slavery fall on his children."

"But our business has nothing to do with Prathe Lendra," Gaultry protested. "What could a slaver want with Bissanty's conspiracies in Tielmark?"

"I should kill him," Tullier said, ignoring her question. "You've already told him too much."

It was late afternoon when the ship nosed its way into Bassorah's inner harbor. A pair of dirty white towers guarded the harbor entrance. For long hours the city had been a low smudge of red tile roof and white towers on the far horizon; now it stretched far and wide, filling the eye. Mud-packed walls marked a low canal that ran away to the west, flanking the city. Ahead, ringing the inner harbor, baked mud-brick walls vied with the pallor of marble facing for precedence.

Gaultry had never seen anything like the scene that spread before her. The sheer number of people was overwhelming. It was market day in Bassorah, and the entire population of the marshes seemed to have rowed their flat-bottomed skiffs down the city's two main rivers to sell their wares. The harbor was crammed with boats that formed a shouting, waterborne marketplace for those who could not get permits to land at the city's wharves. Only the narrow channel to Slaves Wharf was left clear.

"Did you know it would be like this?" Gaultry asked.

Tullier nodded. "Sha Muira apprentices are supposed to spend a summer in Bassorah, learning the city." He leaned over the rail at her side, as fascinated by the spectacle as she. "I never went. The Arkhon chose me for a different service. But it didn't mean I didn't learn about the city, and her market and holy days."

A woman paddled her boat near the slaver, her husband crouched in the stern over a pile of dried fruit. "Crab-queens!" she called up. "Penny for five, twelve for two-penny!"

"Those are good," Tullier said.

Gaultry opened her purse and threw the woman a penny. Crab-queens turned out to be a variety of dark-colored apple, small, tart, and juiceless.

Ahead, thronged marble steps led down to the water's edge and an active fish-market. Slaves Wharf lay beyond, a short stone-clad stub of a landing with a single docking bay. Another vessel had beaten their ship into the dock: a red-painted slaver with a curved prow. Over its rail, Gaultry could see the heads of the slaves who were being unloaded. A lot of scuffling was taking place as they disembarked. It looked to be a more violent affair than she had expected. There were many troops on hand to help keep things under control. "What are they doing?"

"The priests are bonding the cargo as it comes off the ship," Tullier said. "Bassorah City likes a spectacle. They've been denied victories for so long, they think that a train of slaves is as good as a victory parade. But ordinance has it that the slaves must be bonded and safe before they can be marched out into the city."

Their own vessel shipped all but two pairs of its oars and glided to a halt at the entrance to the inner harbor channel. A small boat came alongside, low in the water with the weight of twelve guardsmen. Its Master called to their ship's Captain for leave to board, which was instantly granted. The guardsmen climbed nimbly up to the deck, their master, a fat man in brown robes, close on their heels.

"Wares!" the fat man cried. His voice carried clearly over the noise of the ship and harbor. "Show your wares!"

The crew, working briskly, threw open the iron grates. With the twelve extra men to control them, they got the slaves in order and marched them onto the main deck. The fat man strode up and down the deck, shouting and making them line up in rows.

"Wares!" the man repeated. "Come see the wares!"

Pleasure craft closed in around their ship, elegant narrow boats rowed by showily dressed servants. Gaultry had a brief glimpse of the Bissanty dandies who were their masters, soft powdered men who reclined on plush pillows feigning disinterest in what the new slaver had to offer.

Their bundle of belongings was between them as they stood at the ship's rail. All that remained was for Tullier to give his sign, and over they would go. Fifteen feet below, the brown water beckoned. The gap between their ship's hull and the crush of market-day boats was only two body-lengths. It wouldn't be much of a swim, Tullier had warned her. Beneath the surface of the water, the channel was narrow. After two yards of swimming, they would have to founder through shallow water across a submerged bank of silt, attempting to hide themselves among the bobbing boats before anyone took notice and cried for their pursuit.

The last of the Chauduks, big Kurkut and his chain-partners, were up on the deck, surrounded by a crush of guards. Behind them came the Ardanae, led by the Sharif and her chain-partners, the stout man and the girl with the bandaged ankle.

A great horn sounded across the water. The boat ahead of them, having completed the discharge of its cargo, cast away from the wharf. With its slaves unloaded and no one aboard to row it—some fifty men stood on the stone flagging of the wharf, heads slumped in defeat—it was pulled away from the wharf by two smaller craft. Slowly the ship slipped free, riding high on the water. Its leisurely progress away from the wharf brought into sight the trio of silver-clad priests who stood, two of them holding white basins, the third man tending a brazier with a silver cover, ready to make the god-bond on the next shipload of slaves.

Gaultry found herself searching among the trios of slaves for the Sharif. It was easy to spy her. The tall woman was at the front of the pack, closely studying the spectacle of boats and harbor. Beside her, her young chain-partner was shivering, her stout chain-partner stoic, betraying no interest. But the tall war-leader stared around, still with an air of command, still calculating her odds of escape.

Gaultry, wanting to meet those stern eyes one last time, called a dart of magic. It leapt across the crowd, invisible, questing, and touched the desert woman's shoulder. The woman swung around. Her bright desert eyes met Gaultry's. If the touch of magic scared her, she did not show it. But then, from what Arion had told her, the woman was familiar with the use of magic. She had spoken in the minds of her soldiers—

The desert eyes burned into hers, swallowing her—

There was a frisson of magic, and the woman's spirit revealed itself. She was a great cat, unlike anything that Gaultry had seen, a tawny-colored creature of the desert. The eyes were the same, burning tawny-gold eyes that seemed to perceive infinite distances, to measure the world in the broad scope of the sky. Had the woman owned a tail, Gaultry was sure, it would have lashed furiously against her legs: in pride, in rage, in a stubborn refusal to beg for help.

I could help you, the desert woman said.

A shining flare of magic carried the words between them, unexpected like the bite of a whip. Gaultry would have drawn back, but she had dug so deep in her quest to see the woman's spirit that she could not break free without first untangling herself.

There are too many guards, too many Bissanty, she told the woman, struggling to break the link. A sudden bright image of Martin flashed through her, Martin chained in a dark prison and despairing. She was here for Martin; she couldn't allow herself to be turned from that. *I cannot help you.*

That's not what I ask. The woman's voice was pure magic and air, holding her—but not so tightly that Gaultry felt threatened. She could break free if she willed it— *I can help you. I will give you my sword, my life. Anything. You have the tongue of these people, the words that could hide me. And I could help you. I am strong, my heart is not weak. I could help you.*

The part of Gaultry that loved Martin screamed in protest. Image after image of the big soldier—dreadful in battle, demon-dark, then tender by her side in the aftermath, swept before her. He was bound to her by the geas, by the Rhasan, by a bond beyond magic that was something between love and a hard-learned loyalty. Nothing must get in the way of reaching him, of fighting to free him.

But another part of Gaultry's mind was cool, and it wasn't thinking of Martin. The woman was begging for her aid, refusing to submit calmly to the soul-death of slavery. How could she stand by and ignore that plea? *Make your own freedom,* that part of herself told the woman. *If you can make your own freedom, you can join us.*

Across the deck, the Sharif nodded. She looked down at her chain-partners. Gaultry could see her lips moving—

Then the Sharif flung out her arms and shouted something loud and hard at big Kurkut.

Gaultry did not understand her, but Kurkut's reaction was immediate and rash. He swung round. A chunk of pink flesh tore free from his mouth. Ignoring the injury, he bellowed, furious, and cried out to the men around him.

The Chauduks erupted against the Ardanae, hampered by chains but intent on striking them down. The Bissanty guards

between them were swept up in the sudden clash. They fell
back, struggling to bring their weapons to bear.

Tullier grabbed Gaultry's wrist. "Now," he said.

"Wait."

"What?" He was appalled. "Wait for what?"

The Sharif stumbled towards them out of the melee. She
was alone. Her chains hung off her like ribbons on a lady's
coat; the empty bracelets of her chain-partners clanked
against her wrists. The right bracelet swung open, its lock
picked or broken.

The left was an unbroken circle of steel, sheeted with
blood.

"Are you crazy?" Tullier howled, seeing that the woman
was headed their way. "What do you think you're doing?"

Gaultry thrust their bundle into his arms. "You take that.
I'll help her."

"What!"

"Let's go." She bundled him, still protesting, over the side,
and leapt after, trying to jump far out from the ship.

The water was warm and strong-smelling. Gaultry, coming
crookedly over the slaver's side, plunged under, then fought
· back to the surface, gasping. She flailed around in a circle,
trying to spot the Sharif. Tullier bobbed up to the surface with
the bundle, as capable at swimming as he seemed to be at
everything else he attempted, and his wet head made for a
space between two narrow boats with bright-colored streamers. In the general push to row backwards and to reduce their
proximity to the rioting slave-ship, no one in the smaller boats
noticed or cared that they were in the water. A chaos of badly
steered watercraft churned around them.

Above them, on the rail, the Sharif hesitated, poised
between freedom and slavery, her chains dangling. Something about the water was making her hold back.

"Jump!" Gaultry called, forgetting that the woman
wouldn't understand. She made a curvetting gesture with her
hand. "Jump! Try to reach me!"

The woman belly-flopped awkwardly into the water by
Gaultry's side. Gaultry took a faceful of foul water. The

Sharif, breaching the surface, plunged aimlessly, panicked. It took Gaultry a moment to realize that the war-leader couldn't swim, and then a moment more to realize that shouting not to panic wasn't helping.

Stop thrashing. She calmed herself and tried to touch the woman with her mind. *Stay still. I'll drag you ashore.* The woman's struggles subsided, and she allowed Gaultry to get close enough to grab her. From the look in the tawny-gold eyes, Gaultry saw that her helplessness in the water frightened her more than anything that had gone before.

"Tullier!" Gaultry called. "Come help me here!"

He came back unwillingly, dragging the bundle of their belongings, which still—barely—had buoyancy.

"This is stupid," he said.

"It's ghastly!" Gaultry answered, taking on another muddy mouthful as she struggled to hold up the Sharif's head. "I didn't know she couldn't swim!"

"What do you think desert-bred means?"

Between them, they wrestled the woman across the channel to the sloggy edge of the silt flats. She paddled inefficiently, trying to help them, her legs getting in the way.

Be still, Gaultry told her fiercely. *You should have told me—*

They reached the cover of the mass of pleasure boats. Here the new risk loomed that any one of them would be brained— more likely accidentally in the general uproar than intentionally—by an oar from one of the boats around them. Somewhere off to their left, a boat overturned. Its elegant slave-seeking passengers squalled in panic, demanding instant rescue. Gaultry, one hand on the Sharif and one on their bundle, found herself dropping both to prevent an oar from bashing out her front teeth.

"Go round to the left!" Tullier snapped, paddling beside her. "Keep moving!"

Beneath them was a bare eighteen inches of water, and beneath that, three feet or more of loose silt. The silt was deceptively hard-packed, giving an illusion of stability—an illusion which quickly dissolved with any attempt they made to push off of it. It would have been hard enough ground—if a submerged mud bank could be called ground—to struggle across unburdened. Burdened and in a hurry, Gaultry kept tripping forward, planting her face in the water.

A cry came from behind them—behind them and above, from the ship's deck. Gaultry's heart went into her mouth. Someone had finally noticed the Sharif's escape. She could hear Captain Odipo's familiar voice cutting through the chaos. An oar clipped her ear as yet another craft knocked against them. Gaultry looked up and met the eyes of a well-dressed servant. That clip by her ear had been intentional.

"Hit her again!" his master called.

"Help me," she shouted to Tullier. The boat was heavily overloaded, with three pairs of Bissanty gentry and two servants to row. As she caught hold of this boat's gunnel, already dangerously low in the water, the servant tried to hit her again. She thrust the gunnel sharply downwards. At first Tullier didn't see what she wanted—then he grinned, catching on, and brought his weight to bear. Even the Sharif, mimicking him, tried to help. Water sloshed over the boat's side. The passengers cried in alarm. The young gentleman who had told the servant to attack stood up to kick their hands away, but the moment of return had already fled. His weight tipped the balance, and the boat flipped over.

"And again!" Gaultry found herself mired in a particularly gummy patch of silt as she slopped away to capsize another boat. "Help me!"

The passengers of the boat they'd overturned dragged another boat under in their frantic attempt to escape the muddy water.

"My silks!" someone cursed.

"Let me up!"

In the widening chaos, Tullier and Gaultry dragged away the Sharif and their increasingly waterlogged bundle. Tullier pointed to the piers of a bridge, visible around a cut of the city's docks. It was low, with many arches and a decorative white colonnade.

"If we make it there we'll be safe," he sputtered.

With a goal in view, the struggle lessened. Once they cleared the press of expensive pleasure boats around Slaves Wharf, the watercraft around them were crewed by canny marketers who, ignoring the burdened swimmers, were happy enough to sit dry in their craft and watch the spectacle of Bissanty gentry struggling in the wretched slurry of water without raising a hand to interfere. The Sharif, her panic under control, was quiescent, letting them drag her.

Gaultry felt they were at greatest risk of discovery as they broke away from the pack of marketers' boats and crossed the short stretch of open water to the baked mudflats under the arches of the long, low bridge.

"Why isn't anyone coming after us?" Gaultry asked, risking a look back.

"No one cares except the slavers," Tullier replied. "No one wants to get involved."

As they passed into the bridge's shadow, Gaultry glanced up. Though the bridge was crowded, no one looked down, no alarm was shouted. They paddled the last few yards, under one of the bridge's arches, and came to ground on the far side, where the mud was packed hard enough for them to crawl out. The dirty children who lay in the sun on an abandoned pier nearby stared, but none of them bothered to show active interest, even when Tullier and Gaultry lugged the Sharif out of the thick brown water in her panoply of chains and manacles.

"They'll remember what they see," Tullier said, seeing where Gaultry's gaze rested. "But they won't do anything about it because they don't know what the stakes are."

"How strange." Gaultry's experience of city life was limited to the two weeks that she'd spent in Tielmark's capital after the Prince's wedding. That time had included a trip to the harbor as a member of Princess Lily's retinue—the fisher-child had wanted to visit her old haunts. The dock children in Princeport had not been overly forward. They had kept a suspicious distance from the resplendent party that had descended on them with no warning. But they had been loud and curious. By contrast, there was something lethargic in the way the Bissanty children watched them—something that made

Gaultry deeply uneasy. Where was their initiative, their curiosity?

She should have been grateful for their apathy. Tielmark was far away now. The lack of interest among the crowd of market-boatmen who had allowed their escape should have given her hope. If Tielmaran policy was only of interest to the Emperor and a handful of his cronies, the chances that she would be able to find Martin soon and return to Tielmark safely were greatly improved. But this country—she looked at Tullier's back as he hiked their bundle away from the waterline and realized what was wrong.

Tullier, the trained killer-child who had been raised only for death, was alert and vigorous. These children, in some way that she could not fully understand, were not. That was backwards, evidence of customs so foreign to her that she knew they must be dangerous to her most dearly held beliefs. It frightened her.

▼

chapter 11

They dragged the Sharif up the bank into the shade of one of the bridge arches. Out of sight of the bridge traffic, they dropped down onto the warm earth. In the quiet of the sun-bleached mud bank and the cool of the stone bridge, the tumult of the harbor by the slave pier dropped away.

"What possessed you to come after us?" Tullier asked the Sharif. He sat up and wiped his muddy hands on his legs. "And what possessed you to help her?" The Sharif met the boy's question with a puzzled shrug, Gaultry with a vaguely guilty wave of her hand. "She doesn't even share a tongue with us!" Tullier realized. "Llara help me, what—"

"We can speak," Gaultry said sharply. "She won't be an encumbrance. She did us service, providing cover to escape from the ship."

"Too much cover!" Tullier grumbled. "They wouldn't have cared if we'd slipped away quietly."

Gaultry suspected this was an unrealistic hope but did not want to argue. "It's done," she said. "We're not going to leave her, either, so stop grousing. Let's see if we can get her out of this ironwork before it rusts shut."

Tullier clamped his mouth in an angry line, but he bent to examine the problem without more argument.

The shackles were a jumble of old and new metal. Tullier took one of Corbulo's knives and used it to break up the clumsy locks on the Sharif's leg-fetters. As the fetters fell away, the blade snapped.

"Careful—"

The boy gave Gaultry a cool look and picked the fallen shards up out of the mud.

"You did that on purpose—"

He wouldn't give her the satisfaction of an answer. Moving deliberately, he inserted the longest sliver of sheared metal into the keyhole of the manacle lock that bound the Sharif's right hand. With some experimentation, he managed to shift the tumblers, and the circlet of iron popped open.

The last shackle refused to budge. The manacle on the Sharif's left hand, the manacle connected to the closed, blood-covered bracelet that had bound one of the woman's chain-partners, was of finer quality than anything else on the Sharif's body. "I can't shift it," Tullier said finally, after he'd broken a second shard in the lock. "Maybe it's set with a new kind of tumbler."

Gaultry fingered the closed circle of iron that swung free from its twin on the Ardana's wrist. The river had washed it a bit, but, back on the ship, someone had paid a high price for their leader to be free.

The desert woman reached out and took the closed ring out of Gaultry's hands. Her fingers were strong and hard. The women's eyes met, and the Sharif nodded. *Janier crushed his right hand for me,* she acknowledged, unshrinking in the face of Gaultry's judging gaze. *If they'd reversed the shackles, it would have been Lietha's left. That would have been better.*

Janier. The stout man who had shared the Sharif's oar. Gaultry remembered strong wrists and broad, heavy hands that matched his body. She measured the small circle of metal through which he would have passed whatever had remained of his hand. It was the thickness of her own wrist. *It's revolting,* she said.

The Sharif gripped her arm, preventing her from turning away. The height of the woman, her force, her intensity, bore down on Gaultry like a physical weight. *The sacrifice was not for me alone,* she said. *Janier has three daughters and a son. By his act, they have become mine to protect. After I have served you, and I am free of Bissanty, I will have other debts to pay. Can you understand that?*

"Maybe," said Gaultry, not feeling she could be honest, and tell the woman how disturbed she felt. She wondered how it felt, having a faith that was strong enough to make oneself believe that a mortal sacrifice in one's honor could ever be repaid. "Maybe."

"You're talking," Tullier blurted, perking with suspicion. "Did she threaten you?"

"We've agreed that this last shackle is staying on for now," Gaultry said curtly. She bent to open their waterlogged bundle. "She can hide it under my spare coat."

That didn't satisfy Tullier, but he seemed to understand from her tone that she didn't want to be pushed.

"We should move up to the bridge and mix with the crowd," he said. "If we stay here they won't ignore us forever." He pulled a dry shirt from their bundle. "If she's coming with us, we'll have to find her something to wear. What she's got now isn't respectable."

The Sharif's ragged tunic and loose-woven trousers were falling to pieces after the month or more she'd spent in the confines of the slave hold. When Gaultry offered the Sharif her tar-spattered practice shift—the only garment in their possession long and loose enough for her lanky body—the desert woman stripped eagerly, kicking her discarded rags aside. She had no shame of her lean well-muscled body. Gaultry noticed a deep scar across her shoulders, burned over by the unhealed slave brands she had received at the start of her voyage. There was another across the curve of her hip, and a third ran the length of her right arm. The savage boil on her throat had improved, but there was rawness running halfway up her back that looked deeply uncomfortable. It did not occur to the woman to wash her skin before she pulled her new clothes on over her head.

"She has lice," Tullier observed. "I'd keep my distance."

While Gaultry repacked their bundle, Tullier flung the slave-shackles deep into the river.

"This is the new triumphal bridge," Tullier said as they went up the little stair built into the nearest of the bridge's abutments. "It connects the old quarter of the city to the new."

"So somewhere nearby we may be able to find the Duchess's agent?" That would be a welcome relief.

The boy nodded. "If your friend Mariette gave us good directions."

The white colonnade Gaultry had seen from the water bisected the bridge along its length, dividing the traffic into two counterflowing streams. This allowed the city traffic to move with astounding efficiency. Gaultry found the hectic pace at which the crowd moved unnerving. There was so much to see, and they were passing by it all so quickly. Tullier guided them along in the direction he said headed to the old quarter, but the buildings on either side of the river looked old to Gaultry. Old, grand, much higher, and with many more ranks of windows than she was used to.

Gaultry soon lost any sense of where they were heading. Pressed at every side by a variety of people and trades, she felt almost overwhelmed. The sight of the Sharif, suffering the additional disadvantage of being unfamiliar with the tongue that was being babbled around her, yet still maintaining her composure, forced her to control her panic. The crowd, she reminded herself, was as much a protection as it was something to fear. Bassorah, Empire's center, had market crowds with enough mixed stock that her own bright hair and the Sharif's olive skin could pass without notice.

She wished she had names to put to the faces and races that went by them. The Bissanty features—sallow skin, sloped shoulders, and bony faces—dominated, but mixed in were more exotic types. Many tall, gray-eyed men crowded by her. They had the short, close-cropped heads of professional soldiers atop strong, powerfully built bodies. They would have reminded her of Martin but for their listless demeanor. "Who are they?" she finally asked, dragging at Tullier's sleeve.

"Who?"

"The tall men."

He looked where she was pointing. "They're recruits from Dramcampagna—Bissanty's northern Principality." He paused. "They're mostly farmers, but this year it's their turn to supply troops."

Which meant that these men could soon be on Bissanty's southwest border, pushing the mountain tribes there southward, into Tielmaran territory. "Tell me about the others," she said, not wanting to think about that. "I want to know what I'm seeing."

"You tell me," Tullier said shortly. "I don't recognize half the types, and I need to find this address."

So she was left to wonder. *It's like a play,* she told the Sharif.

It's like a nightmare, the Sharif answered.

It comforted Gaultry a little to know that the Ardana too found the crush of all the people intimidating. The crowd kept pushing past her, too numerous to keep track of. To her left she saw a trio of comely women with bells hanging from their ears; to her right, a wizened, pale-faced man who carried wicker wheels that fluttered with colored tags of paper. Then they turned a corner and were surrounded by a group of tattooed street-performers with brightly dyed hair, skin, and costumes.

Yet despite the press of exotic peoples, the majority of whom were more intent on their own affairs than those of strangers, it soon became clear to Gaultry that their little trio posed a spectacle dangerous to themselves. As they penetrated deeper into a neighborhood of tenement houses, more and more of the faces were sallow-skinned Bissanty, with the set, almost sullen expression with which Gaultry had begun to be familiar. There were few loungers in that crowd—most had an air of knowing their own business—and each time they stopped and Tullier asked for directions Gaultry felt herself being judged by many eyes.

When they arrived at last at the address Mariette had given them for the archer Arnolfo's family, they received the final blow: the small, neatly kept house was shuttered and empty.

"They'll catch us before we find a place to hole up," Gaultry said grimly. They had passed too many faces, been given too many curious looks. "There's no place to hide in this city."

"Shut up," Tullier said, staring at the shuttered door. "You're making me nervous."

"Knock again," she said.

"There's no one there." Tullier kicked the bottom panel, disgusted. "The bar is on the outside—so is the lock."

"So what do we do?"

He gave her a searching look. The green eyes were sharp, intense. "The crowd frightens you."

"You're the expert on fear," she snapped. "Of course it frightens me. Nothing in my life ever made me believe I'd travel to a city like this. Half my magic—" She stopped herself. She did not want to tell Tullier about the limits of her magic.

"Half your magic?"

"Never you mind. Elianté, the Hunt Goddess, is my guide," Gaultry said shortly. "That's enough. I can smell the hunters in this city. They're all around us. But I don't know how to read the signs and see them. That makes me scared."

"Not me," said Tullier smugly. "The Sha Muir training—"

Gaultry laughed, a sour, tired laugh.

"What is it?"

"A killer is not the same as a hunter," she said.

The boy's face reddened. "Why do you always pretend to have more answers than me?" he said. "I was trained to know this city—"

"So find us a place to hole up. Martin's trail is going cold, and I'm too tired to think. We need a good night's sleep. And"—she paused—"you are right. I'm going to have to find my feet in this city before we can go after Martin."

* * *

Finding somewhere to hide themselves proved less of a challenge than they had feared. A neighbor saw them knocking and came to see what they wanted. When they convinced her that Gaultry knew Arnolfo, she told them that the family's next-to-oldest son had been called for an unexpected turn of service and had taken the family with him to a military camp west of the city. No one was due to return for another month. All across the city, it seemed, there had been an unexpected levy of soldiers.

But when Arnolfo's neighbor discovered they needed a place to stay, she gave them directions to another house, a stuccoed tenement that overlooked the loop of the River Bas that ran through the city. The owners were a pair of elderly sisters, one widowed with an army son. With a week's rent paid up front, it was a simple matter to secure a garret-room, high on the fourth floor. The search for Arnolfo's family had brought them to a stolid, quiet city quarter populated by large soldiers' families who were struggling to make ends meet while the pillar of the house was away on an unexpected spring tour of duty. Their arrival had coincided with a time when many households were eager for lodgers.

Tullier told Gaultry they were renting the room illegally. Their landladies were hiding the rental to save themselves the price of the city's stiff head tax—one means by which the government tried to control the city's overcrowding. The woman who had referred them would take a cut of the rent money as well. "No one will want to say anything to the guard," he said. "They'd rather have money in hand than risk fines." Certainly, neither of the elderly sisters showed any inclination to ask awkward questions. They even offered, for a modest sum, to have their personal cook prepare their meals. Later, they offered the services of their own clothier. Behind their faded dignity they were eager for coin and glad to provide their guests anything they might need to make themselves invisible in the neighborhood.

The morning after their escape from the ship, Gaultry, staring out the room's single window after breakfast, listened to the sound of dishes being cleared and sighed with satisfaction.

With a full belly and a night's sleep, her fear of the city had faded. She itched to be out, starting her hunt for real.

It didn't hurt that the three of them were now dressed in a manner that would not unduly call attention to themselves. Their landladies' clothier had proved most efficient, outfitting Gaultry and the Sharif in crisp silver-gray livery, and Tullier in new trousers and a fine jacket that had been abandoned in the clothier's hands, unpaid for, by a former client. From the man's pinched expression and his air of relief when they agreed to take the jacket, Gaultry gathered that it was common custom in Bassorah for those who held rank to order such goods without paying.

The only thing their deceptively proper landladies hadn't been able to help them with had been the Sharif's last shackle. That matter they had dealt with privately, leaving a deposit at a local smithy's for some tools, then taking a quick trip to the river to dispose of the last of the Sharif's slave bonds.

The Sharif. She sat at the breakfast table, struggling to finish the portion of bread and porridge that Agrippilia, the old sisters' young cook, had brought her. Superficially, she looked fine, but she was not in good condition. She was having difficulty keeping any food in her stomach. Indeed, the more Gaultry knew about her physical condition, the more impressed she was by the woman's seemingly indomitable will.

Her time in the slave-hold had taken a severe toll. After they had removed her last manacle, Gaultry had convinced her to bathe. Lice, and worse, had crawled out of her hair. The rash on her back proved to be encysted worms. That last discovery almost made the Sharif lose her regal composure. Barely concealing her half-frightened disgust, she made Gaultry crop her matted black hair close to her skull and burn it, and then she rubbed her entire body with bitter spirits, all in an effort to kill the worms. It was not enough. It was necessary for Gaultry, with Tullier helping, to go over her back with a needle and tweezers. Then they sponged her down with spirits a second time, trying to finish off the worms that had escaped on their first sweep.

Gaultry fervently hoped that they would not have to repeat the process. Last night, while Tullier slept on a straw pallet by the door, she and the Sharif shared the room's single bed. Although the desert woman lay in exhausted slumber, her mind roiled with nightmares of her past month at sea. Gaultry, after lying awake for a long time picturing worms and lice, finally fell into a sleep of fitful dreams, interrupted by snatches of mindcall. That was the Sharif, reliving the horror of her last battle, crying out in her dreams in a way that she would not have allowed of herself while awake. Neither woman mentioned these episodes in the morning, but the Sharif didn't put up much of an argument when Gaultry told her to spend the rest of the day in bed.

Despite her fitful rest, Gaultry was up, alert and eager to go out into the city. With Market Day come and gone, she guessed the streets would have quieted, and she wanted to find her bearings.

Their attic window faced the Bas, upriver from the bridge where they'd pulled the Sharif ashore. A watery morning sun glinted off the white faces of the buildings, burning away the light mist that hung over the river. Day-craft quietly drifted downstream, slipping along with the gentle flow of the sluggish current, in no hurry to reach the market docks. Across the river, rising above the mist, was a low, scrubbily forested hill surmounted by the ruins of a pillared temple.

The ruined temple had been built over a fresh water spring— in centuries past, the only source of fresh water in all the great swamp—that had sprung from the ground on the spot where Great Llara had squatted to birth her mortal son, Meagathon, founder of the Empire. Now the hill was a lonely and desolate place, overgrown by trees and brush and no longer a living place of worship. As the Empire had grown and the needs of Llara's cult became more grand, the old temple's high altar had been moved across the river to the great silver-domed temple that rose over the rooftops on the city's east quarter.

"Why did they move it?" she asked Tullier as he came to stand beside her.

"The temple?"

She nodded. "Why move it, and why let the site crumble?"

"The spring in the East Quarter Temple is bigger," Tullier said. "And by now, in Imperial terms, it has as much history. The 'new' spring was discovered when they built the Imperial Quarter—seven hundred years back. The city needed more water, but the new spring was noisome and unfit to drink. Llara's Heart-on-Earth, the Emperor Livius the First, sent all five of his sons to purify it. They all drank, but only one survived. That was Demetricus the Lion." Tullier raised his hand, tracing the contour of the temple's great dome.

"I could show you," he said, looking a little hopeful. "We could go see the spot where he threw his brothers' bodies into the fountainhead, and their goddess-blood cleaned the water."

From what Gaultry had learned, she understood that the vaunted Imperial goddess-blood, like Glamour, manifested itself as an extra soul. She wondered if those four Princes had sacrificed those souls to the spring willingly. From the tenor of Tullier's story, she doubted it. "You want to see the city?" she asked.

"If nothing else, you need to lose your staring country-look."

"And you want to see the city," Gaultry pressed. There was something odd in his voice, as though there was more at stake here than mere sightseeing.

Tullier did not respond. He had the covert intensity of one who'd once been denied something he'd wanted—perhaps quite deeply.

The silence lengthened. This had something to do with his Sha Muir training. Something he couldn't tell her outright. They were both quiet for a little while, watching the lazy Bas move beneath them, the flow of the boats.

"We'll go," she said. "Of course we'll go." She wished she could touch him—rumple his hair or pat his back. Something beyond words that would show her sympathy. "I want to see the city too."

* * *

Bassorah was enormous. It would have taken them weeks to tour the city properly, particularly considering the wealth of detail that the Sha Muira Masters had drilled into their young apprentice. Tullier seemed to have anecdotes concerning the deaths of every Emperor and Prince for the past century and beyond. For every monument, public square, concourse, bridge, and fountain they walked past, he was able to recite a tale of murder or betrayal, the parties involved, and the methods employed. At first Gaultry found it morbidly amusing. As it went on, it began to fill her with disgust. Her mood came to a head at the pretty statue of a woman in a flowing dress. The statue's site was handsome, at the head of a long, marble-paved street. Gaultry, staring up at the laughing face, the hands stretched gaily to the sky, asked Tullier who had been murdered here.

"No one," Tullier said. "But the statue depicts Sylvie Aronlolia, so I expect fear keeps them away. She was Livius the Seventh's wife, about a century back."

"And?"

Tullier shook his head. "I don't remember everything. She was one of the busy ones. Five confirmed murders, and suspicions of others. She made her husband ghostmonger their children."

"Ghostmonger?"

"That's when an Imperial Prince who is not in line to inherit makes a woman pregnant in secret, and hides his sons, or some of his children. If he gets five sons before the reigning Emperor's heir, the goddess-blood flows to him and the Emperor's heir must cede the throne." Tullier stared up at the statue. "She must have been vain. By the time she had enough influence to make the city put up this statue, she was an old woman."

"What do you mean, when a Prince hides his children?"

"Llara gives five sons to only one Prince in a generation. And five sons is what it takes to make a true Emperor," Tullier explained. "It's not always the oldest Prince who gets them, but usually the oldest is in a position to stop his brothers from trying. Haven't you wondered at the number of monuments dedicated to Tarrin?"

"What do you mean?" Gaultry felt a sick feeling in the pit of her stomach. Tarrin, the White-Faced God of War, had a second title. The Castrated One.

Tullier pointed down the street. "Look there," he said. "And there. See those soldier's slabs up on the second story of that building? Tarrin's mark is on them." The slabs, which Gaultry had earlier noticed on many of the older facades, were memorials put up by soldiers come home safe from war. "Both those were dedicated by castrati Princes."

"You can't be serious!"

"You don't understand." Tullier made a face. "Llara's love of Meagathon's heirs is very strong. The Imperial House has always been prolific. They do what they must to keep things under control."

"No one questions it?"

Tullier shrugged. "Our emperor and his children are not like other men. They are Llara's Heart-on-Earth."

"Let's stop looking at monuments," Gaultry said. "It's tiring me out."

"Can we go to Llara's Temple? I want to see Demetricus's spring."

"Where he chucked in his brothers' bodies?"

Tullier's cheeks flushed. He had mistaken her self-protective flippancy for a genuine sneer. "The fountainhead that was built over the spring is supposed to be very beautiful. And it is sacred to Great Llara."

"All right," said Gaultry, regretting that she had made him feel so defensive. "But that's enough horror stories for now. And lunch first."

Back in Tielmark, Gaultry had given little thought to what it had meant to the thousand-year Empire to have lost control of their wayward southern Principality. The Bissanty were the enemy, Tielmark the victim. Tielmark's greatest Princes were those who had thumbed their noses at Bissanty's Emperors: Briern-bold, who broke the Bissanty army in battle on the centenary of Tielmaran freedom; or Corinne-fair, Prince

Benet's grandmother, who had spurned a scion of the Imperial House on the 250th. Or Clarin himself, the great Founder-Prince of Free Tielmark, who had warred with gods and Empire both to make his land free.

Now that Tullier had pointed out the soldier's slabs that had been dedicated to Tarrin, she began to notice them on almost every street corner. Tarrin's sign, a dark circle banded round with silver and white—the moon in eclipse—surmounted a large proportion of the stones that had been dedicated by Imperial Princes.

But in searching out these stones, her eye began to be drawn to something else. There were monuments to the lost Principality—which the Bissanties did not recognize as lost—on every other street corner. Many of the monuments had been erected centuries before Free Tielmark was born, and the early Imperial signatures—a stout-bellied tree with five branches; a braceleted hand with its fingers outstretched—made little impression. But the more recent monuments, those that had been erected within the latest span of three hundred years, were striking for their sheer numbers.

Finally they came upon a public bathing house that was dedicated to "Llara, the House Imperial, and the five Princes of Meagathon." It was a shining new building with marble towers at its corners. The dome at its center was dedicated to the fifth Imperial Prince. The inscription that decorated its shining marble entrance drove the point home: the bathhouse commemorated the birth, seventeen years past, of Prince Inseguire Pallidonius, the reigning Emperor's oldest son.

Tielmarans, many of whom did not use surnames, knew their first Prince as Clarin. Clarin-the-Great, Clarin-first-Prince, or Clarin-the-Courageous, if they were being formal. But to Bissanty, the rebel Prince of Tielmark was Clarin Pallidonius, youngest heir to Demetricus the Eleventh. As the chiseled letters made plain, despite Clarin's rebellion, the surname had remained in the Imperial family.

A tremor passed through her. Tullier tugged on her sleeve. "If you'd like to see a bathhouse, there's a bigger one on the triumphal way. The ladies can go in there."

"It's not the building," Gaultry said. "It's the inscription. Tullier, does the Emperor's oldest son have a landholding?"

"He's Prince of Dramcampagna."

A little color returned to Gaultry's face. Tullier smiled, unkindly, suddenly understanding her question. "You thought the Emperor's firstborn might be the Orphan Prince of Tielmark?" He laughed. "That's what they call it, you know—the unlucky title that the lowest Prince of Bissanty must bear at every formal convocation. No, these days the Bissanty Prince of Tielmark is the Emperor's younger brother. Sciuttarus's sons have the three highest princeships: Dramcampagna, Montevia, and Averios. Then there's the Sea Prince—the Emperor's uncle, who rules the archipelagos—and last, poor Tielmark."

"Bissanty is never going to let Tielmark go," Gaultry said tightly.

"Free Principalities can be bonded again." Tullier led her on past the bathhouse. "Averios was free for more than a century."

"Averios is the valley Bissanty calls its bread box?"

"Llara mine!" Tullier said. "Don't you know anything? Well before Tielmark ever made any move to freedom, Averios swore itself to Llara's son, Rios, the sword god. Llara made them a free Principality for the span of their hero-prince's blood. The first Sciuttarus, the current Emperor's namesake, butchered the last of that line in his cradle—the hero-prince's grandchild—and brought the land back into the Imperial fold. Tielmark's pledge is so much more fragile—a marriage to a bride of pure Tielmaran blood. You'd think that would be easier to break—"

"Clarin promised the gods' common blood, not pure blood," Gaultry corrected him. "The pledge is meant to honor the land, not good breeding. In Tielmark, we worship our land, not our ruler's godly heritage. That was the point of seceding from the Empire. Our Princes rule for the land's health—not that of their blood heirs."

As she spoke, a sliver of coldness lanced her body. She

stopped, arrested by the pain, and crossed her hands over her heart. "Do you feel that, Tullier?" she asked.

He shook his head.

Around her, the street bustled: merchants, traders—all the busy people of Empire getting on with the day's affairs. But for Gaultry, a stab of anguish had pulled her up short, crushing the breath in her chest. Not a spell—something deeper. A long, slow pulse moved through her, and a resplendent image of the Great Thunderbringer, toiling on a fire-blasted hill to bear Meagathon her only mortal child, flashed before her. The goddess had given her son that hill, and Bissanty in perpetuity.

In Tielmark, Great Llara had ceded the land to her Heavenly Daughters, allowing them to crown Clarin and his heirs Prince. But the Prince of Tielmark did not own the land—he owned the right to defend it, so long as he maintained his godpledges. "Kings and Emperors can bargain with the gods. Not Princes." Gaultry whispered the words the old Duchess of Melaudiere had rasped in her ear the night she'd left for Bellaire.

"What's that?"

"I want to see the temple now. Aren't we almost there?" Gaultry spun around, trying to spot the great silver dome above the rooftops. Oh, Great Twelve take me, she thought, her heart pounding in her chest. The Duchess had been right. While Tielmark was ruled by a Prince, Llara would continue to bless her son-on-earth, the Emperor, with five sons. The fifth son would always hunger for Tielmark's soil. "Is it this way?" she asked Tullier, trying to push the revelation away. .

"Not that way. That goes back to the river."

Llara's Great Temple, the spiritual center of Greater Bissanty, was an ungainly building. To support its mammoth dome, it had to be ungainly. Heavy stone piers buttressed the great silver dome on six sides. Hewn from flawless panels of white marble, the doors that flanked the gaping cavern of its entry rose up more than forty feet. Gaultry had never seen a larger building. Even the Prince of Tielmark's palace, a rambling cluster of buildings that rose upon the side of a hill, would have been dwarfed beside it.

"Are they having a service?" Gaultry asked. Somewhere in the echoing depths of that great central chamber a chorus was singing, the voices high and pure.

"I don't think so. But you may not want to go in," Tullier said. "These precincts are sacred to the Thunderbringer. You may feel her touch. It's like ice and fire together. Pray to any of the Great Twelve here and she will be the one who answers. You might find that unnerving."

"What makes you think I have never felt Great Llara's fire?" Gaultry asked, clasping her hands. They had reached the great marble doors. A cool draft touched her cheek, lifting her hair. It must have been from the movement of the crowds within, she told herself. That, or the movement of air shifted by running water.

Tullier gave her an inquiring look. "What do you mean?"

"I don't mean anything." She folded her arms, palms out of sight, and returned his stare. "Let's go in."

The soaring height of the dome made her head spin. It was painted with streaks of gold and silver. Frescoes on the side walls depicted Imperial triumphs, the touch of Llara's hand on numerous Emperors, and, at the temple's back, in an older, cruder style, an image of a giant, tumbling four smaller figures into a frothing stream.

She had been a fool to come. Llara's eyes were everywhere, and surely she would see Gaultry, the enemy to her Empire. She knew Llara's power. As she had hinted to Tullier, she had felt its touch. It was not like that of the Great Twins, the power she drew on when she prayed to Elianté or Emiera.

Gaultry had felt Llara's hand just once, when she had been halfway up a cliff on Tielmark's border. At that moment, the Great Thunderer had given her just two choices: submit or be dashed to the ground.

The young Tielmaran huntress stared up into the great

dome, awed by the height, the light, the temple the Bissanty people had built their goddess. *You didn't put it to me in quite those terms, Llara-bold,* she said to those airy heights. *Perhaps I could have reached up my hand and found another handhold, saved myself. But I had no faith in that. Wanting to live, I offered myself to you, offered you everything, rather than reaching. Did you spare me on that day so you could bring me here?*

On her hand she still bore the scar where she had been cut by the next spur of rock—the handhold that had saved her. A jagged scar, like the edge of a bolt of thunder. *Why did you spare me?*

No answer. Tullier moved restlessly beside her, not understanding. A priest brushed past them, deliberately knocking Gaultry's shoulder.

"We aren't actually supposed to stand here," Tullier whispered. "We're in the way. Let's find an empty side-chapel."

Gaultry, kneeling beside Tullier in the chapel, could not bring herself to call on Llara. *Elianté, Great Huntress,* she begged. *Lead me to Martin, lead me to the Black Wolf of Tielmark. Let me free him, let me take him safely home.*

And beneath that, the still more involuntary prayer, *O let your Mother's plan for me end swiftly, for I am frightened to discover that I still owe Her service.*

At her side, Tullier knelt, his eyes closed, his lips pursed. His prayers were substantially longer than hers, long enough to make Gaultry, finished with her appeal, grow first impatient and then worried.

As she moved restlessly, he startled, breaking his prayer. He spun around as if panicked, as if he feared that she had left him. He looked astonishingly young. "She hasn't left me," he told Gaultry. The glacial eyes shone with a gladdened light. "I hadn't known I was asking that. But She hasn't left me."

"Bissanty has many troubles," Gaultry said, glancing past the wrought-iron gates of the side-chapel into the great space of the main chamber. "Losing the love of her goddess does not appear to be among them."

They went back to their tenement room past a fruit market,

hoping to get something fresh that would hasten the Sharif's recovery. Gaultry was amazed by the abundant produce. She didn't recognize more than half the fruits, and many of the others on display were not yet in season back in Tielmark. Her mouth watered. There would be something here to tempt even the Sharif's fragile stomach. Delicate spring berries were piled high in woven marsh-grass boxes. There were already melons, peas, sugarcanes—and the small apples Gaultry had first tasted aboard the slave-ship. "There're crab-queens!" she said. "Let's get some."

"There's something Bissanty that you like?" Tullier said, watching her as she tried to pick the sweetest fruits. "How astonishing."

"I like many things Bissanty," Gaultry said. She paid the fruit-seller and took possession of the apples. "I liked Arion, on board the slaver. And certainly I like crab-queens. I even like your silver temple—though a spring where men were murdered doesn't in itself impress me. And what about our silly land-ladies, trying to earn an extra penny by spending four to send us their cook? Those things would be nice, in any country."

Tullier gave her a slightly crestfallen look. "What about—"

A call from behind cut him off. Four street urchins, acting together, had overturned a cart of dried peaches. The cart's owner, bawling to Llara, to the Market Guards, to the Emperor, fluttered about his cart, torn between collecting his spilled fruit and going after the culprits.

The boys were already far across the market square, running in the opposite direction from the market's watch-post. They need hardly have bothered, Gaultry thought. In the post, two soldiers lazily stood to their feet, slow to collect their weapons, and slower to move after the young culprits. The rest of the crowd simply stood back and watched the scene unfold.

"That," Gaultry muttered, "is something I don't like about Bissanty, even if I have benefited from it. People aren't even interested."

Tullier shook his head. "There's where you're wrong.

They're interested. They just know that helping might be more trouble than it's worth."

"Let's take our crab-queens and go home."

"I know how we're going to find Martin," she told Tullier. They were back in their room, eating crab-queens. The Sharif was up, and looking better. And Gaultry had begun to have a real plan. "It came to me when we were watching those thieves in the temple market. No one here acts unless there's a charter ordering it. And even then no one rushes to take action."

"The Sha Muira aren't like that," Tullier said, a trifle smugly.

"Which makes them alone in all the Empire and is no doubt why your Emperor has come to depend on them for his foreign policy. Them and this Prathe Lendra person who controls your shipping."

"The Sea Prince controls the shipping."

"Tell me someone other than Prathe Lendra owned the ship that you and your Master took passage on to Tielmark."

The silence that greeted this was its own answer.

"Where does Lendra live?" she asked. "Here in Bassorah?"

"He has a villa outside the old city walls. In the new quarter. Prathe Lendra was one of the men who mounted the subscription to put in the pilings, the year the Emperor's youngest son was born: Prince Titus Vargullis. The new quarter is called Vargullin in his honor."

"Vargullis is Third Prince?"

Tullier nodded. "There's a daughter as well."

"But his father needs two more male children to get Llara's blessing."

"He'll get them," Tullier said confidently. "It took his father twenty years. It's safer for the younger Princes if the gap is large."

"Why so? What about ghostmongering?"

Tullier shrugged. "There is that worry. But if the firstborn Prince has birthed three or more of his own sons before his father's fifth son is born, his younger brothers are less of a threat. Men of the Imperial House mature young—but no infant known can seed children."

"You're obsessed with potency."

"The opposite," Tullier said. "Our Emperor's curse is potency. He has no choice but to seed five sons. Tielmark doesn't have that problem. Your Princes are practically sterile."

"You didn't learn anything during your visit, did you?"

"Corbulo showed me what to see."

"You rejected Corbulo when you put a dart in his throat."

"You're using what the Sha Muira taught me to your own ends," Tullier said. "Who are you to talk?"

Why are you fighting? The Sharif, who had been watching them from her seat on the bed, got shakily to her feet and moved between them. The day of rest had helped her, but she was still having trouble keeping food down. *They'll hear you downstairs if you continue to shout.*

Gaultry, caught out, scuffed the toe of one of her new boots against the flooring. *We were trying to make a plan,* she said. *Instead, we're trading insults.*

The Sharif grinned, the expression relaxing her whole face. *He'll do what you tell him,* she said. *Anyone can see that. But he has his pride. Tell him he is a good boy. A good boy, and clever. Then he'll listen.*

Gaultry scowled. "That's the last thing he needs to hear," she said.

"What did she say?"

"You don't want to know."

"I do! You shouldn't keep secrets—"

Look at him. The Sharif sat back on the bed, her eyes gleaming with mischief. *He's jealous.*

What! Gaultry snapped. *He doesn't even like me. I explained to you about the soul-bond. He's fighting that; it's difficult for him—*

Harder still when his mistress won't recognize his affection.

"She's impossible!" Gaultry turned back to Tullier. "Not that you're any better. Of course I need you to help me. We're going to be tied together until there's no trace of Sha Muir poison in you, and Elianté only knows how long that will be, with you still sweating black ash. Maybe I should have left you in Princeport, maybe I should have trusted my own Prince not to let his court lynch you.

"But it is not in me to play a game where another's life is the stake. That's a weakness, I know. It certainly means that I can't use my power to bully you, though Elianté knows, you tempt me!"

"You admit it then! I am your slave!"

"Whine on!" Gaultry said, losing her patience. "I'm not going to reclaim my soul-piece before you're fit to live without it."

Agrippilia, gently knocking on the door to bring in their dinner, put an end to their bickering. She'd brought baked chicken, rice, and an orange-colored legume that tasted like parsnips. Everything except the rice was too strong for the Sharif's stomach, so Gaultry and Tullier got her share. The trio consumed their food in silence. There was a sort of strawberry jam for dessert. That, the Sharif could eat.

"So what is your plan?" Tullier said, wiping his mouth on his napkin. The food had settled his temper. "Why do you want to know about Prathe Lendra?"

"He owns the lion's share of the ships that cross to Tielmark. You told me yourself that you came to Tielmark on one of Prathe Lendra's vessels. The Sha Muira who brought Martin back must have returned to Bissanty on one of Prathe Lendra's vessels as well. Remember the morning when the ship's officers left, and that the old man with the thin legs came on board?"

"Angolis Trier."

Gaultry nodded. "Lendra's steward. He brought a big ledger onto the ship with him. It looked like it went with him everywhere. My guess is there's an entry in that book, or another like it, which records Martin's arrival, and maybe where he's been sent."

"That's no good to us," Tullier said. "The records will be under lock and key at Prathe Lendra's offices."

"How difficult can it be to break into an office?"

"I'm not going near Prathe Lendra!"

"That's not what I'm asking," Gaultry said. "We'll keep well clear of him. But Trier wasn't traveling with lots of guards. If we didn't want to draw attention to ourselves, we could probably catch him in the street and take the ledger off him."

"That's a terrible idea. Lendra wouldn't stand for having one of his most important servants assaulted."

"Which is why having a quiet look at the ledger without anyone knowing makes sense." The Sharif was right, Gaultry thought. She was going to have to flatter him. "Just think, Tullier. Picking locks is nothing to you. You had the Sharif's shackles opened in no time, even without tools. Imagine how much simpler it will be with adequate preparation."

"It's not a good idea," Tullier said. "Prathe Lendra's holdings are all consolidated within the grounds at the Villa Lendra: his palazzo, his workshops, his offices and stables. We can't burgle his steward's office without getting far too close to *him*."

"We can find out where the office is," Gaultry said. "It may prove a false lead, but that at least is worth trying. Besides"—her eyes flicked to the Sharif—"another day spent exploring Bassorah will be good for everyone. She can rest, and we can get a better grounding in the city."

"A big help she's proving!"

"Stop being a shrew," Gaultry said. "Another day's rest and she'll be back on her feet."

Gaultry crossed to the window to stare out at Llara's hill, hiding her smile. Tullier, by retreating to complaints about the Sharif, had ceded her the point.

Gaultry's first sight of the Villa Lendra went a long way toward explaining Tullier's wariness of Prathe Lendra and his workings. The villa was far across the city from their comfortable soldier's billet. They had the choice of a ferry ride across the Polonna to reach it or taking the old bridge out of the city and reentering Bassorah from a more recently built city-gate. To avoid passing writs of entry, they opted for the ferry. The villa's gardens could be seen from the ferry's deck: the elaborate marble tiers of groomed garden and ornamental trees rose up, elegant, from behind grimly barricaded fencing at the water's edge. That was as Gaultry would have expected.

But the villa was more extensive than she had envisioned. It was not a house, it was a miniature city: workrooms, arcades, interconnected palazzi, and warehouses built right down to the river's edge, downriver from the barricaded gardens. She began to appreciate Tullier's urgings for caution.

The ferry dropped them at Vargullin Pier, a broad half-circle of marble. They followed paved steps up to a wide avenue, flanked on both sides with well-fortified mansions. The avenue was thronged with foot-traffic. They pushed their way through the crowd. Gaultry was surprised to discover she had already become somewhat accustomed to the press of bodies. Soon, they made their way round to the front of Prathe Lendra's villa. Facing the avenue, a central building formed a U-shape around a gracefully proportioned courtyard. At the back of the U, a magnificent double curve of marble stairs led up to the main entrance, on the second level of the building.

The double doors of the main entrance stood open, giving Gaultry a glimpse of a great space within, and a pair of footmen standing back in the shade inside the doors to escape the heat of the day's overcast sun.

Nothing separated the courtyard from the bustling street, yet the courtyard was empty, a cool, empty expanse of polished stone and tubs of ornamental plants.

"It's not magic," Gaultry said, watching how the crowd stood back, as though an invisible line was there to keep them out.

"It doesn't need to be. No one in Bassorah wants to entangle themselves with Prathe Lendra, unless they are clear on the terms."

Even though Gaultry knew she should be intimidated, she was not ready to give up.

They loitered. Occasionally someone would walk in from the street. They'd ring a gold bell on a pillar at the foot of the double curve of stairs and wait for a footman to direct them. Grander visitors entered via the main entrance, lesser went to a door that was tucked under the curve of the steps.

Just as they were ready to move on, Angolis Trier strolled past them, his stork legs tightly clad in black stockings decorated with gold thread, a fine brocade jacket swinging over one shoulder. Gaultry had been right—the man did not travel with a substantial guard. Today, he only had a pair of boys to keep him company, one in red silk, one in blue.

The boy in blue fumbled with the ledger that Gaultry had seen two days before on the slaver, clutching it clumsily to his chest. It was not the boy Gaultry had seen before: the book was too heavy for this child, and he was struggling. But it was the same book.

"Hurry up!" Angolis Trier called as the boy fell behind. The steward, followed by his boys, disappeared inside the door under the grand staircase.

"Does that lead to offices," Gaultry wondered aloud, "or just a servers' entrance?"

Tullier shook his head. "I don't know. We could ask."

"Is that a good idea?"

"None of this is a good idea."

Two minutes later, the boy in red—the one who hadn't held the ledger—shot out of the door at the top of the staircase. He ran lightly down the steps, then across the yard—so intent on his errand he collided with the gardener, who had come into the court to shift the flower tubs.

"Here, Godo," the gardener barked, giving him a good cuff. "Watch where you're headed."

"Master Trier has an unexpected errand." The boy whimpered, pulling away. "He told me to hurry and fetch round his horse."

"Go on then." The boy, running at a good clip, disappeared into a covered passage that let off one side of the court.

Tullier nudged Gaultry. "Wait by the corner," he said. "Once Trier leaves, I'll ask someone if I can call on him in his office."

"Ask the gardener," Gaultry suggested. Tullier gave her a black look, but complied.

When he met her on the corner, he had news about Trier's office. "You were right," he said. They turned back toward the pier and started walking. "It's inside that bottom door, more or less. The bad news is that the front court is guarded at night."

"We wouldn't be going in the front door in any case."

"The rest of the building will be guarded too."

"We aren't trying to steal anything," Gaultry said. "We only want a small piece of information."

"That's not how Prathe Lendra will view it," Tullier said. "Besides, we've stolen from him already. We stole the Ardana Sharif."

"The Sharif was never his property," Gaultry said. They had reached the ferry pier. The half-circle of marble was empty. They had just missed a boat and would have to wait. Gaultry wrinkled her nose. The Polonna was narrower than the Bas: narrower, slower, and dirtier. Tullier had explained that this part of the city was built over a thick bed of marsh. Pilings had been driven down through more than twenty feet of mud and debris to stabilize the buildings' foundations.

"The villa is certainly impressive," Gaultry said, glancing along the river to the building's barricaded backside. "Prathe Lendra is obviously rich. But what, exactly, makes him so feared?"

"He's a blackmailer," Tullier said. "He's rich because he's a miser with information and extravagant with money. Anyone who takes his favors soon discovers that he won't give them any chance to repay him in coin. He knows everyone's secrets."

"Even the Emperor's?"

"I don't think we've sunk as far as that," Tullier said. "Llara's Heart-on-Earth can keep his own counsel."

"Speaking of which," Gaultry said, "we've seen Llara's

temple, the markets—and now Prathe Lendra's house. When are we going to see the Emperor's?"

"It's not like the temple," said Tullier. "Or even Villa Lendra. There's not so much to see from the outside. It's also," he added, "in the north reach of the city."

"Don't you want to see it yourself?" She did not understand his reluctance.

"We can go," Tullier said hesitantly. "It could be interesting."

Across the river, the ferryboat had finished loading. They watched it make a lumbering turn, pointing its blunt, straw-padded bow back towards them. Tullier's eyes were fixed on the boat.

"I forgot," he said. "I forgot that I could visit it now. Sometimes—sometimes the changes are hard to remember."

Gaultry waited, hoping he would finish the thought before the ferry drew too close.

"Under the laws of Sha Muira and Empire, I cannot come within sight of the obelisk that dominates the palace's front court and expect to live. But—" He hesitated again. "But those laws no longer govern me." He gave Gaultry a serious look. "I am your man, soul and body."

She shifted, uncomfortable, not liking his choice of words. "You're not my man," she said. "We are companions. If you like, I'm your protector. While you continue to need one. Your soul and body are your own." She paused, trying to lighten the trend their words had taken. "Let's get something to eat. Then, if you want, you can return to our rooms, and I'll go on to the Emperor's palace by myself."

Tullier shook his head. "My path is with yours."

chapter **12**

▼

It's not exactly prepossessing," Gaultry said. "But it does make you believe in the Emperor's power."

The Imperial Palace had been built for inaccessibility rather than for grandeur. It sat at the rear of an enclosed court, offering only limited views from the street. At Villa Lendra, the fore-court arrogantly opened itself to the grand avenue it fronted, as if daring passersby to enter. This court made no attempt to acknowledge outsiders: a tall marble-faced wall shut it safely away from public view. The wall was grand but plain, its sole concession to ornamentation a row of statues on its pediment, many of them so worn by time that they were barely recognizable as human figures. The restricted view through the main gate gave glimpses of two gold fountains and, between them, the tall obelisk of which Tullier had spoken. Gaultry had an incomplete impression that the palace was grand as well, but all she could see was a short stretch of the facade which left her no sense of the building's overall design.

"Does the Emperor ever show his face in public?" she asked. They went past the main gate, following the wall to see if there might be another entry where they could get a better glimpse of the building. Several others were taking the same route. From their appearance and dress, they too were visitors from outside the city.

"Not often." The street outside the courtyard wall was narrow and needed new paving. Tullier, who had been almost timid at the gate, crossed to the wall and touched his hand reverently to its smooth marble face. "I never thought to stand here," he said.

"Stop that," Gaultry said, worrying he would draw attention. She could not have told him why that simple gesture made her nervous. Probably it was his wistful tone, his unconscious yearning for his Sha Muir certainties. She glanced up the street, tensing. "Someone's coming." The other sightseers had noticed a disturbance as well. They were moving out of the street. More than one person was coming. She could hear the sound of drums, whistles, and stamping feet. "Get back over here!"

Tullier turned, but it was already too late.

An unexpected throng of people flooded the narrow street, moving almost at a run, separating them as swiftly as a rising tide. Gaultry, struggling to keep Tullier's head in sight over the crowd, found herself dragged along by the sheer mass. Many in the crowd were wearing painted leather hoods, disguising their features. Others were wearing silver-colored armbands and crowns of rags and wire. Someone behind her laughed, and all around her rough voices were calling out. The drum started again, and then the whistles and rough music.

She panicked and tried to fight against the flow of humanity. "Tullier!" she called. "Tullier!" Her voice blended in with the general noisemaking, its hint of desperation swallowed.

As one, the crowd broke into a chant:

> *Sciuttarus had three sons, and fine sons were*
> *   they.*
> *First Prince went to the west to war; he came*
> *   home in stitches,*

The Second had a great amour, throwing off his
    britches,
Third son cried for mercy, fleeing first son's
    tricks
May they live a long life, and water the land with
    their—
Ha-hah, ha-hah!
Sciuttarus had three sons, and fine sons were
    they.

First one burnt his crops down, second took to
    harm,
Third son killed his Princess, calling an alarm.
Goddess see you angry, Llara fare you well,
Bissanty is a prison, and we're off to—

"Gaultry!" Tullier, bursting through the crush to her side, grabbed her by the elbows. His eyes were huge and frightened. "Llara's breath, we've got to break out of this! The guard will come down on them any minute now!"

"What's happening?" It was a struggle even to keep their feet. The crowd swept them along, gaining momentum, then bottlenecked where the way narrowed at a shop that jutted into the street.

"That alley—next to the shop! Cut in there!"

With a goal in sight, they managed to push past the music-makers and out of the stream of bodies. Gaultry's heart hammered in her chest, sped by the music, the press of the crowd, the taste of danger. "Who are they? What do they think they're doing?"

"They're getting the guard called out," Tullier said, "protesting Llara's Heart-on-Earth!" He stared, disbelieving, at the mob that pushed by the alley's head. "They don't think Sciuttarus's sons are good for much. Did you hear what they were saying?"

Gaultry shook her head. "I only heard the song."

"They want the Blessed One to produce another son or cede the throne to one of his brothers. As if the Emperor need prove himself to *them*." The idea clearly disgusted him. "Sciuttarus levied another birth tax for his children. That triggered this."

Out in the street a horn blared, and then another, sounding an alarum. The clash of metal on metal rang out. "Let's move!" Tullier retreated up the alley, his haste and anger making him stumble on the clutter of trash and boxes. Gaultry, somewhat breathless, stumbled after him. More horns sounded. A member of the mob, escaping the street, pushed past them, then another, both faces twisted with fear beneath the ragged crowns. "Faster!" Tullier urged her. "We must keep ahead of them!"

They ran together through the dirty maze of alleys and back streets, discovering more swamp and less pavement in these backways than Gaultry had expected, considering the handsome condition of the main avenues. Gaultry sensed that Tullier was running blind, but the urgency he projected stopped her from questioning their route. Gradually, however, whether by design or chance, they left the rapidly dissipating mob behind. Not long after, they emerged from a sooty byway onto one of the city's wider boulevards.

To the left, the road led down to the Bas. Across the way, Great Llara's dome loomed above the city. "I know where we are," she panted gladly, excited to recognize the landmarks.

"We could have been killed." Tullier was still upset. "What would have happened if I had not reached you so quickly? If the guards had picked us up with the rest of that mob, we'd be for the block."

"Why did it happen?" Gaultry asked. "And so close to the Emperor's palace!"

"Madness. What else could it be? The holy week of the Sciuttarii—the Emperor's children—is almost on us. It's the birthdays of his victory children—the older Princes and the sister. Those people were protesting the levy for the celebrations."

That brought Gaultry to a stop. "What happens in the city during the holy week?"

"Festive parades for seven nights. Torches in the street,

sacrifices to Llara, feasting. It's still three nights away." He spoke reluctantly, realizing as he was speaking that this was information Gaultry would have preferred to know earlier.

"We'll have to visit Trier's office before the celebrations begin," Gaultry said uneasily. "Don't you think Prathe Lendra's house will be a hive of activity once the carousing begins? We can't delay. We'll take the rest of today to ready ourselves. And tonight—tonight we'll break in and have a look at that ledger."

"That's far too soon," Tullier countered. "Our chances for success are better if we take a decent amount of time for preparations."

"Tullier." Gaultry shot him an anguished look, unable to conceal her distress. "Delay is too risky. Time is not our friend here. If Martin is forced to take the slave-bond because I have wasted one day, how will I ever forgive myself? Besides, what more is there that we can do by waiting, other than draw suspicion to ourselves?"

"The whole city will be on watch after that protest we saw."

"Do you think the problem is so widespread?"

"I don't know. But a riot is a serious business. People will be worrying. The Watch will certainly be alert tonight."

"I am not a fool," Gaultry told him. "But we must try tonight, if only to see if it is possible. If there is a guard on every window, I'll accept that our attempt on the house will have to wait."

They completed their journey to the tenement in silence, Gaultry absorbed in her own thoughts, Tullier in his. Gaultry wondered how to interpret Tullier's upset over the chanting mob. Was his unbending acceptance of the Emperor Sciuttarus's right to rule a Sha Muira oddity, or was it a reflexive impulse that all Bissanties shared? In some ways the boy had led a sheltered life, and she guessed that his opinions could not be regarded as characteristically Bissanty. As a Sha Muira apprentice, he had never had to provide for his own food, clothing, and shelter. Among the populace, beneath their air of complacency concerning their Imperial ruler, the Bissanties Gaultry had met seemed deeply discontented, drawing strength from their devotion to Goddess and Emperor, yet highly sensitive to the divisions in their society. That the Emperor was Llara's Heart-on-Earth bridged the yawning gap of discontentment. But if the people came to feel that the reigning Emperor had usurped the place of Llara's true chosen one . . . She wondered how long Sciuttarus could remain in power as Emperor, even behind his high marble walls, if his people lost faith in the Thunderbringer's blessing on his rule.

As they turned into the shabby alley that led to the back stairs of their tenement, she asked Tullier a last question. "Could that crowd have been right? Could it be that Sciuttarus has usurped the throne?"

Tullier shook his head, emphatically. "He has earned the right to rule. He is his father's oldest living son—and no one disputes that his father had Llara's blessing."

"But it's not necessarily the oldest son who inherits the throne, is it?" Gaultry said. "It's the first one who fathers five sons. Maybe one of Sciuttarus's brothers has ghostmongered. You told me already that he has a living brother—your lackland Prince of Tielmark."

"Only one man in an Imperial generation can father five sons," Tullier corrected her. "Once one gets five, Llara won't let the others match him. On the other count, you are right—Sciuttarus has several brothers who are still alive." He stood behind her as she fished in her pockets for the flat iron key that would let them onto the back stairs. "But he took measures that they should not usurp his rights as his father's first heir." He paused. "You won't want to know the details. In Sciuttarus, Llara has blessed us with an Emperor who is jealous in the extreme of any threat to his honor or his standing. His brothers never had a chance to seize Llara's blessing. Anything that might appear to lessen the Blessed One's own glory is dealt with directly. Even Sciuttarus's uncle, the Sea Prince, has felt the bite of his jealous nature." He started up the stairs, as though his explanation was complete, but she held out her arm to bar his way.

"Explain that last bit," she said. "Starting with why the Sea Prince is the Emperor's uncle instead of one of his brothers."

"If the Emperor is lacking sons, there's no rigid precedence for which of his male relations get to sit on the Princes' seats. Sometimes it is even a man's capacity and talents which keep him there. That's why the Emperor's uncle is still Sea Prince." Tullier raked his hair back from his face, the glacier green eyes glinting in the shadowed light of the stair. "Siri Caviedo has served Bissanty as Sea Prince under three Emperors—mostly because there has been no living Emperor's son who was of age during the whole of that period, but also because he is an effective seaman and commander.

"As for the Sea Prince feeling the bite of Sciuttarus's envy . . . When Sciuttarus ascended the throne, he had no children. One year later, following his victory weddings, he had two sons. The Sea Prince made the mistake of getting one of his lovers with child that same year. The Sea Prince's lover, Luka Pallia, made the mistake of giving birth to the Sea Prince's child a month before any of Sciuttarus's wives were brought to bed. Sciuttarus took that as an insult. When Luka died of poison the day of the birth, everyone saw Sciuttarus's hand in it."

"I don't understand," Gaultry said. "Why kill her?"

"It's complicated," Tullier said. She sensed there was something in the story, some ugly Bissanty perversity, that he hesitated to tell her. "Luka was a performer at the great Bassorah theater. The Sea Prince pursued Luka for some time before the relationship was consummated. Siri Caviedo was already in his middle years then, and had never shown any interest in children. When Luka became pregnant, everyone in the streets made jokes about the fire of the Prince's unexpected potency, which Sciuttarus, who had had some trouble getting his wives pregnant, resented. He liked it less when people began laying bets, guessing which of the Imperial consorts would come to bed first—Luka or the Emperor's women. When Luka Pallia delivered the Sea Prince's child before any of Sciuttarus's wives—to Sciuttarus, that was the final insult." Tullier started up the stairs, avoiding her eyes. Gaultry followed, close on his heels. He was hiding a piece of the story, that was certain.

"I'm not surprised the people question whether Sciuttarus has Llara's blessing," she said. "He seems to question it himself."

"Emperors must protect themselves." They reached the top landing. Tullier thrust open the door. The Sharif was dozing by the window, the last golden sun of the day touching her face. She woke as the door opened, and smiled in welcome. In return, the boy frowned. "Whether or not the Emperor has Llara's blessing, that doesn't change."

Tullier spent what little was left of the day meditating in preparation for the mission. After all they had shared in recent days, his withdrawal was disconcerting. When he emerged from his trance, the set of his face brought Gaultry uncomfortable memories of his attempt to desecrate Prince Benet at the Goddess Emiera's feast. He buckled Corbulo's spring-device onto his wrist, intent and focused. To her great surprise, he had made a complete turnabout in his attitude toward the night's work. Jettisoning his initial resistance to Gaultry's decision to break into Angolis Trier's office, he told her he now intended to visit Prathe Lendra's villa alone, and to search for news of Martin solo.

When Gaultry flat out refused, his temper rose.

"You aren't trained," he said. "You'll be a liability."

"I'm usually a liability," Gaultry answered. "But this is not your mission."

"So you won't let me risk my life alone," Tullier said nastily. "Does it make it better if you risk it further by staying at my side?"

"Stay home yourself then if you think it's too risky," Gaultry said, furious that he had learned, so quickly, to turn her own words against her. "Keep the Sharif company. I'll go to Lendra's by myself."

Tullier smirked. "Who will pick the locks?"

Gaultry shrugged. "I may need your help, but I will not require it of you." She pushed her fingers through her hair, distracted. A liability, Tullier called her. It hurt her pride to admit it, but she knew he was right. Partly right.

There was a chasm in her where her Glamour-magic should have been. *Do you think it's fun having nothing in me to power my spells?* she wanted to ask. *Do you think I enjoy being weak? The working half of my Glamour-soul is sustaining your life. Do you think I enjoy being without that power?* Between her temper and Tullier's, she was surprised she managed to restrain herself from spitting out those bitter questions.

With the power of her Glamour-soul, spell-casting had come easily to her, without labor, without struggling. Now, the memory of that case could only hamper her with futile resentment.

With half her Glamour-soul pinned in Tullier's body, she could cast only the simple spells she had learned as a hedge-witch back in Arleon Forest. Those castings had power, but it was power which she called from Great Elianté and Emiera. That power was both less flexible and more limited than the Glamour-magic. Having to fall back on the Great Twins' magic to power her spells was a torment.

Her taking-spell, for example. With Glamour-magic, it was nothing to strip the spirit from an animal, to subvert its will and borrow what she liked of its strength, its quickness, its cleverness. When she called that same spell from the Great Twins instead of fueling it with her Glamour, its power was never so complete. She tended to get slashed by angry sea-gulls, had to battle to keep every spirit she called under control. The negative effects could overpower the positive.

But without calling on that magic tonight, Tullier would be correct, and she would be a liability to him in Prathe Lendra's house. She had not shared every aspect of her plans with Tullier, but when she accompanied him to the Villa Lendra, she intended to bring along the spirit of the meanest, cleverest alley cat that she could find.

She pressed her hands to her temples. Arguing with Tullier

on top of all her preparations for the taking-spell was exacting a toll. For Gaultry, taking from cats was usually difficult because of their cruel independent nature; taking from a half-feral street cat would make the spell maximally uncomfortable. Unfortunately, the night vision, the sense of balance, the intuitive sense of a stranger's approach, the keen hunter's curiosity—all those, in the balance, were enough argument to justify the unpleasantness of taking from such a small, nasty animal for an extended time. It was not an ordeal that she anticipated with any pleasure. She'd have a high pulse and a headache all evening.

Tamsanne, her grandmother, would have laughed. She had often teased Gaultry that she had trouble with cats because she had too much in common with them to enjoy being exposed to their animal honesty.

Gaultry salved her ego with the thought that her grandmother would have known little of the temperament of the average Bassorah alley cat when she had made that judgment.

Villa Lendra's high facade glistened white in the moonlight. The night air was balmy, the moon a gleaming circle that lit the street and the sky. It was a night with deep shadows and silver-lit pavement, inviting wandering—not a good night for skulking and housebreaking.

"Where did the clouds go?" Gaultry sketched the Great Twins' double spiral, seeking assurance.

Tullier, a shadow by her side, shook his head. "It won't matter once we're inside," he said. A strange eagerness for the venture still possessed him. "If we don't do it tonight, we'll have to leave it for a week."

The Sharif, a rather more conspicuous figure at her back, gave Gaultry's shoulder a reassuring pat, as if sensing her nervousness. Gaultry had tried to discourage her from coming with them at all, but the tall Ardana had insisted that she wanted to at least know where Prathe Lendra's house was. Gaultry had not found a successful argument against that.

But you're not coming in, Gaultry told the Sharif once

again. They'd been arguing about this since Gaultry had relayed her the night's plans. *We know they're trying to trace you. Nothing they know now connects you to us for certain, and better for it to stay that way.*

"Gautri," the Sharif said. She couldn't pronounce the consonant group of Gaultry's name. "I wait for you at the ferry." *If you don't meet me before dawn, I will come after you,* she added, so that only Gaultry could hear her.

"Elianté watch over me, that won't be necessary." They made their good-byes and separated, the Sharif heading back the way they had come.

One part of Gaultry wished she was following her.

A wordless, soundless yowl broke that thought. *Shut up,* she willed the yowling she-cat. She had trapped the aggressive, clever, tortoiseshell-colored creature in the alley behind the house where they were staying, and taken its spirit for a night's use. It had not taken kindly to the treatment. After hurling itself repeatedly at its magic bonds, the cat-spirit had given up on trying to free itself and begun to yowl shrilly and complainingly, putting Gaultry's already-stretched nerves further on edge. *Shut up, you,* she scolded it. *You're in for a more comfortable night than I.* The cat's body, curled tightly in a near coma, was safe at rest on her pillow back in the garret—probably spreading fleas, vermin, and the lice she had thus far avoided picking up from the Sharif. She mentally spanked its spirit back to its place, where it could not range and unsettle her mind. *Shut up and make yourself useful.*

She tried to assure herself that the horrible noise would stop once she started making use of the creature's senses and was no longer just holding the cursed animal captive.

Distracted by the cat-spirit, she almost lost sight of the shadow that was Tullier. Gaultry, hastening her steps to keep up, let the cat-spirit slide forward, giving it the control of her vision. Her color sight dropped away, but the murk of the shadows contracted. The cat, sensing a hunt in progress, ceased its complaints. It settled and focused on Tullier's back.

They followed the side of the villa until they came to a place where the white of the walls was plaster instead of stone. Gaultry would have thought the building was a stable, but for the absence of horse smell. Here the great oval curve of one of two connecting buildings met the straight edge of its gabled partner at an acute angle. Tullier pointed upwards.

High above, three stories up, the gabled building was roofed with glass. "I spotted this yesterday," he said softly. "We'll try here first."

"How're we going to get up there?"

"I'm going to climb it," Tullier said. "I don't know about you."

The boy made it look easy. Nudging his body into the tight angle where the walls of the two buildings came together, he began to scramble agilely up the corner. The first few feet were the least challenging. Then a thin ledge—more accurately, a sculptured strip of stonework ornamentation—barred his ascent, about fifteen feet up. It barely slowed Tullier's progress. Reversing the way his body faced in the corner, he expertly swung himself up over this strip, then twisted round to gain a toehold atop of it.

"Watch carefully," Gaultry muttered to the cat-spirit. "We're going to have to do that next."

Above her, Tullier, balanced on the balls of his feet, was a gray shape sharply defined against the white plaster wall. She could see him hunting for fingerholds, then, with surprising speed, climbing another ten feet up to precarious invisible handholds. The glass roof was below him now—canted away at an awkward angle, but below him, where he could reach it if he was very bold indeed.

He jumped. The cat-spirit twitched, its interest fully engaged. Not looking back to see if Gaultry was following, Tullier moved a little way along the roof, stooped, and pulled out his knife, working with it to gouge up the soft strips of lead that held the glass panes in place.

Without the cat, she never would have been able to follow. Tullier's tinkering on the roof had attracted its curiosity—it wanted to be up on the roof almost more than she did. Tentatively, she wedged her body into the corner as Tullier had done, and started up, intensely aware of the stone pavement at the wall's foot. The cat, sensing her nervous commitment to the climb, became maliciously eager to force her higher. She reached the ornamented strip and somehow, leaning heavily on the cat's reflexes, maneuvered her body above it. There was a nasty moment when she tried to reverse her position as Tullier had done, so she could get her feet on top of the thin edge of masonry. Above the fretment, she was relieved to find, the plasterwork was rougher, and the handholds Tullier had made use of so facilely were easier to find.

The jump across to the roof was not daunting as it had appeared from below. The level of the roof's edge was a little beneath her now, making the gap look slightly less impossibly broad. Tullier, busy with the glass panes' lead framing, had spread his cloak on the roof's edge to give her a landing pad. He'd made his own landing soundlessly, somehow managing not to punch out any panes of glass.

Gaultry was not quite so lucky.

She half-landed on Tullier's cloak, the heel of her boot crunching through two panes as it skittered off the padding. The break made a shocking, resounding crack, followed by slithering noises.

The pair froze. Slowly, relieved that she had not cut herself, Gaultry withdrew her boot from the jagged hole in the broken pane. The slithering noises came again, and a very faint jangle of glass landing on a hard surface. Then, blessed silence.

"What happened?" She crept closer to Tullier, away from the broken glass.

"Take a look at where you broke through," Tullier said breathing hard. "Some god made you lucky."

Pressing against the roof where Gaultry had punched through were the branches of a dense, flowering tree. Its untrimmed branches, pushing against the glass, had cushioned and muffled the sounds of the falling glass.

"It's a plant-house."

"Here we'd call it a solarium," Tullier said. "It's for plants that need heat to thrive." He pushed his knife back in his belt and started working with his fingers. "Help me with this." The glass panes had been put up in multipaned sections. By cutting the heads off the metal pins that secured it, and pulling up the lead stripping that had held it in place, Tullier had worked one section almost free. The roof was made up of hundreds—perhaps thousands—of these sections. Gaultry stared warily at the roof, trying to calculate the expense of that vast expanse of glass. When the boy caught the expression on her face, he let out a short laugh. "This is just the roof," he said. "Imagine what the house inside will be like."

"Hurry up," she said. It was too late for her to let herself be intimidated by the power of Prathe Lendra's money. "And stop talking."

Removing that one section of glass made a hole large enough for a human body. Tullier, thinking ahead, had chosen a panel that looked down on a sturdy-looking tree. Indicating that Gaultry should pull the section back into place behind her as she came through, he let himself down slowly through the hole, testing his weight on the nearest branch.

Satisfied, he gave her a curt nod, let go of the pane's edge, and, with a great deal of foliage-ruffling, disappeared from sight.

Gaultry, waiting for him to move his weight off the branch, took a last look at the sky. Though it was a clear night, the lights of the many lamps of the city had dimmed the stars. She could see the brightness of Andion's Eye—the sailors' navigation star—but the familiar constellations of home seemed faded and remote. At the sky's edge, the tiled roofs of the city made a jagged, unfamiliar horizon.

She could smell the heavy scent of the alien tropical plants that filled the solarium beneath her, brought to this temperate city from some unknown land. Two worlds, neither of which was her own.

The trapped cat-spirit hissed, sensing the hunt moving from it. Time to move on. Gaultry sketched the Great Twins' double-spiral in the air, staring briefly at the spot of sky where she guessed that their stars would have shone. "Elianté-bold, play the Trickster tonight," she muttered. "Play the Trickster tonight and get me through this." She thrust her legs through the roof-hole and reached for the branch with her feet.

Inside the dark world of the solarium, moonlight, patterned by the lead framing, dappled down over a mysterious jungle of plants. The flowered tree, where Gaultry had broken the window panes, was a night-bloomer, with pale, star-shaped flowers. Tiny silver-and-black birds perched in its branches, a few of them fluttering dozily, the rest asleep or transfixed, bewildered by the intrusion. Gaultry's cat made a reflexive gesture in their direction.

Ahead of her, Tullier had crossed to another branch, an impossibly thin branch that almost certainly wouldn't take Gaultry's weight. As she watched, he stretched to reach the rail of the high balcony that ran round the interior of the solarium, level with the second floor of the building. "Little bastard," Gaultry murmured, glancing round for an alternate route to the same balcony.

The trees had been pruned to form a canopy over the ground below. Several had substantial branches that leaned over the second-floor balcony—none, unfortunately for Gaultry, attached to the tree she was currently in. Swearing quietly, she descended to the floor, as quietly as the darkness and her haste would allow, and crossed to a tree with better branches up to the balcony. A nameplate nailed into its trunk, some five or six feet above ground level, looked sturdy enough to use as her first climbing hold. She squinted to read it before climbing.

The plate read FIRE-SAP HONEY TREE.

She took a closer look at the tree's bark, which sheathed the trunk with narrow, resinous strips, and reconsidered.

"Hurry up," Tullier seethed down to her.

"You hurry up," she seethed back, crossing to another tree.

"What was that about?" Tullier hissed when she finally joined him.

"No birds in that tree," she said. "I think it's poisonous."

"Really?" Tullier went round the balcony to find it, and snapped off a branch. He paused for a moment, smelling the break. "Not poisonous," he said. "Not poisonous in Bissanty terms, which would mean it couldn't kill you. But it could give you a serious rash."

"Or you."

Tullier shook his head. "Not me. I'm immune to anything except Sha Muir poison. Llara's blessing shields me from all the rest."

"You and the Emperors of Bissanty," Gaultry quipped. "No wonder you think so well of yourselves."

Tullier tucked the oozing branch inside his cloak. "Let's go find Angolis Trier's office," he said.

Two doors led off the balcony. Both let out to a hallway with a richly patterned carpet. The moonlight that slashed in through a high row of windows revealed patches of its pattern: a twined vine in green and black, very fine. Gaultry, who was more accustomed to bare floors and strewn-reeds as floor-coverings, was once again involuntarily impressed.

"This way." Tullier turned left, keeping to the shadows.

"Why not the other?" The wool padding under their feet muffled their footsteps.

He frowned, exasperated. "Because"—he pointed at the blank wall opposite, and down at an angle—"Trier's office is just about *there* in this building, two floors beneath us. I'm supposed to have a sense for it—it was part of the training." His voice quieted, as it often did now when he spoke of the Sha Muira.

The hallway terminated at open double doors. Beyond was a room dominated by a marble staircase, with another hall leading off to the left. Light from a pair of torch-sconces showed red-painted walls and fancy paneling. In deep niches in the panels, marble planters, burgeoning with cuttings from the solarium, made a finishing touch to the decoration. They could hear a whisper of voices from the floor below. Tullier skirted the staircase and took the hall onwards, deeper into the house.

"Look at the coffering on the ceiling!" Gaultry whispered. She guessed they must be in the part of the house kept reserved for large-scale functions, expensively furnished rooms that were kept closed and dusted, to be opened only on festive occasions. Her experience of such places was limited to one ducal seat and the Prince of Tielmark's palace. In both of those buildings, the hand of a single craftsman had dominated. Here, the scale was so grand she could see it would have needed a small army of crafters to have finished it. The floor underfoot was an unbelievably intricate parquet. They passed a second solarium room, this one smaller, more formal, with a black-and-white checkerboard floor. Fancy mullioned doors separated this room from the passage, with more glass mullions forming the far wall. The doors onto the corridor were open, letting in a delicious fruit-scent.

"Oranges," Tullier said.

Gaultry caught his sleeve. "I've never tasted an orange before," she said. "Have you?"

Tullier's pale eyes glistened as he turned to her. "You're crazy," he said. "We're here tonight only for one reason. Concentrate on that."

"Shush!"

They froze. A sudden muttering of voices could be heard moving toward them along the corridor. As one, they ducked into the orange-tree room. Save for the double row of tubs that held the tidily pruned orange trees the glass-sided room had no furniture. The only place to hide was against the wall.

The voices—a pair of men—came closer, passed, and faded.

They waited a long time, standing pressed against the wall where no one who passed in the hall, conversing or otherwise, could see them. "They didn't sound troubled," Tullier whispered. "That can't have been about our break-in."

Gaultry nodded. "Let's wait and see if they come back."

As they waited, she took a closer look at the room. The orangery fronted on a small terrace with graceful marble balustrades. It overlooked the gardens they had seen from the ferry, and beyond the gardens, the Polonna. The view was very beautiful, like an image from a dream. The bright light of the moon cast deep shadows, making everything seem at once serene and mysterious: the dark topiary in the garden; the silver-painted river. Across the river, Bassorah's silhouette took up all the horizon, punctuated by the high shining dome of Llara's temple, the grim hulk of Bissanty's ancient fortress and stronghold, and on the right, barely visible above the encroaching roofs, the white facade of the Imperial Palace with its obelisk. Crowning it all, like a backdrop to the sky, lay the crest of the hill where Llara had come to earth to bear her son.

"There's old magic in this room," she said quietly, staring at the long view with its display of the layers of Bissanty history. "But it's not on the oranges." She twisted one of the fat, brightly colored fruits off its branch and tucked it into a pocket. Tullier flashed her an outraged look. "It's only one," she said. "God's honor, I'll give you a taste when we're safely home."

Tullier made a face. "Let's go," he said. "Enough waiting."

They moved swiftly through long passageways and ceremonial half-chambers, up short stairs, and finally into a fabulous hall. Overhead, dark banners trailed down from high rafters, obscured by darkness. At the sides were double tiers of galleries, at the far end was a grand door. "That must lead out to the front," Gaultry said, "to the entry with the staircases." The party that could fill this room would be large enough to include all Tielmark's nobles and their servers. It rivaled the Great Hall of Clarin in the Prince of Tielmark's palace. That was an uncomfortable thought. At the near end of the hall was a second double curve of stairs that made an architectural echo of the exterior steps.

"Trier's messenger went in the bottom door and came out the main entrance," Tullier said. "So we know we can reach the offices from here."

"If there's a door, it will be tucked out of sight," Gaultry said. "Lendra wouldn't want guests who come here to think he mixes business with pleasure."

It was a canny guess. Out of sight down a side passage, but convenient to the hall, they found the door. A long, ill-lit flight of stairs led them to a plainer, less ornamented hallway, and through an unlocked door into a windowless, airless room that clearly had a clerical purpose.

When Tullier closed the door behind them, they were in utter darkness.

"Wait," he whispered fiercely as she reached for her flint and tinder.

They stood together, their backs pressed against the door. Finally, Tullier touched her hand, indicating that she might risk a light. "Small light," he whispered. "And no talking. I think there's a pallet room right next to us. For the messenger boys."

They had brought a candle with them in a shuttered metal basket. Gaultry lit it cautiously, standing close against a wall, her body shielding the flame, before she risked a look around the room. "We must be close," she whispered. "Do you think Trier's room will have a window?"

The flickering light revealed four standing-height desks and shelves that sagged with heavy sheaves of paper and lacquer-ended scrolls, ornamented with silk tassels. At the far end of the room was a solid-looking double door with a bar on the side that faced them. Tullier went across, a slim silhouette in the hooded light of the candle, and pulled the bar up, locking them in.

"That will slow up anyone who hears us," he whispered.

"But leave us only one way out."

"I'll wedge that door too."

Which would leave them no way out, though Gaultry did not say so to Tullier.

They broke into two more offices before they discovered Angolis Trier's sanctuary. The furnishings were comfortable, though not so fine that they gave a hint of the luxury that was to be found elsewhere in the villa. There was a bookcase of ledgers, similar to the one they had seen Trier's boy carrying. Gaultry gave the candle to Tullier and triumphantly pulled a ledger from the shelf and thumbed it open, scanning down the neatly entered columns to find a date, Martin's entry—

"I can't read this," she said, dismayed. It was written in code or in a foreign language.

"It might be written in Gallian," Tullier said. "That's the tribe of Lendra's father. Make sure you're looking at the most recent book," he suggested, glancing at the door. "Try to find the entry for our ship."

The current ledger was not in the shelf with the other books. It had been left out on Trier's desk, under a pile of loose papers. Gaultry delicately pulled it free, trying to remember how the papers looked so she would be able to rearrange the desk to conceal their snooping.

But, finally, there was the entry. The number seventy, then the numbers thirty and forty, for the numbers of Chauduks and Ardanae.

A note in red ink had been written into the book just below the figures, and then the number twenty-nine, circled for emphasis. "That must be the Sharif gone missing," Gaultry guessed.

Tullier nodded. "Now look for a strange entry, above that. Small numbers. That might be your Martin and the four Sha Muira who brought him back to Bissanty."

"Three," Gaultry reminded him. "Martin killed one in Seafrieg."

"Whatever," Tullier said coolly. "My guess is it will be the only small number."

On what might have been a date four days preceding their arrival, Gaultry found a three and a one, accompanied by another indecipherable note in red ink.

"Copy it out on a slip of paper," Tullier said. "And the note about the Sharif as well. We can puzzle it out later."

There was ground ink-powder on Trier's desk, and water to mix with it. Gaultry took a slip of paper with a blank side from the front office and came back to copy out the writing.

"I don't think that's legible," Tullier said, peering at what she was writing.

"How do you know? Can you read it?"

"No, but you're straightening the curved letters. Let me do it—"

So then Gaultry had to hold the candle while Tullier copied it out.

By the time Tullier had done, they were both eager to be gone. Arranging the office to appear undisturbed, they returned to the front room, each feeling that the other was being clumsy and unnecessarily noisy.

Tullier unlocked the bar to the room beyond, and they turned to the stairs.

"Back the way we came?"

Tullier nodded. "If it's still clear."

They padded up the narrow staircase out of the plain, businesslike world of the ground floor back into the grandeur of the big hall with the banners. The great room seemed quiet and undisturbed, but the cat-spirit, which had been quiescent for some time, jerked Gaultry's head up. High above, the banners were shifting, swelled by an unseen movement, by a current of air. "Tullier," she whispered. "Someone just passed through here."

"We must hurry."

They got only so far as the entrance to the corridor that led back toward the orangery and the solarium when trouble struck. Ahead, they heard sharp voices, accompanied by the chime of a bell. A moment later, the sound of more voices reached them, though whether from the stairs below, the passage ahead, or one of the great number of passages that led off the great hall, they could not determine.

"We're cut off!" Tullier, thinking quickly, grabbed Gaultry's wrist and, dragging her, turned and sprinted up the curve of the great presentational staircase that led to the hall's upper galleries.

They had barely reached the landing at the top of the flight when two separate groups of house servants emerged from passages at opposite sides of the hall. Calling out greetings, they crossed to meet at the foot of the marble steps. Neither group sounded alarmed; Gaultry, peeping over the edge of the top step, could see that none of them bore arms. But it was certain that something had roused them. They lit a lamp at the corner by the door to the orangery corridor. Two men in unbuttoned footmen's coats yawned and leaned back against the doorposts, clearly settling themselves in as sentinels.

"If we go past those two we know we can get out that way without running into locked doors," Tullier said. "We'll have to outwait them. But not here."

The exposed landing was anything but safe.

"Where then?"

"Try a door; find an empty room."

"And if we find an occupied one?"

"I'll silence anyone who tries to stop us, and we'll move on." Gaultry swallowed at Tullier's unmindful cold-bloodedness, but it was not the moment to rebuke him.

The first floor of the house above the great hall had many empty rooms. The first three doors they tried opened into long disused chambers, the beds covered up with ghostly sheets, the windows heavily shrouded. These rooms made Tullier uneasy. "We can't stay here."

"Whyever not?"

Tullier couldn't explain. "It's too empty," he said, shifting restlessly from foot to foot. "It's a disruption."

"And breaking panes in a solarium is not?"

"Necessary for entry," he said. "Disturbing the dust here is not."

"This house is a rabbit warren," Gaultry said as they returned to the corridor. "Can't we find another way to get back around to the other side of the house? There must be a servant's stair somewhere."

Tullier, his eyes closed as if he was trying to envision the villa's layout, took a moment to think. "The big hall," he said. "On this level, it had a gallery all the way around. There might be a second stair at the far end."

"It's worth a try." They had come down a short hall to reach the wing of empty bedrooms. "Let's go back."

The great hall's gallery, like the orangery, was tiled in black and white squares. The surface magnified every sound, echoed every shiver. Tullier and Gaultry kept well back from the railings, out of sight of the servants posted at the door below. Despite their caution, hints that betrayed their passage reverberated out into the hall. The edges of the banners trembled as they went past.

Though the gallery was broad and well-proportioned, it was also surprisingly disorderly. The floor was cluttered with a large number of wooden crates, making it difficult to move quietly. Up two steps was a relatively open space, more tidy, with folding stools and music stands stacked against the rails, and the cases of numerous musical instruments. Two steps down were the brightly painted slats of a puppet theater, designed to be hung out over the railings. Then came rows of artificial trees and an awkwardly packed square of floor filled entirely with metal foil streamers wound onto bolts like cloth.

"What's all this doing here?" said Gaultry, overwhelmed by the sheer mass of materials, all dedicated to transient entertainment.

"Prathe Lendra must have plans to impress somebody with a big party during the holy week," Tullier surmised. "Otherwise, I'd guess much of this would be in storage."

After traversing two sides of the great hall via the gallery, they reached a pair of stone doors clad in metal. One of the doors was ajar, just enough to let in a slash of bright moonlight. "A way back to the solarium?" Gaultry whispered.

"It's on the right side of the house," Tullier said optimistically.

Beyond the doors, the floors weren't being used as temporary storage. The ornamentation was rich, the floor smooth white marble with black veins. Warm night air caressed their cheeks. They had come out onto a covered porch. Two stories below was a paved, oval-shaped courtyard enclosed on all sides by a covered portico.

A fiddler stood at the center of the court, his instrument tucked under his chin, his bow raised. His upturned face was pale in the moonlight, almost mournful. He plucked tentatively at the strings with his free hand, testing his tuning. The notes were sharp and clear, with a hint of a wayfarer's wildness. Tullier pulled Gaultry's sleeve.

"Let's go. Before he starts playing. If we go around to that door opposite, I think we'll be back near the solarium. One flight too high, but near enough."

Gaultry did not have time to answer. Several things happened at once. The musician, his instrument ready, began to play, his music startlingly loud and riotous, considering he was only a single player. Ahead, a door slammed open. A tall man, his lithe body outlined in shining silk, shot out onto the porch and leaned out over the balustrade like an avenging demon, adventitiously blocking their way. Tullier, reacting without thinking, thrust open the nearest door and pushed Gaultry inside. As he pulled the door shut, they heard the tall man's voice. He was screaming at the fiddler, his voice high and screechy as a parrot's.

Lights flickered in the room they'd entered. Gaultry, reacting first, pulled Tullier to his knees, her heart twisting with dismay. They had unwittingly jumped through a servant's door into the very room from which the screamer had exited, and they were not alone.

At first she thought they'd been lucky. They had entered behind a row of servants. The room was dimly lit, and it seemed at first that they might simply be mistaken for latecomers. Then she realized why it was that no one had noticed their entry.

Beyond the row of servants stood a pair of teenage boys, legs entwined, painted faces set and patient, waiting for the interruption to end. Dancers. A quiver of embarrassment darted down Gaultry's spine. The boys wore body paint, feathers, beaded headdresses—and nothing more.

Worse, beyond them, seated comfortably on luxurious mountains of embroidered pillows, was a pair of men smoking long-stemmed clay pipes. One wore a silk hood, midnight-blue, that came all the way to his shoulders, hiding his hair as well as his face. The pipe was drawn to the slash in the cloth, sucked and released, all without revealing the lips that drew on it. His head was turned to the door, watching the shouting man's rear, and his shoulders were slumped, as though he was more than a little drunk. The other man, sitting more upright, was handsome but cruel-looking: of middle years, still strong, heavily built. His skin was healthy and ruddy, not Bissanty sallow.

Outside, the fiddler's music was cut short. There were the sounds of a scuffle, then quiet.

"Thank Llara for that." The man at the door—the man who had shouted—was handsome in a petulant, pretty way, with dark lashes and bright silks and the long, glossily oiled wig of dark hair affected by many of Bissanty's young gentry. He came back into the room, banging the door closed. "What caterwauling."

"I'm sure our host could have stopped it himself, Dati. No need for you to take it on yourself." The hooded man had the voice of an old person.

"He was practicing for the coming fête." Gaultry knew, by the man's voice—his arrogance, his power—that the second pipe-smoker was the Master of Villa Lendra. His voice was gentle but cold. Prathe Lendra gathered the folds of his simple gown of green silk tightly to his body and smiled, showing strong white teeth. "But he should have known it would be an interruption. I'll see the man is punished in the morning."

"After Dati's scolding? I don't think so. Besides, where could you get a replacement at such short notice?"

"No, then? Well, perhaps you are right."

"There's no question of it. Certainly don't do it for Dati's sake."

Dati, returning from the door to the pillows, shot the hooded man a resentful look.

Lendra waved a hand at the dancers, gesturing for them to continue. The one on the left cupped his hands on his partner's shoulders and nodded to the row of musicians, as he shifted his balance and raised one knee. Two sweet sopranos took up a chord, and led the rest into a long-drawn susurrating chant. The voices were like serpentine waves, winding one upon the other, drawing its listeners in. The dance mimicked the movement of the voices. Gaultry took a deep swallow. The boy-dancers were astonishingly supple and strong, their bodies seductively entwining, each movement of the dance teasingly suggesting it would lead to a physical climax, then drawing back. She had seen farm animals rutting a-plenty, but never anything like this.

"Your brothers will be coming tomorrow night," Lendra said lightly, just loud enough to be heard over the singers' sweet voices.

"They are young enough to like a party," the hooded man

said shortly. "I am long past such public pleasures. Come here, Dati."

The sensitive Dati came back across the room and threw himself into the hooded man's lap. "You never think of me," he complained, shuffling pillows to make himself comfortable.

The hooded man laughed and touched Dati's face, along the fine bone of his temples below the black hair of his wig. "I think of you often," he said. "As Prathe himself could tell you."

Gaultry, kneeling in the back row, shot Tullier a nervous look. She wondered if this was his first encounter with such public embraces—it was hers, and she very much disliked it. The room was overwarm, the air tainted with an unpleasant incense that burned her lungs and heated her skin. No one seemed to be enjoying themselves—not Dati, who was fussing and sulking, and certainly not the dancers. The smaller of the boys, beneath his makeup, wore a set look. Gaultry could see that the older boy was hurting him with the pressure of his hands, in the way he bent and twisted the smaller boy's body against his own. The younger's physical control was so intense that despite the pain, his movement remained graceful, full of the appearance of languor.

"You should have told me everything from the beginning," Lendra said as the bigger boy pushed the other over and dug his fingers into his buttocks. The interruption with the fiddler had evidently disrupted an earlier conversation. "Ghostmongering! Who was it? Claudio? Coronne? I cannot imagine it was Coronne. But how can I help now, if the boy is dead?"

The hooded man, intent on the dancers, did not reply. Dati, his fingers busy in his Master's lap, shot Lendra a resentful look.

Prathe Lendra returned Dati's stare, the corners of his mouth hardening and turning downwards. Dati, at first fighting that stare, made an impatient movement and broke the contest. Lendra smiled, a cruel light shining in his face. Then he looked across the room and, almost casually, allowed himself to meet Gaultry's eyes. His gaze was cold, curious, penetrating. She felt more naked than the boys who danced between them, and inwardly was writhing just as fiercely.

He had known she was there, had known that she should not be there, from the moment she and Tullier burst in.

Panicking, she rose to her feet, pulling Tullier with her. As she whirled around, the door behind her opened.

"Master!" It was a house-guard, a short sword unsheathed in his hand. "There's a stranger in the house!"

Startled by the shout at their backs, the singers sprang up in fright, the dancers—the small boy crying in pain at the unexpected discoupling—drew apart. The hooded man leapt up from the pillows, dumping Dati from his lap to the floor.

Tullier killed the guard with a quick, driving blow from his sheath knife.

Gaultry, not waiting for the man's body to hit the ground, scrambled out the door.

Out on the porch, more guards crowded against the railing, waiting for their leader's report. They had weapons, but they hadn't expected the pair of housebreakers to erupt from their lord's pleasure rooms. Gaultry barreled by before they could react.

"Straight on!" Tullier called, running at her side. "The door there!" He pointed. "We can close it behind us."

With their small lead, they got the door shut seconds before the guards caught them. The door had a not particularly solid lock, which Tullier somehow managed to fix shut.

"Now what?"

"With what we just heard?" The boy shook his head wildly. "Lendra will never let us escape."

"Stop that, Tullier," she said. "We're just going to have to keep moving until we're safely out."

They were in yet another hall, doors to the left, doors to the right. Lights blazed from every wall sconce. There was a carpet underfoot: a long red runner with a twined vine pattern. With the room flooded with light, it took Gaultry a moment to recognize the design. Somehow they had come around in a circle and were back in the solarium wing.

"There should be a staircase ahead," she huffed to Tullier.

There was. The same stairs they had passed on their way in from the solarium. They ran down, three steps at a time, abandoning caution, and found themselves on a familiar landing. The room was red-painted, there were niches for planters in the paneling. Ahead lay the corridor that led to the solarium.

"Thieves!" The hall on this level was full of house-guards.

Gaultry, winded, wheeled round, banging into Tullier. "The orangery!" he gasped. "Out the windows to the gardens and down to the river!"

Back at the red staircase room, lights bobbed on the stairs. Their pursuers were closing in.

Running on to the next corridor, their boots clattered at last on parquet flooring. Glassed walls opened to their right. The doors that led to the orangery were steps away—

"They're here!" The corridor in front of them filled with servants, blocking that line of retreat. Behind them, their way was closed off by the house-guards. The fleeing pair darted to the orangery doors. Gaultry felt a hand brush her back as she twisted around that last corner.

Her heart almost stopped with dismay. The orangery seethed with an astonishing number of house-guards. Prathe Lendra's men had planned the ambush quickly, or perhaps they would have set fewer men to wait there, rather than the overkill of twenty or more. Gaultry, thrashing out in every direction, lost sight of Tullier as seven or eight men grappled him down, so many men that they hampered themselves in their own efforts. An orange tree crashed over in its tub. Someone shouted at the culprit to have a care what he did.

Numberless hands groped at her body. She screamed, half-suffocated. The rank of men beyond the knot around her pushed against those who held her, trying to reach her, trying to claim a part in her capture, while those who had a hold scrambled between trying to keep their grip and pushing those behind them back.

Then, somewhere off to her left, someone started screaming. "He hit me, he hit me! Llara help me, my eyes, they're burning!"

Tullier had momentarily freed himself. He lashed out with

the branch he'd torn from the fire-sap tree, clearing a circle around him.

"Let go of her!" he screamed. "I am Sha Muira! You cannot stand against me!"

The room stilled with shock. Those who had touched Tullier cried out with fear. Gaultry wriggled free, leaving her new cloak and one of her sleeves behind, and dragged herself across to him. Wary faces stared back at her, at Tullier.

"It can't be true!" One of the housemen, a short, tough-looking man, pushed his way to the front of the crowd. "He has no Sha Muir blade, and *she* can make no claim to be Sha Muira. Yet they are confederates!"

Tullier shoved her onto the balcony with a strength that was as sudden as it was unexpected. The guards leapt to grab them. Gaultry, feeling the balustrade against her legs, threw herself over it, even before she looked to see what was below.

The next thing she knew, she was tumbling clumsily over rough roof tiles trying to break her fall, no time even to curse her lack of caution. Then she was in midair, the white flash of marble beneath her, rising towards her with a promise of broken bones and broken flesh—

And then she was choking, and fighting, and striking out with her legs in no particular direction, struggling to reach the surface of water that had the clarity of crystal lit by an almost full moon.

"Tullier!" she called, struggling simultaneously to reach the edge of the marble pool and to see the balcony. She could just make out his head, over the balustrade. The boy turned to look at the drop before jumping, and that hesitation—that hesitation sealed his fate. She saw the tops of guards' heads, she could hear scuffling, but the boy did not reappear over the edge of the roof. She clambered, awkward and soaked, out of the water, still calling him. "Come on, Tullier! Come on!"

Off somewhere to her left, she heard deep-throated baying. There were dogs loose in the gardens. The cat-spirit, which had been lying low, recognized the sound before she did, and galvanized into action, exploiting her momentary confusion, her loss of purpose. She vaguely remembered pulling herself up marble steps and trailing wetly across to a garden wall.

There instinct and the cat-spirit took over. She fled pell-mell across the gardens, down over two stone patios and across a prickly rose garden, up over a coarse-surfaced iron wall that tore at her hands, and jumped.

She landed in mud up to her hips, the less-than-crystalline waters of the Polonna churning around her. The cat-spirit, seeing itself safe of the dogs and hating the water, set up to yowl again.

She quelled the wretched thing with unnecessary force, fury and a dagger of helplessness tearing at her. "Why didn't you jump?" she said, facing the high wall over which she had escaped. As if Tullier could hear her. "Why did you have to look before you jumped?"

The full horror of their separation pressed upon her as she struggled along the bank, seeking dry ground. She clutched at her vest pocket, feeling for the scrap of paper for which she had sacrificed Tullier, trying to protect it from the wet. With the information they had stolen, she could finally begin her search for Martin in earnest. The image of the tall soldier's hard face, his deep gray eyes, staring, as if into her soul, flashed before her. Tears of longing traced her face.

Something jumped in the water ahead, bringing her heart to her throat. It was just a rat. The sight of it somehow made her able to think more clearly. She had failed Tullier. His Sha Muir conditioning had trained him to kill, but in so doing, it had dulled his instincts for self-preservation. Knowing this before they had entered the villa, she should not have been so cock-sure, so certain that his skills would help her. She should have considered the price that this night's work could cost *him*.

Besides which, Tullier held half her Glamour-Soul. Even if she wanted to, she could not leave him in Lendra's clutches while he still held that.

A liability, he had called her. And she, looking down into his boy's face, had been dull-witted enough to listen.

The orange had become smashed and ruined in her pocket. She threw it angrily into the river, even that small victory crushed.

chapter 13

It was an hour past dawn. The sun had risen in the east, gilding the dome of Llara's temple and bathing the roofs of the city with pale gold light. Below, the streets were cool and quiet, populated only by scattered servants on morning business. The market crowds had not yet gathered. There had been one exception. Coming down to Great Bas's bank, Gaultry and the Sharif had passed a small, shabbily accoutered parade engaged in a votive ritual. The participants pointed frail spears of woven grass to the heavens as they walked, solemn-faced, beneath the shuttered windows of the early morning streets. Without Tullier, she could only guess at the parade's significance. Its modest apparel and trappings, however, made her doubt that it had anything to do with the proud Emperor of whom the boy had spoken the afternoon previously, or with the birthday celebrations for his children. The pageantry seemed as old as the marsh upon which Bassorah had been founded: the women, who were mostly elderly, wore crudely woven wreaths of marsh-grass, the men had streaks of yellow clay smeared on their foreheads. The early morning traffic made way for them, but no one, save for a few extremely ancient-looking people, stopped to acknowledge the ragged procession.

Down by the river, on the banks where clay-walled pools had been built, the city's women were laying out their laundry.

Gaultry and the Sharif were up to join them. They had chosen the pool farthest from the bridge, which meant carrying their things a little farther but also meant more privacy as they worked. Their closest neighbors, some forty feet away, were a pair of women washing their master's clothes on the ridged laundry-slabs set into the river's bank. Gaultry was in a miserable mood. She slapped the trousers she'd muddied in the Polonna against the flat washing-stone, hard enough to hurt her hands. "I think—no, I know, that Tullier killed one of the house-guards."

The Sharif, standing beyond her, was bending over the primitive pump, trying to comprehend the mechanism. She gave the handle a quick heave, then another. The clay pipe spat: first brown water, then clear, then brown again.

"Don't you hear me?" Gaultry asked querulously. "Tullier killed one of the house-guards."

"I hear you, Gautri," the Sharif said. Not for the first time, either, her raised brows added. "Tullier killed." *Does this pipe bring water from the river or a spring? Clever, I think. The shallows can be muddy, and still there is clean water.*

The pipe takes water from the stream, Gaultry answered impatiently. She pointed at the narrow rippling stretch of water, near the river's center, where the sluggish flow of the river actually maintained a visible current. *But Tullier—*

The mechanism is easy, neat, the Sharif interrupted. Her fingers ran inquisitively over the joint, the small lever where it disappeared into a copper tube. When Gaultry had met her, according to plan, by the ferry-landing, she had taken the news of Tullier's abduction with apparent equanimity, her composure only slipping when Gaultry told her she was determined to go back and retrieve him. But now she contented herself with taking that news too in her stride. Once settled on a course of action, she did not seem to wish to speak of it or argue its merits. Ignoring Gaultry's pointed attempts to talk about Tullier and second-guess the previous night's worst mistakes, she pumped the washbasin full, her vivid eyes measuring each belch of water, calculating the pump thrust necessary to bring each belch up.

Gaultry, in frustration, scrubbed her trousers vigorously. "He's just a boy. I shouldn't have left him."

The Sharif, still watching the water, said nothing.

"He wanted to go."

"He wanted to go," the Sharif agreed.

"It was a risk." The Sharif didn't answer. Gaultry looked up from her washing and saw she hadn't understood. *A risk,* she repeated, peevish.

The tall war-leader nodded. "We get him back." *This device,* she continued, obviously engrossed. *Maybe we go see the man who makes this device?*

But Tullier—

Last night is past. The Sharif stood, her cupped hands full of water, and splashed her face and arms. The pleasure she took in this simple act was plain on her face. *You had good reasons to chance last night's risks. You both gained and lost from last night's actions. We get Tullier; we get your Martin. But after that, you take me back to Ardain, and this device— its workings—comes with me.*

For the first time that morning, Gaultry smiled. As the Sharif's slave-illnesses had faded, the intensity and curiosity that had first drawn Gaultry to her had returned. And the Sharif was right. Reliving every moment over of the previous night's mistakes in her head, trying to understand the moment the decisions had gone wrong, was not productive. Learning how to build a pump—for a woman who one day hoped to return to her desert homeland—was.

In Tielmark, Gaultry said, *a pump-maker can teach you all you need to know about pumps. That I promise you. But the gods conspire—my heart is split. I owe my country Martin Stalker's safe return, and I must not jeopardize that mission. But Tullier—I can't leave him either.*

The Sharif nodded. *Tullier is your man. You leave your man behind, the gods don't forget it. Same in battle for me.*

"My companion," Gaultry corrected her testily, throwing her trousers in the rinsing pool. "I can't leave my companion." The Sharif, of course, did not follow the difference of meaning. She could only follow Gaultry's tone.

"Gautri," she said, her smile serious. "You tell me to rest. Now you need rest too." *Don't worry too much all at once,* she added. *The chieftain who sent you here—she trusted you to judge right in these matters. Honor that faith and trust yourself.*

Gaultry scowled, and slapped the trousers harder. If only it was that simple.

When the clothier understood what they wanted, he was horrified. "In one day?" he said. "It's not possible."

"You don't understand what it is that we want," Gaultry told him. "Besides, we can leave a security for the loan of your merchandise."

"A security?" Avarice, and the thinness of hard times, lit the man's eyes. "What kind of security?"

Gaultry nodded at the Sharif. The tall woman reached into her vest and threw a heavy purse onto the padded table that was the man's workbench. *You'll have to do it,* she had told the Sharif, when they were discussing how to play this scene. *He'll guess if it comes from me.*

The clothier tugged open the purse's drawstring and dumped the contents onto the table. The gleam of gold caught the light as the coins rolled to a rest, bright little suns.

Gaultry turned away. She couldn't bear to watch. With her Glamour-soul split and its magic dormant, she had to strain to trust in her old spells. Without Glamour-magic, her castings seemed thin, powerless, a shadow of what they should be. Now, seeing the coins suddenly, apart from her practice efforts, she was sure she had overdone the color on the silver. She and the Sharif had wavered between robbing their fellow washerwomen and trying this, and this idea had won. Now she was sure they'd made the wrong choice. In his business, catering to a clientele that wanted—or needed—the trappings of society without having the means of affording the payment for them, the clothier must have seen every lie, every cheat, every game. He'd never fall for it. The coins were obviously faked.

"What are these coins?" he asked.

"Chauduki gold," the Sharif said. "You don't know them?"

"Should I?"

"Should you?" the Sharif mocked, standing tall before him, threatening him a little with her height. The man stepped back. The Sharif smiled brazenly, showed her fine white teeth, and, seizing up a coin, she bit it in half. She made it look as easy as it would have been, had the coin truly had the softness of gold. Throwing the split halves on the table, the desert eyes fixed the clothier with an amused look. "You know that, yes?" She pointed to the coin's sheared edge, showing how the pure gold color ran all through the thickness of the metal.

They'd spoiled six silver shillings practicing that.

And wasted half the morning, coaching the Sharif with her lines.

"Too much security for clothes, it's true, but you fight giving it back and you regret it." The Sharif stepped back, allowing the clothier more space at the padded table.

Gaultry envied the tall war-leader's ability, even stumbling in a language she barely knew, to sound threatening and magnanimous together.

"It's not too much if you bring me back spoiled wares." The man sniffed, picking up the half-crescents of metal for a closer look. After turning them over in his fingers, he closed them back in the little bag with the other coins, possessive.

"That's fair," Gaultry said, too quickly, turning around and giving the Sharif a nod. She bit her lip, trying to curb her eagerness to settle the bargain. "Don't you think that's fair?"

"First we see what the man offer us." Where Gaultry was fast and nervous, the Sharif was—from Gaultry's standpoint—excruciatingly relaxed and slow. "Then maybe."

The thin clothier looked from Gaultry to the Sharif, as if

weighing his response. Then he inclined his head slightly to
the Sharif, nodding. "I'll see what I can do," he said.

When Gaultry had first seen the great hall at Prathe Lendra's
villa, it had seemed preposterously large. Now, pressed on
both sides by giggling women and the soldiers who accompanied the honor guard of a Bissanty lordling, she realized that
it was either barely large enough or had been organized to
appear so. The metal foil streamers she had stumbled over
with Tullier the evening before now coiled around every pillar, twined up every glistening marble balustrade, and laced
across the ceiling like a giant shining spider's web, reflecting
tenfold the light of every candle. It was as if they were in a
tent of shining reflected light.

Laugh, the Sharif told her, walking tall by her side. *Join
their merriment.*

"Ha ha," said Gaultry grimly. "Ha ha ha." *Remember not to
put anything in your mouth here. There's a good chance that
everything's drugged or poisoned.*

The Sharif, dressed in a modest gray suit, her cropped pate
hidden under a black wig that had been oiled and curled into
long chevalier's locks, looked at least as masculine as half of
the young Bissanty gentry who pushed in the crush around
them. Gaultry thought she looked magnificent and rather
handsome, and she was not the only one. The tall Ardana was
drawing covert looks from the crowd. There was a fierceness
in her mien that commanded respect, that dignified the cheap
clothes. No one would have guessed that she was recovering
from a month in the hold of a slave-ship.

Gaultry, in a heavier horsehair wig and a cherry-colored
gown with a disgracefully sheer underdress of white tulle—
cribbed together from two separate garments at the clothier's
emporium—was jittery as a scared chicken. She felt her
choice of costume, unlike the Sharif's outfit, had been a mistake. It made her conspicuous, and not in a good way, because
she had no hope of affecting the manners appropriate to the
dress. She could match neither the brittle, artificially stiff car-

riage of the Bissanty noblewomen in attendance nor the studied languor of the assorted consorts and mistresses to the gentry. The clothier had given her a painted fan which she didn't
know how to hold, and a little half-mask on a stick which she
had already tired of carrying. Under the dress, flimsy slippers
pinched her feet, too narrow for her toes.

And, beyond these concerns, once again she was in Prathe
Lendra's house. She remembered the coldness of the man's
eyes as they had met hers, the bitter humor. Would he recognize her in this fancy shell if he saw her? She feared that he
would.

The Sharif nudged her. *You're frowning. Stop it.*

"Let's move over to the stairs," Gaultry said. "We'll be out
of the crush there."

At first the brightly dressed throng seemed to be mixing
randomly, then, as Gaultry watched, clear patterns emerged.
At the foot of the grand double curve of stairs within the
hall—the stairs that she and Tullier had fled up to reach the
gallery, when things had first begun to go wrong—there was
an invisible social barrier to the upper galleries and the pleasure rooms. Somewhere above, music played, and the sound
of laughter filtered down—all sounding much more pleasant
and enticing than the crush that filled the great hall. But the
footmen stationed on the bottom steps were there to politely,
if insistently, turn people back. The public, it seemed, was
welcome enough on the first floor, but was not allowed access
to the inner reaches of the house. Gaultry's heart sank. If
every door was guarded like this, she and the Sharif had
wasted an entire day planning this infiltration.

It had not been difficult to discover that Prathe Lendra was
giving a party in honor of the Sciuttarii births. The references
Lendra had made to it the night before had been easy to con-
firm. From there, it had seemed inevitable that they attempt to
use the cover of the party to locate Tullier. For Tullier, they
knew, was still at the villa. Prathe Lendra had not removed
him. He had not—Gaultry gave thanks to the Great Gods for
this—executed him. Early that afternoon, while praying to the
Huntress, she had discarded her reserve, and finally allowed

her broken Glamour-soul to search for its missing half. It had been a painful excursion, more illuminating than she had intended. She had sought glimpses of the boy, for his location. What she had found had been the tortured knot of his feelings, raw and vulnerable, sucking greedily at the strength of her Glamour-soul like a frightened child at its mother's nipple, driven almost to madness by fear and desperation.

She had not known Tullier carried so much fear. He was like—her mind winced at the comparison—the smaller of Prathe Lendra's dancers: so inured to pain and fear that it hardly revealed itself on his face or in his body. She had seen glimpses of the ordeals Tullier had suffered—and suffered gladly!—at the hands of the Sha Muira. What little she had been able to comprehend of the pain's purposes had sickened her. One actuality only served to salve her worries. The piece of Glamour-soul, still busily consuming dark Sha Muir poison, was also acting to deplete the panicked edge of his fear.

Having found him, having seen an image of the room where they were keeping him, she had broken the prayer link to her Glamour-soul piece. When she had come to herself, she was sweat-soaked and full of grief. She wished that she had known of his internal vulnerability before she had allowed him to assist her in the foray into Prathe Lendra's house.

"Gautri." The Sharif nudged her side. "Look."

At the side of the hall, beneath an arcade, footmen served drinks from three cut-crystal punch bowls. A small band of young people had just drunk from the first punch bowl. At first Gaultry was not sure what had caught the Sharif's attention. The party was laughing, unnaturally loud, and Gaultry could see this was the effect of the drink. Then one girl, downing the dregs of her punch, let out a little cry and fell against her partner's shoulder, her tongue protruding from her mouth, a trace of berry-blue-colored saliva on her lips. Her partner, a tall boy distinguished by the gray pallor of his skin, made a disgusted sound and pushed her away. The girl, deprived of his support, collapsed. "Put her in the gutter," the tall boy called out nastily as a footman came up to remove her. "She's trash fit for a city soldier. What made her think to come here?" The remainder of the party laughed, encouraging him.

"Another round!" the boy called. An unpleasant expression shifted across his face. He turned back to the bowls. "Red cup, this time!" He stepped past the first bowl to the second, and held out his hand for a glass. Once again, he swigged it back.

This time, the drink made him stagger, as if it had brought him to the limit of his strength. That must have been what had caught the Sharif's attention on their first round of cups. He leaned against the table, struggling to recover. At last the gray cheeks flushed with a little color, and an intense, euphoric energy buzzed through him. He smirked and rose, triumphant and unfriendly. His eyes were bright with the punch's effect. "Cori! Roma! Join me!"

The boys he had called by name shot him sullen looks. Grudgingly, both shook their heads. "Not so early," the darker of the pair complained. "We had Blue cup. Let's leave it there for now and go upstairs. What need—"

"Shirker!" The dark boy's consort, a young woman with a merry—if unkind—smile, pushed past him and boldly held out her cup. "I'll take it if you won't!"

The server, a still-faced man with nervous hands, passed her a brimming glass, its contents vivid red. She accepted it resolutely, her smile a little forced.

As she boldly threw back her head to drink it down, a shiver of anticipation ran through her party. She was very pretty, very merry, wearing a rich emerald-colored dress, the white of her skin so pale and fair that blue tracings of veins showed on her temples and throat, her pretty slim hands. The punch looked almost like blood as she lifted it to her mouth.

She drained it in a single draught.

Laughing, she held up the empty cup, turning it upside-down over her head, to show every drop was gone. The party applauded. But it was not enough for her to have passed the test. She wanted more.

"Claudi has lost his partner." She turned back to her consort, the dark boy. "But I don't think that he'll be lonely tonight." She was still smiling the merry, pretty smile, but her eyes were cruel.

The dark boy smiled back, confidently enough, but his eyes flickered to the other party members, gauging their response.

They were waiting, unfriendly.

Faced with the inevitable, he handed his empty glass to the red punch bowl's server.

"Llara watch you, Scalia." He saluted her with the cup and drank it without further ceremony.

His face flushed, and he doubled over, clutching his stomach. Whatever drug had been used to spice the drink, he couldn't take it. Around him, the crowd drew back. Everyone was smirking and staring, coolly amused, the young man's distress and humiliation a public amusement.

His consort's reaction disturbed Gaultry the most. She rolled her flirting dark eyes to the group's leader, the boy who had first pressed the whole party to drink from the second bowl. There was a pause, a moment of calculation. The boy offered her his arm. Then, leading the others, the new red-cup couple went past Gaultry and the Sharif to the foot of the great ascending staircase. The footman welcomed them with a little flourish, took possession of their glasses, and ushered them past. Gaultry stared at their shining faces as they mounted the steps. They were intoxicated with the lingering effects of the spiced punch, the young man they'd abandoned already forgotten. Whether it was the effect of the drink or a natural coldness, for them he did not exist. Behind them, a servant moved the fallen boy away from the punch bowl table: he was an inconvenience to those who came after him.

Gaultry looked at the trio of bowls with new understanding. She and the Sharif, no matter how well they looked or how unconvincing, wouldn't be able to go up the stairs, wouldn't be given a pass to the house, until they could pass the stair-guards. And the stair-guards weren't going to let them by until they had seen them empty a glass of punch.

She looked sideways at the Sharif and saw she had reached the same conclusion. *We'll have to fake it,* Gaultry told her. *There's no other way. Maybe we've already delayed too long.*

Indeed, the first punch bowl—Gaultry guessed it held the least potent poisons—was almost empty.

The longer they waited, the less chance they would have of tasting something they might possibly be able to stomach. As they watched, an elegant pair, a man and a woman together, took from the weakest bowl and were carried out in convulsions.

"Parvenu," said a fat lady as she and her companion passed Gaultry and the Sharif on the stairs. Her thick fingers clenched the stem of a glass with red dregs. "I wonder that Prathe invited them."

"Would you like a drink, Lady Gaultry?"

Gaultry stiffened. She knew that voice. She would have bolted but for the fact that the Sharif anticipated her and caught hold of her arm.

"Lord Issachar Dan," she said, swallowing her fear and turning to face him. The man was a nightmare to look upon: dark, animal lean, with cicatrized scars on his cheeks and a sadist's glint in his eyes. Issachar was the highest-ranked officer that the Bissanties had sent to support Chancellor Heiratikus in his failed plot against Tielmark's throne. The dark lord had worked with Heiratikus to bind Mervion's soul and enslave her to the plan to overthrow the Prince. Gaultry had managed to avoid being soul-broken—but she had not evaded his vicious, animal cruelty. He had tried to beat her resistance from her; indeed, the scars of his attack were only freshly closed. As she looked at him, the hair stiffened on Gaultry's neck.

But he had escaped Tielmark with his life because she had shown him mercy. If she was afraid of him, she could not let him see that. Those dark eyes fastened on hers, alert, curious, but they were eyes of a predator not yet ready to pounce.

"What are you doing here?" she asked.

"I could ask the same of you. Here," he said, "take my glass. I'll go myself for another."

He thrust the glass into her hand and was gone before she could stop him.

"No running," the Sharif said, seeing the panic spread across Gaultry's face. "Not here."

"It's over," Gaultry said. "If he's here, it's over."

Even among the monstrous Bissanty nobility, Issachar stood out. For though the painted crowd who swarmed around them were callous and brutal, there was something cowardly in them, something doubting that made them need to flaunt their power. Issachar did not waste his energy in posing. He acted, and when he did, he did not pause to flaunt his victories. He moved on to his next action.

While Issachar waited to get himself a second cup of punch, two more unfortunates succumbed and were gracelessly dragged away. The weak bowl—Blue cup—was empty now.

Issachar, with his unnatural gray skin parchment-tight over the whipcord of his bunched muscles, his face marked with jagged ritual scars, his crest of black hair, waited his turn at the punch bowls. He looked primitive and tribal, out of place among the urbane and artificial Bissanty gentry. But the most important difference, Gaultry knew, went deeper than dress.

"He looks like a man, but it is not a man's soul that moves him," Gaultry murmured, more to herself than to the Sharif. "Someone split his soul and bonded it with a hawk's spirit." His brutality was on some level innocent, the natural instinct, the impulses, of a raptor's mind. "His soul is a sacrilege against the gods' creation—" Something rose in her, a memory. This was important, she suddenly knew. A kernel, if only she could crack it, that would explain much to her. An answer to a riddle that she had not realized had been posed.

The Sharif jogged her elbow. "Who is?" she said. "Who is?"

The touch of idea dissipated. "Who is he?" Gaultry, knowing the Sharif had managed to follow little of what she had been saying, projected an angry image instead of words. *A storm, thunder and rain. Issachar, burying his fist in her stomach, and then herself, hanging helpless like a lamb from a monstrously large eagle—claws, claws that rent her without mercy, without regret.*

"He almost brought down Tielmark's throne," she said out loud. "I stopped him." She had unconsciously begun to rub her thigh. The claws that had cut her there—those of Gyviere, Issachar's eagle-mount—had nearly cost her that leg.

He's afraid of you, the Sharif said. *Right now he's worrying, wondering what he should do next.*

"Really?" Gaultry said. "A man who can make a choice like that, so easily?" Issachar crossed to the third bowl, the dainty, carved crystal bowl that was filled with the strongest punch. The server at that bowl was a woman with milky cataracts. She took up a clean glass, filled it by weight, and held it out blindly, until Issachar took it from her hand. The liquid swirled in the crystal glass, claret-purple.

A respectful murmur went through the crowd. Issachar touched his lips to the glass and turned to meet Gaultry's eyes. Just for a moment. Then his gaze flickered, and he looked away.

At her side, the Sharif laughed, silently, so only Gaultry could hear her. *Look at him. He's so afraid, he wants to prove his strength to you. Why else take that cup?*

"He could pulp me into mince," Gaultry said, sincerely astonished. "And it wouldn't be for the first time."

The dark Bissanty lord made his way back to them. That drew some attention, but Gaultry at least had a glass in hand now, so they weren't quite so noticeable.

"Why have you come to Bassorah?" he said. He was so dark, so cold, that she could not help but shiver. She tried not to let her gaze rest on the purple drink in his hand. She was finding it hard not to tremble openly.

"I asked you first," she told him.

"I was invited," he said silkily. His tone told her he doubted she shared the invitation. "I am third rank of the Order of Storm." Issachar's eyes slid sideways to single out a stocky warrior on the landing above them. "We are Llara's soldiers. There are four of us here tonight. Master Lendra likes to make a show of his respect for the mother of all Bissanty." Gaultry shot a curious glance past him to the stocky warrior. The man, like Issachar, had jagged cheek scars. And like the dark lord, he wore black trimmed with silver. But though the man was strong-looking, he could not match Issachar's aura of menace and power. Indeed, this man attended to some nobleman's chatter as politely as if it had never occurred to him that anyone might mistake him for a living personification of doom.

Looking at Issachar, the memory she had tried to capture before the Sharif had jogged her elbow flashed on her.

She had thought that the dark hawk-lord was unique. Magic had twisted him into a pattern unlike anything the gods had planned for, something tangled between man and animal, and suffering for it. It had been a comfort to her to think that Issachar's plight was unique, that the man who had committed this atrocity on his soul was safely dead.

But she had seen other magic recently that had sought to undo the line between man and beast.

The deer-boys. The Vanderive deer-boys, back in Tielmark, served up to the Prince's table. Their humanity had been so deeply hidden, body and soul, that not even Dervla, High Priestess of Tielmark, could sense it.

A frightening realization came to her: the day of Emiera's feast, she had been able to sense the magic that bound the deer-boys because of its close relation to the spell from which she had freed Issachar. And not just the spell which had bound Issachar. It was the same magic that had bound the Prince and had bound Mervion, diminishing them to helpless pawns in the great struggle to save Tielmark's throne.

She failed to make this connection before because she had believed that those spells had been created by Heiratikus, the former Chancellor of Tielmark—and Heiratikus was dead.

But now she understood. Whoever had desecrated the bodies of the deer-boys, binding the animal-spirits to their souls and transforming their naked corpses, must have shared another aspect of that power with Heiratikus. That sorcerer had used Heiratikus. No doubt the traitor Chancellor had been chosen for the task because of his Brood-blood. The Bissanties could not have placed one of their own so close to Tielmark's heart without arousing untimely suspicions. But Heiratikus, with borrowed power and castings, had not wielded the spells with enough strength or conviction. He had not been strong enough to trap Gaultry, and with that failure, his plots had collapsed.

She could thank the Great Twins together for that—for giving her enough power that she had survived the dangerous days when her Glamour-soul had first opened to her, and its raw power had not been under her control. A newly frightening thought stabbed her. If she had come so close to defeat by this sorcerer's magic at second hand, what would it be like to face him—or her—straight on?

"You owe me," she said, looking up at the dark lord boldly.

"Not much," he answered.

"I don't need much," she said. "Just the name of the sorcerer who cast a spell."

"You think that because you are overconfident," Issachar said. "You can't help that."

"The gods call it great-heartedness." She held his eyes. "They called me so to my face," she reminded him.

"Much good it will do you. The gods don't interfere often," Issachar replied. "Men can go their own ways. So too can Empires. Else, why would the Goddess of Pure Storm and Sky-Fire allow this?" He drained the contents of his glass and reeled back, clutching at the stair's newel post. The purple drink hit his stomach fast. From the expression on his face, it was worse than ghastly. He swallowed convulsively. For a moment there was human color in his face, shocking in the pale of his unnatural gray skin. Then he wiped his mouth, recovering. His dark eyes brightened with drugged fire. The pain had passed. Euphoria briefly flushed through him, heating his chill, damping the predator.

"Tell me the name of the sorcerer who plays with men's souls," Gaultry demanded, seizing his moment of weakness. She didn't care who overheard. This was too important, too critical. "Who ripped your soul, Issachar? Who paired it with a hawk's? Who stripped even that from your body?"

Issachar gave her a sharp look. The drug passed through him quickly, the coldness of his half hawk-spirit freezing its strength. "I wouldn't advise going near him," he told her. "He is not like Heiratikus, a mewler who doubts the hold of his power. Even you, he would rip to pieces."

"Does he still own you?"

"If he knew you were here, you wouldn't be standing here as a free woman," Issachar riposted. "I would put my hands on your throat and drag you to him on your knees. But, as you have escaped Bissanty chains thus far, you must have learned our ways. We do not act before there are orders."

Gaultry, one hand reflexively covering her throat, was spared answering by a clash of cymbals.

"The Prince! Make way for the Prince!" The crowd bunched away from the great hall's main entrance, poison-drunk nobles stumbling to clear the way. Eight guards marched in, followed by six men, in pairs, wearing purple-and-gold livery. Then came a pause, a knotting in the crowd, and confusion. Something had interrupted the order of the procession.

"The Pallidon!" a man cried out angrily. "Make way for Empire's Heir—"

"Shut up!" another man cut him short. "It is the Sea Prince!"

"Llara on me! It's both of them!"

"Unheard of!" Issachar breathed. "Lendra is asking for trouble if he's invited them together to his house."

There was movement behind them on the stairs. Gaultry looked up in time to see Prathe Lendra step out on the landing where the double curve of stairs met. His face was carefully schooled between amusement and annoyance. "Our bowl of Purple cup is almost dry," he remarked calmly to his steward, as if there was no scrambling confusion in the hall beneath him. Angolis Trier, stork legs and all, was bobbing obediently at his Master's side. Unlike Lendra, the steward looked openly apprehensive. "See that it is renewed. We fail as hosts if we do not have suitable drink to welcome their princely majesties."

Trier, his face pale, pushed quickly down the steps and across to the punch bowls.

There were four men at Prathe Lendra's back, guarding the slight figure of a boy in splendid green velvet livery.

Tullier. His face was white and tired. His glacier-green eyes were huge in his face. Gaultry, her torn Glamour-soul lurching in her, found she had taken a distracted step towards him. *Oh, Elianté!* she cried, deep where only the Sharif could hear. *How are we going to save him now—*

Loud voices cut the length of the hall. The princely entourages, clashing in the street, had evidently sorted through the precedence of entry. Two figures appeared, framed in the great double doors.

"Well met, Brother Prince." Prince Inseguire Pallidonius, First Prince of Bissanty, ruler of Dramcampagna, moved with a lazy saunter well-fitted to his youth and his negligent poise. Pausing in the doorway where everyone could see him, he yawned like an overgrown cat and rubbed his mouth with a golden sleeve. Gaultry did not find him handsome, but the black-haired man-boy cast an impression of smugness, of satisfaction with his state and looks. "Were you expected here this evening?"

"I think not." The Sea Prince, staring over his great-nephew's head, finished dismissing his entourage before he turned his full attention to the young Prince. He was a tall man, loose-limbed, with a strong craggy face and white hair, easily a head taller than Bissanty's Crown Prince. "But I thought it might amuse me to come just the same."

The voice was unmistakable. Gaultry did not need to spy Dati's handsome face at the man's shoulder to know that this was the hooded man from Prathe Lendra's pleasure room. It was there in the voice, in the arrogance of his carriage, in the way he unconsciously turned his body to dominate his imperial great-nephew.

"But I take it you were invited," the Sea Prince said. "Prathe is a gracious host indeed, calling Empire to his home. A righteous man indeed is one who knows his Masters." He turned his shaggy white head to the stairs, fixing Prathe Lendra with an inquiring gaze.

His gaze shifted, lit on Tullier, and then returned to the house's Master. For one moment, his eyes, his glacier-green angry eyes, blazed with killing rage.

They were Tullier's eyes. Tullier's eyes as they would look in fifty years. The recognition sparked a pain in Gaultry that was almost like a surge of magic. Something in her revolted against the identification. Surely this man—one of the most powerful members of the Imperial family—surely this man could not be Tullier's father.

"Lendra!" The Crown Prince had not seen the old man's anger. "Blessings on this house—" He was at the foot of the stairs, bare paces from Gaultry, Issachar, and the Sharif, waiting for his cue to ascend.

"And on you, my Prince." Lendra made a gesture, and his steward pressed a crystal goblet into the young Prince's hand.

Pallidonius threw a full measure of the purple punch back in his throat and handed the glass back to Trier with a curt nod of thanks. "Very fine," he said, wiping his mouth with the back of his hand. The punch, which had made even Issachar reel, brought no other reaction. Trier bobbed his head and shuffled across to serve the Sea Prince.

"Now then, Prathe." The Prince swept up the stairs in a flash of gold cloth. Prathe descended to meet him halfway down. Pallidonius kissed Prathe Lendra's cheeks effusively and shook his hand. "To the feast of Belsarius," he said. Gaultry saw now that the Prince had stripes of yellow clay on his forehead, similar to those she had seen worn by the members of the strange parade down by the river that morning as she had washed clothes with the Sharif. The clay made a strange contrast to Pallidonius's fine silks and gold. "And to putting down your people, only to find, by Llara's blessing, that you master us in trade."

Prathe Lendra smiled, a fixed smile that revealed nothing of his true feelings. "Welcome to my humble house, Prince of all my holdings."

"And who is this you are hiding from me?" The Crown Prince was neither so simple nor unobservant as he pretended. His eye went past Lendra's shoulder, up the stairs, to Tullier.

For one moment, he held onto his smile. Then his charm dropped away, revealing a face as dark and cold as winter.

"My most recent acquisition," said Lendra smoothly. He stepped out of the Crown Prince's way, his face untroubled, his voice even. Gaultry realized then that he had descended to try to prevent Pallidonius from seeing the Sea Prince and Tullier together, something the Crown Prince had been able to intuit from less knowledge than she.

"I want him." The Emperor's Firstborn made a gesture with his hand. One of his guards, unsheathing his sword, drew swiftly to his side. "Llara's heart in me, give him over."

A pause lengthened as Lendra, unmoving, stared at the young Prince, a smile hovering. "You may not have the first claim here," he said.

Slowly, the Prince turned around and looked at his great-uncle, Siri Caviedo, the Sea Prince. "What do you say, Brother Prince? Shall Lendra gift him to me? Or do you have a claim on him already?"

There was no hesitation in the old man's answer. "I? What have I to do with children?" Dati, still at the Sea Prince's side, moved protectively against his Master's shoulder, shooting the young prince a resentment-filled glare.

"Your face says otherwise," Pallidonius spat.

"As you like." The Sea Prince turned to the house's Master. "You can't refuse him, Prathe. Give him the boy."

Lendra nodded infinitesimally, his own face a cipher. Tullier's guards pushed him forward.

Tullier's slim form wobbled down one step to the Crown Prince. He moved as though he was drugged. He did not seem to see the Sea Prince, or Gaultry and the Sharif, or anything beyond the stairs, the man in gold who stood before him, and the swordsman with his naked blade gleaming in his hand.

"What have you to say for yourself, my boy?" the Crown Prince said, gesturing for the swordsman to move forward. The expression on the Prince's face was most peculiar. He seemed at once irresolute and determined. "What have you to say, to hold my hand from killing you here?"

Tullier, dazed, stared at Pallidonius, five steps below him

on the staircase. He could see that the threat was mortal, he could sense bonds upon him that prevented flight, or perhaps even attack. He drew himself to his full—if scant—height.

"I am Sha Muira," he intoned. He shouted a curse in an unintelligible, guttural tongue. It had the sound of metal scraping stone. "I commit myself to death, as I have committed my body twice before to Great Llara who watches above, my protector! Which of you here shall be my companions on my road to Llara's Hall?"

The crowd below, its senses fuddled with poison and drunkenness, simply panicked. The Crown Prince himself stepped hastily back, calling for his honor guard to surround him.

Only Gaultry ran forward. She caught Tullier's hand and tugged him forward.

She could not move him. His feet had been rooted to the steps with a freshly-cast magic spell.

She looked up and met the sinister depths of Prathe Lendra's eyes. He had stepped back, along with everyone else on the stairs, but he wasn't frightened. He had held Tullier in his power for almost a full day, and perhaps did not believe that the boy was Sha Muira. He stood, watching, and rubbed a gold bracelet on his wrist, a bracelet of braided wire.

Gaultry, through the piece of her Glamour-soul in Tullier, suddenly, vividly, felt the tie of the magic that extended outwards from the bracelet as if it bound the whole of her own soul—instead of just a piece of it.

She stared at the certainty in Lendra's face, his amusement at the riot that had broken out in the hall beneath him, and something in her ripped open, like a flash of golden light. Her wounded Glamour-soul, flashing out from behind the weakened caul Mervion had laid over it, reached to its missing piece. "Tullier!" she found herself crying. "Oh, Tullier! I won't let them have you!"

She took him in her arms. Dazed as he was, he didn't seem to recognize her, but neither did he protest. His body was like a limp bundle of sticks. The unbound part of her Glamour-soul slipped against the magic Mervion had set, searching for a point of entry. Suddenly, the two separate halves made a direct, if transient, contact. For that brief moment, the full strength of her Glamour came to life. Instantly it blazed, with radiant fury, drawing so strongly on the strength in her body that she stumbled and almost dropped Tullier down the steps. It raged out, beyond her control, immolating Lendra's bond as if it was a wisp of oil-soaked grass. It had been latent and quiet so long, its flare of power was a blinding joy, almost more than Gaultry could tolerate.

When she was aware of her surroundings once again, every candle, every oil lamp, every light in the whole of the great hall had been snuffed. A roar of angry magic buzzed to the rafters. Panicked cries rose up all around her. She became aware of Tullier's thin body, still clutched in her arms, and then, more slowly, of hands that dragged at her back. Her head knocked against the stone of the stair's banister.

Gautri, she felt the Sharif's mind touch hers, even as she recognized the clasp of the war-leader's hands. *Gautri, are you alive? Andion's eyes—what was that?*

"I'm alive," Gaultry answered. Tears ran down her face in the dark. Inside her chest she could feel the coldness that meant that she was still missing half her Glamour-soul: the spell Mervion had laid had somehow managed to survive the mad burst of power; Tullier still possessed half her heart's magic.

"Where are we?" Tullier said drowsily. He had been heavily drugged. He could scarcely stand on his own feet. "What in Llara's name is happening?"

CODA

"Send him in," said Prathe Lendra, annoyed. The undersecretary, sensing his Master's foul mood, genuflected deeply and hurried from the room. It was not often that Prathe openly vented his emotions on slaves or servants, but his moods were unpredictable, and his servants knew to be cautious. After the wreck of the previous night's party, the escape of the boy prisoner with his accomplices, and the Crown Prince's rage at what he had termed "irresponsibility and endangerment," it was little wonder Prathe was in a bad mood. Villa Lendra was in an uproar as the staff labored to repair the damage caused by five hundred panicked guests—and the opportunists among them who had stripped the downstairs hall of souvenirs. Two of the crystal punch bowls had been stolen—Prathe had humor enough left in him for the irony of that to make him smirk. Those guests could not drink, could not ascend to the upper party—and now they had mementos of their social inadequacy.

Prathe got up from his desk to pace and to prepare for his visitor. It would take the Sea Prince a few minutes to reach him. The servants might complain because Prathe kept his private office in the deepest wing of his villa, but at times like this Prathe could make good use of the distance and the delay it took his visitors to reach him from his front door. It gave him the leisure to prepare for guests, expected or otherwise, and the long walk through the luxuriously appointed hallways of the villa could not help but impress a visitor with the weight of his wealth.

He aligned the ornaments on his desk: the little jade dragon, the gold toad with its ruby eyes, the intricately carved slice of Gallian wood. Reminders of his homeland. Restless, he picked up the dragon, then set it down again, trying to settle himself for the confrontation. It was early yet, and not a good sign that Siri Caviedo had already risen from his princely bed to confront Prathe in his inner sanctum. The Sea Prince was arrogant and careless and lazy, and he liked to pleasure himself and drink late into the evening, but he could also be shrewd, resourceful, and hardheaded. Prathe—he could admit such a thing to himself—had allowed the man's lesser qualities to lull him into carelessness. Siri Caviedo had not remained on the Sea Prince's throne through the reigns of three Emperors because he was soft or stupid. Under the pose of epicurean sensualist, he was true Imperial get, and cold fire burned in him.

Preferring not to linger over this unpleasant truth, Prathe crossed to the divan by the window. A cherry-colored gown with a white tulle underdress had been laid out across its silk back. There was a handful of strange silver-gold coins—one split into halves—cradled in the dress's lap.

It wouldn't do to let the Sea Prince see this.

Prathe pocketed the coins, then picked up the dress and pressed a fold of the material against his face. She'd worn no perfume, the huntress-woman from Tielmark, but he could smell her in the dress's folds all the same. Smell her, and imagine that once again she stood before him.

The night of their first encounter, in the dim light of his pleasure room, she and her companion had been nothing more than muffled shapes. Their mistake, their attempt to avoid Dati and his harangue, had been immediately obvious, but he had felt himself to be in no danger and had chosen to play along. The woman's reactions had been most amusing. When she caught sight of the boy-dancers, she had visibly stiffened. He had been unable to see her expression under the fold of cloth that had covered her head, but he had recognized the reaction. Recognized the reaction and thought her cheap and simple, and wondered at the foolish egoism that had brought such an innocent to his house.

Meaning to expose her, he had deliberately allowed himself to meet her eyes, shadowed in her hood. In those shad-

owed eyes—in the brief moment before she had started running she had stared back—he had seen a glint of something
strange. Something feline, trapped and angry. For that
moment, the intensity of that catlike glare had reduced him to
something hunted, something like a cornered bird. With the
woman's flight, the sensation had dissipated, and he had fool-
ishly allowed himself to dismiss it.

Later when his men had brought the boy to him, Prathe had
been too quick to think that he understood why the pair of
them had ventured into his domain. One look into those
glacial green eyes, burning with pride and fury, and the narrow bony face, and he had known the boy for the Sea Prince's
son. The likeness was too obvious to be mistaken. Siri
Caviedo had come to his house that very night to convince
Prathe to employ his spy network to discover the boy's
whereabouts, dead or alive. Prathe had mistaken that coinci-
dence for a cunning plan, presuming that the boy had dared to
enter his house to be reunited with his father—dangerous
ground indeed, but ground on which Emperor Sciuttarus
would be unlikely to gain wind of their reunion.

The fabulously lucky fortune that the boy had delivered
himself into Prathe's hands before reaching the safety of his
father's side had banished all thought of the boy's partner,
who, he had assumed, had been merely a paid subordinate. It
was evident from the first that the boy had no suspicions of
his heritage—he had not invoked Imperial privilege to be
united with his sire. More strangely, he had sought to protect
himself from Prathe's questions and his whip by claiming a
link to the Sha Muira—indeed, he had claimed to be Sha
Muira himself. Prathe had not deemed this claim credible, the
boy being alive, healthy, and lacking either a Sha Muir guard
or a life necklace to hold back the effects of the goddess-
blessed poison that would certainly have been in his body,
were he indeed Sha Muira as he had claimed.

Prathe—in retrospect, he understood how fully he had
deluded himself—had imagined that, even though he was
ignorant of his pedigree, the boy had been instructed to seek
the Sea Prince's protection. Prathe had imagined that the Sha

Muira story was a desperate pretense to keep the boy alive long enough to effect the reunion.

But now the pieces had come together. The boy *was* Sha Muira—the same Sha Muir boy that the Emperor himself had ordered be shipped to Tielmark. When those orders had first crossed Prathe's desk, he had found them strange indeed, but now they made sense. The Emperor—Llara only knew how—had learned of the boy's existence and had shipped him away on a killing mission to Tielmark. Sciuttarus, Prathe mused, must have intended to strike down two birds with a single stone—new killings in Tielmark to further some Imperial plan, and the elimination of a potential usurper. To Sciuttarus, it must have seemed a flawless plan. The Sha Muira were his servants: if he ordered them to withdraw support from a young novice, they would do so without hesitation or question.

If the Emperor's plan had succeeded, the boy would have died in the course of a routine Sha Muir venture—or have been left stranded where he could not return to Sha Muira Island in time to renew the prayer-beads of his life necklace. The Sea Prince would have had only himself to blame: if he had placed the boy among the Sha Muira for safety, he had also left the boy vulnerable to the dangers of such service.

The Emperor's fatal mistake—a mistake he could scarcely have predicted—had been to send the boy to Tielmark. In Tielmark, the boy had found the one sorceress in all the world with the power to sunder his Sha Muir bonds and leave him living. And he had somehow managed to persuade her—Prathe could only guess at the promises the boy had made in return for his freedom—to use the Glamour-magic in her body to defeat the goddess-blessed Sha Muir poison.

There was a mystery. What could the boy, knowing nothing of his heritage, have promised the Glamour-witch, to buy her support? Perhaps she was a soothsayer as well as a witch? Had she somehow managed to foresee the Imperial prizes that might come to her if she afforded him her protection?

Or perhaps she did not yet understand her power, and she was still vulnerable to coercion? No—that last was too much tó hope for. She knew her strength. He rubbed his wrist. Last night, he had barely rid himself of the bracelet in time. She had, so easily, snapped the bond that he had taken such pains to put on the boy. The bracelet had been destroyed along with its magic.

"Gaultry Blas." The Glamour-soul woman. Her name tasted good in his mouth. He made a place for the dress in the cedar chest near his desk, folding it neatly so the material wouldn't crease. He had not been a rich man all his life, and he could not bear to see the misuse of even such inferior goods as this dress's material.

Thinking on the young Glamour-witch soothed him. He thrust his hand into his pocket to jangle the silver-gold coins, thinking on the irony that the first woman born to the god-challenging power in three hundred years of Bissanty's crippled ruling had resorted to petty trickeries. Last night, in the great hall, the power she had summoned to break the boy's harness of spell, to reduce the hall, in one instant, to darkness, was almost beyond imagining. But this dress . . . Prathe smiled. It was an answer to at least one of his questions. If she had appeared at his house wearing this dress, then she could not yet have arrived at an understanding of the potential reach of her magic. The nap of the cheap velvet had already begun to rub away at the seams and creases.

He would ready a new dress for her. He pictured it in his mind's eye. Not red. He smiled to himself. Not red, not blue, not purple. Deep forest green, for her origins, and her wild spirit. Deep forest green, and her underclothes would be gossamer—

"Master Lendra!"

"Your Most Serene Highness. To what do I owe the pleasure of this audience?" Prathe moved behind his desk, running his finger along the fine leather of its edge.

"I've come to retrieve my boy." The old man, glorious in his blue and silver uniform, threw himself into Prathe's spare chair with the athletic grace of a man decades younger. "And what game did you think to play, exposing him to Pallidonius last night? That young blowhard would have killed him then and there, and you would have let him."

Prathe found himself grinning. "You were eager enough to deny him yourself, if I recall the words—*What have I to do with children?* Old fox! If you had not made such a scene, arriving on his heels to my party, I assure you the affair would have played differently."

The Sea Prince scowled. "I knew you were up to something when you dumped me and Dati out of your house the night previous with so little fanfare. I could smell it on you. You're not so subtle as you imagine, Prathe."

Prathe inclined his head, accepting the words as a mild rebuke. Underneath, he was profoundly relieved that Siri had returned to his usual familiarity of address. He sat behind his desk, gaining confidence that he'd be able to twist this interview to his own benefit. The Sea Prince had smelled something wrong only after he'd wasted a day recovering from his hangover. Then, and only then, had he chosen to move.

"So who was the nursemaid?" the Sea Prince asked. "And where has she taken him?"

Nursemaid. Prathe picked up his letter opener and tapped it against his teeth. He pictured the Tielmaran woman lunging up the stairs, her black hair—surely a wig—flying, her skin powder-white, her eyes a blaze of green and yellow light, her face fierce and determined. He took a breath, remembering the scent of the raw power that had coursed through her, its molten heat an implacable force, consuming the bonds he'd lain on the boy, draining the fire from every candle.

"The nursemaid? That was Gaultry Blas, the Tielmaran Glamour-witch. Didn't you wonder to see your son alive, having been abandoned to his own defenses by the Sha Muira?"

"I had wondered," the Sea Prince said dryly. "Tielmark again. That fly will ever bite us—though this time, I suppose, I must be grateful. What do you think the boy promised to secure her aid?"

"I don't know."

"Where has she taken him?"

"I don't know that either."

The glacier eyes flashed. "Those are not good answers, Prathe. You have the only functioning net of spies in all Bissanty. You want to tell me you don't know where they are? I won't believe it."

Prathe shrugged. "You saw the chaos last night. It will be some time before all is sorted. Anyone could have escaped in that mess. Certainly, my squealers have given me some answers. I know where your son and his witch have been, and I can guess where they're going." *And my web has two more spies*, he gloated privately. *A poor tailor down to his last six bolts of cheap velvet, and a soldier-family's cook. Both of whom had greeted his inquiries with relief once they learned their information would be paid for with silver instead of promises.*

"Then where are they going?"

Prathe Lendra gave the Sea Prince a disingenuously tranquil look. "It surprises me deeply," he said mildly, "to learn that you fathered this boy."

"Does it?" The old man rose abruptly from his chair and crossed the window. Standing there, his body outlined by the morning light, he set his gaze on the distant outline of Llara's temple. It was raining outside, and the storm clouds were heavy. The silver dome appeared as little more than an outline, hovering above the wreathed steam and mist that rose from the city. "I suppose it should. I was never born to find pleasure in the bed of a woman. That's no news to anyone."

"Who better to ghostmonger?" Prathe touched the edge of one of the coin halves in his pocket, thinking again of the woman, the smooth skin of her arms, her face.

The Sea Prince raised his hand as if to hold the far-off temple in his grasp. Then he shook his head, emphatic. "Ghostmonger—no. I was born fifth Prince. That fate suited me well. My father was not a murderer—nor my brother-heir either. They treated me well, and taught me to respect them. I was raised in full awareness that my life was best lived only to follow my own pleasure, and that my pleasure should be to serve

Bissanty. Siri Caviedo play ghostmonger? No. Emperors need sons, and the ambition is not in me to get sons."

"Ambition is only one reason to ghostmonger," Prathe suggested. The Sea Prince was not lying. But he would not be open about anything that approached the truth so easily. "There are others."

"You think I would ghostmonger against Sciuttarus for revenge?" The old man sounded amused.

"Luka Pallia bore you a son. That might have given you a reason." Twenty years past, Luka Pallia had been a sensation on the stage of the Imperial theater, a pretty child whose bizarre boy-girl body had appealed to the jaded tastes of the Bissanty court. The Emperor had him murdered for his audacity in bearing the Sea Prince a child the very year his own Crown Prince was born.

The Sea Prince nodded. "The poor boy was a freak of nature, and Great Llara made my seed strong." He sighed. "I have lived long enough to have learned that the gods do not understand human nature. They understand only that they can dictate man's fate. Just as the Emperor is victim to Llara, and forced in every generation to remake his family in the image of her only mortal-born child and his five sons—so Luka was made victim, when Llara granted him his heart's wish and got him with child. Sciuttarus should have understood that, and left my poor boy alone. There is much I would do to punish Sciuttarus for venting his rage on him. But you forget yourself. You are speaking nonsense: I am an old man—I am not placed to ghostmonger sons. I lost that race to my brother Ighion—Sciuttarus's father. My generation already had its five sons. The goddess-blood bypassed me. The burden is on Sciuttarus and *his* brothers to make the next Emperor, not on me and mine."

"So why this child?" Prathe asked. "Do not tell me you met a second Luka Pallia. The new boy's mother must have been a woman."

The old man threw himself back onto the spare chair, something tired in his expression. His words, when he finally spoke, were barely loud enough for Prathe to hear. "Llara, in her Grace, gave me that first son. It was nothing I wanted, but Luka prayed for it with all his silly, unthinking soul, and the Great Thunderbringer saw fit to answer that prayer. Sciuttarus would have done best to let the matter rest. Instead, he poisoned Luka and castrated our son. That defied Llara's will." The old Prince's eyes were full of wrath—a wrath from which he seemed to gather fresh strength. "If I chose to birth a son to right that wrong, it was and is my own business—and Llara's—not Sciuttarus's!

"I have been Sea Prince for fifty years now. I have served Bissanty well in every port to which I sent our ships. I have served three Emperors—Sciuttarus included—beyond anyone's expectations. And"—the ice-green eyes flashed across the house's Master with a chill expression—"for twenty years the reins have been loose on your trading empire, Prathe, because I found it convenient. If Sha Muira were being sent to Tielmark, my son among them, that should have been in the report you made to me last month."

Prathe felt a chill course along his spine. "I did not know he was your son."

"That was not your business. Your business was to trade with your little ships, to grow rich and fat, and to tell me everything that related to the Sha Muira. When you petitioned the Emperor to end the Sha Muir charter, you did so because I told you I wanted it."

"Your son," Prathe guessed. "You wanted to free your son before the cult risked him on his first mission."

The Sea Prince nodded. "I overplayed my hand. Sciuttarus is no fool. That ploy must have led him to young Tullirius. Llara is with me still—the boy escaped. But now you must tell me where Tullirius has hidden himself."

Prathe reached across his desk and picked up the jade dragon. Siri Caviedo was a good liar. Better than Prathe would have credited. He merged truth with fiction so delicately that Prathe himself could not see where the line was drawn. The story the old man told was pretty: of love enduring and the goddess's wishes honored. Perhaps it was even true. But Prathe was certain that entwined round it was a darker story—a tale of long-laid vengeance.

For years now, desperation had ruled Emperor Sciuttarus's efforts to make new sons. Desperation that had driven him to Prathe Lendra for assistance, bringing Prathe—to a limited degree—into his confidence. Twelve Emperors, it seemed, had held the throne of Bissanty since Tielmark's rebellion— one for every god. The man who followed Sciuttarus to the Emperor's seat would ascend the Imperial Throne as the thirteenth ruler of the broken Empire. Sciuttarus had become obsessed by the belief that the thirteenth Emperor would save or rue the ancient Bissanty bonds. Thirteen was Glamour's number—and it was Clarin Pallidonius, the usurper Glamour-Prince, who had shattered the goddess-bond that had chained Tielmark's lands to Bissanty.

Now that Glamour had again touched the lands—in the form of the Tielmaran Glamour-twins—Sciuttarus was certain that the time had come to regain possession of Tielmark, or to lose it forever. The Emperor was desperate for Llara's blessing and the birth of the two children who would make it possible for his oldest son to inherit the Imperial throne. His brothers had not ghostmongered him—of that Sciuttarus was certain—but still, he could get no sons. His despair had brought him low: to the house of a subordinate tribe. Prathe was a Gallian merchant, and Gallia had never been fully Bissanty. Yet the Emperor himself, like the Sea Prince before him, had been forced to acknowledge that only Prathe could deliver him the information he needed.

Prathe Lendra set the dragon back next to the gold toad on the edge of his desk. He was breathing lightly, disguising his excitement, schooling all emotion from his face. The Emperor had come to Prathe because he feared that Llara was not in him; that his own hold on the Imperial Throne was empty. Why else would Llara refuse to bless him with more sons?

Prathe was sure he had the answer to that question now. The Sea Prince was lying. He must have other sons hidden far away from Bassorah, probably concealed as cleverly as Tullirius, countering Sciuttarus's murderous jealousy with a capacity for risk-taking that took Prathe's breath away.

"Don't waste your time trying to decide what you want to tell me!" The Sea Prince grabbed the dragon out of his reach as Prathe made to pick it up again. "I won't have your fiddling! I want an answer straight: where has my son gone?"

Prathe stuck his hand in his pocket, running his fingers over the coins there. He had to make a decision, and quickly. The Sea Prince had told him true: with a brother who had birthed *five* Imperial sons, Siri Caviedo should not also have been able to father five sons. The Imperial blood should not have been in him to do it.

Yet something was preventing Sciuttarus from having sons, and it was not his own brothers.

Of this, Prathe was sure: either Sciuttarus or the Sea Prince would prove father to the thirteenth Emperor of Bissanty— the Emperor who Sciuttarus thought would repair the wound that Glamour-magic and dispassionate gods had torn in their Empire. He stared deep into the old man's face. He was a trading man, he told himself, and a trader is never much of a gambler. Did he want to lay his bets on the Sea Prince, whose son—whether second or fifth—had been touched by Glamour from the Tielmaran woman, or on Sciuttarus, whose hold on the throne was strong but who had birthed only three sons in twenty years of trying?

"We have served each other well in our twenty years' association," Prathe said, carefully not committing himself. "Neither asking more of the other than could be reasonably delivered."

"Where has the Glamour-witch taken my son?" The Sea Prince stared at Prathe, the pale green eyes unrelenting.

Prathe had no intention of letting himself be forced into any new commitment. But telling Siri where they were heading— that he could do with little harm to himself.

"Dunsanius Ford." It had not been hard to follow the trail that led to the humble priest who had translated his steward's Gallian notes. The huntress and her ex-slave companion had been in a hurry, and not overcautious.

"The gods-crossing?" The Sea Prince could not conceal his emotion. .

"The Glamour-witch thinks she has some business there. Something to do with the blood-prophecy which binds her. Tielmark fancies it wants to make itself a King; Sciuttarus is doing what he can to stop that."

"Stupid bitch!" The Sea Prince never questioned that Prathe was speaking truth. He spat out Prathe's window down into the muddy Polonna, far below. "She's headed right through Sciuttarus's home counties."

"And towards your firstborn son. Do you think brother will recognize brother?"

"Lukas, Luka's son, is not living," the Sea Prince said. "Sciuttarus finished that, long past."

"His magic against that of the Glamour-witch will be something to see. 'With sacrifice comes power,' or so the gods assure us."

"My first son has power. Power and no loyalty to me," the Sea Prince said, his voice faltering. "He'll slave the Glamour-witch and give her to Sciuttarus, and there will be an end to Tielmark's fight to keep itself free. But owning Tielmark will not put Sciuttarus's child on the Imperial Throne." His voice hardened, and he almost smiled. "Only two more sons will do that."

He made ready to depart. Prathe, touching the edge of the broken coin in his pocket, was relieved that he made no more demands before leaving. "Will you go after him?" The question was irresistible.

The Sea Prince gave him a sharp look. "That's not a question for you to ask."

Prathe called his undersecretary to escort the Prince to the front of the house. As the door closed, he collapsed, with great satisfaction, behind his desk.

The Sea Prince could not see what stared him in the face. He was blinded by his prejudices, by the labor it must have been for him to bed the women who had produced his hidden sons.

Owning Tielmark might not get Sciuttarus sons—but owning the young Glamour-witch might serve that purpose. Using the fire of her second soul, she would not need Llara—or the gods—to get herself with child.

The Emperor's plan to kill the Sea Prince's son had gone seriously astray. But the rest of his designs—from what Prathe could determine—were unfolding as Sciuttarus had intended. The boy Tullirius Caviedo—Tullier, the Glamour-witch had called him—was an unexpected factor. But the Glamour-witch had been successfully lured to Bissanty.

His mind flashed to the morning he had gone out to the slave-yard to inspect the yield of the Sha Muir envoy. The Emperor's envoy to Tielmark—knowledge of which Prathe had indeed delayed passing to the Sea Prince—had been curious, and of obvious importance in its curiosity. Prathe had learned long since that indulging his curiosity seldom failed to bear fruit. The visit had been instructive, even without his current knowledge.

Martin Stalker. The man had been born to noble holdings; heir, through his father, to a great sorceress's blood. Possession of that blood would give the Emperor power over the Prince of Tielmark.

The man had not appeared the scion of a noble house when Prathe had come to see him. The priests had prepared him for the slave-bond—stripping his body and chaining his wrists behind his back. Prathe had interrupted them. "Bring him here. I want to see him."

Battle-scars marked most of the man's body. His dark hair was cropped short, like a common soldier's, and his muscles strained as he fought against the priests' hands. Raising his unshaved face to Prathe, the man had laughed like a wild animal: a long, bloodcurdling laugh. Bringing him back to the brazier and its red-hot branding irons, four men had held him while the priests tried to put the god-bond on him, to slave him to Bissanty's soil.

The bond would not take. The flesh had burned under the thunderbolt brand, but the spell would not form.

"Do you suppose it is Tielmark's soil in you that rejects the bond," he had asked the man, "or your own blood, which slaves you to the Tielmaran Prince?"

"It's a deeper bond than that," the Tielmaran had answered, panting, involuntary tears of pain tracing his cheeks. "And a soul-pledge more willingly given. Besides," he added, a strange smile flickering on his face, even beneath the tears, "I have finished with such soul-chains. I will not take another bond that will leave me anything other than free."

"Try the other shoulder," Prathe had said, looking at the chained man sharply. The man's words smacked too much of self-prophecy. "Perhaps the bond will take there."

It wouldn't.

"Do you think she will come after you?" Prathe had taunted him. The man's resistance was unnerving, and it had irked him to be unsettled by a man who lay in chains, the hands of four men holding him against the ground. "The Glamour-witch? If she comes after you, that can only end with her too in chains."

"If she reaches me, every man in Bissanty will regret it," the man had answered.

That day in the yard, Prathe had dismissed the man's words as empty bravado.

Now he was less certain. The Glamour in Gaultry Blas was fated to shake nations. Of that, at least, Prathe Lendra was sure. Would it heal Bissanty or merely cauterize the bleeding wound where Tielmark had been torn free?

He'd prepare the green dress for her, he decided, once again sliding her coins through his fingers. Green for her forest origins, for her wildness. Green for the color of the Lendra livery. And green also for her almost certain fertility.

BOOK THREE

▼

chapter 14

▼

Gaultry trudged along the muddy road, rain streaming down her face and body. The foul weather seemed yet another portent of the difficulties ahead. Indeed, nothing resembling a good omen had happened since their escape from Bassorah. Tullier was not speaking. Between the treatment he had received at Prathe Lendra's house and the discovery of the likelihood that the Sea Prince was his father, he seemed to be in shock. The storm that had now overtaken them had threatened before they passed the city gates, as if Great Llara toyed with the idea of pinning them in place, preventing them from escaping the city. Ignoring the menace of the weather, they'd joined the late moving carts of a grain caravan to the first village north of Bassorah, and there the storm had hit. Waves of thunder had swept overhead, accompanied by downpours so severe, lightning bolts so intense, the caravan had refused to press forward. By morning the storm had not abated and they had pressed on, leaving the caravan, only to discover that the storm had chased every other traveler off the road, leaving them exposed and alone on the increasingly waterlogged track. It had been an exhausting day. The best that could be said was that the rain was warm; it did not sap their strength with cold. The worst that could be said was that the road, which had been elevated through the marsh on a packed dirt and gravel causeway, was no more than a few hours away from being flooded.

Nobody moved in the home counties when the rains fell like this, Tullier cautioned her. And certainly nobody moved on the roads, after dark, in a thunderstorm, when it had been raining all day.

"All the better for us to put some distance between ourselves and anyone who might be following," she answered.

"The marsh will absorb the rain," Tullier said. "Eventually. That's why the rest of Bissanty is waiting in its villages for the storm to blow over. Until then it's dangerous. If we slip off the road the marsh will suck us under."

What is he telling you? That the Sharif, who had been eyeing the rising level of the water with the appearance of imperturbability, was in truth nervous, proved a nasty shock. Following their escape from Lendra's villa, the Sharif had directed their flight from the city. While Gaultry and Tullier had lingered in the aftershock of the flare of Glamour, the Sharif had put their hastily conceived flight plan into action, bullying Gaultry and Tullier into their traveling clothes and getting them safely across the city and onto the back of the grain cart. With her efficiency and steady spirit, Gaultry sometimes found it hard to remember that she understood only one out of five words of spoken conversation.

And that she was a creature of the desert, so the sight of rising water unnerved her.

He says it will subside soon, Gaultry lied.

We should find high ground and wait it out, the Sharif told her. *Look—it's reached the marker stones there.* She was not overstating the case. The water had come up to the lower edge of the painted white stones that marked the limits of the road to either side.

There's plenty of daylight before us still. We must keep going.

"High groun'," the Sharif insisted. "We wait there."

"I can't say I disagree," Tullier chimed in.

"Did Lendra whip your mind as well as your body?" Gaultry demanded. Another unpleasant discovery had been the weal marks on his skin beneath the expensive livery in which Lendra had dressed him. "Do you think he'd hesitate to do it again if he caught us?"

Tullier, his shoulders stiff from the beating, turned up the collar of his jacket and shivered.

Gaultry felt a brute. But this was no time for gentleness.

"Tullier, Prathe Lendra isn't the worst of those who may be coming after us. We may find the Emperor's men on our backs. Only the Great Twelve can know what the Crown Prince made of last night's scene." Or Issachar Dan. The dark lord had hinted that he might, with orders, come after them. She didn't say it aloud, but for the past hours her primary concern had been Issachar. The unstable weather was just what the hawkish warrior, with his great steel-feathered eagle-mount, would glory to ride in. And by now the dark lord could very well have received orders from his Master—whoever he might be—to come after her. "And not just the Emperor's men. What about the Sea Prince? Unless you're expecting protection from him."

"Protection?" Tullier spat, bitter. *"Llara, hold my son, I loved him well."* He had memorized the epitaph he'd seen on the Bissanty tombstone back in Bellaire. The words were harsh in his mouth. "My father loved me so well, he buried me above the ground, committing me to death in life with the Sha Muira."

"If you're not expecting protection from him, you must understand why we have to put Bassorah far behind us."

"I'm tired," said Tullier. He sounded strained. The rain had plastered his black hair against his head, making him look younger, more vulnerable. "You can't understand what I'm feeling."

Gaultry reached for the boy's shoulder, trying to find words that might comfort. He was bundled up with so many layers that touching him was safe. "It would be a vain presumption for me to hope I could guess at your father's motives," she told him. "But he did leave you in a place in which, if you survived, you would eventually become near invulnerable. He must not have intended that you die, and he must have known the dangers inherent in leaving any clue behind that might have revealed your heritage." Tullier's shoulder, beneath his shirt, pressed a little against her. Encouraged, she drew him closer. "I lost my father when I was not much younger than you, Tullier. He too abandoned me with no explanation. That was for my own protection, or so went his thinking. It would have helped me greatly if he had given me some hint of that before he left."

"You still don't understand," Tullier said. He jerked away. "What does my father mean to me? I want Llara's love, not some old pederast's. You are so sure that the gods are on your side. How can you be so confident, loving your twin goddess-bitches? How can you know what the gods think?"

Shocked, she tried to catch him, perhaps to hold him, to let him cry, to offer him comfort, she didn't know which. But Tullier did not know how to share his misery. Letting out a moan of fury and rage, he tore free and ran a few steps down the road. Splashing into a deep puddle, he half stumbled and broke his run. For a moment he stopped and looked back at her. Then a fresh lance of lightning cracked down far ahead on the horizon, highlighting the broad reach of the land in a sharp burst of silver fire. The boy picked up his feet and kept on going. Gaultry took a few halfhearted steps to follow, then sighed and slowed.

"He's got nowhere to go but straight ahead," she said. "He knows the dangers of the swamp. We'll catch up to him when he's ready."

The Sharif, taking off her soggy hat and wringing it, nodded. Whether she understood or not was another question.

"We keep goin'," she said. "We find him."

* * *

After an hour, Gaultry began to worry. The intensity of the
storm had not diminished, and Tullier was nowhere to be
seen. Soon it would be nightfall. Although the sky was a
strange light silver, as if the wild storm had thinned and clear
sky was almost managing to break through, beneath that shining sky the winds had picked up and the weather was
appallingly fierce. She sensed that night would come quickly,
thickened by dark storm clouds. They would have to find
shelter before the way became obscured by dark as well as by
rain.

At the side of the road, the marker stones were half submerged. The rising flood had begun to encroach on the road.

"Look," said the Sharif, pointing through the slashing rain.
"Is it Tullier?"

"High groun'," she said. "Maybe Tullier there."

The Sharif, accustomed to the bright reaches of the desert,
had impressive sight for distances. It took Gaultry another
ten minutes to make out, even dimly, the bouldery hump of
land that the tall Ardana had spotted. Anywhere else, it
would have been an insignificant hummock; here, it was an
amazing relief to see something that wasn't rain-beaten
marsh grasses, waterlogged road, or slowly submerging road
markers. An overgrown path led off to the rise, complete
with its own markers. The remains of a small building could
be seen at the top of the hump, half hidden among the boul-
ders.

"Shelter!" Gaultry picked up her pace. Despite her desire
to press on, the unrelenting pounding of the rain and wind
had made her eager for a respite. Picking up their pace, the
two women jogged up the path and along to the ruined building.

"Tullier!" They found him huddled miserably in one corner, under the remains of the roof, knees drawn to his chest,
his expression part rebellion, part shock. Despite his general
rain-washed wetness, his face and hands were black and
sticky. In the intensity of his emotion, his body had newly

purged itself of its internal poisons, dark and strong as the day of Emiera's feasting.

"I'm never going to be free of the Sha Muira," he said, his voice leaden and tired. "I'm as full of poison today as I was when you first lent me your Glamour-soul. It's never going to end, and one day you will have to take your soul back. I've known that since the moment you touched me on the stairs at the Villa Lendra. I could feel it trying to break free and go to you." He turned his face to her. "You should have let me die in Tielmark. I'm afraid of the pain now. Why would you want to do that to me?"

Gaultry came to look at him more closely. He was a shocking sight. The slick of poison had made a sheet of dark oil on his face and hands, and a little on the front of his shirt. She wanted to touch him, but didn't quite dare.

"The Sharif and I will try to get a fire started. In the meantime, you go out in the rain and try to clean yourself." She wished there was something she could say to reassure him.

Together, the women went outside to gather a pile of sodden marsh grass. They brought it in and stacked it in the center of the floor where there was a depressed area that had evidently been used in the past as a hearth—perhaps by earlier travelers seeking shelter. The Sharif doubted they could get a fire going with wet grass, but Gaultry proved her wrong. Back in Arleon Forest, she had learned how to get even the dampest wood started—and the marsh grass, which had been dry before the rain had come, was excellent fuel. At first the flames were feeble, but any fire at all was bright and warming, and Gaultry's success at getting it started cheered them both.

As the fire strengthened, detail in the room became easier to pick out. The ruin was built of crumbled yellow stone, little harder than unfired clay. The flames gained, illuminating a painted frieze, high on the broken walls. In better days the building had been a small temple dedicated to Llara. A section of the roof which had at first appeared to be collapsed proved to be three holes of equal size, designed to open the building to the sky.

"I hope it was properly deconsecrated," Gaultry said. She eyed the frieze uneasily, looking for a symbol that might indicate that such a ceremony had taken place, closing Great Llara's eye to this forlorn place. Signs in the hearth confirmed that they were not the first to use this place for shelter. But the thought that the Thunderer's presence might linger made her uneasy. Jittery, she rose for a closer look at the frieze, a twist of flaming grass in her fist. The pale blue and gray of the design, a serpentine geometric pattern, gave little hint of its meaning. Then the light caught the edge of a deep scratch. Her breath caught in her throat. Carved clumsily into the soft stone, overlying the faded frieze, was the silhouette of a bird with outstretched wings. *We can't stay here,* she told the Sharif. *Do you recognize that glyph?*

That is Rhasan magic, the Sharif answered, equally alarmed. *The sign of Great Llara.*

Gaultry nodded. *That glyph is a spell, waiting to release itself.* Gaultry recognized it from the hexes she had seen her grandmother set at the bounds of her land. *We mustn't panic. We are not the first travelers here. If we are quiet, and move on quickly, we won't invoke it. We'll wait for Tullier to clean himself, then leave. Don't let him see it. He is struggling with himself. I don't want to give him another shock. We will let him dry himself, and then we'll press on.*

The Sharif nodded, agreeing. *He is near despair.*

After a time, Tullier returned. He'd scrubbed himself with a handful of coarse marsh grass and looked pale and somewhat cleaner. The paleness, however, was due to more than newly scoured skin.

"This is Llara's house," he said, hesitating by the broken door. "I blasphemed her here."

"She'll forgive you," Gaultry said, trying not to provoke him. "You were rightfully upset."

"No," Tullier said. "That's not what I mean. I've been to this place before. Three years ago, when I had my six months off Sha Muira Island. They put me in a big house on a half-ruined estate rather than giving me a year in Bassorah City. I guess we know why, now. My father didn't want to risk me in the city."

"Is the house nearby?"

"Not far. I should have recognized the road earlier. And this place. But this temple was newly abandoned then, and it looked different. Without floodwaters around it, even more so."

"Who owned the house?" Gaultry asked, curious. "Could we get shelter there?" Her eyes slid to the Rhasan glyph. She would suggest anything that would hasten them away from this place.

Tullier, lost in memory, was unaware of Gaultry's and the Sharif's anxiety. "Maybe. I don't know. When I was there it had been rented to a drunk with four noisy sons. They had house-parties for the duration of my stay. I was supposed to learn manners from them, and courtly ways. But I'd learned all I was going to learn in the first week. After that, my stay would have been a waste if the house hadn't had a big library—and good horses in the stables." He stared around the ruined room. "I came out here because I was lonely," Tullier said. He sat next to Gaultry and held his hands to the fire. "You saw what Lendra's party was like. People feigning they have a hint of Llara's blood, and testing it against poisoned drink. Well, for six months it was like that every day. I didn't understand why the Sha Muir Arkhons had chosen to deny me the city. I never believed that Llara would hear me—"

"If she heard you," Gaultry said, rising and picking up their bags. "She would have known you were young, and being very harshly tested. Shall we be on our way? There's not much grass left for the fire." She met the Sharif's eye, and the Ardana stood up.

"Why aren't you taking my suffering seriously?" Tullier flared.

Gaultry saw that it had been a mistake not to warn him about the Rhasan glyph. "This is not the moment, Tullier," she said. "Llara in you, be quiet. This is a dangerous place for an argument—"

"You're wrong!" Tullier shouted. "I am old enough to know the fragility of the gods' blessings. How can you know what Llara thinks? I'm cursed—"

Something in his shout caught the rhythm of the wind. Gaultry, staring round, felt a sizzle, as of long-quiescent magic, thrumming in the building's stones. "Be quiet, Tullier," she said, reaching for him. "For the love of the Great Twelve, shut up. There is a spell—"

"You can't stop me!" he cried, so angry that he no longer attended her words. "I'm cursed!"

As he screamed, a blast of wind struck the building, shaking it on its foundations, followed by a loud crack of lightning and thunder, striking somewhere very near in the swamp. The light slashed in through the roof, through the open door behind Tullier, freezing them in a terrified tableau of silver chased with black. Tullier's last words echoed through the room, which suddenly seemed more open and unsafe than the whole of the day's travel out in the flat plain of the marsh.

I'm cursed! the wind sang. It tore the fire apart, whirling showers of sparks and burning grass across the room. *I'm cursed!* It whipped flames that should have been dying into a bulging cone of fire, burning white hot, shot through with brighter skeins of pure light. As the yellow and red died in what was left of the fire's flames, the room blazed to light with shining silver magic.

A new voice, formed of wind and fire, cried out above the storm: *I prayed to Llara to save me, and still I'm cursed!*

The Sharif backed against the nearest wall, crying out in her own language. Gaultry stumbled up, shouting for Tullier to protect himself. "Huntress," she panted out. "Huntress, help me!" The wind whipped the prayer away. Gaultry had felt the touch of the Storm-Goddess once before, in the frozen slash of scar that still marked her hand. Now that strange cold touch burned through all her body. Half-blind with the shock of light and power, she could not turn away from the roil of magic that had consumed their hearth-fire.

A shape appeared within the cone. A spectral bird, a hawk, its black feathers shot through with silver, fought the wind, bold, strong, making a little headway. A second bird joined it, this one small, ghostly white, too weak to fight the battering tempest. The black hawk struggled against the wind, as if trying to seize it, but the wind only laughed and ripped them farther apart. *Help me,* came a weak voice, barely audible above the wind. *Oh Goddess, help me.* That was the small bird, a white dove, its voice almost lost as it faded and sank down.

Goddess be cursed, that she should allow this outrage. And that, in a voice Gaultry clearly recognized, was the black hawk. Issachar Dan. The dark lord's voice curdled with unfamiliar human despair. *Let me die,* the voice said. *Let me not suffer this cursed life. Oh Goddess, why have you allowed this desecration? I have been, always, your servant—*

The cone spun and rose. As if the whole sky had taken a breath, it funneled through the open ports in the roof and vanished.

The magic had run its course. On the wall, the Rhasan glyph was scorched and black. The stone it had been scratched into was crumbled so that it was no longer recognizable.

The Sharif huddled on her knees, palms lifted outwards, sunk in prayer. Tullier stood, face pale and haggard, staring at the ceiling. "What was that?" he said shakily. "Did I trigger it?"

"Leave it, Tullier," Gaultry said, her voice irritated and tired. "This was my fault. I should have warned you. Instead, I let you trigger it. That could have been avoided." Doubt curled in her. "Or maybe it was meant to happen. I don't know. It seems you weren't the only one who cursed the gods in this place." She trembled, unsure whether she'd been shown a punishment or a warning. "What was it? It was a Rhasan spell. Someone did a reading here, and then left that mark so someone who followed would bear witness to what had occurred. Though why Great Llara allowed a

Rhasan reader to work a reading in this place, I don't know."

"The Sha Muira don't believe in the Rhasan," Tullier said. "They believe Llara is the highest power—"

"The Sha Muira would disbelieve their own noses, if the Emperor decreed it," Gaultry said. "I hope you never have a Rhasan reading, Tullier. The card you pull from a Rhasan deck molds your future. You keep touching back to the image—to fight it is madness, or worse." She shook her head. What did the vision mean? She was not sure whether the birds were Rhasan images or something else. The pairing of birds in flight suggested a bonding of futures—just as she and Martin had been bound, Orchid to Wolf.

"Let's get out of here," she said aloud. "Let's go down the road and find this house of yours. They may give us shelter, or they may not—but anything's better than waiting out the rest of the storm here."

The Sharif and Tullier were for once in total agreement.

They saw the wall long before they reached the estate's entrance. Constructed of the now familiar yellow stone, it stretched on for more than a quarter mile before it came at last to the front gate. The tops of mature cypress trees jutted up from behind the wall as they followed the road alongside it. Tullier explained that the estate sat on a table of high ground, with the brick wall running most of the way around, except in the back, where a deep slough made such a barrier unnecessary.

The wind had gentled slightly, but the rain continued and the weather had taken on a chilly edge. Nightfall was overtaking them. Everyone's spirits had reached their lowest ebb.

"How much longer now?" Gaultry asked.

"Not far."

They had walked almost to the gate when the barking began. First one dog, then two, then an entire pack. The noise was deep and spine-chilling; not being able to see the animals that produced it was unnerving. Gaultry found herself imagining huge, monstrous animals with slavering, toothy jaws. The pack, tracking their progress, matched the weary travelers pace for pace on the inside of the wall.

"There were no dogs when I was last here," Tullier offered, as one low growl particularly made her shiver.

Gaultry, who seldom feared animals, shrugged, wishing she had hidden her fear better. "I'll try to turn them against each other if they come after us."

At last they reached the gate, a heavy, oiled grate of iron. The dog pack pressed against it from inside, the bolder members poking their blunt muzzles through the bars, still growling. They were the largest dogs Gaultry had ever seen, with solid, heavy heads and loose skin on their bodies and necks to show that they had been bred for fighting. Mean-looking canine eyes fixed suspiciously on the intruders. Gaultry regretted having spoken aloud her confidence that she could handle them. These animals were the size of undergrown ponies, brindle-coated and muscular. She could smell their musk, their stink of aggression, even from outside the gate.

Beyond the dogs, a gravel drive curved away towards the dark silhouette of a squat, hulking house, set back from the road behind clipped hedges and broad earthwork terraces. In all the mass of the dark house, they could not see the glow of a single light.

"Very welcoming," Gaultry said. She looked back at the dogs, trying to assess if it would do any good to try to spirit-take from them. Their leader was a lean, rawboned bitch, slightly shorter than her mates but obviously dominant. Her doggy lips curled and the hair on her spine stiffened as she met Gaultry's stare, recognizing the threat of magic. *That's right,* Gaultry warned her, letting her see a narrow channel, a channel that she could have thrown open to strip the beast's spirit raw. *Even if I could not fight your pack, I could take you.* Aloud she asked, "What now?"

"There's a bell," Tullier said. "We could ring it." By the

gate, he pointed to a long cord with a ring tied to its end. The other end of the cord disappeared up into a little box.

"Will they be willing to offer travelers shelter for the night?"

"If they know me, they'll let me in," Tullier said.

"Are we sure that's a good thing?"

"We could always spend the night lying on the road, or in a nest of wet grass by its side," Tullier said nastily. "But I thought we'd decided we were against that."

"I am cold," the Sharif interjected, trying to follow what they were arguing about. "Why wait?"

"We need someone to control the dogs," Gaultry mused. "We won't get past them otherwise." Still dubious, but not seeing they had another choice, she reached out and gave the bell cord a quick series of tugs.

After a long time, a single figure came out of the house, shoulders hunched against the rain, a shuttered lamp in one hand. "Quiet!" a man's voice raised above the dogs' growls. "Quiet, I say!"

The pack, grudgingly obedient, drew away from the gates.

"Who is it?" The night-porter unshuttered his lantern. A streamer of light struck Tullier full in the face, lighting the pale green of his eyes. The man gasped and almost dropped his light.

"Domitius," Tullier said, recognizing him in return. "Let us in."

"Tullier Sha Muira." The porter drew back. Spider-thin, he was bundled up in a pale gray coat, already darkened with spots of rain, a necklace of keys dangling in his hand. "What brings you here—and on such a night?"

"Who is at the house?" Tullier replied, imperious and cool. The tone belied his obvious soaked misery, the disarray of his clothing.

"The new Master. Aron Masonillius. He's been here just on two months."

"I need lodging. My companions need lodging. Open the gate."

"I'll need to ask the Master—"

"It's cold out here." Tullier's voice was lethally polite. "Let us in."

"The Master can't be disturbed," the man said, apologetic. "He started a party before the rain set in."

"So let us in," Tullier said. "If he's been in a party for a full day, he won't care if he has extra night-guests. Morning—or noon—tomorrow will be soon enough to ask him."

The expression on the porter's face suggested that Tullier had spoken something near truth. He rattled his heavy necklace of keys, thinking. Then he began to fumble among them for the gate-key, tucking the lantern against his spindly legs to steady it as he searched. "I shouldn't," he said. "I really shouldn't." He was speaking to himself. "But, Llara bless me, the rain is pouring so! The Master can see you in the morning just as well."

"If he's fit for visitors," said Tullier. His politesse with the man held no hint of his earlier broken-spiritedness. With the porter deferring authority to him so politely, the boy seemed as though he had already been dry an hour and was dressed in a fresh suit.

The gate opened with a squeal of protesting metal. The dog pack, growling quietly, drew back to let them in, and then came and swarmed closely around them, large damp noses sniffing and invasive. They stared up into the visitors' faces with hooded, unfriendly eyes. The lead bitch, keeping safely to the outer edge of the pack, sent Gaultry an evil glare and made her pack bunch the trio uncomfortably close within the weak circle of light cast by the porter's lamp.

They began to hear the party music as they reached a low earthwork terrace ornamented with terra-cotta pots, just by the house. A low, bone-resonating sound, it reminded Gaultry uncomfortably of the singers who had accompanied the two boy-dancers at Prathe Lendra's. A few steps on, the first caws of raucous laughter reached their ears. Although the house was shuttered and closed against the wind and rain, evidently the weather had not dampened the revelries. Gaultry gave Tullier an anxious glance. Prathe Lendra's party had been enough for her. She had no desire to attend another Bissanty house party, this one at a private home, played out over days. She didn't want to imagine what debaucheries it might encompass.

Tullier, reading her expression, turned to the porter. "Show us straight to our rooms," he said. "My companions are women of virtue. I don't want them mixing with the guests."

The man nodded. "That would be better, I think. They've got Thalia dancing on the table in the long room." He paused and made a flutter with one hand. "Your old quarters are empty. I'll take you there and send someone to make up the beds."

"Thalia? It's all the same servants?"

The man sighed. "We're land-bonded here, Master Tullier. Of course it's the same servants. Only the Master changes."

They had reached the front door. It was a curious construction of highly varnished marsh-grass woven into a single basketwork panel. Gaultry guessed it was tight and strong enough to turn the blows of an ax. The porter tried to push it open, failed, and fumbled again with his keys. "If you prefer, we could put you in the green suite," he said, balancing the lantern awkwardly on his knee. "The beds are already made there—for guests who never came."

Tullier shook his head. "Put me in my old rooms."

The porter nodded. "Good. The front wing is full, and you'll be more comfortable there in any case. The ladies can have the back room—"

The door was abruptly yanked inward, sending the porter sprawling, and two mocking drunken faces bobbed into view. "Didn't you wonder that it was locked again, Domo?" the taller taunted. For all the frills of lace that fronted his coat, he was a hard-faced man with rangy shoulders that suggested unusual strength. His skin had the strange gray cast that Gaultry had begun to associate with Bissanty nobles who could take their poison strong and lethal.

"My lord," the porter said nervously, gathering his spider limbs and recovering the lamp.

"What a pretty boy!" That was the other man, a balding horror, both his face and the naked skin of his scalp flushed with the red of drunkenness. As he stared at Tullier, his smiling mouth was moist, and even redder.

"Go away, ugly," Tullier said coolly, taking the man's measure. "You're not wanted."

The bald man purpled. "Puppy!" he snarled.

Tullier darted forward and seized the man's wrist. Whatever he did, it must have hurt badly. The drunken eyes glazed, and the breath whistled asthmatically between the bald man's teeth. "Go back to the party," Tullier said. "Go find Arno, or Grissius. We're not here for your games." He released the man and stepped back.

Baldy gave him a resentful look and rubbed his wrist. "There's nothing for us here," he said, tugging at his partner's sleeve.

"The woman is very pretty," said the other, staring at Gaultry. "I could use—"

"She's not for you," the bald man said, almost in a panic. "Come away now!"

Even under his drunkenness, his partner sensed the urgency in his friend's voice. That whetted rather than dulled his interest. He looked at the companions with deepened attention. "Masonillius has left us with only feeble creatures. I have tired of that sport. Now, a woman who is not a slave—"

"Llara on me, leave them!"

Casting them a final look, the gray-faced man allowed his partner to drag him away.

"It's been like that all day," the porter gasped, hurrying them along a corridor with a smoothly tiled floor. "With the poor weather, they're getting bored." Massive stone walls, unplastered and rough, stretched before them. Instead of wooden wainscoting, the walls were inset with thickly lacquered grass panels, the stems cut and woven in a seemingly infinite variety of patterns. Unlike Bassorah, with its proud monuments of marble and granite culled from the quarries of the outermost provinces, this building seemed to have been constructed entirely of local materials. Gaultry guessed that the ground floor of the building and its foundation were ancient, perhaps the remnants of an older, more heavily fortified building. The walls were thick, as though they had been built to support a taller building than the house, seen from the gate, had presented in silhouette.

"Here," the porter said. The wall was so broad that the door he thrust open seemed to be set deep in its own passage. Domitius darted in and lit a table lamp from the flame of his lantern. "Come in, take off your wet things, make yourselves snug. And lock your door," he added nervously. "You have seen already that the guests are wandering tonight. I'll see that dinner's brought to you from the kitchen. You will want to dry your things. Shall I get someone to build you a fire?"

"My women can do that," Tullier told him.

The porter was gone before they could thank him.

"This isn't so bad," Gaultry said, looking around at the spare lines of the room, its simple furniture. Here the grass panels were woven with an elegant design of running horses, reduced to simple geometric patterns to fit with the weave. The room's two windows, without glass as was the common Bissanty fashion, were tightly shuttered against the weather. "This is where you stayed when you lived here before?"

"That's right." Tullier stripped off his jacket and threw it onto a drying rack by the shuttered windows. "And that's not the only advantage to having old Domo stick us in here." He pulled open his pack and wrinkled his nose as he pulled out his spare shirt. It was almost as wet as the shirt on his back.

"What do you mean?"

"In a minute." Tullier dumped out his pack and spread out his clothes. "Aren't you tired of being wet and miserable?"

"Tullier!"

"All right," Tullier relented. "I'll show you." He went to one of the lacquered panels by the door and pressed hard on the rump of one of a pair of woven horses.

With a creaking sound, the panel swung back, revealing a narrow, dust-filled passage inside the thickness of the wall.

"We don't have to wait until tomorrow morning to find out

what sort of a house-master this Aron Masonillius is or how he'll receive us. We can go and take a look. Right now, if you are in such a hurry. Or"—Tullier snapped the panel shut—"we can wait until Domitius's message gets through to the kitchen, have some dinner, and then go."

That was the easiest decision Gaultry had needed to make in a long time.

"Let's build up that fire," she said, "and have something to eat."

chapter **15**

▼

Tullier's dinner consisted of roasted quail,
spiced bread rolls, and a glass of wine. For Gaultry and the
Sharif, there were bowls of barley and vegetable stew and
hunks of more plebeian coarse-grained bread. The former had
been gleaned from the remnants of the feast that had been
served for the party; the latter was kitchen food.

The man who brought their food was a gray-haired giant
with hands like spades and a graceful carriage that belied his
bulk and age. He had no tongue, and his features showed that
he was not Bissanty-born. He proffered Tullier the fancy food
and the others the plain, shaking his finger warningly as he set
Tullier's food before him.

"He's reminding you that we can't share," Tullier said.

"I don't need to be told twice," Gaultry snapped back.
Whenever she began to slip and imagine she had inured herself to Bissanty customs, there was always some terrible
reminder of the society's hopelessly inhumane protocols: an
old man taken, long past, into slavery, food that could not be
shared by those not born to privilege. Trust the Bissanties to

poison-season their food so that only the highborn could enjoy the luxury of meat and sweet-cakes.

Not that the bowls of stew, after a long day of walking through wind and rain, were not delicious. Gaultry, still concerned about the Sharif's health, was pleased to see the woman clean her bowl with a crust of bread as she scraped up the leavings. The desert-woman seemed more sensitive to the cold than either Gaultry or Tullier. Gaultry hoped that the woman's prolonged exposure to the rain would not trigger a relapse of the slave-sickness that had bedridden her in Bassorah.

Before they ate, they had pushed the drying rack close to the fire. By the time they finished, their wet clothes had begun to steam. Gaultry, putting her bowl down, got up to pull the rack away from the flames.

"Shall we foray out to find the house's Master?" Tullier asked after they'd rested themselves in front of the fire for a time.

"Would it be better to wait until the house has quieted?" Gaultry asked.

"Sure," said Tullier. "If you don't want any sleep tonight. It won't quiet until toward dawn."

"Let's go now then."

The boy sprung the panel, showing Gaultry and the Sharif how the catch worked. "The passages run behind most of the walls on the ground floor in the oldest part of the house," he explained. "There are a few places where they extend up to the second floor. Stairs climb up and down over the doorways—or underneath, but that's just in one place. Only one passage goes into the new wing, but it leads directly to the Master's private chambers. In older times, the family who owned this house must have used the passages to spy on their guests. But tonight we can use them to spy on the Master."

"Whoever rents the house doesn't tell the new Master about the passages?"

"Not in my time," said Tullier. "I think they fell out of use long past. When I explored them, I made the first footprints in dust decades old."

She wanted to ask him how he had first made the discovery, but he had brushed off her other questions about his time in the house, so she restrained herself. Had he considered them a place to hide from his vile hosts or an intriguing maze opening new doors to exploration? Perhaps both.

Tullier stepped into the passage, turning his body sideways and ducking his head. Gaultry came after him, mimicking his posture. It was narrow and dirty, with a low roof. The Sharif, in the rear, forced herself about four feet into the cramped passage, then balked.

It's too tight, she protested. *I'm too tall. It's tighter even than my quarters aboard the slave-ship.*

Gaultry looked back. The Sharif was at least half-a-head taller than the passage.

"Stoop." She demonstrated. "Duck your head."

No. I'll wait here. The Sharif backed out of the passage into the room. Her handsome face showed a twinge of panic. *It's too close. Why should I go? You are only going to scout.*

I don't want us to be separated.

"You go," the Sharif said, stubborn. *You went to Villa Lendra without me.*

"That was before—" There was no point in arguing. If the Sharif was claustrophobic, there was little to be gained by forcing her to come. "All right. Keep the door locked."

"They all drunk out there. Maybe you find a chance to steal me a sword." The Sharif, grinning, indicated with her hands the length of the blade she wanted.

A sword. In Bassorah, even the most brittle blade had been beyond their means.

"Tullier?" Gaultry asked.

"We can get weapons," he said, his face lighting. "There's a storeroom I can get into—if it hasn't been opened in the past three years and emptied."

"That sounds more important than spying on the house's Master," Gaultry said. "Let's try for that first."

The Sharif pushed the panel shut behind them, closing them into the dimly lit passageway. Though the grass panels were at least half an inch thick in most places, and in some as much as an inch thick, speckles of light leaked in through the weave and through small patches of clear or translucent lacquerwork, giving them, when the rooms and corridors they passed were well-illuminated, enough light by which to see. Where rooms outside the walls were dark, Gaultry held the back of Tullier's shirt and let him lead her, since the openwork meant that they couldn't risk a torch or taper of their own. Fortunately, they were able to see most of the time, and enough noise echoed in from the party that even had Gaultry been constantly tripping on Tullier's heels, she doubted that anyone would have heard them.

"You must have loved knowing about these passages when you were here before," she whispered, peeking out at a room where swift-working servants tidied away the remains of a feast.

"I saw some things nobody would have wanted me to see." Tullier replied.

The last part of their route led through a totally dark passage, climbing rough, unfinished steps up between coarsely-finished masonry walls. There were no grasswork panels or illuminated openings to relieve the darkness. The narrow stair was hot and stuffy. The air felt stale. Gaultry, with rough stone brushing her on two sides, could feel a slick of dirt and sweat accumulating on her skin. She caught her temple on an unexpected spur of stone and winced, stars in her eyes momentarily brightening the darkness.

"Is it far, Tullier? I just hit my head again." The oppressive dark had begun to wear on her nerves. Even with a hand upraised to protect herself, she kept banging into stone. Tullier had it easy. Not only was he familiar with their route, but his slim body made him better suited to the scale of the passage.

"We're here," Tullier whispered back. "Put your hand out." She reached out cautiously. Her fingertips, roughened by the walls, brushed a surface that was slick with lacquer. She felt a faint draft, as if from a void beyond the lacquerwork. "Be quiet. If this room has been turned to another purpose since my last visit, there may be somebody inside."

They waited in the dark, cramped behind the panel, straining for any telltale noise. Finally Tullier whispered, "I don't hear anything. Let's risk it." Through the dark, Gaultry heard a click, and knew that he had sprung the catch. The panel creaked open, terrifyingly loud.

Tullier, bumping gently past her, stepped out into the void beyond the panel. The noise and sparks of the flint and tinder seemed exaggeratedly loud—and then the candle was finally lit.

"Come see," he said. "It's safe."

The storage chamber was a boxy room with roughly plastered walls and a barrel-vaulted ceiling. They had emerged opposite the room's only door. Dust lay thick on the floor, dust and a clutter of boxes, some covered with cloths, others buried under bundles of paper and scrolls. Tullier set the candle on one of the boxes and went confidently to a tall case that was wedged against the wall near the hidden entry panel. "I don't think anyone's been here since I last visited. Come see. I used to look in this one often," he said, "thinking how I would be punished if I took anything without asking."

"Well, we're not going to ask now," Gaultry said.

"Different circumstances." Tullier shrugged. "Back then, I knew there was no point. Sha Muira apprentices don't have the privacy of possession. I couldn't have kept anything I'd taken once I was back on Sha Muira Island."

He cracked open the tall case, his eagerness obvious as his fingers fumbled with the latches.

Inside was rich red velvet lining and places for twelve blades, seven filled by swords in greased silk bags.

"Whoever left this here knew they weren't coming back for a long time." Gaultry picked up a blade at random and slid it out of its sack.

It was beautiful and delicately balanced, the hilt a joy of open metalwork and crystals. The artistry with which the chamfered blade had been forged was obvious. Whether that meant it could do business in a fight was another matter. She swung it experimentally, wishing she knew more about weaponry and swords. "What do you think?" she asked Tullier, offering it to him hilt first. "It's not like a knife, where all the weight is in your hand and wrist."

He took the blade and tested its flex. "Still fresh," he said, and ran his hand lovingly along the flat. "They're all beautiful, to my memory. But maybe something less ostentatious?"

"Why not take two?" Gaultry said. "That way the Sharif can choose. And something for yourself."

"Really?"

"Why not? If we're going to take one, we may as well take another. Along with anything else in here that might prove useful." She ran her hand down the smooth wood of the sword-case, then absentmindedly rubbed the dust onto the leg of her trousers. "I want to get through this venture and be able to get myself home when it ends, and that's looking increasingly unlikely as my coin diminishes. Tielmark—" Her voice caught, and she found herself choked by an unexpected wash of emotion. "I'm needed in Tielmark. Tielmark needs Martin too. We must not lose any Broodblood to the Emperor. He'll make use of any hold he can get—"

"What about me?" Tullier asked. "What will become of me?"

"You'll come to Tielmark with us. Then, when we finally sweat the last of the Sha Muir poison out of you, I'll take my Glamour-soul back. After that—" Gaultry gestured to the boxes. "You'll take your fine Bissanty sword, and whatever else here takes your fancy, and you'll have to decide for yourself what you want to do."

Tullier had a second sword in his hands, this one with a plain hilt. He tested its edge gingerly, head bent, eyes down. When he spoke, his words were so soft that Gaultry had to strain to hear him. "What if I want to stay with you?"

She bumped awkwardly against the case, startled. "What

makes you think you'd want to do that once my Glamour-soul no longer binds you?"

Tullier slid the sword back into its oiled bag, an angry motion. "Forget it," he said. "Forget I said anything."

Gaultry pressed her lips together, swallowing her instinctive urge to say words that could only be falsely reassuring. There was no knowing how Tullier would feel or act when his body was cleansed of Sha Muir poison and she took back her piece of Glamour-soul.

For almost a month now, her Glamour-soul had served as a shield against the poison that riddled his body. It had freed him from the soul-grinding, constant physical pain that had been his lot as a Sha Muira. But it had also served as a leash to curb his murderous ways. He had grown accustomed to that leash, and learned to wear it lightly. But how would he feel once that restraint was lifted? Would he want to stay in Tielmark with her then?

"Tullier," she finally said, "your Sha Muir conditioning is who you are. You grew to fit it—just as I grew to fit my life as a forest hunter. Those years won't ever stop influencing the choices you make."

"My Sha Muir Masters told me that I could never leave the order." His voice shook. "Never leave. Not even through death. That I must live as an assassin, always in pain. In death, I would be transported to Llara's Feast. Llara's touch was as simple to me as the easing of the pain that lived always in my body—a reward for good service. The Arkhons called that anodyne the silver fire—*her* silver fire. But your magic soothes the pain of poison in my blood—more richly even than Llara's blessing.

"I could stomach that when I despised you. You destroyed my bond to the Sha Muira. I told myself that you were trying to sully my bond to Llara. I thought that I could withstand that. But now—we know now I was sent to the Sha Muira for political reasons that had little to do with keeping Llara's faith. Was Llara never there to help me? Was everything my Masters told me lies?"

"Tullier," Gaultry said helplessly, "how can you doubt that Llara loves you? Not all her blessings are poisonous." The boy had been in shock since he'd learned his father's identity. It had all unraveled, revealing itself to him, too quickly: his torture at Prathe Lendra's house, the sight of his father on Lendra's grand staircase, his rescue, the storm on the road, and their retreat to this house. Focusing only on his personal pain—mental and physical both—he had yet to assimilate the implications of his parentage. The Blood-Imperial, Gaultry guessed, laid more intractable bonds on a man's soul than even the Sha Muira cult. She was sure, in time, Tullier would grow to understand his responsibilities to his heritage.

Which probably wouldn't include living under her wing in Tielmark.

"My upbringing didn't prepare me to face the secrets of my blood any more than yours did. I'm just as confused as you are," she admitted, knowing that he wouldn't find her words reassuring, hoping that they would shut him up. "But being a hunter—somehow it has helped me survive the struggle to keep Tielmark's Prince free. Maybe your training will help you survive the intricacies of Bissanty rule."

"It's not the same," Tullier said. He hid his face from her. "You have never doubted that the Great Twins love you. Which is why you don't understand those doubts in me."

"I have doubts," Gaultry said. "But I try not to let them paralyze me. Which is what having this discussion in this place is doing to us now."

Tullier knocked over a pile of rugs, pretending to resume his search. His frustration and confusion showed clearly in the set of his shoulders.

They found a cache of armor in one of the boxes at the bottom of a large pile. Most of it proved big and cumbersome, but there was a mail shirt at the bottom that Gaultry guessed might fit the Sharif's tall but lean frame, and perhaps even travel well. Gaultry put that on the pile of things they wanted to take. In addition to the weapons, the room was stacked high with furniture, papers, rolled-up carpets, gilded picture frames, carved wooden fetishes, and metal equipment stands. Six cedar chests packed with fragrant shavings held men's clothing, fine and sumptuous, most of it richer than anything Gaultry had seen, even on the Prince of Tielmark's marriage day. Velvets edged with gold braiding lay atop whisper-soft silk, some of it so delicate with age that disturbing it made the threads crumble. Gaultry, hoping that she was not spoiling her luck by presuming on it, pulled out a suit of the plainest shirt and trousers she could find.

"For Martin," she told Tullier, "if ever we find him." As she folded the find compactly for travel, she stroked the soft nape of the velvet, picturing the tall soldier: the lustrous gray eyes, the fast-moving expressions of his face, his soldier's hardness, but also the trust he had put in her, his tenderness.

In the weeks that had led up to the Prince's marriage, when Martin had been geas-bound to her protection, she had given him much heartache by insisting that he allow her to match him in every risk he took. She had not understood then how she had set the geas's power warring in him, as its power tore him between protecting her feelings and protecting her body. She frowned and rubbed the smoothness of velvet against her cheek, remembering. That pain, he had told her, and the reward of happiness that had risen out of that pain, had given him the courage to feel once more, to break free of a decade of dedicated soldiering in the Prince's service. Indeed, it was his passage through that pain that might make him a man of greater parts than soldier, if only he could overcome the emotional reflexes that had made him such a successful soldier.

Was that what Tullier was experiencing? Was her Glamour-soul forcing him to consider, as her father's geas on Martin had done, unfamiliar emotional needs beyond his own person?

She looked up sharply and discovered Tullier was watching her, his green eyes fixed and intense. He looked away guiltily when he saw she had caught him.

"Magic feeds some strange bonds," she said, pretending she thought nothing of his stare. "But true friendship survives beyond those bonds. I would have come farther than this house for Martin Stalker, Brood-blood aside."

"Then why did he break his sword for his wife?"

Gaultry shrugged, not wanting to answer the raw challenge the boy's words offered. Tullier was speaking with more ardor than she was comfortable with, and she could not help but feel invaded. She lay the clothes on top of the rest of the takings, smoothing her words as she smoothed the cloth. "He did not break that sword to save Helena," she said firmly. She shut her eyes and pictured the wash of blue magic that had spirited Martin from her, the cascade of shining metal shards that were all that had been left to her when he was gone. "He broke it to save himself. If the Sha Muira had killed Helena, he would have had to empty his life for her, dedicated himself only to avenging her." She smiled ruefully. "I wish he had taken me with him. It might have spared us both this trip."

Feeling obscurely that she had said more to the boy than she had intended, she reddened. "Don't just stand there," she snapped, discomfited. "See what else you can find that might be useful. You know what's in this room better than I."

"Not really," Tullier said. "When I was last here, I was interested only in the weapons."

"All the more reason not to stand around."

Tullier, taking her hint, began to rummage into a large pile of furniture. Behind him, Gaultry closed the trunk she had pilfered and pushed it back how she had found it.

"This might be interesting." Tullier resurfaced with a delicately built lap desk of richly inlaid wood. It had been well hidden under boxes and a broken-backed mahogany sofa. When Tullier shook it, a sound like loose coins rattled within.

"Here's something that'll be more useful than all these

heavy things," Tullier said, tinkering with the lock. "I'm sure I can unlock it—"

The lock clicked and opened. A little needle darted out, piercing Tullier's thumb. He swore, slipped the abused digit into his mouth to suck it clean, then spat.

"Lucky that was you, not me," Gaultry joked nervously. "All that Sha Muir poison-training has to be good for something." Then she caught sight of the boy's face. His cheeks had gone the color of uncooked dough. "Tullier!"

He squatted weakly on his heels, letting the desk fall with an incautious crash. Gaultry caught his shoulders, barely quick enough to prevent him from sliding onto the floor. His hands reached out, spasming, and curled into the front of her shirt. "It hurts," he said, his voice a surprised whimper. "Llara watch over me, it hurts."

Gaultry clutched him to her, appalled by the poison's swift progress, and tried to reach out with her remaining Glamour-magic. *Help him!* she pleaded to the part of her that was in Tullier's body. *Mervion set you to burn poison, why aren't you doing it?* She pressed her cheek to his, oblivious to the risk, trying to warm him, praying to the Great Twins—and suddenly, with that contact, she could see the curdling poison, like a black serpent racing in his blood, making for his heart. Panting with the effort, she flattened her palms against his chest, willing whatever force she had left to protect him. The black force of the poison met her, redoubled, and rushed onwards, barely checked.

But that scant moment seemed enough. As if from an ambush, the golden Glamour-force rose up, bound round the blackness with sheets of bright fire. The snake of black poison flashed iridescent as it fought.

Kill it! Gaultry willed with all her strength. *Kill it!*

The head of the poison flared open like a cobra's cape, momentarily engulfing the Glamour, but the move created a thinness where there had been none before—gold fire flared and blistered through. The edges of the hole glistened with power, but still the black snake of poison regrouped and fought back, constricting the burn hole like a noose to choke the gold flames.

Gaultry let out a muffled cry, realizing that the Glamour-strength would not be enough. "Tullier!" she called. "You have to fight it too!" The boy's body shuddered, as though he barely heard her, but within, there was a sudden response. As the balance of power tipped towards the black, the dark snake of poison growing ever stronger, from within the gold, like a chrysalis creasing open and parting, a purple fire burst free.

At first it was no more than a flaring spark, but the spark quickly ignited and roared to vivid flame. The black poison cowered like a living creature, shriveling, making itself small, but the purple fire had no mercy. It lashed out, violent and potent, and dashed the black power into jagged pieces.

Then, turning, it wound its way back to the tatters of gold strength—the strength that had kept the boy alive against the poison's first onslaught. Gaultry had an impression of gold and purple forms furling, binding together like skeins of silk. She felt, like a distant shivering echo, a sensual pulsing warmth. The purple strength seemed almost to be nursing the gold, urging it to regroup its strength—

Then the vision faded. Slowly, she became aware of the box room, of Tullier shifting weakly in her arms.

His ashen face was cradled to her own, his pale eyes staring into hers, terrified.

"It's over," Gaultry said, pulling back and patting his head. "It's over." She had never told him so great a lie, and her cheeks flamed. The poison was defeated, but a latent force had been raised. Could the boy feel it himself? Did he know what it was? She suspected she did: it had to be his Imperial goddess-blood, finally manifesting itself. What did that mean? Had his Sha Muir training been actively suppressing his blood-heritage? "You're starting to sweat," she said. "That's good, but I can't touch you when you sweat." She paced away from him, then returned, afraid for him, afraid for herself. What did this mean for the piece of Glamour-soul she had lent him? How easy would it be to reclaim her power from him now? Exhausted and scared, she laid Tullier on a dust cover that they'd thrown over a pile of rolled carpets. "Lie a while and recover yourself."

"That could have killed the Emperor himself," Tullier whispered faintly.

"I'm sure you're right," Gaultry said. She stared at him, as if trying to see him anew; to see a change, but externally he seemed unaltered. "Tullier—" She could not explain what she had witnessed. The purple force that had come to life in him—that had nothing to do with her magic. She sat by him for a moment, resting herself, listening to him breathe. She forced herself to smile. "There had better be something important in that desk," she told him.

She peered at it cautiously. With the lock sprung, the lid had cracked open just wide enough to wedge a blade in. Getting up, she chose a short sword from the tall sword-case to pry the inner compartment open, not wanting to spoil the edge on any of their own weapons.

There was loose coin inside—the bait that had tempted them—a small accounting book, and a pair of scrolls. Curious, she uncurled the first scroll that came to her hand.

"Fructibus Arbis," she read the first line. "What's that?"

"The name of this estate," Tullier told her. "Its wealth used to be from its orchards. They've mostly been cut down."

"I think this is the estate's master-deed." Gaultry, puzzling through the archaic writing, did not realize for a moment the significance of the paper she held in her hands. Then a single name leapt out.

"Tullier," she said, bringing it to him. "This whole estate belongs to your father."

"That's impossible," Tullier said. "He's Sea Prince, and these are the Emperor's home counties."

"Impossible or not, that's what it says here. I think." She held the scroll out to him. "Tell me if you agree. He owns it under another man's name, but I'd say it's his all right. He bought it—paid for it in one lump sum—about twenty years ago. Why would he have done that?"

Tullier sat up weakly and reached his hand out for the document. "I don't know," he said peevishly. "Give me that."

She handed it over and returned to investigate the desk's other contents. The account book was filled with lists and figures to its last page, twenty years outdated. It appeared to be the former owner's reckoning of the estate's affairs before it had changed hands. The coin was a mixture of gold and silver, fallen free from a little silk bag. She pocketed it without hesitation. The last scroll was sealed within a leaf of oilpaper. The seals, which were black waxy blobs, looked poisonous.

"What do you suppose that is?" she asked, nudging it with the tip of the spare sword.

"Is there an insignia on the seal?"

"A crown," Gaultry said, not liking that she had to stoop close to see. "Surmounted by two lightning bolts and a little bird."

"Don't touch it," Tullier said suddenly, making a move as if to stagger up. "I know what it is. Don't touch it."

Gaultry closed the lid of the desk with the tip of the sword and came to sit next to him. "Don't get up yet. But tell me—"

Tullier grimaced and nodded acquiescence. He pushed the hair back from his face with a clammy hand. "Do you understand what it means, that my father is a ghostmonger?"

"I think I do. Hidden sons, and an attempt to take the Imperial Throne."

"That's right," Tullier said. "That's what it usually means. But why ghostmonger, if you are not trying for a seat on the Imperial Throne? Llara's law on him, my father shouldn't be in any position to do it. Ghostmongering is for brothers, struggling to birth five sons, and my father is Sciuttarus's uncle, not his brother. By rights, my father lost his chance to birth his five—and to pass on the Blood-Imperial to his children—when his brother, the old Emperor, sired his fifth son."

"Tullier," Gaultry said carefully, not wanting to interrupt his flow of talk, "I think the Sea Prince *must* have had five sons. Something is blocking Sciuttarus from having more children. And there are other hints . . ." The image of the purple power coiling itself protectively round her torn Glamour-soul came back to her. She could not help but shudder.

Tullier nodded soberly. "Llara's hand is in this," he said. "Sciuttarus, by his spiteful acts, must have forsaken the Great Thunderer's blessing. It is nature among Bissanty Princes to jockey for power amongst themselves, but Sciuttarus went beyond that when he castrated my father's first son. That child was not in line to challenge Sciuttarus's power. Granting the Sea Prince a full five of sons in payment for that transgression may have been Llara's punishment on him."

"Was the child Sciuttarus castrated Luka Pallia's son?" Gaultry asked. "The theater performer Sciuttarus poisoned? You told me about her back in Bassorah."

Tullier squirmed. "I didn't tell you everything. I didn't tell you the most important thing: Luka Pallia wasn't a woman— or rather, Luka was something formed between a man and a woman. It was pretty clear the Sea Prince never expected that Luka would be able to bear him a child. Sciuttarus interfered in something that was never the Sea Prince's will."

"The mother was a boy?" Gaultry asked, torn between pity and disgust.

"Mostly a boy."

Realization slashed through Gaultry like a shock of lightning. "Luka Pallia must have prayed long and hard to the Mother Thunderbringer for the blessing of a baby."

"That could be," Tullier said.

"If that was so, Luka's pregnancy would have been a god-granted miracle, a mercy, to answer his prayers." She looked gravely at Tullier. "Sciuttarus must have been mad, desecrating that prodigy. What Sciuttarus did to the baby must have driven your father to beg Llara's blessing and try his luck at ghostmongering. Even knowing that he wasn't in line to do it."

"Maybe," Tullier said hesitantly. He obviously found it difficult to talk about his father in this analytical way. "Rumor had it that the Sea Prince's love for Luka Pallia was not inconsiderable. He could have done it to avenge that death.

"Whatever his motives," said Tullier, staring at the roll of paper, "ghostmongers usually keep secret records that detail the births of their sons. My guess is that the scroll documents the birthing of the Sea Prince's sons. Probably including me."

"Then we have to see it," Gaultry said, excited. "To take the guesswork out of your parentage. Will it tell us who your mother is?"

"I'm not interested," he said. "That black seal means something is poisoned about that scroll—poison that could probably kill anyone short of the Emperor."

"Tullier," she answered him, very serious, "what do you think you just survived? Even Imperial poison won't touch you. Your interest here is not casual. The risk is well worth taking. You may have brothers. You should know where they are hiding, where your father has placed them."

Tullier picked up the sealed scroll, an apprehensive crease knitting his brows. "You could be right."

"Are you worried there is a spell as well as poison?" Gaultry said. "I can try to cloak you with my magic. I think that helped with the lock poison."

Above the scroll, the pale eyes met hers, lighting. "Let's read this scroll together."

Gaultry stood behind him and carefully clasped her arms round his body, avoiding his bare skin. She pressed her palms flat against his rib cage, just over his heart. Beneath her hands, his heart hammered, from what emotion she could not tell. It occurred to her uncomfortably that this was probably the closest Tullier had been to another person's body in all the remembered years of his short life.

Unless, of course, that person had been Sha Muira and equally committed to death.

They clung together for a long moment, Gaultry sinking deep into herself, trying to open a channel for her magic to run out to him, should he have need of it.

Tullier tore the oiled paper cover open. He threw it down and away, maybe too hastily.

Nothing happened. The pair stood, waiting, intense and focused. Tullier's body quivered; whether from tension or eagerness, Gaultry could not determine.

Still nothing.

"Well, read it then." She unclasped her arms and let him go.

Tullier cautiously unrolled the scroll and held it so she could read with him, over his shoulder.

It was a short list of names, with dates and notations.

The last name on the list was Tullirius Caviedo and a date just over fourteen years past. Next to the name and date was a note recording that the baby had been sent to Sha Muira Island.

A note below that commented that his mother had been strangled and given a private burial directly after she had delivered the baby.

"Huntress help me," Gaultry breathed into Tullier's hair, holding his chilled body tight against her own as she scanned the rest of the list. "Look at that. Your poor brothers."

The three boys before Tullier. Half-brothers. All strangled as they were born, with a priest of Llara presiding. Their mothers strangled with them.

"That was clever," Tullier said, hollow-voiced. "The Emperor would have trouble tracking those births." He paused. "What made him keep me alive?"

Gaultry scanned up to the first name. " 'Lukas Caviedo,' " she read, " 'born to Luka Pallia, castrated by the hand of Enolias, Priest of Tarrin, the day of his birthing.' " Her throat felt parched. That was all the answer Tullier would get from this document. With his first son castrated, the Sea Prince needed at least one other son alive.

" 'Sent by my Imperial brother's hand to Dunsanius Ford,

the summer of Sciuttarus V's coronation,' " Tullier read the next line. "That's brother in the titled sense. He means Sciuttarus."

"That's where we're going," Gaultry said uneasily. "That's where Prathe Lendra sent Martin. What exactly is Dunsanius Ford?"

"It's a monastery," Tullier said. "The monks worship Tarrin the White God. Sciuttarus had the boy's faith dedicated to one of the lower gods, so he could never have a dominating role in Bassorah politics, even if he rose high in the priesthood."

"A castrator's house?" said Gaultry, alarmed. "And they've sent Martin there? Would they— Could they—" The question was too painful to put in words.

Tullier, guessing the source of her worry, shot her an irritated look. "Why would they bother, if it's his blood they want? Unless he decides to convert voluntarily to the White God's service.

"Dunsanius Ford isn't far from here," said Tullier, looking back at the list. He traced the names of his three dead brothers and then paused, marking the line that recorded the birth of Luka Pallia's son. "Do you suppose that's why the Sea Prince bought this house? To be near"—Tullier's voice stumbled—"to be near Lukas?"

"I don't know," Gaultry said. She brought the paper close to the candle, looking for any last clues. "What's this last note?" The ink was different. Paler, faded, hard to read—it had been rubbed out but not entirely effaced. Gaultry read it aloud. " 'Lukas's sister is the image of Luka P. I could not have her killed.' That's more personal than the other notes. The Sea Prince's first son had a sister? Wasn't Luka Pallia poisoned soon after he gave birth?"

"There was no girl-child that I ever heard of," Tullier said. "But that doesn't mean anything. Who cares about a girl-child in the Imperial house? The Emperor—and Llara—want sons, not daughters." He saw the look Gaultry gave him and shrugged. "Your not liking that doesn't change anything."

"We'll burn this paper," Gaultry said. "It's too dangerous. What the Great Twelve know does not need to be kept in man's records."

"It won't be the only copy," Tullier said. His manner, as he held the paper, was reluctant. "And the paper itself might be poisoned."

Together they decided that the safest thing would simply be to leave the records and deed where they had found them. Closing the lap desk and jiggering the lock shut from a safe distance, they buried it under the pile of boxes where they had found it.

Then they began to bag their loot so they could carry it conveniently, although the swords made this more awkward than they had expected. In the end they made two clumsy bundles out of dusty furniture covers.

"There's nothing else you want to take?" Gaultry asked, sneezing a little from the dusty cloth. She scanned the room, her eye falling at the last moment on a small box that had fallen and wedged between two rolled-up carpets. "What's that?"

Inside was a pair of matched daggers. The hilts glittered with blue and white crystals, the sheaths were ivory and hammered silver. "You should take these," she told Tullier. "As a present from your father."

"I don't want them. Not from him."

Beneath his sullen expression, an acquisitive light belied his words. "Then take them as spoil," she said.

Tullier, no real heart in his initial refusal, needed no more encouragement to stuff them into the breast of his shirt.

They could do nothing about the dust they'd disturbed on the floor, but they tidied the room as best they could and tried to cover the evidence of their visit by scuffing up the dust all the way across to the room's door to make it appear their entry had been made through that ingress. Through the door's lacquerwork panel they could hear music, still playing, in the house beyond.

"Let's go see if we can make any discoveries about the man

your father is currently renting to," Gaultry said. "And whether or not we want to avoid seeing him in the morning."

"That won't be difficult," Tullier said. "The passage to that room is not far from here."

Despite the music they'd heard outside the storage room door, once they returned to the more heavily paneled wall passages, they found the house had quieted. Heavy drunkenness, or druggedness, had settled over the houseguests, and the mood had soured. People had started to retreat to their beds. In the Master's bedroom, a woman lay sprawled across the bed, her clothes in disarray. "Someone has been at her," Gaultry said, disgusted. "Do you think she was awake enough to know?"

Tullier bent to look through the peephole. "She might have been," he said coolly. "Not that I'd guess it would make a difference."

"What are you saying?"

"I know her. She's the wife of the youngest son of the man who was renting the house when I was here before. She's been in this state before. Many times."

Gaultry gave Tullier a hard look.

"We should go back," Tullier said, shifting, impenitent, beneath that look. "There's nothing more to be learned here."

"I'm learning," Gaultry said, "more than I wanted."

"We couldn't all have your sheltered upbringing." If Tullier had spoken the words less bitterly, she would have felt sorry for him. As it was, she regretted her words, but had no desire to retract them.

No longer speaking, they retraced their steps to the passageway that would take them back to the junction where they had left their bundles. There was a convenient place to peep out there, into a well-lit parlor, empty save for an elderly servant nodding by the fire and two men bent over a small table, wine bottles rolling around their ankles on the floor.

"Our best plan would be to leave in the morning before any

of these fools are awake." Tullier sounded as though he was still angry with her.

"That would be lucky." Gaultry picked up the bundle that had the two swords for the Sharif, getting a good grip by finding the hilts within.

"Luck? Hardly," Tullier snorted. "No one but the servants will be up before noon." He took a few steps down the passage, then stopped and came back to her. "There's a shortcut from here," he said tauntingly. "Not that you'll want to take it." She heard the taunt, and still she could not stop herself from rising to it.

"Why not?" she asked.

"We'll have to pass some bedchambers. You won't like that."

Gaultry liked his tone even less. "If there's a shortcut," she said curtly, "we should take it. If there're bedrooms, we won't have to look."

"It's your choice."

"We're wasting time talking."

Tullier picked up his bundle again and nodded at her to follow him.

The shortcut was a narrow stair that crossed above the big doors that separated the two large salons where the party had been at its wildest. Going over the doors meant they wouldn't have to circumnavigate the larger of the two rooms. Even Gaultry, who had lost her sense of direction, could tell that taking the stair cut a big loop out of the distance back to their suite.

But, as Tullier had warned her, this route passed bedchambers immediately after the rise over the stairs. They went through a tightly fitted interior door and came into a somewhat wider passage with extensive paneling on both sides, creating an almost comfortable space. It had very obviously been built as a spying room. Many tiny peepholes gave a flickering view of the pair of bedchambers that flanked the hidden passage. To the left, a well-dressed man and woman sat in a glassy stupor, their gaze fixed on a pair of numb-faced servants who were mechanically performing a sex act; to the right, two men and a woman rolled on a bed, the woman's body sandwiched between the men. "They're hurting her," Gaultry said, catching the woman's expression. "Does anyone do such things for joy in this country?"

"What would you imagine?"

She gave Tullier a sharp look, fully aware that he had brought her this way intentionally to make her witness the things he had been compelled to see as a child. But it was more than that. Her comment outside the Master's bedchamber had made him angrier than she had realized. He wanted to watch her squirm with embarrassment, wanted to punish her.

"Hurry up with that lock," she hissed. He was fumbling inefficiently with the panel that blocked their way onwards.

"Shush," he said. "I can't find the spring."

I'll bet, she thought grimly. It seemed Tullier held them trapped in that awful, claustrophobic space forever, listening to the grunting sounds that emanated from the rooms to either side.

Finally Tullier opened the door, and they were able to continue onward.

They went on a little ways, past quiet rooms with occupants drunk and insensate or not yet come to bed.

Then, passing through yet another interior door, they heard very clearly the sound of someone crying.

"Shut up," someone said, loud enough for them to hear the words clearly.

There was a nasty slapping sound, and the crying stopped.

Gaultry tugged at Tullier to stop. "What's that?" she said.

Then, again clearly, they heard the sound of ripping cloth.

"Let's go," Tullier said, taking a hold on Gaultry's bundle and trying to pull her away. His punitive urge seemed to have faded. "We've seen enough."

"You wanted to show me those awful things." Gaultry's face burned. But fury filled her as well as embarrassment. "You thought you could play a game with my feelings."

"I didn't—" The way his shoulders hunched, half guilty, half defiant, she knew her suspicions were right.

"But none of this is a game. Someone is getting hurt in every room here." The cry came again, high and desperate. And there was more than that. There was something—some magic—that made her feel the terror of true desperation in that voice. "And that one worst of all!"

"It's not our business—"

"You made it our business," she said savagely, "by choosing to take me this way." Gaultry backed up four paces, saw a flash of light, and discovered a narrow slot in the wall. There were lacquer panels a few feet along, panels that looked out into the room where the crying had come from. She forced her body into the slot. Tullier, still reluctant, followed her.

Through the panel, she saw the lurker who had opened the door on the porter when they'd first arrived. The big man whom Tullier had teased. He'd lost his balding partner, but he was recognizable enough, even from behind. His naked back was to them, smooth skin with an unhealthy gray pallor and a knobbled arching spine. The high rangy shoulders were flexing, exerting pressure. He'd put aside his wig. The cropped hair on his scalp was iron-colored and wet with sweat.

Bile rose in Gaultry's throat.

His long body almost obscured the slender girl who shuddered beneath him, her thin legs twisting to avoid him, her dress shoved high up over her hips. Her face, contorted with pain, was half turned into the pillow, masked by tresses of silver-pale hair, prematurely white.

"That's Columba," Tullier said coolly, trying to pull Gaultry away. "A half-wit. She comes with the house. This has happened before. Come morning, she won't remember anything."

Gaultry touched the panel, numbness running through her, something—Llara's scar—burning on her palm. "Does this open?" she asked. "Can you open it?"

"It opens," Tullier said. He put his hand over the spring to stop her from using it. "But it's not worth interfering. This isn't new to her."

"What do you mean?" Gaultry said. "He's going to kill her."

"Don't be stupid," Tullier whispered. "He won't—"

The man shifted on the bed, suddenly intent and active. "You little bitch," he hissed. "You temptress bitch. Llara sent you to test me, didn't she?"

There was a knife in his hand. A copper-handled knife. He rubbed the edge against the pale woman's throat, drawing a line of blood. "Llara take you, bitch," he said. "She'll have you right after I do."

Gaultry put her hand on the hilt of one of the swords they'd stolen for the Sharif. "Open it," she told Tullier.

"Gaultry—"

The girl began to scream. High, piercing, frightened screams, cut through with pain, shame, and hopelessness. A red cloud descended across Gaultry's vision. Something moved in her—something that was more than her own volition. The palm of her hand—the hand that held the sword—went cold. A touch of cold lanced through her arm into her brain. She found she had crowded against Tullier, that she was fighting him for the latch, and then, suddenly, she was out in the room. The girl on the bed cried out, struggling to hold back the knife.

"Thunderbringer! Thunderbringer! Oh Llara! Don't leave me!"

Something in Gaultry responded—something she did not control. The sword was in her hand, the man's broad, gray-tinted back before her, the girl was screaming still—

Then the man's screams joined the girl's. Gaultry drove him forward onto the bed, slashing furiously at his back, the blade glancing off his shoulder blades, his spine, no soldier's art in it, no single blow hard enough to kill. He arched up, trying to wrestle around. The girl beneath him, delirious with fear, clung to his knife arm, hampering his efforts to protect himself.

Then Gaultry severed something in his neck with a lucky blow, and he collapsed on the bed.

"Elianté, help me." Gaultry stared down at her hands. The hilt of the sword, where her left palm had gripped it, shone with silver light. An imprint from the scar on her palm. She threw the weapon onto the bed, frightened.

Tullier came into the room and looked at the bed. Intent on the wounded man, he did not seem to notice the weapon or the fast-fading crescent of light on its hilt. He bent and listened to the man's gurgling final gasps. Then he went to the door and turned the key in the lock.

"They won't be investigating the noise, with what he was doing," he said, and threw the key onto the bed. "But someone might want to come join the fun."

Gaultry moved weakly toward the basin on the room's sideboard, her stomach heaving. Tullier, merciless, stopped her. "You can't do that here," he said. "Too suspicious. You've done what you wanted. Now we're both going to have to clean it up."

chapter 16

▼

The man's neck was broken. Tullier jerked the pale girl roughly off the bed and sat her in the room's lone chair while he tied the man's body into the top sheet on the bed. "Stay there," he told her.

"What are you doing?" Gaultry asked. She lurched against the carved sideboard, held onto it for support, and resisted the urge to make use of the basin. Blood roared in her ears. Her scarred hand was like a block of ice. She tucked it into the warmth of her armpit, afraid that Tullier would see it and know how little of herself had controlled her attack.

"Trying to contain the blood," he said. "We'll pull the body into the wall and leave it there. That should buy us the time we need to move on."

"I'll help you," Gaultry said. She stood away from the sideboard, ignoring the lights that shimmered before her eyes.

"Take hold of his shoulders then. I'll take his feet." The warm slack weight made the ice of her hand feel that much colder, that much sharper. Tullier saw the spasm of pain on her face and gave her a disgusted look, not understanding.

Together, they wrestled the body through the narrow slot in

the wall. The man's wide shoulders scraped nastily against the rough stone. Gaultry's stomach once again threatened to empty itself, but they were in the dark now, so Tullier didn't see. They humped the body along to a stretch of passage that had no openwork panels. The pitch black of the passage there made the body seem larger, more cumbersome. Gaultry scraped repeatedly against the unplastered walls, struggling to hold up the deadweight. Between the horror of the murder and the pulse of power that had forced her hand, she wanted to let herself faint—but there was Tullier, tugging the other end of the body, not letting her rest.

At last, Tullier stopped and spoke through the dusty darkness. "We can leave the body here. It's well enclosed. The smell won't get out for a week. Maybe more."

Gaultry dropped the dead shoulders and leaned against the wall. Her hair and spine were soaked with sweat. The fancy struck her that the sheen of moisture that coated her flesh was the dead man's blood. She shivered.

"Should we prop him up against the wall or just leave him?"

"Leave him," Tullier answered. He clambered over the man's body. Gaultry groped for his hand. Her fingers brushed his sleeve. "Don't touch me," he said. "I'm sweating. It's still poison." His voice sounded tired.

They stood for a moment in the darkness, trying to collect their wits. Tullier's ragged breathing fell into a rhythm, then quieted: his Sha Muir training. She envied him that—the ability to quickly regain physical control.

She slumped against the rough masonry wall, her head rushing with the memory of the cold fire that had overrun her senses. The image of the man's heaving back flashed once more before her. She shuddered with guilt and self-loathing. She had allowed the goddess to force her hand. Fighting against that thought, she pictured the scene again: the line of blood the man had drawn across the girl's throat with his knife, the girl's terror. Something in Gaultry calmed. The man would have murdered the girl if she had not intervened. There was a measure of comfort in that.

But even now the brand of ice in her hand mocked her tumult of feeling, her horror. What had she relinquished, that day she had bought her own life with faith, high on the crumbling rock cliff? When would that price be fully paid? She was glad for the darkness that veiled her fear, her uncertainty. A prayer rose, unbidden, in her mind. *My soul belongs to Tielmark, to Elianté the Green Huntress.* Her distress gave her prayer force, the strength almost of a spell. She could feel it, blossoming in the dark, soothing against the heat of her wall-chafed skin. That strength flushed her with a momentary confidence. She knelt and fumbled to touch the sheet-wrapped form of the man she had killed, pressing the hand that Llara had branded with her mark against that cooling skull. *You did this, Great Llara.* She did not know where she pulled the courage to make her prayer an admonition, but the words poured from her as she bent over the body, and she could not make herself stop. *You called me in the dark to protect your devotee. I answered your call.*

I could have fought you, Thunderbringer. The woman would have died if I had hesitated. But I let you rule my will, and now this man is dead.

The darkness that enwrapped her seemed to thin where her hand clutched the skull. Gaultry concentrated on that point, something more than darkness, less than light. A thing, a force, spread her fingers, as if it was using her hand to feel the man's death mask.

Gaultry understood, with a sudden heady clarity, that Gray Llara was truly in her at that moment. And the Great Thunderbringer would take hold of more than her hand, if she did not fight.

My soul belongs to Tielmark, Gaultry chanted in unspoken prayer, trying to clear her mind, *to Elianté the Green Huntress. On Llara's Ladder, the Great Thunderbringer showed me Her grace, and for that I owe a life debt. I will repay this debt. But I will not be plaything to any god. I will not. I will not let any god force my hand again. Even to save a helpless girl.*

Great Thunderbringer, this man was a brute. Gaultry

forced her hand away from the skull and clenched her fingers into a fist. *If we had fought, he might have killed me. But even so, he should have been allowed his death fight. His death was not just.*

Pain flared, flexing her fingers wide. Gaultry gasped, recognizing a force beyond anything she could hope to overcome. As if there was any hope in challenging the gods—

Then the dagger of cold in her palm was gone, and the point of silver light vanished.

She fell back against the wall, stumbling blindly, wishing desperately she could know for sure what the release signified. Yet among all her doubts, she had one answer: in Llara's eyes, she had not murdered a man. She had saved a woman's life.

"We have to go back for the girl," Gaultry said, surprised at the steadiness of her voice.

Tullier abruptly squeezed by her. His rough movement jarred her against the wall. In that brief moment of contact, she felt his young body, rigid with inheld anger. "Columba is a land-bonded slave," he gritted. "She's not like the Sharif. She's not salvageable. We can't take her with us. The only act of mercy we could grant her would be a sword through her neck and an end to her miserable life."

"We're going back." Gaultry reached through the dark and gave him a push.

"You were sent here from Tielmark to free your precious Brood-blood from the Emperor's grasp." Tullier stood in her way, blocking the passage. "You told me you agreed to come to Bissanty because you owed Martin Stalker a debt. But now that you've almost reached him, now that you have weapons and gold in your pockets and perhaps even a chance of success, you risk everything again. To no purpose. To help no one."

"I'm not going to waste time arguing," Gaultry said, pushing past him. "The goddess moved me. I have no better answer to offer you."

"These are not Elianté's lands," Tullier spat, mistaking the deity she had invoked. They had reached the first pinpricks of light, the slot in the wall that led to the fateful chamber, to the pale waiting girl. "The Huntress has no province here in Bissanty." Light struck his face as he turned, light that caught the ice green of his eyes, the pale, soot-stroked skin of his face. He seemed tall, a taut arrow of death, the true Sha Muir dagger trained for Llara's left hand.

Gaultry caught her breath. If she did not stop him right away, he would see that he had scared her, and she did not want him to know that he could do that.

"What makes you assume it was the Huntress who moved me?" Gaultry took a step towards him, forcing him to tilt his face up to hers. "What makes you think it is only the Great Twins who speak in me, through me?"

Tullier's mouth opened. No sound came out.

"A man died today under my hand," Gaultry said bluntly. "I am not a killer—born *or* trained. I will not pretend I understand why I was chosen to break that man's neck. But that girl was begging mercy from the Thunderbringer. I'd say that Llara answered her."

"I dedicated my life to Llara," Tullier said. "She would have asked me first—"

"Maybe," Gaultry said, losing her temper. "Maybe she thought that what you had to offer that poor girl wasn't worth much."

Tullier went livid. "You are so certain the gods favor you—"

Gaultry made a tired gesture with her hand. "Oh, stop it, Tullier," she said. "I don't want to fight about that—"

"You can't help every outcast."

"I don't want to help every outcast," Gaultry said. "Tullier, face the truth! I'm no warrior. If I had been moved by my own will in this, I would be dead now, and Columba with me."

That shut him up, even if it did not settle the crux of the argument.

The pale girl hadn't moved since they'd left. A half-wit, Tullier had called her. Looking into her listless eyes, Gaultry was struck again by the enormity of what she had done, saving this girl. She saw again the man's arching, sword-slashed back.

How could she believe that Great Llara herself had touched her, reaching through her hand to save this half-empty bag of bones?

Tullier had every reason to be angry. When they'd rescued the Sharif, there had been something impressive, both brutal and magnificent, in the force of will that had driven the tall Ardana to seek them. Balanced between the fire of the slaver's brand and the brown water of Bassorah Harbor, the Sharif had made her decision: she had plunged headlong into the water—and risen, determined to make it safe to shore.

This girl had none of that self-motivating fire or will to make her own freedom. She huddled passively in the chair where Tullier had pushed her, thin arms clasped around thinner body, waiting to be told what to do. In all the time Gaultry and Tullier had struggled in the wall-passage with her attacker's body, she had done nothing to help herself: nothing to repair the disarray of her dress; nothing to tidy the signs of the struggle that still littered the room.

"Do you remember what happened?" Gaultry asked. As she touched the girl's shoulder, she realized that stillness was unnatural; something distinct from shock, not even a stunned, numbed inability to accept her circumstances. The tears had already dried on her cheeks; her face was smooth and composed, as if the horror and pain she had so recently experienced were wiped from her consciousness. Struggling to understand the girl's state of mind, Gaultry went down on one knee and touched her hands. "Do you remember what happened?"

"I told you," Tullier said, efficiently tidying the floor and the bed. He tore off the second bedsheet and added that to the growing pile of things they would need to hide in the passage.

"Be quiet," Gaultry said, trying to concentrate. "I asked her, not you." Columba's dark eyes stared through Gaultry, wide and empty. Gaultry wondered if it was the torpor of some strange Bissanty fatalism, some conviction that this attack was as it should be.

Yet she had cried to Llara to save her when the knife was at her throat. There was something in her that did not simply drift and accept her fate.

It was hard to be gentle with Tullier standing impatiently behind her, finished with his work, ready to move on.

"I have some clothes," she said to Columba. The girl shifted, uneasy. "They're men's clothes, but nicer than what you're wearing." The front of the girl's dress was sticky with the dead man's blood. "If I help you, will you put them on?"

The dark eyes turned to Gaultry and focused, as though the mind in that pale-haired skull was moving slowly toward her from across a great distance. "Thank you." Her fingers tightened in Gaultry's. Her voice was a soft whisper, a murmur, a shy coo. "I would like to dress."

"Where are the things I brought for Martin?" As she turned to speak to Tullier, the girl made a sudden, darting movement—not to escape, merely to draw away. Gaultry, struck by sudden memory, spun round and stared. For a moment, the painted bedchamber seemed to drop away, and she was back in Arleon Forest, reaching out with her mind to entrap a wild bird, to hunt its spirit with her magic—

Columba was bound by a powerful spell—by perhaps even a web of powerful spells. It was not simply a Bissanty slave-bond. It was something more familiar, a layered shadow on her soul. Yet somehow the casting seemed distant, almost buried.

"Here." Tullier dug the stolen clothes from the bundle and threw them noisily at Gaultry's feet, breaking the line of her thoughts. "Hurry up. We should be out of here before someone comes knocking." He bundled up the sheet and dumped it somewhere out of sight inside the panel. Coming back, he splashed his hands clean in the basin, dumped its contents in the passage, and, wiping it dry, returned it to the sideboard.

"Can you undress and put these on?" Gaultry asked the girl.

Columba shot a timid glance at Tullier, delicate lids flickering to hide the fear in her eyes.

Gaultry rounded on Tullier, already annoyed with him for interrupting her. "Wait in the passage."

He flashed her a disgusted look but did as he was told.

"Go on." Gaultry gazed at the slim girl. "Columba, hurry up. We're trying to help you."

Columba stared back, as if Gaultry's words were beyond her comprehension. "Help me?" she said. Again, Gaultry saw the hunted bird-flutter in her—like a pigeon tied to a string to draw a hawk.

"Columba, is there a spell—" Even as she asked the question, Gaultry pressed forward with her mind, snatching at the whisper of bird-spirit, trying to understand this magic, locked so subtly on the girl's soul. The girl cocked her head nervously, sensing Gaultry's probe.

Then she drew her dress down off her shoulders, and Gaultry found herself snared, from beneath the strand of bird magic, by a second spell.

The luxury of the painted bedchamber whirled. Gaultry lurched, sensing the spell as it slipped like a silk noose on her throat, but not quickly enough to prevent it from seizing her. A thick scent, somewhere between flowers and musk, filled her nostrils, choking her breath, and suddenly all she could see was the bending outline that was Columba's thin body, barely masked by her cheap servant's dress.

One part of her mind was sheltered from the assault on her senses, and she clung to that, trying to focus, trying to unravel the web of spells that cocooned the girl's mysterious essence. She sensed something in the girl that the huntress in her should be able to fix on. A soft flutter, the form of an animal mind moving, familiar, as if through a forest of twisted branch and briar. Gaultry reached out; her magic seemed to touch a warmth, a gentleness—

The outline of the pale girl's body sharpened. Her dress was off her shoulders. A prickle of unease tickled Gaultry's spine, her senses flooding with awareness of Columba's dangerous beauty.

Beneath the tatters of dress was a woman's body. Gaultry could see now the refinement in Columba's thinness, the grace and beauty that ran deeper than trauma. Her skin was pure and smooth, her silver-white hair gleamed, falling gently around her shoulders. She was delicate and ethereal. Her undressing was a dance that stroked the senses. Despite the bruises on her arms and neck, the ugly red gouge across her rib cage, and the line of blood on her throat, Columba drew Gaultry to her. The young huntress felt an unnatural, unwanted press of attraction. Her body warmed; the urge to hold Columba's thin frame, to stroke that pale skin, pushed reason away. She wanted to cover the girl's mouth with her own lips, to possess her beautiful spell-sexed body—

"These are your new clothes," Gaultry said, her voice rough with fear. "Put them on. They're going to get soiled in the wall-passage, and there will be no change of clothes for you after." She wanted to be unkind, wanted to shove the woman away from her in any way she could. Dropping the clothes at the thin woman's feet, Gaultry stepped away, unpleasantly aware of the bed, of the intimacy of the room, of the tang of scent on Columba's flesh.

This was not Columba's invitation, she told herself harshly. The mass of magic that tugged at her senses was there to divert attention from the fleeting feather-light presence, to conceal it. Still, the potency of the sexual lure unnerved her. Gaultry, struggling to throw up her mental shields, began to babble, trying to hide her fears behind words. "Tullier said you were a bond-slave," she said. "Less than a servant."

Why, then, the powerful skein of magic? Why the cold dagger of power that had forced Gaultry's hand to protect her?

Needing to do something with her hands, Gaultry pried the ruined dress out of Columba's hand, quashing down the impulse to rub her own hand along the line of Columba's throat. "Less than a servant." She repeated herself, struggling to resist the skein of spell. The magic that bound the woman was insidious, like lapping waves against a beach. Despite all her efforts, she caught herself watching Columba's body again, watching the girl—the woman—twist and bend as she pulled the stolen clothes onto her body.

Columba, unaware or unconcerned by Gaultry's scrutiny,

stooped to pull on the trousers. They were too long for her. As she bent to roll them over her ankles, the woman's shoulder blades fluttered and tensed, the bone painfully close to the surface of her skin. Bruises showed where her attacker had dug in his fingers.

Gaultry, staring at that smooth skin, realized with a start what it was that she wasn't seeing. "Tullier," she called, struggling not to raise her voice. She took two steps to the open panel and called again. "Tullier, she doesn't have a slave-brand."

Tullier poked his head into the room, impatient. "She's a slave," he said. "She has a brand."

Columba had the shirt on. The sheen of blue velvet looked good against her skin. Too good. Gaultry, struggling against her own senses, made her pull it up to show Tullier the unscarred skin of her shoulders.

"Where's her slave-brand?" he asked. He took the shirttail out of Columba's hand and covered up her back. His nostrils quivered. "What's that smell?"

"What smell?" Gaultry snapped, embarrassed to see how easily Tullier dropped the woman's shirttails, how easily he let himself cover that ivory skin.

"It smells like musk."

"It's some sort of magic," she said grudgingly. If Tullier couldn't sense the pulse of sexual power the woman radiated, Gaultry wasn't up to explaining it. "You told me that what happened tonight had happened before. That's not surprising. There's magic on her strong enough to call a choir of priests to rut."

"Magic?" The coolness of his tone, a contrast to her own heat, was infuriating.

"Tell me, Tullier. Why would this woman have drawn a sorcerer's attention?"

"A passing guest's whim?"

"That's not good enough." Suddenly she was angry again. "I said this magic is strong—"

"Piron!" A rapid knock on the door interrupted them.

Somebody tried the knob, discovered that the tumblers of the lock had been turned, and began to curse and hammer. "Piron, let me in!"

More swearing. Then the distinctive sound of keys fumbled and scratched against the lock.

Moving as one, Gaultry and Tullier seized the pale woman's arms and hustled her into the secret passage. Tullier got the panel sprung back into place just as the door rattled and burst open, its knob crashing against the wall.

The bald man from the front entryway blundered in. "Piron!" he cried, more gleeful than pained. "Why did you leave me?"

"He's drunk!" Gaultry whispered.

"Do tell." Tullier had his knife out. He jammed it into the panel's latch, breaking the mechanism so it could not be opened.

The drunk man was in his own world, barely able to walk and happy for it. He caught hold of the door and slammed it shut. The crash made him laugh; the laugh made him stumble. He blinked, owlish, and threw his coat onto the floor. "Piron?" he called, tugging at the laces over the crotch of his trousers. "Where have you crept off to?" He shook his boots off his feet and sent them skittering under the bed. "Piron, Piron, where have you gone?" The words were more a drunkard's rhyme than a true call for his friend.

He careened across to the wall sconce and tried to snuff the candles. "Llara's blight!" He had burnt his fingers. He damped them on his tongue and tried putting the little flames out again, this time successfully. He banged over to the lamp on the table next, the room's last light, and snuffed it too. In the space behind the panel, total darkness trapped them. Beyond the panel, the drunkard, mumbling incoherently, crashed towards the bed.

The dark and their sudden constraint behind the panel were unsettling. Columba's breath shuddered, too loud, as though she was slipping towards panic. Gaultry reached through the dark to hush her. Her fingers brushed the girl's lips, and a lance of pure pleasure ran through her, to her loins. Gaultry jerked back, bumping Tullier.

The magic that held Columba in its clutches laid in wait just beneath her skin, unrelenting. When it was roused, the girl could not have human contact without involuntarily drawing a sexual response. Gaultry leaned against the wall to steady herself.

After a time, Tullier tapped Gaultry's shoulder, a light, questioning touch. Gaultry pressed her hand over Tullier's, grateful for the simple contact. Almost a month had passed, and finally she could touch his hand—when he wasn't sweating.

That, she thought somberly, was the Bissanty curse. Simple contact: poisoned by spells and by poison and by rigid social barriers. What was wrong with the Bissanties that they were so eager to perpetuate and proliferate such a curse? Was the Emperor so insecure that he needed constantly to put his subjects to the test of poison, proving to them again and again that there were some protections Llara afforded only to him and his blood?

She wished she knew what it meant to Tullier that he could reach to her in the dark, reach to her and tug her, gently, in the direction of the slot that led back to the main passage, letting her know it was time to risk moving again.

She squeezed his hand back and followed him into the main passage.

▼

chapter 17

Columba accompanied them docilely through the passages and walls. Tullier led the way, moving quickly, as if to compensate for the time they'd lost in the painted bedchamber. Gaultry brought up the rear, struggling with her thoughts as she watched Columba's back moving ahead of her.

In the narrowness of the passageway Columba moved deftly, so deftly that Gaultry, who was both the tallest member of the trio and tired of bruising herself against the rough stone, assigned her to carry the bundle with the two swords. Descending through a hole in the floor that gave onto a short ladder, fragile with dry rot, they reached a constricted chamber at a crossing of passages illuminated via two high panels that filtered in a welcome patch of candlelight.

"Are we almost there?" Gaultry whispered testily across Columba's head to Tullier. "I'm tired of stooping."

"Soon. Don't you see where we are? This is where we came first, before we went to the storage room."

The passages had become so monotonous that Gaultry had not recognized it.

Relief and welcome suffused the Sharif's handsome features when they pushed the last panel open and stepped out into the chamber. *At last.* Spying Columba, confusion wiped the relief from her face. *Who is this?* she demanded, unfriendly.

"This is Columba," Gaultry said. "She may be coming with us to Dunsanius Ford." Tullier understood that, even if the Sharif did not. He gave Gaultry a sharp look.

"Col-umpah?" The Sharif sounded troubled. *She is bones and skin, and weakened for it. Do we need another companion?*

"Columba," Gaultry repeated, ignoring the Sharif's question. She did not need the Sharif to pressure her as well as Tullier, questioning her decision to help the woman. "It's a Bissanty word." *It means dove,* she added, picturing the bird so the Sharif could recognize it.

Like Issachar Dan was the hawk?

Not like Issachar— As Gaultry shook her head, a gesture caught the edge of her vision, a flutter, a sharp motion. Columba, her head ducking and her eyes turned down. Wild bird. White dove. Gaultry started and looked at the woman directly. The impression had already faded, leaving only Columba's wasted flesh and downcast face.

But that did not mean that Gaultry had missed it.

"Columba." The huntress rolled the woman's name on her tongue, tasting it. "How many layers of magic have been laid on you? I've sensed two so far."

The pale woman shifted, fumbling with her bundle. "Can I put this down?" she asked.

"On Llara's name"—Gaultry took a step toward her—"and all the Great Twelve, tell me, if you can. What chained you to service in this house? Who cursed you to this life?"

The dark eyes fixed on the young huntress's face. Columba's slender fingers twisted in the canvas cover of the bundle. But she did not have the strength to stare Gaultry down. "I cursed myself," she confessed softly, and dropped her eyes.

"I don't believe you," Gaultry said. "You don't have the strength."

"I did once—"

What are you saying? The Sharif, moving closer, pulled the bundle out of Columba's hands. *There are swords here— where have you and Tullier been?*

Columba used the interruption to retreat to the window, where she fixed her gaze on the closed shutter and began to rub her palms, agitated.

Gaultry, fearing she would rouse the rutting-magic, told her sharply to stop. Then she turned to the Sharif. *The house is peopled with degenerates. We'll be leaving in the morning before they are awake. And this woman may come with us, if we can pry some answers from her first.*

That woman's so cold I could believe she was soul-empty, the Sharif responded, unusually hostile. *Not like your Tullier, who has a beating heart beneath his angry armor. I could feel the void in her the moment she entered the room. Don't waste your sympathy on her.*

She is enchanted, Gaultry told her. *The gods pity her.*

Not me.

"What are you saying?" This time Tullier interrupted. Gaultry, pressed from both sides to play interpreter, threw up her hands.

"Be quiet, both of you. Columba needs to give me some answers." The aggrieved look Tullier and the Sharif exchanged at her outburst made her even angrier.

Columba, frail and yielding, made an easy target for that anger. "You!" Gaultry rounded on her. "Stop equivocating, and tell me how you came to this house!"

Columba shrank from her, cowed. Fortunately, unlike the Sharif or Tullier, she responded positively to bullying. "I was brought here to guard my mother's shrine. My mother's tomb was charged in Llara's name to be guarded by one who was pure. Pure of heart, body, and soul. I was pure once—and fit to guard her. I used that power to profane her."

"What shrine?" Gaultry asked, clutching at the one shard of real information in the woman's babbling. "Do you mean the old temple on the highway?"

Columba blanched. "That place? Oh, no—I mean the cata- comb—here in the house."

"In the house?" Gaultry looked at Tullier.

"She's addled in the head," he said. "There is no cata- comb."

"Could it be hidden in the passage walls?" She turned back to Columba. "This place—it's somewhere in the wall- passages, isn't it?"

"It's a secret place," Columba said. "I can't—"

"You were familiar with the passages," Gaultry pressed her. "I could see that in how you moved."

"But the dust wasn't disturbed," Tullier protested. "Not in all the time I lived here before. And not now, when we went in."

"But Columba was already like this when you came here," Gaultry reminded him. "If she ever walked the wall-passages, it would have been before your arrival."

A passage-creature, the Sharif put in. *A white scorpion who never sees the light.*

Gaultry did not know what a scorpion was, but she guessed from the Sharif's tone that the comparison was not a flatter- ing one.

It had been an exhausting night. Gaultry crossed to the basin on the room's sideboard and dipped her hands in, trying to give herself time to think. A vial of cleaning grease had been placed on the sideboard next to the basin, and a towel. She used both to wipe her face. The black that came away on the towel appalled her. Sweat and dirt, mixed with dusty soot. She glanced over at Tullier. He too was filth-covered from the passage. Columba, by contrast, was white and clean—save where the bruises showed.

"Look at her." Gaultry pointed. "Tullier and I are sorry sights, but look at her. Look how clean she is. Even carrying a bundle, she hardly has a smudge on her."

"I once lived half my waking day in this house's walls," Columba admitted.

Tullier made an angry noise, as though he disbelieved her.

"So the shrine is there?" Gaultry pressed. She gave the boy a look to warn him she had had enough of his interruptions.

"The shrine is there. But it was closed to me. Long ago. Before even that one came to this house." Tullier shifted under her sliding gaze. "Once I took the curse, my mother's tomb was denied me."

"Could you at least show us how to find it?" Gaultry asked.

Columba squirmed. "I can't go there. I'd make it unclean." She sketched the lightning bolt of Great Llara with the edge of her hand. "Nothing in me is pure—not my heart, my soul, my body . . ."

Gaultry looked at Tullier. "What is she talking about?"

"What do you think?" Tullier asked caustically. "That Piron wasn't the first man to tup her. What could be pure, after years of a life like that?"

"Her heart could certainly be pure—the Sharif at least thinks she's coldhearted."

Her soul is cold. The Sharif, who had followed only the general outline of the conversation, nodded.

Columba's eyes flickered, as if she had heard or sensed the animosity in the Sharif's unspoken sentiment.

"Well, I want to find out what this shrine is," Gaultry said. "Whatever the two of you say. The magic that binds this woman reminds me of something. If you two would shut up, even for a minute, I might remember what it was."

"But if Columba can't go—" Tullier broke in.

"She can show us to the shrine's entrance," Gaultry cut him short. "We can find the last part of the way ourselves. And I think this is important. It must be. A secret burial place has to be important. Use your imagination, Tullier. If the Sea Prince knew of such a hiding hole when he purchased this estate, who do you imagine he might have buried there?"

Beneath the ash and dirt, the boy's face paled.

"So you are going to show us the entry to your mother's tomb," Gaultry told Columba firmly. "You have nothing to fear. No one will make you go in."

Gaultry touched the Sharif's shoulder. *There's a burial ground hidden in this house's walls,* she told her. *The Sea*

*Prince—Tullier's father—may have buried his wives there.
Before we leave, we must see it. Columba will show us where
it is.*

*So I have to crawl like a scorpion through a dark crevice
after all,* the Sharif complained.

You can stay here—

And leave you and Tullier alone with that creature? The
Sharif snorted. *Not likely.*

The choice is yours—

"I come with you, this time," the Sharif told Tullier. "You."
She turned to Gaultry. "You show me these weapons."

Gaultry, seeing the woman had made up her mind, undid
the bundle for her.

The Sharif unsheathed the blade that Gaultry had used to
kill Piron. Her warrior-hardened hands made the motion
graceful. She ran her fingers along the flat, testing it. The
metal had been rubbed clean, but something in its feel made
the woman give Gaultry a sharp look, as if she could tell that
it had been recently covered with blood. The young huntress
shrugged, tired of explanations.

*Take whichever weapon you prefer. Tullier and I have to
go back into the walls. I want you to come with us, if you can
make yourself face the dark and the walls, but I don't want to
hear any more complaints.* "Tullier," she added aloud, "if
Columba will show us where this shrine is, we're not leaving
here without seeing it."

Their path took them deep into the foundations of the house.
Stone underfoot gave way to earth, and the ceilings lowered
dramatically. Gaultry had to walk with a stoop and the Sharif,
clearly unhappy with the closeness but determined to accom-
pany them, had to walk bent almost double. But there were
also no lacquered screens in these passages, so instead of
stumbling along with intermittent windows of light they traveled with a pair of hooded candles. The flickering lights, shining upwards, cast ominous shadows on the rough walls. A
suffocating weight of earth pressed on them from all sides,

and the dusty air, heavy in their lungs, intensified the oppressive atmosphere. Gaultry felt far from home. She was shamed to find reassurance in the doubt on Tullier's face. Though they passed no obvious door or turning, there came a point when the boy touched the rough stone of the passage wall and pulled his hand back, alarmed.

"I have never been to this place," he whispered. "It is ancient. Older than any of the house above by centuries."

Ahead of them, Columba paused. Unlike Tullier, her face was a passionless cipher. The candle she carried tipped downwards, revealing narrow, undressed steps, cut straight into the claylike yellow earth. Over the steps was an ancient-looking arch, crudely chiseled from pale reddish stone.

"You go alone from here," she said, standing aside to let them by. "For me, the passage beyond is forbidden."

"Is it magic that holds you back?" Gaultry questioned her. "Or your own promise?"

"Only the pure may enter the catacomb," Columba intoned flatly.

"That's not helpful," Tullier said sharply. "Tell us what holds you back. Shame? Sin? Magic?"

Columba blinked and looked confused. "I don't know," she said. "I only know I cannot pass this arch."

"We could force you," the boy said. "And see if there's truly anything you need fear."

"Stop that, Tullier!" Gaultry said. "You can wait for us here, Columba."

"She'll wait," Tullier said. "We'll take her light." He twisted it from her fingers.

"Take it," Columba said, her face controlled and blank. "I don't need it."

She can move in the dark. The Sharif put her hand on Columba's shoulder and pushed her against the wall. *Why bother taking her light?*

Tullier whirled round to Gaultry, disbelief on his face. "I can hear her," he said. "She doesn't like Columba either."

"There's a breakthrough," Gaultry said resentfully. "At last you two have found common ground. She can only touch the minds of those with whom she shares a trust."

I'll stay with the woman and watch her, the Sharif told them. *Leave me a light, and the two of you can go on.*

"Fine," Gaultry said, irritated by the Sharif's phlegmatic acceptance of Tullier's new ability to share her mindcalls—as if shared distrust of Columba could have been expected to set that affinity between them. She plucked Tullier's candle from his hand and pushed it at the Sharif. "I don't guess we'll be long."

Twelve steeply descending steps took them into a corridor with a low, arched ceiling supported by thick trusses. A pair of marble caskets lay in the recessed alcoves between the trusses nearest the steps, one to either side. A statue of a reclining lion surmounted the first, the second had a female figure with staring owl-eyes and a necklace of four rings chiseled on its chest.

"This place looks as old as Tielmark's founding," Gaultry said, her voice barely above a whisper.

"It's older than that," Tullier snorted.

"I didn't mean as old as Tielmark's freedom." She stared at the tomb with the owl woman. "I meant its founding, when it first got borders, back at the beginning of Empire. There are ruins all over Tielmark dating back toward that time. Not like the aqueduct we saw at Bellaire. More ancient." She looked at Tullier, trying to explain the strange feeling that the owl woman put on her. "Back in Tielmark, I lived in Arleon Forest, near what you probably call the old Imperial border."

"I knew that," Tullier said. "Corbulo knew."

Gaultry nodded. It did not surprise her that the information had been passed along. Then she shivered, realizing that her lack of surprise was in its own way a big change. A month ago, that news would have astonished her. It had not taken long for her to learn how intricately entwined Tielmark's politics were with Bissanty's.

"The land by the border is almost entirely wooded. Deep greenwood forest to protect the southern farmers from the land across the border." She traced the curves of the owl-eyes with her fingers. "When the Bissanties held sway there, they protected the border with great pillars of stone. Old Bissanty stone, with carvings styled like this woman. The woods have grown up and covered those stones, but you still come across them sometimes. Once when I was hunting, I almost fell over a carving like this on a stone that was three-quarters grown into the bole of a great oak. A woman with four rings and an owl's head. When I came home, I described the stone to my grandmother. Even though night was coming on, she insisted I take her back to find it. But somehow I'd lost it. The trunk that had grown over it was near seven feet wide." She pictured it in her head, wondering again at the mystery. "We eventually found something that seemed like that tree, but there was no stone. We never saw it again."

"Owls are for wisdom," Tullier said.

"Probably why my grandmother insisted I keep trying to find it," Gaultry said wryly.

They left the owl-figure and ventured on. A series of lidded tombs lined the walls, separated into niches by ancient earthwork buttresses that had been plastered and stabilized with clay-hardened reeds. The buttresses meandered left and right, irregularly formed. Shadows obscured the corridor's farthest reach.

Gaultry rounded what turned out to be the last corner and stumbled, coming to a halt.

"What now?" Tullier grunted, walking into her back.

The catacomb's corridor ended in a rough circular chamber. The walls were naked, packed-clay earth, clear of the clayed-over reedwork that elsewhere reinforced the walls. Their dun-colored surface was carved from the substance of the land itself: flattened, shriveled-looking earth. Gaultry had seen earth like that only once before—in a small grotto that her sorceress grandmother had carved into a hillside with no tool other than powerful magic.

"This chamber is not more than a decade or two old," Gaultry whispered. "Somebody hollowed it out beyond the old terminus of the catacomb."

Someone who had wanted a secret place for a coffin. The back wall of the chamber housed a deep, if plain, funerary niche. A lightning bolt painted with age-tarnished silver gilt on the wall above was the room's sole adornment.

The air smelled heavy with old incense and earth. More than ever, Gaultry felt the pressure of earth over her head— with no supports or trusswork, it was magic alone that kept the ceiling from collapsing. Columba's admonition that the crypt was only for the pure temporarily froze her on the threshold. Huntress help me, she thought. That could mean anything! Tullier shot her a nervous look, and she knew that he too was recollecting the pale woman's words. Not wanting to reinforce his uncertainty, she gave him what she hoped was an encouraging grin.

"Here's where we find out what pure means." Taking a deep breath, she set her eyes on the casket niche. Then, clenching her hands to steel herself, she stepped over the threshold.

The magic chamber's reaction was immediate but not catastrophic. In a golden bowl that had been positioned in the center of the niche shelf, a bright light leapt to life, illuminating both niche and chamber. Gaultry startled, then realized it would not hurt her, and released the breath she had been holding in her fear that the ceiling would fall in.

"It felt me." She looked back at Tullier. Her heart was beating wildly, whether from fear or the room's strong magic, she could not tell. "But I guess it forgives my transgressions. Your turn now."

"I'll watch from here," Tullier said, wary. "Why test me? I don't even know what you think you're going to find."

"Very sensible," she said, frowning. By now, she thought she knew Tullier well enough that she could judge it safe for him to enter. She felt his reluctance as an affront to her judgment. "You wouldn't want to drop the roof on me, eh? Fine. Stay where you are then."

Turning her back, she walked deeper into the room. Fitted into the niche, behind the bowl, was a short, magnificently embellished casket. Unlike the stone tombs they'd passed to reach this last chamber, this coffin was constructed entirely of dark, age-hardened wood, richly inset with gems and semi-precious stones: carnelian and malachite and lapis and many pieces of a deep purple stone unlike anything with which Gaultry was familiar. She suspected that it implied something Imperial.

She crossed the short distance to the coffin and the glowing bowl and looked down, expecting to see either true flame or magic fire.

Instead, the light emanated from a little statue, drowned in clear liquid at the bottom of the bowl. It was a shrunken figurine, no larger than the length of a child's little finger. A silver shape that was half-woman, half-bird.

"That's a soul-figure," Gaultry said, instantly recognizing the shrunken form. She touched the edge of the bowl, gingerly tilting it towards the arch so Tullier would see it. The metal was cold beneath her fingers, belying the flame within. She shuddered. Her sister's soul had been trapped in such a figure. Her sister's, and her Prince's, and almost her own. Her neck prickled with fear. "Columba's soul-figure."

"What's a soul-figure?"

"You don't know? The Chancellor sent by Sciuttarus to twist Tielmark's rule did. The trick of forging the metal for the figure itself was beyond him, but he had strength enough to wield the spell that bound a soul into the metal." The figure lay face upwards, glittering, the mouth a round circle of agony. "There is a sorcerer in Bissanty who has discovered a way to trap the human soul outside the human body," Gaultry said grimly. "That's what a soul-figure is. A repository for a human soul. It's a means of control."

"But the figure doesn't look human," Tullier protested. "The arms are like wings."

"It shouldn't look fully human," Gaultry said. "Half Columba's soul has been replaced with part of a bird's spirit. The sorcerer who did this—he must have practiced bonding animals in this way first. Then something that was animal, and also a little bit human. Later on, he didn't even need the scrap of animal-spirit to pry free the soul."

"How do you know all this?" Tullier stared across at her from the threshold.

"I don't know. I'm guessing. From things I saw in Tielmark—and from things Issachar Dan told me when I was at Prathe Lendra's in Bassorah. The sorcerer who paired Issachar's soul with a hawk's spirit was the same man who stripped that two-parted soul from his body. It must have been the same sorcerer who did this to Columba. The style is identical—and don't forget the vision we saw at the temple. Hawk and dove—that must have been Issachar and Columba."

"Taking a human soul from its body isn't possible!"

"It shouldn't be possible," Gaultry agreed. "But I've seen it done. Even to the Prince of Tielmark. Thankfully, the process can be reversed."

. Tullier struggled to accept the implications of her words. "I don't believe you," he said. "Or I don't believe this is Bissanty magic. I won't believe Llara sanctions it."

Gaultry, reaching to take the figure from the bowl, touched an oily surface that repulsed her contact. Layers on layers of spell. Oil slicked nastily onto her fingers, exuding rancid perfume as it tainted her skin, but her fingers would not dip beneath its surface. An unseen barrier prevented her from touching the figure. She plucked the bowl from the shelf. The liquid sloshed in a single viscous wave, casting up more rank scent. But she could neither empty the bowl nor retrieve the figure. "Why do you say not Llara?" she asked, setting the bowl back on the shelf.

"You say you saw this magic in Tielmark. Were the deerboys I delivered to the Prince's table a part of that?"

"They were. The Great Twelve only know what was left of the soul in them. I was only able to sense that they were human because I had seen their maker's work before."

"That spell was not Llara's magic." Tullier said triumphantly. "I was there when Corbulo cast it. I know—"

"What do you mean?"

"That spell belonged to the Huntress. Your Goddess. You even said so, looking at the dagger that held the spell. You

said the spell had been summoned from the Huntress, as sacrificing mother."

Gaultry stared at him, remembering the dark night they had
shared in the Tielmaran inn: Corbulo dead; Mariette
wounded; herself and Tullier, sifting through Corbulo's
belongings. "That bone dagger held the spell that transformed
the Vanderive boys?"

Tullier nodded. "So it wasn't Llara's magic."

"I don't know why you are being so smug about Llara, Tullier. Does soul-splitting shock you? I don't see why. You say
you were there when Corbulo cast that spell. That makes you
accomplice to that desecration.

"My Huntress would not perform such magic either,"
Gaultry added defensively. "Tielmark is her Prince. She
would not act to defile him. And that night at the inn—" She
struggled to remember what she'd said. "I'm sure I never told
you it was Elianté's spell. That broken spiral—maybe that
was Elianté's. But the spiral was banded with silver and
black, and that magic is Tarrin's!"

"Defend your god," Tullier said. "I need not defend mine."

"Say that again once you've stepped into this room,"
Gaultry mocked him. "My heart and my conscience are pure.
I show how I trust my goddess with action, not words."

He spluttered, and could not find an answer. Turning her
back on him, she fixed her gaze on the casket. Better to look
at anything that wasn't Tullier.

From the shape of the coffin, she guessed, the corpse had
been folded with the knees hunched to the chest. She'd seen
bodies buried so before, though it was not a common Tielmaran custom. The inlays were elaborate: flowers surmounted tiny masks, masks like those she'd seen crowning
the front of the Imperial Theater in Bassorah, smiles and
frowns and grimaces. She traced the vines that ran underneath
the flowers with her eye.

They were letters. L-U-K-A-P-A-L-L-I-A, once, then a
break of flowers, then repeated again.

"Columba is Luka Pallia's daughter," Gaultry breathed,

rubbing her hand against the cool wood and stone inlay of the coffin. She turned to Tullier. "Columba is your half-sister."

Tullier turned whiter than Gaultry had ever seen him. "She's the house whore!" he spat. "It's disgusting, the things she's let them do!"

"She has been the pawn of power," Gaultry said. "Do you imagine she courted her own dishonor?"

"She would," Tullier said angrily, still hesitating on the threshold. "She has."

Something in his voice caught Gaultry's attention. "What do you mean it's disgusting, Tullier?" She studied the boy intently. His eyes were wide, somewhere between frightened and defiant. "You watched her, didn't you? From behind that panel between the bedchambers. Didn't it ever occur to you that it wasn't what she wanted?"

"She's foul! She let it happen! She encouraged it."

"She's under a spell, Tullier," Gaultry told him stiffly, her voice rising despite her effort to remain calm. It was good the walls were thick earth here, the crypt a secret. They were openly shouting. "That was your half-sister who you so casually watched debauched!"

"You're wrong!" Tullier screamed. Tears streamed down his cheeks; clean tears that tracked pale trails on his dust-smeared face. "She was willing! She chose!"

"Degradation?" Gaultry hurled back. "Rape? Huntress help me, my guess is once the poor thing grew breasts your father couldn't stand the sight of her!"

"She wanted what happened!" Tullier spat. "She still does! I saw her! She wanted you, even with the blood of a dead man marking her. Don't tell me you didn't feel her wanting. And you wanted her back." That last was an accusation.

Gaultry looked at him sharply. "Is that your problem?" she demanded. "I thought you couldn't feel it. But you could, couldn't you? Even not knowing her for your sister, you couldn't bear the idea of your pure Sha Muira flesh wanting someone you despised as a whore! Couldn't bear the idea that you were not in control. Did it never occur to you that there might be something wrong in that? Something unnatural, something beyond what unaided flesh could reasonably desire? Didn't you wonder? Is your weakness to her enchantment part of what makes you doubt Llara loves you?"

Tullier sprang at her and chopped her across the cheek with the hard edge of his hand. "How dare you!"

"You're a young hothead." Gaultry clutched her face and stepped away from him, wary of striking back. She could not match Tullier in hand-to-hand combat. "Thinking and acting are not as far apart as you imagine." She shot an anxious look at the ceiling. The chamber's magic had shifted. Was Tullier's entry the cause?

"Look!" Tullier swung around. "Look at her! It's her, not me, who is wrong!"

Despite her earlier insistence that the catacomb was forbidden her, Columba was standing at the threshold, watching them intently, the dark eyes dilated, the white skin paler than ever. Gaultry, spotting her, swallowed. "Where is the Sharif?" she asked, her mouth suddenly dry.

"It called to me!" the white woman keened. She had shed her clothes, and her hands and knees were torn, as though she had been crawling. "Oh, lost, lost! It called to me!" So close to the source of the spell, her ivory skin was aglow, her silver-white hair a cloud of light, flowing down over her breasts and outheld arms. Wordless, she held her arms open to the boy and the huntress both. "Oh, help me!"

"There!" Tullier ranted. "You see!"

"See what?" Gaultry shouted. "I see only a woman who is suffering under powerful magic!" In her fury, she raised her hand.

Behind her, the oil in the gold bowl flared, sending out a pulse of power.

In the archway, Columba cried out and fell to her knees. Two forces seemed to be struggling in her for ascendancy: one that wanted her to enter the room, another that would not let her cross the sill. "Oh, Goddess, help me," she whimpered.

"Go on," Tullier sneered. "Go help her. Hit me if you like."

Gaultry, facing him with her hand raised, felt the chamber air thicken. She shot a reflexive look upwards. The spell that supported the ceiling had pulsed and faltered. The magic warped, unforming, releasing an unbodied cry of anger and despair and separation. *Oh, Goddess, help me!* Columba's words echoed and reverberated through the chamber, shaking the walls. Memory flashed: the white bird, the little dove, whispering as it lost hope in the cone of light at Llara's temple.

Tullier was deaf to the resonance—or he simply didn't care. "Give her the help she wants," he said derisively. "Give her a candle, or the pommel of your knife, since you can't offer her the other yourself."

Gaultry rounded on him. "You!" she swore. "You are too young to understand, and yet old enough that you should know better." She grabbed him by his shoulders and gave him a hard shake. "I have given you a month of life, and still you understand nothing! Alive today, because of me, because of my sister's love for me, Mervion who set the spell so I could soul-share with you!"

A pulse of gold fire burst between them. Gaultry gasped. The absent part of her Glamour had lurched toward her. Tullier, feeling it move as well, let out a sudden cry, as though something in him had broken. "Take it!" he screamed, sobbing, half clawing at her face. "If you love the white bitch so well already, take it. I want to die!"

"Elianté in me! You're jealous, and for what?"

Columba, keening with pain, or with desire, or with something between the two, was suddenly between them, having broken through the spell that denied her the room. Her slender sylph body and silky naked skin and burning dark eyes seemed everywhere between Gaultry and Tullier, madness burning in all of them. "Me!" the tremulous voice cried. "Help me!"

Gaultry barely heard her. Tullier's right hand was clasped in her own. A channel had broken open between them. A channel that was wreaking havoc with the bonds Mervion had set in place. "Tullier!" she cried. "Let go!"

But Tullier only cried harder, great clear tears that splashed down his cheeks. "You hate me! You hate me!" he shrieked.

It was too late to stop. Gold light flooded her vision, and the dun-colored walls of the burial chamber dropped away. Her missing Glamour-soul crowded to her, a glory of light and power that swamped her senses. For a moment she imagined something purple and powerful sought to chase it, fought to retie the broken spell that had bound it, then that power abruptly fell back. She could not feel Columba's skinny arms around her neck, could not smell the sweet rank scent of that spell-ridden body. All that was left was the grip of Tullier's hand and the power that coursed to her through that contact. She forced her eyes open. Tullier's pale eyes loomed before her.

The glacial green was washed with tears, full of wonder. As the magic left him, he felt its full strength for the first time. He had not really understood what Glamour was. Had not believed her when she had told him what force kept him alive. It had not been real to him. Not until this moment, as the gold fire left him. Gaultry began to laugh, hysterical. The poisons in Tullier had been a dark bridle indeed, if he had not been able to feel the potency of Glamour until this moment.

Then that thought too spun away and all she could feel, finally, was the magic that flamed through her body. Sighing, she luxuriated in glorious sensation of union, of reclamation, as the torn halves of her Glamour-soul melted together. Too soon, the fusion was complete, the gold light dimmed, and once again she had her full sight.

Yes, Columba's arms were around her neck, the woman's soft body pressed against her own. Gaultry stared at the curve of her back. She was beautiful. Or she had been beautiful. Too beautiful for her own good.

"The dove," she said, her words a caress against the woman's hair.

Tullier shot Gaultry a look, a look that said he had been betrayed, and dropped her hand.

"Columba," Gaultry said, this time firmly, mentally shutting out Tullier and his pain, and concentrating her own power—power that had been denied to her for far too long. "It is time you had your will and mind again."

"What are you doing?" Tullier said. "You can't challenge the gods! This woman is cursed! The gods have cursed her."

Gaultry swung round, allowing the slim woman to cling. The golden bowl was in her hands. "Not the gods!" she said firmly. In the first flush of returned power, she was a tower, a bolt of lightning, a lance from a god's quiver. "The curse is a sorcerer's work, and it can be countered. By my power, by Mervion's. I call on all the Great Twelve to help me here, to make this woman whole!"

With a blaze of light, the Glamour-power in her focused and ignited.

She plucked the soul-figurine out of the golden bowl. The oil burst into blue flame, licking up her wrist. Ignoring it, she pressed the finger-length of silver against Columba's unsteady palm.

There was a blaze of light and fire, then the candles were out, the bowl-light was out, and the crypt pitch-dark.

For Gaultry, the dark was lit with a brief vision of a black hawk and a white dove, rising together in a spiral that was at once courtship and flight.

Then that vision too exploded, and the darkness that took her was unconsciousness.

chapter 18

▼

Gaultry awoke, stiff and uncomfortable, with her cheek pillowed on her hands and her head pressed against a velvet cushion. The floor beneath her body, polished wooden boards, shook and jumped unaccountably. Cracking open her eyes, she discovered someone had laid her down on the floor of a moving carriage. In front of her face was a muscular pair of ankles.

The Sharif.

Gaultry rolled onto her back. "Where are we?" The last thing she remembered was the flush of power: the missing half of her Glamour-soul as it had flooded her senses, the leaping hope that she could be whole and that Columba could be whole. Those two things together had twisted into a wrenchingly strong wave of magic. "There was a dove," she said out loud, remembering, "and a hawk. Flying together."

Her throat felt parched and cracked; her body ached as though she had been beaten with a broom handle. Raising her hands to rub her face, Gaultry saw for the first time their appalling condition. There was a dark crescent of blood under every fingernail. Her own blood, as though some internal pressure had burst her nail-beds.

Above her head, as if in mocking contrast to her ragged figure, the carriage's ceiling was a delicately painted panel of blue sky filled with butterflies. The clouds behind the colorful butterflies carried an ambiguous suggestion of faces. The gods, smirking down from the heavens. The painting, a courtier's trifle, mocked an eternal truth. Who knew whether—or when—the gods were watching?

"Where are we?" she asked. She coughed, clearing her dry throat, and struggled into a sitting position. "How did we get out of the catacombs? Whose plaything is this carriage?"

The frames of the seats were richly appointed with gilt. Wine-colored silk curtains fluttered in the open windows. Everything was exquisitely luxurious and clean. Nothing could have been more different from the primitive clay-walled crypt where Gaultry had last known consciousness.

The Sharif sat alone on the forward-facing seat, her strong legs sprawled and relaxed. She nodded and gave Gaultry a smile, the picture of ease and contentment.

Dunderhead. The woman's relaxed body concealed burning anger. *You gave me no warning, no warning at all.*

What? Gaultry pressed her hands to her temples, trying to beat back the unexpected wave of rage.

Why did you leave me alone with her? You might have warned me she was sexed like a mad desert-weasel. The Sharif, still in perfect control of her expression, nodded across the carriage and smiled. *We have names for her kind, where I come from.*

Columba sat where the Sharif was looking, pressed into one corner of the rear-facing seat. Her face had altered in the hours since Gaultry had last seen her. With her soul returned, her dark eyes seemed to have a deeper luster, but new melancholy marked them. Age had touched her—age and cares. She seemed both more fragile and more intense.

Do you still think she's soul-cold?

The Sharif made an impatient gesture. *She's worse now.*

You have made an enemy. And Tullier—why did you let him slip his leash so soon? For Columba's sake? That was no bargain.

Tullier! How is he? Tullier was sharing the rear-facing seat with Columba, hunched in the opposite corner from her. The boy had fixed his gaze to a point outside the window. Though he clearly knew she was awake, he refused to meet her eye.

Where are we? Gaultry asked again.

In the carriage of the man you killed last night. At the house, they imagine that he is with us. Here, his servants think he is at the house. A satisfactory arrangement.

How did we get here? She recollected that the Sharif and Tullier had been able to understand each other, if briefly, the night before. *Can you and Tullier still talk?*

The Sharif shrugged. *He doesn't talk, that one. He argues. But Andion smiled, letting us have that link before you went unconscious. After you fell, we had to drag you back to the room. From there, planning would have been a challenge without communication.*

Your Tullier is jealous, she added. *He would have left us all behind if he hadn't needed our help to get you out of the house.*

So they had dragged her through the wall-passages. Little wonder her entire body felt abraded and sore! Rubbing her elbows, Gaultry heaved herself up to the seat beside the Sharif. *Jealous?* she asked.

Don't play the fool. The Sharif shot her a disgusted look, breaking her external composure. *He owes you his life, and he never had a life while he was Sha Muira. He would kill us all to make you his.*

I don't believe that, Gaultry said. *He's struggling. With me as much as with you.*

We are not so fair of face as thee, the Sharif answered, drawing herself tall on the seat. *We did not erase unceasing pain from his life. He did not know that life without pain was possible. Pain-bearer is the very definition of Sha Muira.*

They grow to believe the pain is not there, to believe that death is a relief—

He shouldn't have tried to leave you behind, Gaultry said. She did not want to think about Tullier's past. It was too depressing, too strange. *But that doesn't mean he is jealous.*

You cannot be that naive, the Sharif said grimly. *With your power, your skills—*

We will discuss this later, Gaultry cut her short. "You're alive, I see." She turned to Tullier. He'd cleaned his face since the crypt, but her memory of the clear tears marking his cheeks was vivid. "Glamour-soul notwithstanding." Tullier shifted in his seat, but his sullen expression didn't flicker. "And so are you," she told Columba. "How do you feel?"

Tullier's half-sister lowered her eyes. "How do you imagine I feel, Glamour-witch? When we last spoke, my suffering had a purpose. And now—what do I have now?" ·

"You have your soul," Gaultry said, dismayed. "The lure-curse is broken."

"Once I thought the gods cursed me. Now I know it was only a man who wanted my power."

"What do you mean?"

"I am Siri Caviedo's daughter," the woman said, faded pride rising. "The Blood-Imperial once flowed in me, strong as a second soul. That prize was worth something, don't you think? I ceded it willingly. In return all I got was a false god-curse." She sank back, hooded and miserable. With the lure-curse stripped away, Columba's pale beauty seemed a haunting, an accusation.

"Who made you think there was a god-curse?" Gaultry asked.

"You haven't guessed?"

"The sorcerer who bonded Issachar Dan?"

"That's one answer." Columba stared out the carriage window, pursing her lips.

"Where are we headed?" Gaultry turned from her, irritable with the knowledge that her actions on Columba's behalf had contributed to, rather than lessened, her misery. She picked at the blood under her nails, uncomfortably aware of her general shabbiness.

"Dunsanius Ford," Tullier answered. The look of surprise on her face stirred him to more words. "It's less than a day's journey from Fructibus Arbis, traveling with a carriage. The choice was between this and walking." He twisted one fist nervously in the other. "The storm ended early this morning. We left the house just after dawn, while the house's guests and its Master were still asleep. Did I do rightly?"

"Were we followed?"

Tullier mistook the question for a criticism. "Llara knows! I was just trying to guess what you'd want me to do. Who knows if I thought of everything? After the magic fire went out, when I got the candle lit, I could do nothing to wake you. There was blood coming from your nose, your ears, your nails. And her—" He gestured to Columba. "She was wailing like a woman who'd lost her reason. When I finally got you out of the catacomb and found the Sharif, if we weren't being followed, it can only be because no one was sober enough to want to investigate the noise."

"She did lose her reason," Gaultry said quietly, trying to ignore the aura of rebuke that was being projected by Columba's melancholy figure. Louder, she said, "You did well." Her voice sounded discouraging to her own ears. No wonder Tullier thought she was expecting too much. "I'm impressed that you managed to keep everyone together. Thank you."

Tullier shot a suspicious look at the Sharif. "It wasn't easy," he said. "What did she tell you?"

"She's glad the two of you can share words now. That sharing was a relief to her, gaining exit from Fructibus Arbis."

"She's all right," Tullier conceded. "She helped a lot, getting things organized."

Outside, someone gave a shout. The carriage slowed. A servant knocked on the door's panel and popped his head in the window. "The road's underwater, Master," he told Tullier, ignoring the other passengers. "Coachman thinks we can make it through, but the going will be difficult."

"That's fine," said Tullier. As always, with servants, his voice was cool, self-possessed. "Move on as you can." The servant tugged his forelock respectfully and ducked back out of sight.

For a time it was quiet in the carriage. The foursome sat, not speaking, listening to the sounds of debate from the driving box, and then to the sound of the horses being whipped forward, the splash of the carriage and team together in the water. After an encouraging start and good forward motion, the carriage began to settle, with a sort of slow inevitability, onto its left wheels.

"Try the right side of the road!" Someone shrilled from the driving box, loud enough that his words could be heard in the carriage. Gaultry and the others shifted their weight to that side of the seats, trying to help reestablish balance—to no avail. A few yards farther on, the carriage lurched to a complete stop.

"We're mired," Columba said flatly. Her toneless voice made it sound like a moral pronouncement.

"Give them time," Gaultry said.

They sat in their cushioned seats and waited as the coachman and the two side-servants struggled to break the carriage wheels free. After a time, words of encouragement for the horses were replaced by the sound of a whip lashing flesh. The carriage began to rock but not to move. Restless, and not liking the sound of the whip, Gaultry jumped up and craned her head out the window.

Three matched, coal-colored horses were hitched to the carriage: a leader and a pair. The coachman was next to the lead horse, in muddy water up past his knees, beating the animal's hindquarters and back.

"Wait!" she called. The coachman, turning around to see who had spoken, started as though he thought she was a madwoman.

"You're supposed to be my lackey," Tullier reminded

her. "Also, you're supposed to have taken ill, which is why we've pushed forward this outing to Dunsanius Ford, instead of waiting out the flood on high ground like reasonable people." Gaultry shot him a quick look. He wasn't smiling, but there was at least a shadow of amusement in his face at her unintentional display of non-Bissanty manners. "The monks at Dunsanius Ford are best known for their healing," he explained, "so I thought that would make a decent cover. But you're not playing a sick person very convincingly."

"That was clever," Gaultry said, relieved to see him emerge from his gloomy mood. It was clever, but it was also confusing. Why would the Bissanties have sent Martin to a house of healing? "It would have been more clever if you had given me some warning."

"Lean out and tell them I don't want the horse whipped." He glanced at Columba. "Let them think they misunderstood. She can be the sick one."

Gaultry nodded, craned out the window, and waved to catch the coachman's attention. "The Master wants us to lighten the coach before you try that," she called. "Wait there. We'll come out and help."

She shucked off her boots and rolled up her leggings. *We have to help free the carriage,* she told the Sharif. *Take off your boots.*

She swung open the carriage door. They were at the bottom of a shallow area between two gentle rises. A dark roil of floodwater spread away from the carriage on all sides, broken by outcrops of earth and the tips of rain-beaten marsh grasses. The tops of the road's marker stones were just visible, delineating the course of the roadbed. Looking back, she saw that they had made it more than halfway along the flooded stretch before becoming mired.

The rain clouds had moved to the north, but the sky was still heavily overcast with dense towers of cloud.

"You stay here," she told Columba, as if the woman had offered her help. "The Sharif and I will do it." She tried not to mind that the woman did not respond to her.

The Sharif, at Gaultry's shoulder, gave the water a gloomy look. *Water again. You go first, and show me the depth.*

"It's perfectly safe," Gaultry said as she stepped down. The water was warm and full of brown silt. She took a cautious step forward. The current was sluggish and the roadbed underfoot was seemingly solid. "Come on." She gestured for the Sharif to follow and took a few splashing steps to prove that she wasn't exaggerating. "It's not even cold."

The Sharif and Tullier traded a look and, Gaultry guessed, a few words. The big Ardana turned to her and grinned. *Go a little farther. You have a tendency to want everyone to rush out with you before you know the ground's safe.*

"It's fine," Gaultry said, frowning. She wasn't sure she liked that the Ardana and Tullier could now share secrets from her. *Absolutely safe.* She took two giant steps to prove it, and discovered that the footing was looser than she'd imagined. *Of course it may be best nearest the carriage—*

Her feet suddenly found the muddy rut the carriage was mired in, and she sank in over her knees, soaking her rolled-up leggings. Dismayed, she tried to scramble back to drier ground, slipping once more, and succeeding only in getting wetter. Above her on the carriage steps, the Sharif began to laugh. *Absolutely safe, you say? You should see your face!*

"Easy for you, long bones," Gaultry grumbled as she finally regained her balance. *Come on. We don't want to wait out the rest of the day here.*

The Sharif, still grinning, climbed down and moved carefully along the side of the carriage, trying to avoid Gaultry's mistake.

"Keep pulling," Gaultry called to the men by the horses, "and we'll go to the back and push."

From the carriage's rear, they could easily see the extent of the problem. Both wheels on the carriage's left side had lodged in the rut into which Gaultry had stumbled. The efforts by the men at the front of the carriage had only served to grind away more of the road's gravel bed without moving the wheels forward. Gaultry made the Sharif rock the carriage box gently while she grubbed in the water and tried to wedge handfuls of gravel under both of the back wheels. After a time, their efforts were rewarded. The straining horses ground the wheels against one wedge of gravel, then the other, inching the carriage forward. With an ungainly lurch, the wheels regained the gravel paving. The carriage broke clear and began to accelerate, wheels splashing, horses churning. The coachman cracked his whip, not wanting to chance slowing down to allow the women to reboard while the carriage was still in danger of sinking into another submerged rut.

Watching the carriage rush away, water splashing, the horses whinnying, pleased to be once again moving, Gaultry's heart unexpectedly constricted. Somehow, the clumsy acceleration of the horses brought it home that Tullier was no longer bound to her.

She kicked at the mud underfoot, disturbed by her reaction. It was not unlike the way she had felt when Martin's geasbond had left him—as though in her hidden heart she preferred the certainty of a magic binding rather than to trust his own desire to remain loyal. Why should she crave anyone's loyalty in that way?

Was it a desire to control? If so, she was a nice one to prattle on about the evils of slavery and bondings!

Staring after the carriage, she forced herself to remember that the reason she and Mervion had set the Glamour-leash on Tullier had been to save his life, nothing more. With that reason spent, however it might have suited her purposes to retain that hold on him, there was less to justify it. Indeed, Tullier had accused her of compelling him to help her often enough—how could she continue to claim that accusation as a false one if her heart felt regret at having freed him now, when he was safe from Sha Muir poison?

At the Sea Prince's estate, when they had plundered the box room, Tullier had asked if he could come to live with her in Tielmark. At the time, his question had seemed strange.

Strange, she admitted to herself now, because some part of her had not wanted to acknowledge that he was with her for reasons other than coercion. Her cheeks flamed. No wonder he had been angry! She, who had lectured him so calmly, telling him she didn't own him, and yet had reacted with incredulity the moment he asked her to consider the possibility that his loyalty to her might continue outside a forced bondage.

How did he feel now that the bond was sundered? He was free of the poison of Sha Muira, but now he had to consider the more serious tie of his Blood-Imperial. His father had plotted and sacrificed three sons to see him reach his manhood. If that secret came out, blessings of the Great Thunderer aside, he could expect the full weight of Emperor Sciuttarus's fury to fall on his shoulders. Whatever the course that Llara's blood had chosen to run, Gaultry doubted that the sitting Emperor of all Bissanty had any intentions of ceding his throne without a fight.

Ahead, the carriage rattled up onto dry gravel. The coachman reined in the horses and gestured to the women to hurry. Tullier stuck his head out the window, looked back to where the two women were sloshing along in the carriage's trail, and cracked a smile. He said something to the coachman, and the coachman's shoulders quaked with laughter.

"I shouldn't have taken my Glamour back to break the spell on Columba," Gaultry mumbled, staring across the stretch of muddy road to where the carriage waited. "Freeing Tullier to play in Imperial court games didn't help Tielmark. I should have left the leash on him until after we rescued Martin." Not, she thought, that that would have protected her from her conscience.

"Gautri?" the Sharif said, curious, sensing her unease.

"Nothing." *Nothing.* Cloaking her worries, she reached out to the Sharif. *I don't like the dove woman.*

Her soul is withered, the Sharif agreed.

Gaultry shook her head. *That's not fair,* she answered. *She's suffering from what a sorcerer has done to her. Her soul is bonded to a piece of animal-spirit. Somewhere, a dove lives, a dove with half a woman's soul, half its own spirit.*

Truly? the Sharif asked. *Why is Tullier jealous of such a person?*

Elianté knows that better than I. Or Llara. Why should he envy Columba?

He told me Llara moved you to save her life.

Gaultry shrugged. *He doubts the Mother Thunderbringer's love. That's not my fault. If Llara's intervened to save Columba, it does not mean that Columba is more favored than he—only that for that moment, she needed more help.*

They sloshed the rest of the way to the carriage without more words.

Tullier leaned out the carriage door to greet them. "Well done." The Sharif accepted his tone as praise and nodded. She clambered past him to take her seat. Gaultry, a few steps behind her, hesitated.

"You look tired," Tullier said. He reached out his hand.

"I'm muddier than the Sharif," Gaultry said. "That was hard work." She looked past Tullier's outstretched hand into his eyes, remembering what the Sharif had said about jealousy, about possession, not sure she should let him touch her. "Let me clean myself first, to spare the carriage."

"Forget about the carriage," Tullier said sharply. "I've waited for this moment a long time now. Let me help you."

She looked at his outstretched fingers—the lean young hand, the muscular wrist. Everything had changed for him. That change was her responsibility. She had wondered what choices the boy would make once her Glamour-soul leash had been loosed. This reaching hand, it seemed, was a part at least of the answer.

She could not refuse him this small thing. Taking hold of his hand, she let him pull her up.

It was noon. The carriage had stopped at a wayside farm, a lonely, unkempt place on an elevated table of land. The carriage servants watered the horses at the pump while Tullier and the Sharif went round to the public room to try for some provisions, leaving Gaultry and Columba together in the yard. It was the first time the women had been alone since they'd met.

An awkward silence stretched between them. "Let's walk a little," Gaultry said, the inactivity making her nervous, "and stretch our legs."

A hard-packed path led them away from the yard to the top of a low knoll that lay across the road. Turning back, they stood, watching the shortened figures of the carriage servants as they came and went, changing over the carriage's lead animal. Around them, the rise of the farm's land marked the beginning of a plateau: sparse wheat fields which sloped gently up from the great marsh plain that they had crossed from Fructibus Arbis and from Bassorah, now far behind them in the east. Beaten tracks, like the path they had followed to the knoll, revealed the contours of the land, narrow goat-paths that crisscrossed the graveled causeway of the main road.

"It's so empty," Gaultry said, staring at the lonely sweep of the empty fields and marsh. "I never pictured Bissanty lands as being so big and empty."

"You don't understand what you're seeing," Columba said. "The marsh still has some salt in it here, but the plain is full of rice. At harvest time, all this stretch of land before us will be teeming." An indecipherable emotion fluttered in the woman's voice. Gaultry was not sure if it was longing or pain. "When I was a child, the peasants outside the estate used to petition the house's Master to rub their rice-rakes against me. It was quite a performance. They would tell the master that my service to my mother meant that Llara was in me, that it was that for which they sought my blessing. Then they would take those rakes and come out here to bring in the harvest, and the estate-masters all around would cry out with amazement at the bushels of grain they would collect, and raise the levy. Those were good days. Long gone now of course. It's been years since the peasants brought their rakes to me."

"Why did they stop?"

"The peasants can feel it when the Blood-Imperial moves on."

Gaultry did not understand. "You said they brought their rakes to you because of your bond to your mother's tomb—"

Columba laughed, bitter. "I only said that was the excuse the peasants gave their masters. What do peasants care for someone else's dead parents? They knew it was something to say that the Master would like hearing. No—they worshiped me because, from the day little Tullier was born, the Blood-Imperial was alive in my veins. That was the magic that they wanted to aid them in their harvest." Her gaze, which had been scanning the waterlogged plain, suddenly fixed, riveted, on a distant hummock. "Oh Llara," she whimpered, the pride that had so briefly risen in her dashed. "Am I never to know peace—is it too high a boast in me, even to have loved my past?"

"What is it?" Gaultry could not see what she had spotted.

"There!" Columba said. "Look there!"

Far across the marsh, back the way they had come, the sun broke through the clouds and thrust down a single lance of sunlight. For a moment, at the top of a far hummock a figure gleamed, caught in the light. A single figure, with a hint of movement next to it in the grass that might have been goats, dun-colored like the grass and all the landscape. Together the two women stared at that far spot.

Then the cloud-gap closed, the light was gone, and the impression of the distant goat-herder vanished.

"What was that?"

"That was a marsh-witch," Columba said. A gust of wind lifted her pale hair, revealing her face. Something hard flickered in her expression, quickly followed by a fearful grimace. "Maybe she sensed my release. There's a new torment for me."

"Why do you say that?"

"She called the sun so we would know she was there."

The hair stiffened at the base of Gaultry's neck. "How would anyone know what I did?"

"This is not about you," Columba said scornfully. "It's about me. For all that the Blood-Imperial is gone from me, perhaps the earth still knows me, still can feel me—and my release. If the earth feels it, a marsh-witch would feel it too." She turned to stare at Gaultry, one thin brow lifted, suddenly arrogant. "Did you have no idea what you were freeing when you released me? Was your motive only pity?"

"That wouldn't be the worst reason to try to heal a troubled soul. But no, my motive wasn't pity." Gaultry pressed her palms together. The woman's unstable moods unnerved her. There was no way she wanted to explain to this woman that Gray Llara had forced her hand. "When I destroyed your soul-figure, I knew you were Tullier's sister," Gaultry said cautiously, "and Luka Pallia's daughter."

"You were clumsy when you released my soul," Columba said bitterly. She threw out her arms, and once again, eerily, Gaultry saw the dove-spirit move in her. "Clumsy and slow. You know more than you claim, Orchid-bearer. You have revealed more to me than I revealed to you."

"My Rhasan card," Gaultry stuttered. "How did you know?"

"We'll be at Dunsanius Ford soon," Columba said, as if that was an answer. "Do you expect to find your Black Wolf there?"

Gaultry stared at her. "You know about my Rhasan reading."

"I wonder, could you really have been in control of what you were doing when you released me? Would you have shared so much with me if you had truly been in control? Now I know about your Rhasan reading, and I know you know about mine. What did you imagine was being shown to you at Llara's roadside temple?"

"Dove and Hawk?" As Gaultry spoke the words aloud, the pieces fell into place. Columba and Issachar. That was what the vision in the temple had signified: like Martin and Gaultry, Issachar and Columba had shared a Rhasan reading, a reading that had bound their paths together. But from

Columba's expression, Gaultry guessed that her bond had brought her more pain than joy.

"Rhasan readings can be interpreted in many ways," Gaultry said, struggling to find some sweet in the sour. "The Rhasan Dove is a symbol of strength."

Columba jerked her hand angrily in the Thunderbringer's sign. "I was told that once," she said. "But it was a lie. The dove is only a bird for sacrifice. And I was sacrificed. Look at me, Huntress of Tielmark. I was born to the Blood-Imperial. Do you know what that means?"

"How can I know?" Gaultry said honestly. "I've been told that it's like having a second soul—but how can I know?"

"No." Columba threw her arms wide. A silver light flickered, as though Llara had briefly touched her, and Gaultry had a dizzying sense of a void in the woman's chest and body, an enormous void such as she herself had felt when half her Glamour-soul had been missing. "That is what it should mean. That is what it once meant. But I gave up that soul; I accepted humiliation and a harsh curse. All because I broke the oath I had sworn to guard my mother's resting place, and I was made to believe that the gods demanded my total submission in atonement. But you, Glamour-witch, you broke that curse. And now I see—my submission, my humiliation—they were for nothing."

"Where is your goddess-blood now?" Gaultry asked.

"My brother has it." She saw Gaultry's startled expression and laughed unpleasantly. "Not my little black-haired brother, your puppy Sha Muir boy, if that's what you're thinking. No. My brother Lukas has it."

"Luka Pallia's son?"

"Who else? And I see now what he did." Columba stepped close to Gaultry, so the young Tielmaran woman found herself forced to look deep in the woman's pain-touched eyes. The bird-flicker that she saw there made Gaultry draw uneasily back. "Lukas bribed a Rhasan reader to bind me to Issachar Dan, the hawk-lord. With that done, that transgression, I was clay for his molding."

"The Rhasan doesn't work like that," said Gaultry, remembering her grandmother's deck. To see the face of even a single card, Tamsanne had to expend a frightening amount of energy and magic. "You can't choose which cards to pull. Try that, and the deck will punish you."

"The Rhasan! I curse it!" Columba seized handfuls of the pale hair at her temples, clutching at it as if she meant to tear it from her head. "And the marsh-witch who made our readings—she ruined us all. She tricked us into thinking that it was a game. A game indeed! It transformed my brother into a monster!"

Gaultry stared, disbelieving. "You played with a Rhasan deck," she said. "You, who pride yourself on your Imperial blood, played with a Rhasan deck? Had no one warned you how dangerous that could be for you? Shouldn't you have been more careful?"

"We all played! It was not just me!"

Gaultry, looking into the woman's angry face, could not understand her defiant tone. Unless, of course, it meant that Columba had known of the danger—and ignored it. She did not know what to say. "Tell me what happened."

"I will tell you the story—though if you plan to set yourself against Lukas, it won't help you. But if you truly want to know how I came to have this animal-spirit bound in me—"

"I do," Gaultry said. "How could anyone but a god split a person's soul?"

"I will tell you. You have made my life a ruin—a conscious ruin—but I will tell you.

"It was never a secret that I was the Sea Prince's get, but despite this, my life was quiet at Fructibus Arbis. Only the lowest peasants gave me any regard—and who pays attention to peasants? I tended my mother's grave, and that was all. Except that every summer Lukas came to visit. Sometimes with his friends, sometimes alone. His visits, of course, were one of my life's greatest pleasures." Columba was a vivid storyteller. Gaultry could almost see the house, its summer visitors. She had something of a troubador's magic in her.

Watching her as she warmed to her story, Gaultry could see that her performer mother's blood, as well as that of her Imperial Father, ran strong in her veins.

"The summer I became a woman," Columba continued, "everything changed. Lukas was a month late for his visit, and when he finally arrived, nothing in the house could please him. He wanted only new diversions. Then the marsh-witch came and offered to tell our fortunes."

"Who was she?"

"A wanderer. She had goats," Columba said, flinging wide her hands. "She was like that one in the sun's stream—there but not there. We never knew when we would see her. She came and went from Fructibus Arbis all the month that Lukas was with us, bringing us stories from Averios, Lanai, Tielmark. Borders were nothing to her. She claimed she could see our futures, even without reading from her deck.

"Before the month's end, Lukas succumbed to temptation. He followed her into the marsh to have his reading. Oh, he was excited when he returned! His card had prophesied magics that had not been seen in many generations, power, even god-hood. I laughed and did not believe him. Then he showed me how.

"Our father had ghostmongered and stolen the Blood-Imperial. Lukas had always used that second soul to make magic—now he showed me that he could draw on my Imperial Blood as well, to make magic of astounding force. Not since Clarin Glamour-Prince has there been a man who wielded the power of three souls—and never has there been a man who turned that power to magic.

"Lukas used that new power to split Lord Issachar Dan's soul. Oh Llara, that was awful! Issachar did not believe he could do it. He was a fool twice over: first, to doubt my brother's power; and second, to indulge him in what the dark lord thought was only a game."

A gust of wind, as though something unseen had passed them, brushed Gaultry's cheek. She started, and stared around. The land had dropped away from the little knoll, the sky had darkened. The farm across the road seemed far away;

she saw the figures of Tullier and the Sharif, coming into view around the side of the farmhouse, as if they were across a border in another land.

"What brought Issachar Dan to Fructibus Arbis?" Gaultry asked, her mouth so dry her voice cracked.

"He was part of the house party. Lukas had invited him for the summer's hunting with three other gentlemen. It was not an unusual thing—any more than games and divertissements were unusual things. That was how my brother tricked Issachar into submitting to the hawk-bond. He pretended that it was a game.

"When Issachar understood what my brother had done, he would have cut him down where he stood—but my brother held Fontin, the great falcon, where half Issachar's soul was trapped, and Issachar could not fight Lukas while my brother held Fontin. The dark lord would have turned his sword to his own heart then, when he saw how lightly he had given over his deepest treasure. Lukas calmed him with promises that all would be well—if only he went along to the marsh-witch and submitted in his turn to a reading. Lukas sent me with Issachar to keep him company—telling me I must make sure the dark lord's card was read. I followed his order—never intending to have a Rhasan card pulled for me. My future was at my mother's graveside. I needed no Rhasan card to tell me that. I did not suspect that my brother had a deeper purpose, sending me with Issachar."

Gaultry pictured it in her mind's eye: the dark, hawklike warrior; the pale, delicate girl, just on the cusp of womanhood. Walking out into a marsh, going to meet a witch. A witch with a fortune-teller's cards. Cards that had the power of the gods vested in them.

"You met her in that old temple of Llara's," Gaultry guessed.

Columba nodded. "She was waiting for us. An old woman, thin as a stick. When she saw us, she had two cards ready, even before we could tell her why we had come. Mine was the Doves—two white birds, standing on a sword's edge with the blood flowing from their feet. But Issachar's—" She shook her head. "I won't tell you. You know what it is to share cards with a man. For a short while, that sharing was a wonderful revelation."

"I think I know," Gaultry said shyly. "But if I do, I don't understand how such a reading could be a sin against your oath."

"Perhaps it would not have been," Columba said, grimly. "Save that she pulled a third card for us, and the third card told us what to do. It was a lovers' card." Shuddering at the memory, she clasped her thin arms tight around her body. "I cannot tell you how much force that card held. No one on earth could have resisted it."

"So you became lovers?"

Columba laughed derisively. "Right there on the floor of the temple, after the witch left us. Lukas walked in before we were finished. His rage was high and righteous. He had been out flying his little sparrow hawk, and he held a living dove in his hand as if by chance. He made me submit to his will, there and then, binding my soul to the dove-spirit, and forcing the concession of my Imperial blood. And the punishment seemed just. Lukas was shining with power and light. It was easy to believe the gods spoke through him."

"He was lying!" Gaultry spluttered.

"That is true," Columba said. "Having tasted power when he tied Issachar, he did not want ever again to have to beg for that share of my strength—he wanted to own it. Though he at least was kind enough to leave me believing that my suffering might, in time, atone for my offenses. Now even that comfort is denied me."

"We're going to Dunsanius Ford now," Gaultry said. "Your brother is there—"

"Perhaps that will prove my release from this nightmare. Your magic broke his spell, it's true. But that was at a distance. He has the power to make it whole again."

"Not if I have anything to say about it," Gaultry said stiffly. "I'm not going to let that spell take you a second time."

"Even if I want it?"

"You don't want it," Gaultry said. The woman's embittered assurance grated on her nerves—as if words became fact because she spoke them. "When you saw Piron's knife, you called to Llara, begging release. How dare you question the fact she answered your prayer?"

There was a long pause. Columba had tears on her cheeks. Like Tullier when Gaultry had first met him, she didn't seem to understand the sadness revealed by her crying.

"You can't save me," the pale woman said. "Close in, Lukas will rip your soul into pieces. He was powerful before, when he was first learning soul-taking. Imagine the strength he has learned in the years since then."

"I'm afraid of him," said Gaultry. "That doesn't mean I will turn back."

"You think your Glamour-soul will save you?"

Gaultry looked at her coldly. "You know that Martin Stalker is at Dunsanius Ford. Your brother doesn't waste time with animals these days—he seems to think that any soul is his for the taking. He did that to my Prince. He did that to my sister. If he has done it to Martin, I will find some way to make him regret it."

Columba met her gaze, equally cold. "I'll warn you once: you don't have the strength to face him. I have seen the limits of your power—I touched it in the catacomb, when you broke my soul-figure. Lukas is my twin, and I tell you now, you cannot match him."

A coldness touched Gaultry's spine. "Your twin?" she stammered.

"My twin. So I understand you, Glamour-witch, better than you think. I, like your sister, had the misfortune to be born the subordinate twin. You and Lukas—you are alike. You think it is your right to sap your twin for her strength."

"I would never do that to Mervion!"

"No?" said Columba. "Then what is this?"

She reached into her sleeve and pulled free the soul-figurine that Gaultry had first seen in Luka Pallia's crypt.

Then, it had been shaped like a dove melded with a woman.'

Now, all semblance of the dove was gone and half the figure was formless slag. The other half was still discernibly female: long hair, a graceful shoulder—

"What is that!" Even as she saw it, snatched it from Columba's slender fingers, she knew.

It was half a Glamour-soul. Half of her sister Mervion's Glamour-soul.

Horrified, Gaultry's memory flashed to the day on the Prince's feasting grounds. She had begged Mervion to help her save Tullier, offered half her own Glamour-soul, if Mervion would only use her skills to bind it to him. Then, when her twin had hesitated, she had demanded that Mervion help her, sure she was right to do so, fearing that any delay would doom the boy to death.

She had not understood that the power needed to withstand Sha Muir poison was stronger than her Glamour could stand, that the magic needed was more than what she alone could offer.

"I didn't force Mervion to sacrifice this to me!" she said, appalled. "She could have told me I was asking too much!"

"Yes," Columba agreed. "She could have told you. Yet she agreed to cede it to you without telling. Just as I could not argue with my brother when he told me that I must cede my Blood-Imperial to him, in payment for my sins. You are the dominant twin. How could she refuse you anything?"

"The dominant twin?" Gaultry laughed nervously, trying to cover her rising horror. "Hardly. Mervion was out of Arleon Forest and at the Prince's court before I was brave enough to haggle the price of the eggs from the local farmwomen."

Columba nodded, the maddening self-possession deepening. "Just so. A vain attempt to escape before you stole the best of her soul and magic."

In Gaultry's fingers, the little soul-figure was cold. So cold it burned. "I won't believe that!" She closed her eyes and clutched the figure tighter, ignoring the pain. The darkness behind her lids swarmed with images. Her sister, beautiful and composed. Her sister's voice inside of her, sharing the vision of Tullier as the black puppy. *You are asking more than you realize,* her sister had told her.

Her sister's tone had been a warning. She had ignored that warning and forced Mervion to finish the casting.

But confronting that memory, her unthinking impetuosity in forcing her sister to act, Gaultry found suddenly that a deeper truth was revealed.

She opened her eyes. It no longer hurt to hold her sister's half-formed Glamour-soul figurine. "You are wrong," Gaultry said, looking deep into the Bissanty woman's dark eyes. "But I will not blame you for being wrong. Just as I do not understand Bissanty ways, you do not understand those of Tielmark. I am not like your brother. If I mistakenly forced my sister to give more than she desired, that was not because I wanted to fatten my own strength.

"My theft was not a malicious act. My intention was to lessen a suffering boy's pain. Even so, I will see my debt to Mervion repaid when I return to Tielmark." She clenched the figure in her fist, touching it gently with her mind, taking comfort from the warmth that she knew was her sister's love.

"Mervion could have told me what she had done. If she kept the information back, it must have been because she knew it would weaken my resolution: my choice would have been to protect her power, rather than to ask her to sacrifice it to save Tullier. She did not fear to share her strength. She knew I never would knowingly misuse it.

"My sister trusted me to use her power wisely. I will repay that trust in full."

Gaultry turned, suddenly aware of another presence. Tullier stood at the top of the path, listening. She wondered how much he had heard.

"The carriage is ready," he said, "and the farmer gave us some food."

"We must be on our way," she told him. "I have had some disturbing news. It is more important than ever that we find Martin quickly and return with him to Tielmark."

"What's that?" Tullier pointed at the soul-figure.

"Sha Muir poison that possessed you was very strong, Tullier. It took more than half a Glamour-soul to turn it back. This—this was a gift from my sister so that you could be saved."

"Did she steal it from you?" He cast an unfriendly look past her to Columba. "I saw her pick it up in the catacomb."

Gaultry shook her head. "No, Tullier. You should thank her. She kept it safe. She knew she would need it to teach me a lesson. Thank Elianté and Emiera both, it wasn't the lesson she imagined it would be."

"So what was it?" Tullier gave Columba another hostile stare.

"My sister loves me. And I have to take care that she does not sacrifice too much for that love." Gaultry tucked the little figure securely into the breast of her shirt. "Probably that's a lesson that you don't see people work their way through so often, here in Bissanty."

chapter **19**

▼

It was late afternoon when the carriage reached the end of the farmed plateau and descended once more into flooded land. This was a new kind of swamp, less broad, more broken. They had left the last vestiges of salt marsh behind. Now deciduous trees and brush crowded the high ridges of rock that studded the landscape and long raised mounds of earth radiated out from the high road, giving the land an appearance of imperfect cultivation. Every mile or so the carriage would rumble through a small hamlet with ingeniously constructed buildings of age-darkened marsh-grass lattice, many of them battened down against the passing waves of storm. Passing these, Gaultry had the impression of worn, elderly faces staring out, watching the carriage with the same listless disinterest she had seen among the Bassorah street-urchins. When she asked Tullier about this, he reminded her of Bissanty's mandatory conscription. "The regions take turns sending their men to Bassorah for tours of duty. When the men go, they bring their families. Only those who can't travel stay behind. It's less of a hardship than you imagine," he added, seeing Gaultry's response. "The wages are generous, and few of the troops actually see fighting. Mostly those farm families spend three months in Bassorah or one of the border towns, living the good life and occasionally doing some training. It can be like extended holy days for them, if they get really lucky."

That didn't seem unpleasant, but the emptied farmhouses, like the empty rice-plain, left Gaultry with a melancholy feeling. It was very different from the rhythm of life that she knew in Tielmark. ·

The sun was dipping toward the horizon when the coachman called another halt. One of the coachman's skinny lackeys knocked at the carriage door. "We've reached the Locatus Feeder," he told Tullier, touching his forelock respectfully. "And this is Dunsanius Ford. The ford's flooded. Will you cross to the monastery afoot, or wait at the staging house for the waters to recede?"

"My woman has not much recovered," said Tullier. He cast a quick glance at Columba. "But night is coming on us, and it may be that we have come too late to be welcomed at Dunsanius's House. I need to stretch my legs. Run down to the staging house and ask how late the god's house accepts supplicants. I'll decide what to do when you bring me that answer."

The man made a short bow to acknowledge the order and ducked away from the door.

Telling Columba to stay in her seat, Gaultry, trailed by Tullier and the Sharif, got down from the carriage to stretch.

They had stopped on the road a little way above the staging house. From the sloping roadside, they had a good view of the low-beamed, rambling house, its comfortably appointed yard, and the carriage-lackey, jogging briskly ahead to discover the answer to Tullier's question. For a moment Gaultry wondered why the coachman had stopped so early, then, looking ahead to the yard, she understood. They were far from the only ones to be balked by the flood. A crowded tangle of wagons and carriages had accumulated in the staging house's yard, ranging from a simple pony cart through to a carriage that was almost as elaborately gilded as their own stolen rig. From the settled-in look of some of the con-

veyances, several at least had been camped there since before
the rain had begun, two nights back. Their coachman had
wanted to give them a chance to decide whether or not they
too would be joining that makeshift camp.

Ahead, a swollen mud-brown river barred the road, leaving
only a precarious crossing via a narrow plank bridge. Upriver
and down, the waters had long since broken the river's banks
and spread onto the floodplain, temporarily creating a broad,
rushing lake. Across the river, in front of low brown hills that
receded into the distance, was a wedge-shaped rise of land,
screened by cypress trees. In contrast to the untended landscape all around, the ridge of land had a tidy look, the grass
beneath the trees trimmed and raked, the scrub pruned and
tended all the way down the side of the hill to the angry, risen
edge of the water. At that edge, a flooded boathouse and
abandoned farmshed suggested where the river's natural bank
might lie.

Two golden onion-shaped domes peeked above the trees at
the top of the rise. Beneath, a glimpse of the rosy-orange
brick wall that enclosed the domes and a cluster of more modest buildings with red tiled roofs could be seen through the
belt of cypresses.

"That's the monastery," said Tullier. "What now?"

Gaultry found herself staring at the swollen river, almost
mesmerized by its force. "This river feeds into the Locatus?"
she asked, recollecting the carriage-lackey's words. Unlike
the sluggish waters that had flooded the saltwater marsh, here
the rushing power of the swollen river was almost hypnotic.
"Elianté in me, the Locatus must be fearsome broad." The
mouth of that great river touched the sea less than a day's
march from Tielmark's border—as had been proved, to Tielmark's detriment, in one of the largest battles of Briern-bold's
war against the Empire, two centuries back.

She looked nervously at the water and the rise of land
beyond it. They had finally reached their goal. Somewhere up
on that hill, Martin was a prisoner—Martin, her black wolf,
the man she had pledged herself to save. The lackey had disappeared into the yard. She was ashamed to find herself hop-

ing that he would bring back the news that the monastery was closed for the night, the ford was uncrossable, and they would have to wait. She shivered at the irony of this last obstacle. Martin's god was Allegrios Rex, the water god. The spectacle of this angry river would not have daunted him. She must not let herself be set back, even by a torrent of floodwater. A plan began to form, unbidden. "Is the Locatus navigable in a flood like this?"

"It depends on who's doing the navigating."

To her eye, this fast-running flooded river did not look navigable. "And this river?"

"The answer is the same."

Staring at the unmerciful current, the greedy way it had spread across the floodplain above its banks, tearing at the land that flanked it, Gaultry felt distinctly queasy. The Locatus, fed by this and other rivers, would possess even greater power.

But the Bissanties too feared a flood. She had seen that in the way they clustered in their villages and staging points while the great Thunderbringer shook water from the heavens. If they succeeded in rescuing Martin, braving that angry river could prove their best means of escape.

Or, indeed, their only means of escape. What other choices did they have? Pressing on westwards and reentering Tielmark through the Lanai Mountains? Returning east to Bassorah?

This river runs south to feed a greater river. Gaultry told the Sharif. *That second river flows almost to Tielmark.*

The tall woman turned her desert-bright eyes to the huntress. She smiled uneasily. *A path of water. Is there no other way?*

It could be the first step of the journey that takes you south to Ardain. Gaultry did not want to say more than that, but the Sharif, detecting that she was trying to give an evasive answer, demanded an explanation.

What does that mean, my journey to Ardain? Could I follow a path of water without you?

Gaultry swallowed. Mind-touching with the Sharif was not

the ideal way to speak of things she wished to keep hidden—
the fears that she was not ready to acknowledge, even to herself. She spoke aloud, trying to keep her words simple enough
for the Sharif to follow. "Up there on that hill, we will face a
soul-breaker, a man who steals souls so that Imperial power
can flourish. I came to Bissanty to rescue Martin—a man
whose soul is bound to the fate of Tielmark's Prince. The
soul-breaker must not claim Martin's soul.

"We've reached Dunsanius Ford sooner than I had hoped.
Time is not our friend after what happened in Bassorah. Too
many people know that I am in Bissanty—and that Tullier is
here with me. We don't think we were followed out of Bassorah—but many of those who saw us at Lendra's party know
that the Emperor himself will reward them if they track us
down. The Great Twelve have been with us, finding us shelter at Fructibus Arbis and setting us on this road. We've got
this far playing gentleman-with-a-sickly-servant. But that
cover—how can it last us even another night? We can only
pray that it will last us up the hill through the monastery's
doors.

"Columba warned me that I won't be able to match the
soul-breaker's power. She might be right. If I can't, there is
still a course that is open to me—and to Martin. If that happens, someone will have to take Mervion's soul-figurine
home."

The Sharif did not immediately respond, as she puzzled
through the meaning in Gaultry's words. When at last she
reacted, it was to reach out and press her strong palm to the
top of Gaultry's head. Something in the motion suggested ceremony, an act the war-leader might have performed for one of
her own warriors back in her desert homeland. *Young one,* she
said. *You speak of releasing your soul, and your man's, to the
gods. Buying safety for your Prince and his lands with your
deaths.* A tiredness emanated from the woman, a tiredness
that touched at her eyes, the carriage of her shoulders. *That is
an honorable pledge. Greater than the pledge Janier gave to
me.*

Gaultry squirmed, and would have turned away, but the

Sharif grasped her hair with her strong, muscular fingers, and would not let her go. "Slaving made Bissanty sick," the woman said aloud. "Men or land, it made Bissanty sick." *In Ardain, we say the last journey runs down a river of light to the feasting grounds.* She nodded to the flooded stream. *I will brave this river for you, Gaultry Blas, if you must wade those waters.*

"What is she saying?" Tullier demanded. "What is she telling you?"

I would like to fulfill my promise to Janier, the Sharif continued. She paused, as if remembering the stout warrior who had destroyed himself to buy her freedom, then went on. *But I will strive to complete my promises to you first.*

Tullier grabbed at the Sharif's sleeve, disliking that she was shutting him out. The tall war-leader gave him a short reprimanding glare. The boy's anger subsided. Gaultry understood from his change of manner that words had accompanied the Sharif's sharp look.

The pair made another exchange. The boy turned to Gaultry, with an expression in his eyes partly distraught and partly furious.

"You're planning to sacrifice your life for that man? Even if it means he dies too? Is that what you meant when you said there was another course open to you?"

"I can't leave Martin alive in Bissanty hands," Gaultry told him. Put so baldly, she felt her stomach turn. "For Tielmark's sake, if not his own. That is the stake here, Tullier. That has always been the stake. I didn't travel all this way just to familiarize myself with your country's customs. I'm not going to lie to you or the Sharif—or to myself. I have broken this sorcerer's spells several times now. But that has little bearing on whether or not I can best him in open battle—or even if I will be allowed the opportunity to fight him on such ground. The Great Twelve only know how many men he has to reinforce his power up there on that hill. Our best chance lies in the fact that he might not expect us yet—or if he does, he won't yet have received extra support from the Emperor in Bassorah."

As she spoke, she drew Mervion's little soul-figurine from

her belt. "Will you give me your hand?" she asked Tullier.
The green eyes were suspicious, but when she reached for his
hand and took it in her own, he did not resist her. "The power
in this figure made the spell which bound my Glamour-soul
in you," Gaultry said. "It belongs to my sister." Her fingers
clasped Tullier's; both their hands together clasped the figure.

She could not meet his eyes. There was too much she
wanted to ask him. For vengeance, if the Emperor's sorcerer
killed her or Martin. For support. For too much. It would not
be right to ask anything of him that would further tangle the
web of Imperial deceit in which his father had meshed him.
"If I do not live to take this to Mervion, you must promise on
your goddess to take this to her yourself." She tried to smile,
but it came out crooked. "If it's vainglory for me to have
hoped that I could rescue Martin, she shouldn't have to pay
the price."

"I'll swear more than that," Tullier said hoarsely.

"I won't accept any greater promise." Gaultry blinked back
tears. She tried, unsuccessfully, to hide them from Tullier.
The boy shuddered, as though something unfamiliar had
passed through him.

He turned to face her and raised his right hand. "On Llara
Thunderbringer, Gray Mother Llara whose blood runs in my
veins, I will take this to Mervion. But, Gaultry, you have
overstepped yourself. You cannot limit what I choose to
pledge. To you, I promise—" Something moved in him,
something that choked off his words. His eyes glistened with
silver light, and a strange set appearance cast itself across his
features. Gaultry and Tullier, startled, drew apart, Tullier with
Mervion's soul-figure in his hand. "To you, I promise—"

Again that movement in him, and the words choked in his
throat.

Gaultry recovered first. "Tullier," she said weakly, "I'm
beginning to suspect that your Sha Muir poison was a rein on
more than your body."

The boy looked shaken. "I did not believe." He threw back
his head and stared up at the sky, at the thick bands of cloud

that hung low across the great vault of the heavens. "My Mother, I did not believe."

Gaultry thought of the story Columba had told her of the peasants secretly bringing their rice-rakes to be blessed by her body, of how they no longer come to her after they sensed that that power had passed on. The purple fire that preserved Tullier from poison in the hidden room could only have been one thing: the boy's awakening Imperial blood. Would the peasants be bringing their rakes to him now? Where did that leave the Emperor Sciuttarus, sitting on his throne, surrounded by three sons, in the Bissanty capital?

"That mob outside the palace in Bassorah had their blood up for a reason," she said. "The peasants near Fructibus Arbis must have known something when they gave Columba all that attention. That started just about the same time that you were born, you know, and finished when her brother bound her. Which all makes sense if she really did possess Imperial blood."

"I heard," Tullier said. "I heard much of what she told you. But I didn't believe it. When I came to Fructibus Arbis, she was already one of the house whores. How could I have known who she had been?" He touched his neck, as though feeling the place on his throat where his words, his attempt to promise himself to her, had been stopped. "But this—this power in me means that my father has blocked the Emperor Sciuttarus from fathering an Imperial heir. Yet Columba's brother is allied with Sciuttarus. Why else should the Emperor have sent Martin to Dunsanius Ford, Sciuttarus the Emperor who wants to regain Tielmark almost more than anything in the world?"

"Tullier—why should Luka Pallia's son be a threat to Sciuttarus? The boy—your brother—can't do anything other than magic with his Blood-Imperial. The Emperor castrated him. Doesn't that mean he's no longer in the Imperial line?"

"The Emperor should not be that stupid!" Tullier exploded. "If Luka Pallia could pray to Llara and bear twins, who knows whether or not that freak's son can seed children or no? Llara on me, there is a precedent. Even White Tarrin, the castrated one, was healed for a time—by your own goddess, Elianté. Who knows what is possible?"

"That is not a nice story," Gaultry interrupted him. Indeed, it was one of her least favorites. The wounded God Tarrin, condemned to wander in the lands by the sea, had stumbled upon the hidden bower where Elianté, Huntress Goddess, trysted with Cyronius, her mortal lover. Tarrin had contrived to take Cyronius hostage. He had forced the goddess to barter the healing powers of her body in exchange for the mortal man's life. Elianté submitted as Tarrin had planned, but Cyronius did not. The story ended with Elianté raging, Cyronius dead, and Tarrin healed—though through the cycle of time, his affliction returned to him again. Gaultry shook her head, not sure why Tullier should have mentioned the story now. Those events were long past. Elianté had forgiven Tarrin his trespass. The gods did not hold grudges.

Such forgiveness was a small thing—the gods could leave petty matters of revenge to be handled by those who worshiped them.

"Who cares if it's not a nice story? Bissanty doesn't have a nice history," Tullier continued. "And Tielmark's bid for freedom has made things worse. The Emperor's bond with the land is compromised, but not broken. Why else would Llara continue to grant the Emperor five sons, if she does not want the Empire to take Tielmark back? Tell me that!"

"Llara conceded Tielmark to the Twin Goddesses," Gaultry said hotly. "It was her Heart-on-Earth who refused to honor her pledge! Why shouldn't murderous sons and a poisoned land be her punishment on the Emperor for refusing to recognize a three-hundred-year-old god-pledge!"

The Sharif stepped between them. *The man comes,* she told them. *He must not see you fight.*

The trio fell silent, watching the skinny lackey labor towards them up the road.

"The monastery gate will be locked at sunset," he called. As he came closer, he genuflected to Tullier, taking that moment to catch his breath. "There is still time to cross, if you hurry. They will rent you a stretcher to carry the woman across the stream, if you like. And there's room in the yard for another carriage."

"Fine," Tullier said. "Then that's what we'll do." He spun on his heel and stalked back to the carriage, not waiting to see if Gaultry or the Sharif followed.

The Gray One touched him, the Sharif said, running her hands through her dark cropped hair thoughtfully. *When he tried to pledge himself to you, she touched him.*

Gaultry nodded. *Llara is in him. She wants him for herself. He wasn't ready for that.* She stared at the stiff line of the boy's proud, angry back, turned from them as though that denial meant he could avoid that truth. He should have been ready for it, she mused. Ever since they had read the birth roster back at Fructibus Arbis, he should have been ready for it.

The staging house had been built with a large, sheltered yard and well-ordered places to set up campfires when the house's rooms were full. Clearly, it was accustomed to accommodating the travelers who were halted there by floods. It was equally accustomed, it seemed, to supplying the needs of those supplicants to the monastery who did not feel they could wait out a flood. It was a seemingly simple request to hire a litter and litter-bearers. Soon after they entered the yard, a servant brought them a canvas-and-pole litter and showed them how to assemble it.

"We've sent for the carriers," he told them, standing back from the assemblage. "They will be here shortly."

When Tullier protested that they could make the crossing without bearers, the man laughed. "Only if you want your lady dumped into that flood stream! I assure you, sir, we won't be wanting to lose our litter that way!"

"Is it so dangerous?" Gaultry asked.

The man gave her a sharp look. "The river is strong here," he told her. "The Emperor would have put up a bridge long past, but, Allegrios Rex! The gods don't want it, and the Lord-of-all-Water chief among them. His Holiness—Dunsanius himself—he bargained with Allegrios for the crossing stones when he founded the monastery. Be thankful for that saintly man's forethought, without which you might be waiting here another week, your woman wasting to nothing all that while."

Gaultry thought of several responses, all of which she choked back.

"We'll accept the litter men's services," Tullier said.

After despatching the carriage-servants to the staging house's kitchen they retreated to the private space behind the carriage to finalize their plans.

"You'll have to keep pretending to be sick," Gaultry told Columba. "Can you manage that?"

Columba already looked ill. Her dark eyes were huge in her thin face, and she was shivering restlessly. "Lukas will know me if he sees me," she said, lying obediently between the two long poles of the litter and arranging her skirts to cover her legs. She seemed grateful for the cover of the blanket, pulling it up over her body with a hasty tug. "It does not matter whether he thinks I am sick or well."

"Will he be at the door, greeting every supplicant?" Gaultry asked testily.

"They'll have a gatekeeper." Columba sounded astonished that Gaultry should ask such a question. "Lukas would not stand at the gate."

"Then the risk that you'll be seen before you're settled in the sick ward is a small one. After that, we'll just have to see what happens. Lie still." Gaultry threw a second blanket on top of her and busily tucked it around the woman's slim body. "We're not going up there to confront your brother. We're going there to rescue my compatriot." They had decided not to share their escape plan with Columba, but that much she could tell her.

"I don't know why you brought me away from Fructibus Arbis."

"Do you want an honest answer?" Gaultry tucked in the last blanket corner. "One part of the answer is that I hope we might help you reclaim your Blood-Imperial. Maybe that will weaken Lukas a little if we end up in an open test of power."

Her voice sounded harder and less sympathetic than she wanted. "That's the selfish side of why you are here. But it's more than that. After I killed that man, we couldn't leave you. There must be some punishment they mete to a slave who has contributed to the death of one of her master's guests. Are you telling me you want to go back and face that?"

Columba shut her eyes, as if to pretend she hadn't heard. "I am a sick woman," she said softly. "A supplicant to the holy house. You should be gentle with me." The skin seemed somehow to strain over the flat, pale features of her face; the wan color in her face drained, leaving only her lips pale red, a sickly contrast. "I am a supplicant, seeking healing." Gaultry stared, fascinated. Before her very eyes, Columba's flesh seemed to wither, her body to shrink. She was ignoring Gaultry now, the role that Gaultry had called for her preoccupying all her attention.

Gaultry turned to Tullier, astonished. "Is it a trance?"

"The freak who birthed her was Bissanty's greatest actor," he said, watching the transformation alongside her. "It wasn't done with spells—it was something inborn. He could take on any role and make it seem like nature. Indeed, with his pregnancy, his role as mother *became* nature. Maybe she has something of that power too."

"It's frightening," Gaultry said, annoyed when Columba, still sinking in her stretcher, seemed to react to her words with a subtle smile. She remembered, back when they had seen the distant goatherder, how Columba had made things seem true just by describing them. Thinking on that, she shivered. "She shouldn't be able to make herself look sickly just by thinking it."

"Why not?"

"I don't know," Gaultry said. "Isn't that a power best left to the gods?" Columba really did look worryingly sick now. "What if it were to stop being playacting and come true?"

"Don't tell me you never played sick to avoid chores once in your life!" Tullier laughed at her worried expression. "Even among the Sha Muira, we could do that!"

"Not like this," Gaultry muttered. "Goddess take me, where are those litter-men!"

Something in Columba's transformation was truly disturbing her—something in the way the woman had retreated from conversation into an invented role. "I'm going to take a short walk," Gaultry said. "I want a last look at the monastery. Call me when the men get here." Leaving the trio behind her, she went swiftly out of the yard onto the open road. The crush of people was suddenly suffocating.

Outside, the heavily intermingled smells of cook-pots and horses behind, she felt a little more comfortable. But she stared at the monastery across the river and could not push down a stab of fear. She feared that everything she had done since leaving Tielmark was a fool's game, that she was a worse fool still to think she could challenge the weight of Bissanty authority—its magic and military power combined—and win.

"I have not gone against the gods," she told herself, fixing her gaze on the larger of the gold onion-shaped domes. "I never flattered myself I could use my magic to mold prophecy to my own interests."

Self-flattery. Back in Tielmark, the Duchess had warned her against that. The Duchess, who had seen her sons die in battle for their Prince.

"I don't know if I can overcome Lukas Soul-breaker by myself," Gaultry whispered. "What if he can make things true, just by believing them? Huntress help me, I am afraid. But I cannot leave Martin alone up there on that hill."

"The litter-men have come." Tullier shifted into her line of vision, blocking the onion domes temporarily from her view.

She nodded. "Then there's no reason to wait."

Their swords, Tullier's and the Sharif's, went into the blanket that padded the litter. The Sharif, who would be carrying the heavier end of the litter once the litter-bearers had helped them get it across the plank bridge, arranged both hilts where she could reach them once she took over the back end. When Gaultry met her eyes, the Ardana smiled, a little sad.

We will give them a good fight today.

It shouldn't come to that, Gaultry answered. *This is a place of worship, not a military encampment.*

The Sharif shrugged. *Your man will be guarded. Perhaps by ones such as he.* Her eyes were on Tullier.

Sha Muira? Elianté grant that not be so!

And Andion above.

Columba's words, her brutal accusation, echoed unpleasantly in Gaultry's head: you are the dominant twin. Leaving Arleon Forest was Mervion's attempt to escape before you stole her soul.

Gaultry looked up at the onion domes. Not the dominant twin, she thought wryly, but most definitely the dumb one.

Ah, Mervion, she prayed. *Forgive me, please, as I will not forgive myself if I fail you here.* She sketched the double spiral of the Great Twins on her palm and rose to her feet.

"Has everyone finished their prayers?" she asked. "If so, let's go."

Tullier called the litter-bearers over. They were pleasant-faced, unhurried men, pleased about the extra coin they would be earning this evening.

"Strange times, these," the older of the two commented, picking up the front end of the litter. "Freak storms and thunder. What's making Llara want to slow all the business of her country to a standstill?" When he saw that none of his new employers meant to share his conversation, he stopped talking.

From the yard, the road dropped quickly to the river. It was unpleasant going, the earth beneath the gravel spongy. As they approached the edge of the flood, Gaultry looked ahead to count the crossing stones. She stopped at twelve, which would have taken her less than halfway across. The plank bridge, laid across the tops of the stones, looked unstable and weak. Each board stretched from one dark, mossy stone to the next, held in place by rust-dark pins knocked into the top of the stones. In places, the stream lapped no less than inches beneath the wood.

"Has the flood crested yet?" she asked fearfully. The brown

floodwaters curled beneath the boards, seemingly threatening to tear them loose.

The older litter-man cast her an amused look. "The boards never go under," he said. "The same can't be said for those who try to cross without a calm head. It will be one at a time from here." He squinted at his partner. "Who do we take across first?"

"I'll go," Tullier said. "My women will come behind."

The man handed him a copper-green amulet on a worn leather thong. "Slip this over your head, sir, and we'll be on our way."

Tullier's walk on the bridge across the stream was reassuringly uneventful, though Gaultry, watching the boards wobble under his feet and the spray of foam from the rushing water brushing at him, began to think that it would have been a better idea if they had sent the Sharif across first. When he was halfway across, she began to think—surely it was her imagination?—that the river was toying with the frail bridge, sending up little gouting waves just where they would unnerve the crosser most. But Tullier progressed across smoothly and safely and at first the men who went over with Tullier—one before, one behind—did not seem to pay it any heed. On their return, however, one of them put his hand inside his jacket, a nervous gesture, as though he touched an amulet at his own throat.

"That was deftly done," she said as the two stepped down onto the muddy bank.

The man who had been touching his amulet gave her a hostile look. "The litter next," he said. "The water runs high. We must be quick."

"It's not raining anymore," Gaultry said. "What do you mean, the water runs high?"

Ignoring her, the men picked up the litter, hefting Columba's weight to determine the center of the litter's balance. Gaultry, realizing that they saw no need to explain to her now that they had taken Tullier, her "Master," across, bit back a curse.

On this crossing, the water splashed higher, wetting both

men's boots. The wind seemed to have picked up. Halfway across, the man in front slipped, dipped one foot into the river, and almost dumped Columba out of the litter into the stream. The other man, shouting, twisted the litter upwards until he recovered his footing.

After that, Gaultry thought they would be slower, more careful. Instead they moved faster. When they reached the far side, they did not immediately set the litter down. Gaultry saw Tullier wave his arms—an angry expression—but no words came back across the roar of the passing water.

"What's happening?" she said impatiently.

They don't want to come back for us. The Sharif, standing well back from the river's foaming edge, made an angry gesture.

"What do you mean?"

"Tullier tell me. He angry."

"You can hear him?"

The Sharif nodded curtly, trying to concentrate. "Those men afraid now," she reported. "Tullier boast that he Sha Muira to make them come back for us."

As they watched, helpless, the men dropped Columba and the litter on the muddy ground, and they came hastily back onto the bridge, half running. Before they had taken care not to disturb the boards, placing the heels of their boots carefully—now Gaultry saw the edge of one plank tip up behind them and almost tumble free of its pins into the water.

Don't let them pass us, Gaultry said, moving to block their way.

The men might have made an attempt to sweep by Gaultry, but, taking one look at the Sharif, they slowed, twenty feet back from the shore.

"Get out of our way!" the man in back called.

Gaultry, staring past them to the surging water, did not know what to do. Any disturbance they made would surely be noticed by the monks up on the hilltop. "We can't leave the Master," she told them, hoping that would make them pity her. "You must take us across."

She did not like the pleading sound of her own voice, but

the man in front—the older man, who had spoken to them earlier—shifted uneasily. "Your Master must be a hard man to serve. Still, you'll have to join him tomorrow. Today—the stream's awake. It's out of the question."

"Don't the amulets appease him?"

The man laughed, a little bitter. "The river is stronger than a broken sliver of glass. Now, lass, let us by."

"We'll cross without you," Gaultry said. "If either of us slips, our deaths will haunt you." She tried to keep her voice steady, still hoping she could sway him, but the man just shook his head.

"Llara on me! I have no part in any pledge that lies between yourself and your Master! If you must brave death to follow him, that is no fault of mine!" Behind him, his angry partner whispered something in his ear. Again, the man shook his head. He met Gaultry's eye. "I will give you my own amulet. Tonio, here, will give the tall woman his. That is the best I can offer."

"And another shilling to cover their value until you return them!" the second man spat.

For some reason, that struck Gaultry as humorous, the seriousness of the situation aside. "The Great Twelve seal your words! There's a bargain." She nodded for the Sharif to step out of his way.

The front man, relaxing a little, caught something of her humor. His pleasant face was composed as he stepped off the last plank onto the shore—almost as if he was smiling. When the second man made an angry move to push past him, he laid a calming hand on his arm. "The river is behind you, Tonio." He fumbled into his jacket and pulled free a blue sliver of glass tied to the end of a black string. It glinted in the fading light as he held it out to Gaultry. "By Dunsanius's blessing, the danger of crossing is in your own head," he said. "But— look at that stream! It is no surprise that Tonio and I have had enough for the day."

Gaultry dug a shilling out of her belt and exchanged it for the piece of glass. "It's your river," she said. "You know better than I when to trust it."

He grinned then, and gestured for the angry man to give his amulet to the Sharif. He tucked the shilling into his purse. "You have a steady head," he reassured her. "You'll make it over. Great Allegrios won't pull you in. Then you can go finish your business up the hill. They say His-Highness-on-High hasn't been feeling too well these last few days," he said. "Headaches come on him, you know, and he's down for days. It's not like the old days, with Gregorius—the old father made a point of touching hands to every case that came through those gates. With this one, you'll be lucky if he walks past the end of your bed."

"You've said enough," Tonio cut in. "Now leave them to join the demon they call their Master."

"The Great Twelve bless you," Gaultry told the older man. "Thank you for your help." She stepped back, and looked at the two men, where they stood side by side on the bank. They were much alike. Perhaps brothers, sharing that pleasant face, broad back, and strong arms, well fit to carry any load. One smiling, one with his face set in a frown. The good Bissanty man and bad. Fear, or the ability to overcome it, made the difference between the two.

She turned to the Sharif. *Are you ready for this?*

The Sharif fingered her amulet—a round pebble rolled smooth by water, a hole bored through, a leather lace through the hole—then slung the lace over her head. *No. But I will follow in your steps.*

The first planks were the easiest. The water was shallow beneath their feet, the tips of grass stems, bent over by the current, reassuringly visible beneath the surface. *In Tielmark,* Gaultry told the Sharif, *there is a sorceress of such strength, she could spell all this water to support our weight.* Of course, the wild water that ran beneath them was nothing like the placid lake that she had seen Martin's grandmother ensorcel, but the Sharif did not need to know that.

Give me a mud hole, the Sharif answered, *a box of sand, and a fine-wove cloth to strain it. That is water enough.*

Beyond the grass tips, the water darkened and deepened. Gaultry, staring down at the well-aged grain of the plank beneath her feet, tried to focus on anything that wasn't the floodwater. This was, she realized, the most wood that she had seen since leaving the slave-ship behind them in Bassorah Harbor. Her Tielmaran breeding had not let her notice it as an anomaly.

"Where do they get the wood?" she asked out loud. It was a fine, dense, hardwood. A tree she did not recognize. She wished she had asked one of the litter-bearers. Now it was too late.

Gautri. The Sharif called her name in the faintest flutter of mindcall.

What?

Gautri, the man said that the river would not drag us down. But, Gautri—what would he say to that? She pointed up the river.

Upstream, caught in the current and rushing towards them, was an imposing tangle of brush. A cord—something—had bound it together. "It won't hit us," Gaultry said, tracing its path with her eye. "But goddess—if it hits the bridge! Tullier will be stranded!" *Run!* she told the Sharif. *We must pass in front of it!*

The boards seemed newly slippery under her feet. She had a vague sense of Tullier on the far bank, shouting words of encouragement, of the Sharif keeping with her, trusting her to keep her feet, but she was running blind, her mind's eye filled with the vision of the impending collision of brush and board. The plank she was on was at an awkward angle—the crossing stone beneath had an edge that jutted out above the others, making the footing more unstable than ever. She tripped, and ran forward into that motion, trying to give the Sharif room not to run into her. On her knees, a splash of water surged, wetting her head. She felt the Sharif's hand on her shoulders, helping her up, then she had gained her feet again. She ran on, skidded, and cried out as her lead foot plunged off the bridge into the water. Nothing could save her now—

"Gaultry!" Tullier was there, grabbing at her sleeve. "What happened?"

She had not reached the far bank. But she had made it to the shallows. Grass stems, bent by the current, clutched at her ankles. She was standing, stunned, just over her knees in the river. "I don't know," she said. "You tell me."

"The brush—a wave tore it apart just as it would have hit you."

Gaultry slumped against the edge of the plank, too shaken to pull herself out of the water. She could see the high crossing stone where she had stumbled. The brush must have impacted with the bridge just at that point. "Maybe there's a submerged stone in the water there," she said. "I can't see what else would have saved us."

"It was the wave," Tullier insisted. "Not a stone."

"If you say so." *What do you think?* she asked the Sharif.

All I saw was your back. The Ardana reached a hand down to her. *Let me help you.*

Gaultry grasped her hand and allowed herself to be ignominiously pulled back onto the plank. "Where's Columba?"

"Still playing sick."

The slender woman had not even got out of her stretcher. Propping herself up on her elbows, she had watched everything unfold from her cocoon of blankets. Looking at her, Gaultry did not know whether to be glad or angry. "Well, if anyone was watching from the monastery, our story won't have been compromised."

Tullier and the Sharif waited while she emptied her shoes and picked the marsh grass out of her clothes. Her hands were badly grazed where she had fallen on the crossing stone. She reached inside her shirt. The litter-bearer's glass amulet had scratched her chest. "Did you protect me?" she asked it, rinsing it and her hands clean in the water. "Allegrios Rex, did you protect me?" She sighed. "I hope so, for Martin's sake."

She tucked the amulet in her belt pouch, where it would not scratch her again. "Let's go," she said. "It will be dark before we know it."

With Gaultry and the Sharif carrying the litter, they started up the well-tended path that led up the rise to the monastery gates.

* * *

The gatehouse was built of the same rosy-orange brick as the outer wall, with grass thatch roofing the short towers at either side. The gate was constructed of intricately carved posts—more wood than Gaultry had seen used in construction since they'd left Bassorah City. The gatekeeper, a paunchy man in dull gray robes, stood behind the carved lattice, watching as the pair of women toiled up the road with the litter, Tullier at their heels.

"White Terrin's blessing on you," he called out to Tullier as they neared.

"We seek housing for a blighted soul," Tullier answered, his intonation more formal than supplicative.

"The house is full."

"Piron Aldinus has sent his woman for curing," Tullier said. "He will not be gainsaid."

Tullier had warned Gaultry that these negotiations had a form that must be followed, and that it would take some back-and-forth before they would be allowed to enter. Listening only with half her attention, she let her gaze rove past the gatekeeper into the irregular rectangle of the yard beyond. It was a pleasant, sheltered place with buildings on four sides, two with covered loggia. At the far end, a little to the right, was the drum-shaped round of the temple, beneath the larger of the complex's two domes. She could see the door that led in, with the carved figure of a man holding a horn over the lintel. In the late light, with its long shadows, the rose-orange buildings seemed serene. She fancied for a moment that she could feel the gentle whisper of the many healing prayers that had been called here over the decades.

The wind had died to nothing. The belt of cypress trees afforded them some protection, but it was not merely that. A stillness radiated from the monastery grounds as though the gatekeeper, haggling with Tullier to ensure that he knew the form, was the only thing moving in all the compound.

A false impression. Even from where she stood, she could

see monks in the eastward loggia, heads bowed, robes rustling. Yet still—

Her eye lighted on a lone sparrow. It had taken refuge in the carved fretwork of the temple, in the deep cranny that was the mouth of the god's horn. It was the first bird she'd seen since coming across the ford and passing the flooded plain to climb the monastery hill.

The poles of the stretcher jerked in her hands. She glanced back and saw that the Sharif had pushed to get her attention. *Go on,* the Sharif urged.

"Wake up." Tullier sounded annoyed. The gate was open. This was not the first time he'd spoken. "Wake up."

The sparrow. A little male with mottled brown feathers. Gaultry stepped forward, barely aware of the gate as it closed behind her, her concentration focused on the bird. She scanned the yard, trying to understand. From within the loggia, bland priestly faces stared back, politely curious, but not intent.

"Over there to the left," Tullier said. "We go through that archway to the dormitory."

The archway led to a muddy yard, the service court for the monastery. Gaultry took a single step in that direction. Then, almost without thinking, she turned back to the sparrow. "Wait—"

The casting leapt up like warming fire in a grate. Rich Glamour-power sang from the center of her chest, called to its first casting since her renewal. A fierce gladness swept her. Any regrets she might have had that Tullier was no longer bonded to her by magic burned to nothing. Tullier was alive—and she was once more whole. She reached to touch the sparrow with her mind, sending out the leash of magic as easily as she could have thrown a snare or a line of cord, and with truer aim. The little bird, peeping wretchedly in response, welcomed her. It was not *her* the sparrow feared. *It did not resist her taking.* She felt its ruffled feathers, its misery—

And saw the image of the silver hawk that had driven it to the safety of the deep cranny.

"Tullier!" She grabbed his arm, dumping Columba's litter. "Not that way! Get your weapon!"

As Tullier half turned, angry, words of recrimination rising in his throat, a knot of armed men crowded the archway.

At the center of the knot was Lord Issachar Dan, garbed in silver-and-gray armor. A small hawk clung to his shoulder, hissing and bobbing fiercely. The hawk that had frightened the sparrow.

The storms that had swept them across the marsh to Dunsanius Ford had been nothing to Issachar, mounted on his great, steel-feathered eagle.

"Gaultry Blas." Issachar signaled to the men to fan out. "It would have been wiser for you to return home after our last meeting."

Gaultry backed against the litter poles, sensing Columba at her back, wriggling to free herself from the tangle of blankets. Gaultry drew her knife. "A monastery should be a place of sanctuary," she said.

Issachar laughed. "A month of travel and still you know nothing of Bissanty ways. Sanctuary? On the altar, perhaps, but nowhere else." He gestured to the great bear of a soldier at his side. "Take the boy. And you and you—" He gestured at two others. "Take the tall woman."

"There are four of them?" A voice called. "Who is the fourth?" Behind the screen of soldiers, a thin, lightly built figure appeared in the archway.

Columba's twin.

The soldiers fell back to make way for him.

Lukas Caviedo was radiant. His eyes shone silver, and silver lit his skin from within. The front of his robe was embroidered with a dark circle, banded round with silver and white. The moon in eclipse. The symbol of the castrated god, White Tarrin, in his aspect as earth-wanderer.

Lukas's was the face of a man who imagined himself a god fallen to earth. "My guests!" he said warmly. "Welcome to Dunsanius House. It seems I must ready another place at my table!" Pride of power burned in him like a lit torch.

Issachar stepped forward. "Your weapon," he said to

Gaultry, smirking. "There will be no knives at my Master's table." Then his eyes met Columba's and opened wide in disbelief.

"You said she was dead." He swung round to his Master. "You swore on your mother's grave that she died."

"The Columba that you knew is dead," Lukas answered coldly, and raised his hand to Issachar, palm open. "Does it matter that her flesh is walking still?"

"Filth!" Acting without thought, the dark lord lunged to strike the smaller man, but Lukas took a graceful step back and brought the tips of his fingers together, his hand a claw.

Magic swirled, potent enough to fog the air between them. Issachar staggered as though struck, his arms mantling like outstretched wings, his mouth opening to utter a hawk's cry.

When he turned to face Gaultry, there was no glint of human reason in his eyes, just the maddened, merciless anger of a raptor raised to cold fury. He cocked his head, scraped his feet in the grass—and then, suddenly, human reason was back in him.

There was sweat on the dark lord's face, but his composure had come back to him.

"There will be no knives at my Master's table," he repeated, holding out his hand to Gaultry as though nothing had happened.

Gaultry, not knowing what else to do, handed her weapon to him, and nodded for Tullier and the Sharif to do the same. They could not fight against these odds. For the moment, they would have to play Lukas Caviedo's game. Tullier gave her an angry look and kicked the swords out of the litter blankets for a temple man to pick up.

"The Prince of Tielmark sends his welcome," Gaultry said, bowing slightly, trying to put the best face on the turn of events. "I am here, as you must know, as his envoy. The Prince has sent me to bring his man home."

Lukas Caviedo bent his shining head and smiled. "In good time," he said. "But first, you must avail yourselves of the fine hospitality of this god's house. Have you eaten?" he asked. "After such a long day on the road, you must be hungry."

"Can we trust your meat?" Gaultry said sharply. "Considering the viand you prepared for my Master's table, I think not."

To her astonishment, Lukas laughed. "The Vanderive boys? No—this table is simple grain and honey. Food from the Golden Age, fit for the gods. Come and eat with me—we must eat before the rising of the summer star! I will feed you from my own mouth if you distrust me. . . ."

There were more men behind her now. A pair of large, bear-bodied men were at the Sharif's shoulders; Tullier was flanked by slim, fast-looking men; as for herself, Issachar loomed, ever threatening, at her side. Only Columba was left unguarded—but from the look of open despair on her face, her dark eyes following Issachar's every movement, it was clear that she did not mean to fight.

The meal was served in a small court behind the main buildings. Gaultry and her companions sat miserably in their places. Despite Lukas's insistence that they dine with him, the strange Tarrin-worshiper did not seem to notice that they sat dully in their places, not lifting spoon to mouth.

There was no conversation. Only the slow dropping of the light, the slow thinning of the cloud, the sky brightening to reveal its first stars, and Lukas Caviedo, sitting at the head of the table, shining with silver light.

"Beauteous Lady," Lukas said, turning to Gaultry at last and lifting his glass in a toast. "You are like the Huntress born to the earth, in your grace and manners. How far you have come—How far indeed!—and all to play in my game!

This was a nightmare come to life. A game such as Issochar had played, to lose dominion of his own soul? Gaultry did not see how it might be in her power to escape, to end it.

▼

chapter 20

"Your loyalty to your Prince intrigues me."
Lukas, setting down his empty wineglass, leapt lightly
to his feet and threw down his napkin. The silent men who
had guarded them throughout the meal shifted at their Master's signal, once again alert. "You are bonded, but surely
you have power enough in you to wear thin a cycle-old
bond?"

"Age makes some bonds stronger, not weaker," Gaultry
replied. She stared down at the mess of untouched chaff and
honey that had been served onto her plate. Columba's brother
had meant it literally when he had told them they would be
served the food of the gods. She wondered what his cook had
prepared for his plate—from the eager way that Lukas had
consumed his meal, she did not believe that he too had been
served with unhusked grain. "My grandmother made a
promise, and I honor it. I would not choose to dishonor my
grandmother's promise."

Lukas nodded and made a lazy gesture with his hand. "My
own familial relations are infinitely more complex," he said,

his eyes sliding to his sister, "but I take your point." He took
two steps to the left, then changed his mind and turned to the
right, back to Gaultry. "You will come with me and see now
how I play. All of you," he added. Four men stepped forward
to move out the guests' chairs. Gaultry jumped up before her
brawny footman could pull out her chair, and motioned for
her companions to do the same. Issachar, she noticed, was
behind Columba's chair, his cicatrized face utterly devoid of
expression. Guards and guests together eyed Lukas nervously, as if uncertain where his attention would next fix, and
to what effect.

He's mad, the Sharif's words were the barest thread of a
whisper, as if she sensed Lukas might hear even this faint
mindcall. Gaultry, who had almost reached the same conclusion, infinitesimally nodded her agreement. The strange silent
meal had unnerved her. Lukas had been waiting for something; she was not sure what.

The night shadows had grown, while they had sat at the
table watching Lukas eat. As they stood to leave, a pair of
men bearing lanterns joined them. Several of their escort
shifted uneasily, as if something in the flames made them nervous. Those men faded to the back of the uneasy train, which
had Lukas at its head, then a knot of men, Gaultry and her
companions, and more guards at the rear.

Lukas, surrounded by his silver aura, did not need a torch
to guide his steps. He moved lightly and confidently, his silk
robes fluttering. Gaultry had somehow expected that he
would take them to the temple under the large onion dome,
but instead he led them to the broad wooden door of the hall
at the temple's side. This big door had a second smaller door
set into it. Lukas pulled the smaller door open. Inside it was
dark, with a rich musky smell with acrid undertones. Gaultry
recognized it at once as the scent of animals. Many animals:
their dung, their fear. The guards, with nervous attention on
their Master, hustled her forward, Tullier and the Sharif at
her sides. She entered the door after the Sharif, before Tullier. Just inside, she could not help but come to an abrupt

halt. A feeling somewhere between horror and wonder touched her.

She stood in a great vaulted chamber, divided into aisles of closely interjammed boxes, tanks, cases, and cages. All these cages were filled with animals. Gaultry had not felt such rich, teeming life since she had last been in Arleon Forest. For a moment, the sheer familiar presence of the animal warmth made a delicious feeling wash through her.

Their entry had startled the animal in the nearest cage, a creature with striped fur, a long tail, and clever limber hands. It jumped down off its perch and up onto the bars at the front of its cage, curious. Above a sharply pointed snout, vivid, smoke-colored eyes with staring slit pupils reflected the lantern light. In the next cage, four paces on, sat a tired-looking wildcat. Beyond that, another unrecognizable: a creature like a sturdily built weasel, or a slim badger with soft fur.

Gaultry, thrilled by the exotic striped creature, the intelligence she saw reflected in the smoky eyes, reached reflexively to touch it with her magic. "Is it from Bissanty?" she asked Tullier, even as she opened a channel towards it.

"No—"

The strange animal mind twisted and tried to bite her. "It's very clever!" The realization came as fast as her sense of its anger, its wildness to be free. She shifted, enjoying the familiar sense of give-and-take between herself and an unknown animal as each of them learned the other, and she tried to impose her will. The creature's mind seethed with images of a forest with strange, broad-leaved trees, a high green canopy, the heat of an unfamiliarly warm sun. She could feel its memories, dampened and mysterious. Despite its intelligence, this should be a gentle beast. A honey-eater, a climber. Instead it was consumed by deathly anger that repulsed even a gentle overture. Perplexed, she widened her channel to it, calling deeper power. It was a small beast, delicate even. Determined will was not the center of its spirit; it should not have resisted her.

Then, as she probed, she became aware of something between herself and her probe. The creature was deeply bound by a spell, by something that impinged on her casting. She touched its spirit through a tattered net of spell and magic, a net so subtle at first she had not been aware of passing it. Curious to know if she could free the gentle creature, and her awareness of the form giving the spell-net substance, she brushed against one bright strand—and recoiled, deeply shocked, into her own body.

The pulsing web that bound the creature's spirit was formed of a piece of a human soul, a soul that had been torn and drawn in horrible, pain-filled strands.

"The gods must be asleep," Gaultry said, her voice louder than she'd intended. "It should not be allowed."

"Go on," said the man behind her. "Move. Follow the bright one."

"What is it?" Tullier whispered, trying to keep with her.

She shook her head, not wanting to answer.

Cages. So many cages. Lukas led them on down the center aisle. They passed big cages, small, strong-built, fragile. A huge aviary cramped with birds in brilliant colors crowded one side of the aisle; beyond it, a tank of snakes. Big animals, small, clever, dumb—Gaultry had barely suspected the world held such variety. Tiny monkeys chittered from above, clinging fretfully to wire perches at the top of a tall cage; mournful deer with branching antlers trapped in a too-small cage tried to hide behind the scanty cover afforded by a screen of long-dead branches; farther on was a seething case of rats, yellow teeth gnawing hopelessly at the metal grate that fronted their case. Gaultry stared around. Surely every creature among them did not represent a bound human soul?

"Tell me!" said Tullier. "What are you looking for?"

The next cage held a pair of bears. Gaultry recognized them at once. "Tullier," she said, "look at the men who are guarding the Sharif. Then look at these bears and tell me what you see."

Without being told, even Tullier could see the bears were connected to the men. His face went very solemn, and he caught for a moment at her hand. "How many are there?" he asked. "All?"

Gaultry started to walk faster, trying to crane down every aisle, to scan the larger cages. Where did Lukas keep the big predators?

"All of these?" Tullier said, jogging at her elbow. "Are all of these bound to men?"

"Not all." Gaultry stopped as she reached the end of the aisle, sick-hearted. "Not that one."

"That one" was a thin black puppy with spindly legs too long for its body. Sensing their attention, it pressed itself against the far side of its box, afraid.

"The dog?" Tullier said. He did not understand what he was seeing. "He looks lost among all these exotics. What's he doing here?"

"He's waiting for someone whose soul mirrors his spirit," Gaultry whispered. How had Lukas been able to match, so exactly, the vision that she had so briefly conjured, the day she had made Mervion help Tullier. Except for the color of the puppy's eyes—dark brown—the skinny animal exactly matched her spirit-vision of Tullier.

Ahead of them, Lukas stood on the first broad step of a winding flight of stairs. Next to the step was a large cage, cramped with five vigorous looking swans. "These beauties are my pride," he said, gesturing with an arm, a flowing sleeve. His eyes fixed on Gaultry's. Something he read in her expression made him smile. "But I see you love them all, which well meets my desire."

The swans were beautiful. Gaultry did not on the whole like swans. She considered them bullying, ill-tempered birds, and she did not think much of the walnut-sized brain that controlled their big strong bodies. But they were beautiful. These birds were white, their feathers glossed with a golden iridescence. Four of them—cobs, she guessed—had topknots of black feathers. The biggest of the four had a particularly proud, malevolent gleam in his eye. He hissed at Lukas when the sorcerer ran his hand along the bars at the cage's top—and Lukas hastily drew his hand back. The single female had a gold patch of feathers at the base of her neck instead of the topknot.

"Gaultry," Tullier said faintly, "those are Imperial swans. Only the Emperor, or his immediate blood, can own them."

"But Lukas is the Emperor's man," Gaultry said. "Why else would Martin be sent to him?"

"He might be playing at being the Emperor's man, but if Sciuttarus caught him with those birds, he wouldn't be able to hold up that face for long."

Lukas started up the steps, seemingly oblivious to their conversation. The guards at their backs pushed at them, impatient. Gaultry glanced at them, guessed at least two of them— a short, dark-brown man and a stout soldier with green eyes— were soul-bonded to creatures caged somewhere deep in the menagerie. Animals that were fierce but shy of fire.

She paused briefly at the cage of swans and looked in. The proud old cob hissed. At his side, three younger cobs and a small female. Looking at the three young males, it was easy to guess which one might be intended for Pallidonius, the flashy young man she had seen facing down the Sea Prince at Prathe Lendra's party. That swan was clearly ready to challenge his father's right to rule the cage, and preening himself for it.

The stairs, worn from the passage of many generations of monks' feet, had small niches, irregularly spaced, at the sides. Gaultry blanched. They held empty soul-figures: blank slaggy shapes ready for soul-taking. Then she shook herself and reined in her panic.

Lukas had staged this scene in a deliberate attempt to frighten them, and he had certainly succeeded. But if he had taken them this way in order to play on their fears, he was neither so confident nor so mad that he did not feel the need to overawe them—and maybe there was some comfort to be gleaned from that. If not—she could only hope that the pattern he saw in these events was one that she and those she had brought here with her would survive.

She did not want to look at Tullier, the Sharif, or Columba. It was her fault that they were here with her now. That thought depressed her most of all. She had not saved their lives so Lukas could make them his pets.

Ahead, Lukas passed through a door with a pointed arch. Gaultry, following him, found herself in the monks' chapter-house—a round room, beneath the smaller of the two onion domes, with stone seats all around the dome's perimeter. Tonight, however, the room had been turned to another purpose. Sheets of silk had been spread across the stone floor. The air was heady with incense, and three graceful-looking men clustered near the rank of narrow windows at the room's side, playing, very softly, a flute, a double pipe, and a reed pipe.

Gaultry shuddered. The music was very pretty, but she was sure, at least, that the man with the double pipe had been soul-bonded to a mockingbird, and she could not help but hear mourning in the tone—the same song she had heard, so many years back, when she had discovered a female bird crying over a destroyed nest and a dead mate.

Lukas seemed oblivious to the music's mournful under-tone. As Gaultry and her companions were ushered into the room and bunched together against the wall on the far side from the windows, he moved restlessly around the great circle of the room, unable to settle.

Finally he came to stand in front of Gaultry.

Though he and Columba were twins, they were not very much alike. Lukas topped the slender woman by a hand's-breadth. Where Columba was still and slow, her moods changing faster than her body, her brother's body and eyes moved constantly, echoing a mind in constant motion within. At long last, he struck a commanding pose, and turned to her.

"What do you think of my present?" he asked Gaultry, so abruptly she started. She had thought his attention had moved back to the narrow windows—but no, suddenly, it was centered on her.

Her stomach lurched, queasy. "What present?"

"The musicians. I made them for you. Here—" He spun round. "Is it not enough? Watch. I can make you another."

He reached out with his long limber fingers and grabbed the Sharif's throat. He made it seem a spontaneous act, but Gaultry, crying out, could see that it, like so much else of Lukas's posing, had been highly orchestrated to heighten its drama. There were men behind the Sharif to ensure she could not leap free of his grasp, that she could not strike him; there were two more men on the stairs, hauling up a creature that snarled and spat. Everything happened quickly, smoothly, as though no other course was open, as though it was all inevitable, the will of a god come to earth, but that was only true because someone had calculated and shut down other possibilities. Columba had been mistaken to say that the story of how she had lost her Blood-Imperial would be of no use. In it Gaultry saw the actions of a careful man who trusted little to the gods—and even less to chance. His 'play' was the fruit of careful planning.

That didn't make what happened next any less distressing. The Sharif, pinned by her guards where Lukas could grab her, shrieked angrily and collapsed. The animal exploded in at the door in a hopeless, tawny-furred ball of rage, rage that subsided depressively into a mewl of fright. It was a huge, maneless, desert lion.

What did he do? Gaultry called.

The Sharif's first answer was a wordless yowl, more mind-shattering than the spirit of the strongest alley cat in Bassorah City. Gaultry, involuntarily pressing her hands to her ears to shield herself from that soundless cry, stumbled back.

"Help her up," Lukas said impatiently, gesturing to the sprawled desert woman. "What's so shocking?" He was clearly upset that some studied effect had not come out as he had staged it. "It's always like this with the big predators," he told Gaultry peevishly, bending and taking the Sharif by her chin. "Get up, silly, get up." To Gaultry, "They can be unpredictable, you know, but they offer such good service, once they settle to the bond."

Gaultry was only steps from the mewling animal that the men had dragged up from the menagerie. She bent to calm it, reaching within to feel the creature's befuddled, frazzled spirit. Trying to soothe the great cat—anything was better than trying to understand, even with the staging, even with the preparations, the power of Lukas's casting. To think of that power—to think of setting herself against it—who was she, thinking of such things, to say that it was *Lukas* who was mad?

Pushing that thought away, she concentrated on the cat. Inside, it was like the striped honey-eater: strips of a shining, angry soul that she easily recognized as the Sharif's lashed round the ragged edges of the half-spirit which Lukas had left it. A reciprocating image of what must have been done inside the Sharif. But what was holding the animal back? What Lukas had done had been a shock, but the big cat was alive and furious, and the Sharif was alive and furious. Why had the soul-net and the half-spirit beneath it not colluded in their fury to lash out at the man who had bound them?

The spirit of the big cat regained a little of its composure at her touch. The animal abruptly stopped its mewling cries. Gaultry, her hands warm in the thick fur of the creature's neck, found herself staring into narrowed, yellow eyes— eyes in which she could see enough native intelligence to suggest that the creature understood a good part of what had happened to it. It stared at her, still not gathering its strength to rise, grappling with the situation, not liking it. Gaultry, looking guiltily back into those eyes, felt herself blush. Cats were her least favorite animal to take from— and she had never seen a cat as large and powerful as this one. Its look made her feel almost as much at fault for its plight as Lukas. She knew from the creature's mental images that it was a kind of desert panther. She had never seen a panther outside of the pages of the bestiary at her grandmother's cottage.

Glamour-witch—the word rasped, barely intelligible, in

Gaultry's mind. She managed with an effort not to startle, but it indeed was the great cat who had spoken. Oddly, and with the word barely formed, but still recognizable. A hint of the Sharif's voice beneath the growl of the cat. *Look here*—

There was a moment of focus, quickly past, but clear enough that Gaultry understood what she was being shown.

Lukas had only a tenuous hold on the cat. What he had was a thin, carelessly looped leash of magic, wrapped loosely around the outside of the package of spirit and soul. He had an awareness of the shape, and, if either cat or Sharif misbehaved, he could tighten that leash, incapacitating them both. But it was a clumsily done spell, ill-fitted to such a large, proud animal.

No wonder Lukas found the big predators unpredictable. No wonder his menagerie included so many birds. A clever animal would at once be wriggling in that leash's coils, testing its limits. Perhaps they could not entirely escape it—but they could shift it subtly so that the stranglehold could not be quickly tightened, so there were moments of free will. Gaultry cast a puzzled look at Lukas's back. Was he even aware of the risk he was taking here? The spell itself was a weak one—laughable next to the power of soul- and spirit-breaking. There was no tailoring to it: he had not even bothered to name it to the great beast. It was an unnamed spell: it could have been cast on any predator.

"This is a present indeed," Gaultry said aloud, releasing the cat's head and rising. Lukas used animals freely, but he did not understand them. She wondered how differently his path might have gone if he had bound Issachar—his first experiment—to a great cat like this, instead of to a hawk. And Columba—doves had a sort of brutal stubbornness in them. They might peck each other to death on their dovecote perches. But they were not smart animals, and they were happy in a small cage, a small sphere. She guessed Columba would not have stayed at Fructibus Arbis house so long—

even with the lure-spell on her—if Lukas had bound her to a
bird that was less suited for domestication, even in a place
where it was tortured. The Rhasan image of the dove showed
the bird perched on a sword's edge, blood running from its
feet. That had been Columba, staying on at her father's estate
after her Blood-Imperial had been stolen. But Gaultry
guessed that Lukas had chosen the dove because its name
was already Columba's and because the marsh-witch had
pulled her that card, not because he had any awareness of the
compatibility of the little bird's temper with his long-term
aims.

"You like it?" Lukas hove back into her view. He gave the
cat a tentative slap on the shoulder. "If you like it, then you
must thank me." He turned his head, offering his shining
cheek.

He meant for her to kiss him. Gaultry counted the guards
swiftly—a full dozen men—and came back to the same conclusion she had already reached.

She stepped quickly to him and brushed her lips against his
cheek.

It burned. His shining skin was like hot metal. She let out a
cry and would have dragged herself away, but he caught hold
of the hair at the back of her neck and forced her mouth onto
his. For a horrible moment, she felt the looming weight of his
overblooded mind, his soul-heavy body. Then she found her
strength and tore free, pressing her hand to the painfully
scorched skin of her mouth.

"It begins!" Lukas burbled excitedly. "It begins!"

"Don't you touch her!" Tullier was suddenly between
them, reaching up to grab his brother's throat.

"Tullier!" Gaultry tried to pull him out of the line of
Lukas's focus. "It's too dangerous!"

Neither brother paid any attention to her.

"I wanted to bond Imperial blood," Lukas said, "and here's
my father's last fetus to give me practice."

At the door was a new man, bearing in his arms the skinny
puppy. "You bastard!" Gaultry shouted out, trying to draw

Lukas's attention from Tullier. "You planned this! Your mother was a theater whore, and you are her natural son!"

Lukas, focused on his young brother, did not seem to hear her.

Brother was not equally matched to brother. The force of Lukas's magic beat Tullier to the ground. Gaultry was sure it was all over. The puppy yelped in terror, Tullier cried out—

Then Lukas released the grip he'd gained on Tullier's throat, shaking out his limber fingers. For the first time, his composure slipped. "What did you do?" he screamed at Gaultry. "You stupid bitch, what did you do? What loyalty do you have to this mass of birthing tissue? Don't you recognize that *it*"—he meant Tullier—"is nothing more than that?"

Tullier stumbled back against Gaultry. "I didn't mean to—" he started to say, shooting her an apologetic look. He pressed his hand to the lump at his belt where he had secured Mervion's half Glamour-soul. Gaultry knew from the way he touched it that the little soul-figurine once again was empty, that Mervion's half-soul was somehow back in Tullier, that her sister's magic had somehow served to protect him. But with Lukas ranting over them both, there was no time to think of that.

The veneer of pleasantries had vanished. Lukas's face was twisted and horrible. "You cannot thwart my will!" he screamed. The puppy he had meant for Tullier was crying in fear; the bird-musicians were cowered back against the wall. Even their guards, many of them under tight leashes, looked frightened. Gaultry, standing with Tullier, the Sharif, and Columba, the big cat on the floor in front of them, did not know how to respond. She called the puppy to her to make it shut up—that was nothing. All she had to do was open a small channel, and it ran to her with eager relief. She gave it a nervous pat. Around her, it seemed, an abyss loomed. She could only wish that she knew where its edge lay.

"You'll have to tell me what your will is before you can accuse me of thwarting it," she managed. These words seemed only to inflame him.

"I was not going to threaten you," Lukas hissed. "I too know reason, and I was not going to threaten you. But now, I see, threats are the only leash you will bear." He waved a hand, and two of his men went quickly to the wall near Gaultry's back. They folded open a panel, raised a little above two of the chapterhouse's monks' seats, and stepped back.

The panel covered a window, a window that let out high in the side of the temple beneath the great onion dome. Lukas gestured for Gaultry to look. She stepped near, the puppy at her heels, and looked down.

The temple, with its great gold dome, was dimly lit. She squinted, trying to penetrate the gloom. It was hard to see the walls, the painted frescoes. But she could see the altar: a great circle, white banding black banding white. There were two figures chained to the altar: a man and a wolf.

The man barely looked up as the window opened. The wolf was calm. At first Gaultry was frightened by their lack of response. Then she saw that their chains were arranged so that if one pulled, the other suffered. They had worked out a truce. Both were at rest, and apparently comfortable.

"Look at that!" Lukas jeered. "The savage man and the savage beast! That was how I would have matched them, even without the Rhasan deck!"

Gaultry looked at Martin, and he at her. She thought her heart would burst. He was naked from the waist up. Horrible unhealed burns marked his shoulders and his back—like slave-brands, only worse. He was dirty and unshaven, one eye socket crusted with blood beneath where his brow had been split. But when he looked at her, she felt somehow that he was smiling, deep in whatever soul was left to him beneath Lukas's bindings. It was water for a thirst for him to see her.

She looked away. It would do neither of them good for her to betray her feelings. She looked at the wolf, Martin's soul-partner. It stared back, its intelligent predator's eyes level and calm.

"You will obey me!" Lukas planted his hand on her shoulder. Tullier hissed, but the guards were at his elbows, and he could not move. "I have the trump card in the deck, the hostage who will make you yield!"

Gaultry stared at him: the burning silver skin, the mad eyes, the nervous energy that coursed through his body. "You think Martin is my Cyronius? That I will agree to play Elianté to remake your manhood?" Was that his game? It was.

Lukas nodded. "See?" he said. "You already know your lines."

She glanced once more into the temple. The wolf was there, watching her—perhaps Martin's eyes were on her too, but she would not allow herself to look at him again. She opened a channel, felt the big, muscular shape of the wolf's spirit. Carelessly torn pieces of Martin's soul were strapped around it. Beyond, even more carelessly formed, was the loose loop of magic which kept the great creature under Lukas's control. The wolf had nudged it subtly so it was very slack. She saw, then, what she must do.

"Huntress on me," she said. "I must submit to you."

"Bow to my will, then," Lukas said. "Bow!"

She wanted to strike him. Instead, curbing herself, she dropped to her knees. The channel to the wolf was still open. As Lukas gave a crow of triumph, she began her work. Martin's soul—it was familiar to her. It was a small matter to draw the tortured strands back, to ease the wolf spirit free and then to loop Lukas's clumsy leash of magic, with a quick flicker of power, around the whimpering spirit of the puppy who had taken refuge at her knees.

Lukas, ordering servants, looked up for a moment, confused. The puppy whimpered, as if it felt a constriction in its chest. Gaultry felt her own heart jump in her throat, waiting for the shining madman to discover her. But Lukas only shook his head dismissively, not able to determine just what was amiss. He wiped his palm against his cheek, and shouted at another servant, the moment for discovery slipping from him.

Gaultry stroked the puppy's head, watching Lukas with narrowed eyes.

Maybe he did have the power to grind her soul into paste. She didn't care. There was one advantage at least that she had over him.

She could tell the difference between a dog's spirit and a wolf's.

If Lukas didn't, that might well be enough to break him.

She wondered how long it would take Martin and the wolf to tear themselves free. Looking at Lukas and his preparations, she prayed that it would not be too long.

chapter 21

Lukas was having his men prepare a bed. A silken bed, with a down-filled mattress and innumerable quilts. Gaultry glanced past Tullier, past the Sharif, and found her eyes fixing on Columba and the dark lord, Issachar, who stood at her back. It disgusted her that Lukas wanted them to watch, though she guessed that Luka Pallia's son could not bear to perform any important act without an audience.

Lukas glanced up from his work and saw where she was looking. He made an impatient noise. "I should have called the marsh-witch! You want our bond to have the strength of theirs, and I could have arranged it!"

"That's a different story," Gaultry said, feeling queasy, "and I don't have your skill at this game. I can only play one role at a time."

"It is an inborn skill," Lukas said, without evident irony. "But I do not think you would want to have any part of the sad ending to that love."

At their words, Issachar made an impatient movement. There was a new weight to his motion, as though all the time Gaultry had known him something in him had been straining, unknowingly, skyward, and now he had come to earth. He stood by Columba, her slight, pale figure emphasized by his darkness and muscular bulk. For a moment his eyes met Columba's in a lingering look that Issachar had not allowed himself since Lukas had subdued him, down in the front court. For that moment, it seemed they were reading each other, reaching out across their years of separation.

Then Issachar's head made a small, almost invisible shake, and he turned away. Columba blanched. She made no sound, but her eyes slowly filled with tears.

"You don't need me here," Issachar addressed his Master coldly. "I am not a maker of beds."

Lukas, his eyes fixed on a new layer of red silk that was being laid out, nodded. "Send Chlymas up. He can stand witness in your place." He looked round. "But quickly. I must have my twelve witnesses."

Issachar nodded and disappeared out the arched door to the stairs.

"What did you mean, you could have called the marsh-witch?"

Lukas gave Gaultry an impatient look. "Do you want me to call her? There is no time. The summer star is rising—look out the window if you doubt me. She can bring her cards and weeds and goats another day."

Gaultry did not know what he was speaking of, but she went to the window. The casing was narrow—less than a head's width. The view faced east into the yard and back across the river. From this distance the river, still turgid and full, was flat gray under the full clouded sky. Beyond, the lights of the staging house were visible, and a few scattered lights on the plateau. No stars were in sight. Below her, in the courtyard, stood two soldiers. They did not look like monks— indeed, none of the guards Lukas had put on them looked like monks. Gaultry wondered what the monastery brothers made of their leader's bizarre preparations, his shining skin, his meals of honey and wheat. What did they make of his menagerie, the strange soul- and spirit-bound men? One of the soldiers in the yard looked up and saw her there, framed in the window. She stared back, curious, noting the heavy sword, the dark breastplate, and finally, the striped baldric, looped loosely across his chest. The soldier looked away and trotted off across the court.

"I don't see any stars."

"They are there. The summer star is there." Something in his voice made her turn around. Lukas had draped himself elegantly across the bed. He had donned a thin silver-colored robe, loosely closed by a silk cord tied at the waist. Suspended from the front of the cord were two gold pods, just large enough that they would have fit into the palm of his hand. "Where's Chlymas?" he said petulantly. "Why hasn't Issachar sent him up yet?" The pods clicked against each other as he shifted on the bed.

Gaultry looked at the man's sprawled body, fascinated by his costume, the golden pods. The thought of lying in bed with him disgusted her, but she was not frightened as he might have expected her to be frightened. She was a witch—no man could force her against her will—and Lukas, whatever role he sought to play, had been castrated. He could work himself into a frenzy between her legs for all she cared. He would not be able to push his maleness anywhere farther. Her greatest worry was that she might inflame his temper.

He could want no more than for herself and him to pose together, two players on a stage, pretending they were gods. She did not believe he had eaten the chaff on his plate. She did not believe she could return his mutilated flesh to life.

Then she shivered, not sure if she should be so certain. On Prince's Night, the night Benet of Tielmark had taken his wife, she had watched two priestesses die. The traitor Heiratikus had convinced them that they could play the part of the Great Twins in the ritual marriage ceremony. Their apostasy had been cruelly punished. When the Great Twins incorporated themselves in flesh, come to earth to receive the Prince's marriage vows, the goddesses had entered through the bodies of those foolish women, tearing their living bodies to pulp as They became manifest. Those woman had believed that they could dance without reprisals in the roles of the gods—and they had died for that belief. Gaultry had seen their faces as they died—their disbelief that legend could become real.

Here, she realized—here in this dark chapter house, with the summer star rising outside, the problem was no different. She did not believe that playing at the gods could be other than a game. But Lukas. Lukas was in earnest. He expected—he was making himself believe—that the god Tarrin was alive in him. Gaultry thought back to the moment behind the carriage, when Columba had lapsed into illness. The woman truly had been as one ill—incapable even of struggling out of the litter when she had been dumped on the riverbank. And here was her brother, striving to draw the gods' eyes to them.

Gaultry licked nervously at her lips. Perhaps she was right. Perhaps there was no harm in playing at gods. But perhaps Lukas, in his intensity, in his belief—perhaps Lukas had the power to draw the gods into them. His mother had been born to that power. In Luka Pallia that knack had been strong enough to swell his male belly with a child. What if that power lived in Luka's son's veins, heightened to new strength by his Imperial blood? What then?

The image of the priestesses, who had died on Prince's Night, of their shattered limbs, rose before her.

Elianté, she prayed. *This man, in Tarrin's guise, would lie beside me in your name. Hearten me. Tell me that this is not a blasphemy.*

"I can't do it," she blurted. "I won't risk it." Across the room, Sharif and Tullier moved restlessly, eyeing the guards nearest them.

Lukas scrambled onto his elbows. His voice was firm. "You have no choice. If you fight me, your lover will be served as Tarrin-White served Cyronius! A sword through his neck, and then through his bowels!"

Gaultry glared. "Much lasting good that it did Tarrin, god of the ever-wilted staff!"

Lukas was out of the bed and across the room to her. For a moment they tangled, Lukas throwing his power at her like a curtain of engulfing flame. Gaultry, who had been waiting for this, lashed back. But not at Lukas. A scythe of brilliant Glamour-power flared out—not at Lukas, not at his armored front, but at the hundred glittering strings that sprang from him, invisibly tying him to the menagerie. That scything blow stopped him cold. He looked at Gaultry, his face twisted with inhuman rage—and certainly not at all smooth and godlike. "That was Fontin," he said coldly. "And others who I would not have separated from me at this moment. But not your wolf-hearted lover. So your insolence can be punished—" He made a chopping gesture with his hand, jerking cruelly on one invisible thread.

The puppy, who had darted over to the wall when Lukas had advanced on her, reciprocated with a shrill squall of pain. Lukas turned to it, at first uncomprehending, then, as the pup threw itself down and began to desperately rub its head against the floor, as if it felt itself aflame, he understood what had happened. His silver aura took on a fresh radiance. "You match me!" He laughed. "You snuck and exchanged the pup for the wolf! The marsh-witch did not lie! I will be healed!"

Gaultry, squealing with frustration, struck again. The magical line to the puppy severed—the still-frightened animal leapt up and scampered away—but she had failed to break the tie that would have freed the Sharif and the great cat, and Lukas, guessing quickly at her intention, was fast enough to raise a counter-spell, sweeping the remainder of the unsevered ties out of her reach and securing them with a fresh burst of silver strength.

"Not so quickly!" He chortled. "We must wait for our last witness—"

From beyond the room, there came a resounding crash, louder than thunder. Silver light flashed in through the narrow windows, and suddenly, out in the yard, the sky was full of rain and storm. A second flash rang out, and there was an unpleasantly loud crackling sound, as if of a series of explosions. Pungent smoke swept in through the windows, overwhelming the chapterhouse's incense-and-wax scent.

"Issachar!" Lukas said angrily, his head snapping round at the great noise. "What is he up to?" He looked round at the remaining guards. "Don't leave them! Don't let them move!" Gathering his robes above his knees, he ran out lightly onto the stair. His men, staring after him, exchanged nervous looks.

Gaultry, temporarily reprieved, waited until Lukas had reached the bottom step, and perhaps a little more. Then she turned to the big cat. With sudden directed pulse of power, she snipped the magic leash that bound it.

It snarled, ferocious, and flung itself on the unlucky man who stood nearest. The poor man's sword was sheathed, and what little chance he had, he wasted trying to draw it. In the stunning moment in which he met his death, the others reacted. The two nearest the door bolted. The men on Tullier threw him to the ground. The Sharif, moving with unnatural animal quickness and grace, disarmed the man to her left and got in her first cut on his shoulder.

The bear-bonded men were nearest Gaultry. One grabbed her with his meaty hands, pinning her. Gaultry grunted with pain and retaliated, throwing open a channel, tunneling deep into his mind. There, as she expected, was the mass of torn soul, spun round with strips of bear-spirit. Bears were easy—dumb and quick-tempered. She unwound the ursine strands—a little clumsy in her haste—and massed them together, giving them the form and strength they would need to flow back to their missing half, somewhere down in the menagerie. She finished none too soon, feeling the grip of the man's hands on her slacken as he lost his bear-strength.

Tullier was up. He had managed to kill one of the men who had thrown him down, and taken his sword. The Sharif and the big cat were working together, driving another man onto the stairs, killing a man who lagged behind, not quick enough to escape.

There were three spirit-bonded men left—four, including

the man who had lost his bear-strength. Something had gone wrong for them. One man was rolling on the floor—just as the puppy had done when Lukas made it think it was on fire. Two others were trembling; the fourth, the former bear, screamed.

"The menagerie is on fire!" someone called up from the stairs. Somehow that stopped the fighting.

"Let them go!" Gaultry said. Another man was dead, but as she spoke, there was a rush for the stairs, men slipping on blood, tumbling over themselves in their hurry.

Gaultry rushed over to the paneled window that opened into the temple, looking for Martin, and almost cried in frustration. Though the lights had been removed, she could see, in the temple's dimness, that the altar was empty. The soldier and the wolf had disappeared. Did that mean that they were free, or was it a bad sign?

What now? the Sharif asked.

"Down the stairs!" said Gaultry. "It's the only way out!" She stared around the room. The bird-musicians were huddled against the narrow windows, as if they sought to escape through that egress. She darted across to them. "Come with us," she said, touching one man on the arm. "The stairs are the only way."

A movement in the yard below caught her eye, and she released the player. She looked down. The yard was aswarm with men in striped baldrics. "Tullier!"

"We can't help the players," Tullier said. He was at the door, impatient, calling for her to hurry. "They're Lukas's men. Let them burn. Gaultry, let's get out."

"No—come here Tullier. Who are those men?"

Grudgingly, he came to her side. Looking down, his manner changed. "Oh Llara," he said. "That is the Imperial Guard."

"Not more of Lukas's men?"

"No. Those men must have followed us from Bassorah."

"How did they manage to follow us across the river?"

Tullier did not know the answer to that question.

Raging fire lit their passage down the steps. The menagerie's roof was already in flames, raining gouts of burning thatch onto the cages beneath. At the far end of the main aisle, the big doors were open, creating a devastating draft that swept the fire to new heights. Out the doors, in a rain that seemed to be doing nothing to stem the flames, the yard was crawling with a mixed battle, men in baldrics against robed warriors and priests.

The bear-men, maddened with pain, were trying to wrench open the door of the bear cage. The large cage, with its clumsy bars, had taken a direct hit from a flaming hunk of thatch. Gaultry, trying to decide what to do, caught sight of Columba.

The woman had been so quiet, so little of a presence in all the sparring with her brother. Now she stared at the flames, transfixed, somehow helpless. Gaultry took a nervous swallow. Somewhere in the gathering inferno there was a dove, imprisoned in a cage, hypnotized by the power of the jumping light.

"Start opening cages," she ordered Tullier. *Open the cages,* she told the Sharif. "These are men as well as animals; we can't let them die like this. Look at Columba—the bears—we can't leave them."

Tullier looked at her, quickly studying her face, guessing if he could argue, could turn her mind. Seeing that he had no hope of dissuading her, he shrugged, ran lightly to the bears' cage, and threw open the complicated latch. Men and bears together rushed for the patch of fresh air, lashing into the fight. "Let's do it!" he shouted. "Let's let them all free. It will add to the confusion, and that can only aid us!"

Gaultry sprang to release the catch on the cage of the Imperial swans and threw back the cage's lid, not stopping to see whether they flew to freedom or cowered in their cage to burn. Those were only birds—she reckoned that any creature with a human soul binding it would have enough sense to make its way to freedom.

I'm going down this aisle, she told the Sharif. *You take the other side. Look for the predators—most of Lukas's men were bound to predators.*

It was terrifying among the cages. She bumped against a

case—looking down, she saw it was the rats. She fumbled for the catch, then threw open the lid. Four out of the hundred seemed to know which way to go: they guided the others. Other animals were more confused by the flames, more frightened. Gaultry tried to hold her mind open, to offer them direction. But this was increasingly difficult with smoke drifting against her face, gouts of flaming roof dropping at every moment. She freed delicate deer, foxes, four cages of birds. A flaming hunk of thatch the size of a hay bale demolished the last birdcage before its denizens could escape.

Animals around the room screamed in pain and fear. Someone—perhaps Tullier—opened the main aviary, and a large number of birds winged for safety. Others, confused by the flames, flew straight into the heart of the fire.

As Gaultry opened a cage that contained a striped cat, something pressed against her ankles—Tullier's puppy. It had followed them from the chapterhouse and had chosen to stay with her. "Idiot," she told it, "you'd be better off outside." It would not heed her.

She reached the end of the aisle. Four cages, wedged into shelves, blocked her way on. Mice in one, and a tortoise. She let out a despairing laugh: the tortoise had no chance of making it. She would have to leave it. There was no helping everything. Time to turn back. She whirled around.

Behind her, blocking her way, was Lukas. Lukas, with his robes blacked with ash, a look of fury on his face. This time, wasting no time in talk, he threw himself at her, all the power of his Blood-Imperial, Columba's, and his own soul lashing out to subdue her.

"I am Tarrin!" he hissed. "You will play the goddess for me, and I will heal myself in your loins!"

"You're nothing!" Gaultry spat back, as she was thrown against a metal shelf. "A pretty boy dolled up in a god's clothes! You fail even to honor your mother's prayers!"

Astonishingly, a balance hung between them. Lukas's magic did not seem to have the power to force her back. Her mind, clearing of her fears of fire, of flame, of the crazed animal cries that surrounded them, became slowly aware of the glowing colors of their combat: his magic white and purple, Hers Glamour-gold, the green magic she called from the Great Twins . . . and twisted all around those colors, a bright band of silver.

Her heart leapt. Llara Thunderbringer was repaying her debt.

For a moment, the joy of the power that pulsed through her disjoined her from the combat. Then a drop of sweat spattered against her face and she became aware of Lukas's face, close to hers, his cheeks flushed. Against her stomach, she felt the coldness of the gold pods he had tied to his waist outside his robe.

"This is how it was meant to happen," he panted, triumphant. She felt the edge of the tortoise's cage against her spine as he pushed her against the shelves. "In the fire's heart, the gods' house. Every drop of our magic engaged, the symmetry perfect. And now I can prove myself on you, as a man must do on a woman."

Gaultry realized, panicking, that although, with Llara's aid, she equaled him in the balance of her magic, Lukas outmatched her in his physical strength. She should not have needed to fight him—she was a witch, and no man could rape a witch who had any corner of her magic free to protect herself. But now—she had no magic to devote to that protection. Her magic was fully engaged, consumed in the battle to force Lukas's power back, to prevent him from taking victory in the battle of their magical strengths and minds. She did not possess the physical strength that she would need to stop him. A part of her, bound in the fabulous struggle of green and gold and purple and silver bloods and magics, seemed to watch their struggling bodies from above, observing, almost with disinterest. Lukas crushed her viciously against the shelves, punching her—once, then twice—in the stomach, and tearing her clothes. She tried to lose herself in that magical battle, tried to pretend that her body was nothing, that she did not care that he was forcing her legs apart, that he was biting her neck, that he was shrieking to Tarrin in triumph at the bolting power of male strength that, for the first time ever, was building in his groin.

"Leave her alone."

Lukas glanced round. It was Tullier. One of the boy's hands was empty, the other held only the slim bar that he had been using to pry open cages. "Puppy!" Lukas snapped at him. "Don't interfere in matters that are beyond your comprehension."

The glacial eyes narrowed. "I understand well enough. I want you to leave her alone."

"You can't stop me!" Lukas panted. He shifted his weight on Gaultry's body, and she felt the golden pods, obscenely, slide on their cord so that they had moved between her legs. Gaultry tried to wriggle free of him then, but he rammed his fingers into her throat, forcing her to stay still while he spoke. "You were born only to give me the Blood-Imperial! Your life purpose is done! Why Father let you live I do not know— you should have been aborted with the rest!"

Tullier's face went black. "None of that matters to me," he said. "Just get off her."

Lukas made an impatient frown. Perhaps he felt his new man's strength fading. Perhaps he really thought Tullier would not try to stop him. Gaultry, looking into Lukas's dark eyes, finally found, beneath all the weight of their titanic magical battle, the strength to scream.

Tullier lifted his wrist, pointing angrily at Lukas's back. Tears clouding her eyes, Gaultry saw a brief motion, a quick flick of his hand. From the cuff of his shirt flew one of the Imperial daggers she had encouraged him to take from his father's storeroom, the gemstones on its hilt glittering, fiery and vengeful, in the light of the menagerie's flames. Lukas's body jerked against hers as the slender blade pierced his back. "You *will* leave her alone," Tullier said. He ran quickly forward and yanked Lukas's body off her.

Lukas tried to fend Tullier away, but already his strength was fading. "Blasted puppy!"

Tullier grabbed the dagger by the handle and twisted it
deeper in his brother's back. "I did not train twelve years as
a Sha Muira for nothing," he said. "You are dead now." He
dragged the dagger free. "But it will be slower than you
like."

Gaultry, on the floor, felt a rush as the purple-and-white
force of Lukas's magic disengaged. Tullier, keeping an eye
on the fallen sorcerer, helped her up. "The roof has fallen in
on the right side," he said. "It's time for us to leave. We've
done all we can."

"You've done too much!" It was Columba, Columba with
a dove clutched tightly in one fist, its feathers streaked with
soot. Behind her were Martin and the Sharif, flanked by the
wolf and giant cat. Luka Pallia's daughter pushed to her
brother's side, knelt, and took his hand. "This is my twin!"
she cried. She bent to look in his face. Lukas seemed to
acknowledge her, his fingers feebly clutching at her, and
something unspoken passed between them. A look of disbelief crossed Columba's pale face. "You want my life?" she
asked him.

Lukas shifted slightly. The obscene pods at his waist, soot
obscuring the gold, clicked together and slipped out of his lap.
"The blood of Great Llara is in me." His words were slurred.
"I will be Emperor, I will be a god . . ."

Columba's fingers tightened over his. Even colored by the
ever-encroaching flames, both hands seemed very white:
Lukas's bloodless, yet still gleaming silver, Columba's
unnaturally pale. "You were not a god when you forced me
to take a lover," she hissed. A sulfur smell flared up, as if
something between them was burning. "You were not a god
when you relegated me to whoredom and misery. You had
my power already. You did not need to do that." Weakly,
Lukas tried to free his hand. Blood, deep purple painted
black in the flames, seeped from between their clasped
palms. Columba's Blood-Imperial was returning to its
source.

"You're killing him faster," Tullier observed. "Llara's
blood is all that holds him here now."

Columba's face flushed with emotion. She clutched at her brother's hand, harder. "So be it!" she said giddily. "He's dying! He does not need it! He's not going to Llara's Feast. He's going to Achavell, to perdition!"

Martin, who had been keeping himself aloof, strode forward and jerked her away from her brother's body. "Don't be greedy," he said. The tall soldier's wrists were smeared with blood. Deep scratches marked his hands and wrists. "Take your own, but no more."

"It is my due!" Columba said curtly. She slapped the tall soldier to force him to free her—slapped him with a white and unblemished palm. "Leave me be. You do not know what I have suffered. I am a Princess. It is my turn to taste power. You think—your bitch Glamour-mistress thinks—that you have done me a favor. But I am Blood-Imperial. I acknowledge no debt to you!"

"Fine," Martin said. He jerked the slender woman away from Lukas's body. Her frail strength was no match for his own. "That doesn't mean I'll let you fatten your power on this man's corpse. Bissanty will survive another generation without a double-blooded heir."

"Tielmaran pig!" Columba gouged her fingers into the wounds on his hands, trying to force him to release her. "Let me go! It will be too late!"

Gaultry, who had been tempted to intervene, stepped back, shaken by the vehemence in Columba's face. "Columba!" she said. "Calm yourself! Your brother is dying."

Columba, tearing herself free from Martin, spun around. For a moment, she and Gaultry faced each other. Columba's features twisted with confusion, as though, for a moment, she had a decision to make, and she did not even know what a decision was. Then she made her choice. "Guards!" she shrieked. "Help me! The Tielmaran spies are here!"

Her confusion undid her. They were deep in the maze of flaming cages. There was no one to hear her screams. Gaultry looked at the girl, remembering how frail she had been when they had saved her, how helpless she had been beneath her Bissanty rapist's thrusts. She thought of the power that was in

the woman to remake herself, to take on, as her brother had
done, any role up to that of god-hood. "Llara saved you
once," Gaultry said, looking down at Columba's impassioned
face, "working through my hands. In that moment, the Goddess-Queen taught me much, and I know now I can't risk
leaving such power in your possession. She chose me to be
your judge. I think that you are evil, that you will use your
Blood-Imperial only for the bad. I don't have the strength or
will to kill you, but I can leash your power in at least this
way." She reached out, faster than Columba expected, and
plucked the dove from the pocket where she had tucked it for
safety, as, vampirelike, she had sucked at her dying brother's
blood.

"Huntress Elianté in me," Gaultry intoned. "To her I make
this sacrifice." With a quick, practiced motion, honed though
years of readying food for the pot on her grandmother's table,
Gaultry wrung the white bird's neck. "Half your soul to the
gods, Columba, and half of this poor bird's. That is your payment for this betrayal."

Columba began to scream, high, keening screams
between pain and tragedy. There was theater in the
screams—theater that reminded the young huntress too
much of Lukas. Gaultry gave her a quick, unsympathetic
look. "I would have tried to help you," she said. "But I will
not risk Tielmark's future to the conscience of your regained
strength."

The flames were hemming in the aisle. Gaultry doubted the
roof would hold much longer. She touched Martin's arm,
gently, above the scratches. "We should get out now."

He nodded. "We don't want to go through the yard. It's still
full of fighting. There's an unguarded door in the temple. We
can slip out that way." He prodded Lukas's corpse with his
foot and cast Columba a brief glance, where the woman had
crouched down, whimpering, by the wall. "We should kill
her," he said.

Gaultry shook her head. "I made a promise to a god. We
can't. But the irrevocable binding to the dove-spirit—that
weakens her in ways beyond our understanding."

Martin nodded, satisfied, then stooped. He plucked the golden pods free from Lukas's waist and threw them deep into the flame, where it spiraled highest, above a row of broken cages. "When I saw you up in the chapterhouse, I made a promise to a god too," he said. He shot her a fierce look. "I just fulfilled it."

Lukas had been a fool. He had thought Martin a savage, bonded to a wolf, a truer savage. She rested her head against the big muscle of Martin's arm for one moment, hiding her face. Lukas had known nothing of wolves. They were savage to their enemies, but they would do anything to protect the members of their pack.

"It's time to move," Martin said. "I assume this lot are coming too?" His glance took in the Sharif and Tullier. Tullier, eyeing Martin's arm around Gaultry's shoulder, scowled, but he kept his mouth shut.

"That's about it," Gaultry said. *We're going,* she told the Sharif.

We're not taking the bitter woman? the Sharif asked.

She has twined her fate with that of this bitter land, Gaultry answered. *I am going home to Tielmark. She is no longer my concern.*

A single figure watched them go. His white head was slick with rain, throwing his handsome profile into starker relief. He watched them slip across the yard, then along the garden wall, making their way down towards the river. That was wise, he mused. The Imperial Guard would not imagine that they would turn to the river. They would scout the road westwards. The Sea Prince grinned. He would happily help the Imperial Guard scout the road westwards, after all, he was not the leader here. It was just too bad that Sciuttarus had forbidden him to bring more than a handful of his own men—men who might helpfully have aided in a pursuit that followed the Tielmarans south down a flooded river. He was going to enjoy telling his Imperial nephew how they might have taken the Tielmaran spies if only he had allowed him his own men, who had experience navigating floodwaters.

He looked back at the confusion that reigned still in the rain-filled yard. Bleating, cowering animals butted against the monks and defeated warriors who crowded the loggia, trying to gain a place out of the wet. The storm had finally begun to make headway against the fire, and the last of the monks had been subdued. Much of the Monastery was in ruins. It would be many months before the hostel at Dunsanius Ford could reopen.

His squire came pattering up, nervous and eager. He did not have his Master's confidence, so he was still worrying that the old man thought things had gone amiss. "What are you going to say to the Emperor, Your Highness? They can't find the Tielmaran spies anywhere."

"We will tell him the truth," the tall man said. He grinned. In the dark, his teeth, like his hair, flashed very white. "The Sea Prince rode out with his men to suppress his own son. He performed that service successfully, ever faithful to his Emperor."

Overhead, the clouds opened just a sliver, allowing them a glimpse of the moon. The waning disk was surrounded by a pale corona of white light—Tarrin's emblem. Although everyone aboard the little boat was intensely aware of the sign, no one commented, not certain whether the omen was a good sign or a bad.

They had argued in the boathouse, and then again as they chose the boat, bailed it, and shunted it out into the swift-flowing river. They were too tired to argue now.

Gaultry and the Sharif huddled in the bow of the boat, the big cat curled around the war-leader's legs. Tullier's puppy nuzzled against Gaultry's side, its nose tucked into her armpit, seeking warmth and a contented sleep. It had been the puppy who had fetched Tullier when Lukas had attacked her, braving flames and falling roof thatch to show him the hidden aisle where Lukas had trapped her. For that alone, they owed the animal rescue.

She was less certain about the striped honey-eater, furry monkey, and colorful songbird that had chosen to come with them. In the hectic retreat down the hill, sliding in the dark, bruising their shins on stones and ornamental shrubs, she had been unaware of the additional animals who had somehow become attached to the party until they were in the boat, well away from the shore, and the monkey and honey-eater began a protracted squabble as to who would get to occupy the little cubby under the front seat. Perhaps later she would be able to send them home, like the Sharif.

Martin and Tullier, in the stern, were still arguing, putatively about the navigation. Gaultry found their bickering obscurely soothing. That at least was not her problem. She had no claims to those skills. Perhaps, after they reached the Locatus, she would have to get up again and take her turn at one of the oars. For now she was pleased that all she had to do was watch.

Looking at Martin, she felt sleepy and happy. There, at least, they had been spared the drama of another animal companion. The wolf and the great cat had categorically refused to enter the boat together. Gaultry had not had the energy to untangle more than one of the warrior couples—and logic had all gone towards freeing Martin. Logic, because the wolf was a Bissanty creature, with no need of a ride downstream. But it had also been her desire.

The act of freeing him had not been so straightforward. It was not merely relief at touching Martin's body, the knowledge that he wanted her, that she wanted him. His worries that he was too cold to love—at some point in his ordeal he had stopped teasing himself with that. In that moment she had stood with her body pressed against his, feeling for the edge of his soul-strips, the edge of the wolf's spirit-strips, the cold soil of Bissanty had warmed beneath her feet. Like her own, Martin's blood was bound to Tielmark. Touching him had made Bissanty fade. His shoulders were savagely burned where the slave-bond had refused to take on him—touching his soul, she had seen why that bond had not set on him. Tielmark's bond preceded it.

When it was finished, the wolf slipped shyly away among the trees, leaving Martin tall and strong before her, back to arguing about the boat. "That's your province, not mine," she had told him, relieved by the relief from constant responsibility.

A stray thought nagged. Gaultry reached into her belt purse and brought out the sliver of glass, the amulet that the litter-carrier had given her. She had wondered at its shape when the man had handed it to her, but there had been no time for questions. Gingerly, she held it in her fingers, watching it catch a hint of blue spark from the moon. It reminded her of something—but she was too tired to think what.

"I know nothing of water magic," she said softly, staring down the length of the boat. "But there was something strange as I soothed the wounds of your soul, Martin. I think Lukas was not the first to touch you there."

Quietly, she slipped into sleep, blissfully blind to the look of raw jealousy that Tullier, under the guise of arguing points of navigation, was throwing into Martin's face.

CODA

When Mariette burst into the Duchess's rooms, her grandmother was sitting by the window, one hand trailing in a basin of pure white marble, an abstracted expression on her wrinkled face. Despite the dramatic entry, old Melaudiere barely glanced up. "It's you," was all she said. "I suppose you have news for me?"

"I do."

"Well I have news for you," the old woman said querulously. "I expect you will find it of as much importance. But—gods on us—I won't come running to ruin the plaster on your walls."

The young woman gave her grandmother a curious look. Melaudiere had seemed well enough this morning, now she seemed almost ill. Mariette's eyes flickered to the basin by her grandmother's hand. The old woman had been struggling for days to open a window to Bissanty. Did her mood signify yet another failure, or success and bad news?

"Martin had better make it back to Tielmark in one piece," Mariette said brightly. "I have business I need to settle with him." For example, the young woman thought grimly, the decision she had come to in Bellaire, during the week she'd spent fighting doctors in order to convince them they didn't need to chop out half her bowels to save her. She had not wanted to live a cripple, a laughingstock with a bedpan tied to her belt. It was a realization that had profoundly changed her. There were many ways of being a cripple. Without Seafrieg, knowing Seafrieg was in the hands of someone who should not own it, she could never truly be whole. To recover herself, to recover her birthright, she was going to have to fight her brother's ex-wife for the right to the title that Martin had abandoned.

Martin would not be happy. But her brother—he had already broken their father's sword. She could no longer stand aside and allow him to break the Seafrieg land as well, leaving it in the hands of a woman and a child who did not have the strength to manage it.

Besides, Helena had been rude to her as she made her recovery.

She grinned fiercely, thoughts of that coming battle—a battle which she was sure to win—tumbling in her head. Those were thoughts for another time. Seafrieg was weak; it needed her—but other parts of Tielmark were weaker, and those would have to be dealt with first. "Tell me," Mariette said, walking over to the window. Melaudiere's rooms were some of the best in the Prince's palace, with a long view, out across the cliffs, to the sea. "Do you have news of Martin? I thought you lost sight of everyone from the moment they disembarked in Bassorah City."

"I had my first flicker this afternoon," the Duchess admitted. "I thought I would try something new."

"It worked?"

"Beyond my expectations."

Mariette, confused by her grandmother's dull manner, took a covert look into the font. She had no talent for sorcery—none of Melaudiere's grandchildren did. Perhaps something from the old Duke's side had blocked it—in Mariette's dim childhood memories, he had always seemed a vividly nonmagical sort of person, committed to honor and war. There were times, however, when, looking into one of her grandmother's fonts, she picked up faint images on the water's mirrored surface, like the afterglow of light burning her eyes on a sunny day. Or at least could go so far as to envision the mirror that the water became! So perhaps the magical family talents were merely lying low. Today, dim in the evening light that slipped in from the window, the font water was transparent. But that transparency . . . Mariette bent and looked closer. A sliver of metal rested on the font's bottom. As she stared, it glinted. It still held a faint gleam of blue-and-green power.

"Did you save all the shards from Father's sword after Martin broke it?"

The Duchess, seeing where her granddaughter's gaze had fallen, expelled an angry hiss and came back a little into herself. "All the shards! What are you saying! I was on my knees for an hour, collecting every sliver. You do not understand the power that was vested in that weapon."

"Small surprise," Mariette said sharply, "when you remember that you and Martin decided together not to pass it to me, when he renounced possession of everything else."

The Duchess rose abruptly from her seat. "Martin could not give the sword away. I had my reasons for making him keep it. They were good ones." Refusing to elaborate, she swept up the shard, wiped it on her sleeve, and tucked it away in a hidden pocket. "So turn yourself to other news. Martin and Gaultry are on their way back to Tielmark," she announced. "They are in the arms of Allegrios Rex, even as we speak—Llara's children will not take them, now they are safe in the water god's arms. So—at least for a time—Tielmark's flank is safe on the north."

"Grandmère!" Mariette swept the old woman up in a relieved hug. "Why didn't you say so first off!"

"So tell me your news." The Duchess returned her hug, but not before Mariette noticed that she wanted to change the subject.

"My news—" Mariette frowned. "I have a great deal of news, little of it good. Tamsanne of Arleon Forest is just arrived at court." Her grandmother had told her once that the Blas twins' grandmother was the most powerful of the surviving Common Brood. She was not sure how her own Grandmère would take the news of her arrival. "That means that the Prince has succeeded in calling the last of the surviving Brood to court."

"Except Richielle," the Duchess said.

Mariette shrugged. There had been much debate at court about Richielle. Fifty years ago, when the Common Brood had formed, Richielle had already been old. The Duchess was among a slim handful who believed it possible that the woman was alive. "No one in Tielmark has seen the goat-herder for fifty years," she told her grandmother. "If she's alive, there's no way to get her the message that the Prince wants her at court."

"Richielle would know," the Duchess said. She brushed her marble basin with her foot. "She did not have my gift of far-seeing, but she had something else. She was a part of the land—more even than the rest of us. She would feel it, if the Prince wanted her."

"Even in her grave?"

Melaudiere met her granddaughter's eyes. "Perhaps so far as that. But Richielle—she always liked having the last word. If she comes to court, you can be sure that she'll be the last to arrive. And Martin and young Gaultry aren't here yet."

Mariette shrugged. If her Grandmère wanted to clutch at such fancies, that was her own problem. The country would have to face worse. "The last news—it's the worst.

"You've been worrying about Kings, Grandmère. Well, the news is, there is a King in Tielmark. But he's away on the west border, and he's wearing smeared red paint on his body, and he's hurling his spears at Haute Tielmark's finest troops.

"The Bissanty made a secret move of half their troops into the mountains. They burned the Lanai fields deeper up in the gorges than they've ever done in twenty years of fighting. The mountain King of the Lanai has promised his people new farming grounds. He's run his warriors down from the mountains and invaded."

To Mariette's surprise, the Duchess burst out laughing.

"There is nothing fun about death and burning," the young woman said angrily. "I'm heading west with the rest of the army this summer, don't forget."

The Duchess's laughter faded as quickly as it had risen. "Mariette," she said. "Believe me, war is not my joy.

"But the first birthing signs of our free nation! What is a season of war, next to that!"

Mariette looked at her grandmother and sighed. I hope you know what you are talking about, she thought. You—you and every member of the Common Brood who wields magic. You have been wrong before. That last thought, as she stared out the high window to the sea's distant horizon—that thought was not at all comforting.

About the Author

Katya Reimann lived for six years in Oxford, England, where she wrote a Ph.D. dissertation about pirates. She put this knowledge to active use in founding the (now defunct) Kamikaze Punt Club.

In the past she worked for a monument company lettering and designing tombstones. She also paints and works in stone. She and her father—a distinguished sculptor—recently completed work on a major commission for the Massachusetts Port Authority.

She enjoys going down caves and up mountains, being out of doors and in boats. She shares ownership of Cheka, a red-and-white Basenji—the most catlike of dogs.

A Tremor in the Bitter Earth is her second novel. Katya currently lives in St. Paul, Minnesota, where she is working on *Prince of Fire and Ashes,* the next book in the Tielmaran Chronicles.

TOR
BOOKS The Best in Fantasy

CROWN OF SWORDS • Robert Jordan
Book Seven in Robert Jordan's epic *Wheel of Time* series. "Robert Jordan has come to dominate the world Tolkien began to reveal."—*The New York Times*

BLOOD OF THE FOLD • Terry Goodkind
The third volume in the bestselling *Sword of Truth* series.

SPEAR OF HEAVEN • Judith Tarr
"The kind of accomplished fantasy—featuring sound characterization, superior world-building, and more than competent prose—that has won Tarr a large audience."—*Booklist*

MEMORY AND DREAM • Charles de Lint
A major novel of art, magic, and transformation, by the modern master of urban fantasy.

NEVERNEVER • Will Shetterly
The sequel to *Elsewhere*. "With a single book, Will Shetterly has redrawn the boundaries of young adult fantasy. This is a remarkable work."—Bruce Coville

TALES FROM THE GREAT TURTLE • Edited by Piers Anthony and Richard Gilliam
"A tribute to the wealth of pre-Columbian history and lore."—*Library Journal*